FOREVER
Auburn

A NOVEL

SANDRA WADE

LUCIDBOOKS

Forever Auburn
A Novel
Copyright © 2018 by Sandra Wade

Published by Lucid Books in Houston, TX.
www.LucidBooksPublishing.com

ISBN-10: 1-63296-311-6
ISBN-13: 978-1-63296-311-6
eISBN-10: 1-63296-264-0
eISBN-13: 978-1-63296-264-5

Special Sales: Most Lucid Books titles are available in special quantity discounts. Custom imprinting or excerpting can also be done to fit special needs. Contact Lucid Books at info@lucidbookspublishing.com.

I want to thank my husband, Delbert R. Janik.
He inspired me to write this book and
has been my constant support and
my love for almost 30 years.

TABLE OF CONTENTS

CHAPTER
ONE

River Bend was a large plantation with the Mississippi River bordering the west side. In the summer, as far as the naked eye could see, the cotton fields glistened like snow as the bolls split, bursting into a fluffy white mass of fibers. William Wilde and his family lived on the plantation with his parents. His grandfather had settled in Natchez in the 1700s and built a six-bedroom, two-story mansion on the high side of the river. Imported marble embellished the large entry floor enhancing the wide winding staircase. Each room had beautiful rugs that graced the oak floors and exquisite furniture purchased in Europe. Live oaks outlined the stately house with its porches wrapping all four sides, providing shade and outside comfort for the magnificent view of the fields and river. William marveled that three generations now lived in the old home. Through the years, River Bend had seen many balls and picnics with families from along the delta attending. The Wilde family worked hard to maintain River Bend as the most productive cotton plantation in the South.

William's life seemed perfect as he mounted his horse and headed for the fields. His wife, Reginia, waved goodbye from the porch before returning inside to read to the children. Reginia thumbed slowly through the book, reading each line with enthusiasm as the children sat attentively at her feet. Suddenly, there were loud poundings against the front door. Reginia quickly turned her head toward the sound. Two more alarming thuds and she dropped the book on the floor and rushed to the door, bolting past Laudie, the house slave who had cared for William since childhood. Reginia pulled the door open swiftly, finding Ben, William's brother, slumped to his knees with his head hung low. "Ben, what is it?" Ben did not look up. He just held his head in his hands and began sobbing at the sound of her voice. She began to reach for him when she caught sight of the buckboard. Her hand rested on his shoulder but her eyes focused on the two lifeless forms, covered with a blanket, lying in the back of the wagon. Her heart began to beat rapidly fearing one was William. Reginia proceeded down the brick walk, never taking her eyes off the covered bodies. She hesitated, and then with all the courage she could muster, she jerked the blanket back. Her eyes turned to steel. There lay William's parents, blue with the color of death. How did this happen? A lump formed in her throat. She remembered Ben on the porch and turned abruptly. She bumped into Laudie who, unbeknownst to Reginia, was standing right behind her. Laudie stood paralyzed with shock. Reginia trembled as she took Laudie by the arm. "Fetch Master William. He's in the fields. Quickly, Laudie, quickly."

Laudie hurried, shaking her arms in the air and wailing for Master William. Reginia reached Ben and urged him inside. She waited for William to return home before asking Ben what he knew about the death of his parents. There was little need for Ben to have to explain the tragedy more than once. Reginia summoned Samuel to bring the bodies into the house and place them on the large table in the library. She then rushed upstairs to Ben's wife, Elizabeth, and explained what little she knew about the accident. Elizabeth broke into tears.

Reginia put her arms around Elizabeth. "We must be strong, Elizabeth. Ben is taking this very hard and William will need our support," Reginia stated as she wiped the tears from Elizabeth's face. "Now come downstairs with me. Ben is in the parlor."

William rushed in to find Reginia guiding Elizabeth down the stairs. Laudie was too hysterical to give William any information. She had only told him that a terrible thing had happened and he must get home. Elizabeth left Reginia's side and went to Ben.

William turned to Reginia. "What is going on, Reginia? Laudie is hysterical. Is something wrong with the children?"

"No, the children are fine. There has been a terrible accident, darling." She began to explain as she reached for his hands. "Your parents . . ."

"My parents? What about Mother and Father?" His eyes shifted, glancing toward the library where his father had so often sat. He caught sight of his parent's bodies lying on the big table. He bolted to their side with Reginia behind him. He stared at their lifeless bodies in disbelief, taking his mother's hand and holding it tightly, fighting the tears from his eyes. "How did this happen?"

"I'm not sure. Ben knows but I didn't ask the details. He's taking this very hard." Reginia took William's arm. "Come into the parlor. Ben's waiting for you in there."

Ben pulled himself together and described his parent's death to the best of his knowledge. His voice quivered as he told them about the accident. "Mister Smith found the carriage turned over in the deep creek. Father evidently suffered a strong blow to the head when thrown from the carriage and Mister Smith had to pull Mother out from beneath the carriage." He swallowed hard before continuing. "She drowned, William." William put his arm around Ben's shoulders. "Mister Smith didn't know what had happened, unless the horses were traveling too fast when they came across a hole in the road. It was in the curve and this must have caused the carriage to break loose from the horses and flip into the creek. Mister Smith sent his slave to get me to come with a wagon." Ben began to weep, as his head slumped against William. William fought back his own tears of grief. He, being the oldest, was now the head of the Wilde family. He could not break down. He had to be strong for the others.

William made the preparations for the burial. He wanted his parents buried by his grandparents on the knoll overlooking the home they had shared for so many years. Many friends gathered at River Bend sharing in the sorrow and great loss of these two magnificent people.

The day after the funeral, William thrust himself into working the plantation. He knew his father would want him to take charge and not sit grieving. Cotton was plentiful the following years, making the Wilde family more money than they ever dreamed. They had hundreds of slaves. William was good to the slaves, attaining great loyalty from them. One slave, Samuel, had been a house slave for ten years. He was slight of build and light in color. His demeanor was quiet and well mannered. Samuel and William had grown up together, fishing and playing. During the evenings, when no one could see them, William would sneak out of the house with a book to teach Samuel how to read and write. They were best of friends and had a great understanding of one another and of the differences in their cultures. Their friendship gave William the ability to work his slaves without punishment and cruelty. He even allowed Samuel to teach the young Negro children to read and write, which most plantation masters forbid.

Laudie was the main house slave for William's family, continuing her duties after the death of his parents. Laudie was a large woman, dark in color, with a strong, stern voice that rang throughout the house. Reginia laughed to herself quietly when she heard Laudie scold their daughter, Sarah. "Miss Sarah, stop that runnin' up them stairs. You walk like a lady with your head held high. You ain't no common folk, so quit behavin' like one." Reginia did have to admit that Sarah was a handful. She could hardly believe Sarah was three years old. Sarah preferred running through the woods or riding her horse as fast as the big gelding could go, with her long auburn curls blowing in the wind. Her eyes were dark brown and freckles dotted her fair skin. She was a beautiful and free-spirited child. Their son, Alexander, was tall and lanky for five years of age. His dark hair accented his blue eyes. Reginia imagined Alex would grow into a stately man with perfect manners, as this was a trait he already exhibited. Laudie and Samuel supervised the house help. Samuel gave quiet instructions while Laudie demanded perfection with her stern voice.

Over the years, William became wearied with River Bend. The death of his parents had left a void in his life. He needed a change. Reginia did not know what to do for her husband. While in Natchez one day, William heard the news that Stephen Austin was taking colonists into Texas. The stories intrigued William. Later, his friend

Joe Bell, who had gone with Stephen to settle Texas, wrote to William about the new land and the Spanish land grants. Joe's letters convinced William to go to see for himself the vast land of promise.

William and his friend Joseph Riley went to Texas. Reginia was glad. She knew William needed a change; she just did not know these changes would affect her life. William loved Texas and wanted a particular piece of property that bordered the Brazos River. The land he wanted belonged to a gentleman named Mr. Foster. He offered him a fair amount for one thousand acres and Mr. Foster accepted.

William returned home and explained to Reginia what he had done. She could not believe what she was hearing. "Darling, you purchased land? Does this mean you will be gone a great deal?"

"Just for a while." The smile on William's face soothed Reginia's concerns. She had not seen him this excited in many years. William took Reginia into the parlor and told her all about Texas, the land he had purchased, and his plans. "I will take slaves and clear the land and build a big home for you."

"For me? You plan to move us to this place?" She never dreamed of being uprooted from her home.

"Don't fret, Reginia. It will take several years for this to come to pass. By the time I take you to Texas, there will be many people and the land will be civilized and our plantation will be as beautiful and productive as River Bend."

"I don't know about this, William. What about the children . . . their friends . . . their education?"

"Darling, this is the opportunity I have longed for. Something I can achieve on my own. You know Grandfather did the same thing when he came to Mississippi and you love it here. You will love Texas even more, because we will have created something together. Something we can be proud of."

"All right, my love." She smiled and realized she would never win an argument with William. Reginia could see the excitement in him and knew the Mississippi plantation was a constant reminder of his parent's tragic death. Texas might be fine and if it weren't she knew they would always have River Bend to come home to.

CHAPTER
TWO

The years passed too quickly for Reginia. William had taken slaves and his overseer, Ransom Hall, to clear the land for planting. They had worked the land almost three years before building the main house. William had been back and forth to Texas, and over the last year, he had remained to oversee the finishing touches before bringing his family to their new home.

He left Ransom in charge of the planting. He knew when he got home things would be in order. Ransom had worked for the Wilde family for twenty-five years. He was a dedicated and loyal hand. Ransom had insisted on going with William to the new frontier to help build the plantation.

Reginia had depended on Samuel so much the past year, and of course she had depended on Laudie too. The sacrifices made the prior year now seemed worth it. William had finally returned. It took a month for William to conclude his business in Natchez and prepare for the move that was now only hours away.

Everyone was in their bedrooms sleeping as Reginia gazed about the parlor and into the foyer with its grand staircase, reflecting upon the days with family, friends, and children scampering about among sounds of laughter. Crashes of thunder and wild streaks of lightning broke her thoughts. Night had fallen dark and dismal that March of

1829. Clouds hid the stars and the smell of rain was prevalent. The March air was still cool as Reginia relaxed in the overstuffed chair by the redbrick fireplace. Her long auburn curls hung freely down the back of the chair as the burning logs brought warmth to her soft white skin. Her brown eyes sparkled in the dim light of the flames as she began to imagine a new life on the frontier. She had heard tales of the wilderness, the Indians, and the uncivilized land and wondered why her beloved husband wished to move them away from their family and friends. Suddenly, the thunder roared and a streak of lightning lit the room. Reginia looked to the clock and could not believe how much time had lapsed. She eased out of the chair and headed up the stairs to join William.

Thoughts of the unseen land raced through her mind as she prepared for bed. William had warmed the room with raging logs in the fireplace. Reginia crawled into bed gently, trying not to disturb him. It felt so good to have William in her bed again. She quivered thinking of the passion between them his first night back. The hot coals added a soft glow to the room as Reginia snuggled deeper beneath the covers.

She felt William's arm embrace her as he mumbled her name softly. She had fallen in love with William the first time she saw him. He was handsome and stood tall with perfect posture. She felt as if he could see right through her with his deep-set hazel eyes. She remembered how his mustache tickled as he kissed her and how his muscles bulged when he playfully lifted her, carrying her about the room. His touch still excited her after all the years, and oh, how she still loved when he took her long auburn hair in his hands and gently pulled her close for a tender kiss.

Reginia's body ached from exhaustion as she nestled closer to William. The last week had been a challenge, to say the least. They had a grand ball and all their friends and family came. It was the last time Reginia and William entertained in the big home she had come to know and love. They had spent the remainder of the week packing their belongings in the canvas-covered wagons William had purchased. They were the finest wagons money could buy and William bought well-bred thoroughbreds to pull them. Her thoughts became faint as she felt so comfortable wrapped in her husband's arms, and as she dozed off, she wondered if she would experience such comfort ever again.

The morning sun peeked through the shutters, filling the room with a soft glow. Reginia arose to discover William had left their bed. She stretched her arms high above her head, yielding a large yawn. The day had come to leave her cherished home. She shook her head and shoulders with a quick twist and rushed to dress, for the girls would be upstairs soon to strip her bed. It would be the last piece of furniture moved.

The smell of coffee and bacon cooking filled her nostrils as she descended the staircase. Upon entering the kitchen, Reginia saw William, Sarah, and Alex sitting at the table. "This is the first and last time we will eat in this kitchen," she thought. The kitchen was a place where the slaves ate, but with the dining room furniture loaded onto the wagons, they had no other choice.

"Good mornin', Miz Reginia, I cooked up some bacon, eggs, and corn muffins." Laudie's voice rang with excitement. "You need to eat somethin' before we leave."

"I think I will just have some coffee and a muffin, please," Reginia said with a smile. She was trying to appear excited, but inside she feared the new adventure.

"Reginia, Big Bo is going to move the last of the furniture and Laudie will make sure Fancy and Batha will pack the last of our clothing." William was so calm as he spoke. This was very reassuring to Reginia. She knew he could always sense when she was anxious over something. "We'll be leaving in about one hour. Children, are you ready to leave for our new home?"

"Yes, sir." The children both responded to William at the same time. Sarah could hardly wait to explore the wild frontier called Texas and Alex imagined new friends to play with. Fancy and Batha were stirring about frantically making sure they had not forgotten anything. Laudie would have their heads if she found something not packed. The slaves took great care in packing the china, crystal, and silver. Samuel inspected all the furniture, ensuring that each piece had a blanket bounding it for protection.

Samuel entered the kitchen with words Reginia was not anxious to hear. "Master Wilde, the wagons are loaded and the livestock is rounded up and ready to leave." William had rounded up many wild cows in Texas over the last four years, but he wanted to take some of the fine-bred cattle from home with him to Texas. "Thank you, Samuel. We'll be out in a minute."

Reginia watched as the children rushed to the head wagon with great joy. She took a few minutes to walk through the house one last time. What memories she had to cherish. As she walked out the front door, she saw William proudly sitting in the first wagon. His look of confidence reassured her. She turned cautiously toward the wooden door, paused, and very gently closed it. "Goodbye, old home, I will surely miss you," Reginia whispered, then stood for a moment with her hands pressed against the door. She turned slowly and walked to the covered wagon and took her place beside William. She never looked back.

William slapped the reins on the backs of the horses, shouting, "Get up." Suddenly, Reginia's stomach tied in knots with the suspense of not knowing what her future held. They were Texas bound. William told Reginia that only a few settlers were in Texas but he guaranteed her more would come.

As the wagons moved down the road, William eagerly began telling Reginia all about the Texas plantation. "The bottom lands are fertile and produce a generous amount of cotton and the house sits on a hill overlooking a clear creek. I feel confident in this decision to move," he stated firmly as he patted her lovingly on her leg. William's excitement brought an unexpected smile to her face.

William knew this move would bring hardships but they would make the best of them. He had left Reginia behind until he had overcome some of the adversities. The land was producing now and making a large amount of money, the house was complete, and he had eagerly prepared to move his family.

Joseph Riley and his family would be leaving for Texas shortly after them. The Rileys' homeplace was near the Wildes' plantation and for this Reginia was grateful. The horses pulled the wagons westward as she daydreamed of her future. William said it would take almost three months to get to their new home. He wanted to arrive before the hot summer set in. This was a good idea. That would give them all summer to get settled into their new home. Reginia had requested a large home with wide, long porches and tall columns. In her confusion of leaving, she forgot to ask William what kind of home he had built for them. She turned at once toward him with a childlike curiosity in her eyes. "My darling, what about the house? You must tell me about it. Is it grand, with large porches? Does it have large columns?"

"Reginia, I wouldn't disappoint you. You'll see," William replied teasingly.

Oh, she just hated when he would not elaborate. "You're such a scoundrel. I've never known anyone who enjoys creating a surprise more than you." He laughed and Reginia knew she would have to wait and see for herself what he had built.

They traveled due west across Louisiana from Natchez. They stopped along the way, staying one or two days with other plantation owners. This made their travels much easier. Spring had been good to them with moderate showers and cool days. They could not have asked for a better trip. April was ending, and Reginia had not seen the river they had to cross to enter into Texas.

They had been traveling the trail most of the day, when suddenly she heard the sound of rushing water. "William, is that the river?" she exploded with excitement.

"Reginia, honey, we're here. We've reached Texas. The river is right up ahead." William was so proud—or relieved—she wasn't sure which. They were so near. The sounds of the water increased until suddenly, out of the woods, the river appeared. "I can't believe we're here," Reginia whispered. She felt apprehensive about crossing the river. It was deep and the water was flowing rapidly. Large flatboats made of timber waited to carry the wagons across the river, but the livestock would have to swim across. With the wagons on the flatboats, and the horses unhitched and on the shore, they were ready to cross. Reginia felt a rush of fear as the current tugged against the large wooden flatboat. She held Alex and Sarah tightly, closing her eyes until they were across. She stood on the bank with the children watching as William directed the slaves to bring the livestock. The animals struggled against the river's current, but all of them crossed successfully. Amazement filled Reginia at the God-given instinct the animals had to swim and survive. Nightfall was near and William decided to camp overnight by the river. Texas appeared wild and primitive. She could hardly believe what she saw. It was nothing like Mississippi.

Reginia was restless all night; there was also the fear of Indians, which did not help matters. Every noise roused her as William slept soundly. She tossed and turned all night until the morning light appeared over the river. She turned toward William, caressing him. She thought how silly she had been to have worried and deprived herself of sleep. "William, wake up. It's morning," she said softly. He turned over and gazed into her beautiful brown eyes. He held her close for a minute, grateful for a wife such as Reginia. She woke the children and prepared them for travel while Laudie prepared the breakfast. As they ate, William informed them of the day's plan.

"We'll travel today to San Augustine. However, I've changed my mind about the length of stay there. We'll stay a week or possibly two. I want to rest the livestock and visit with the other Texans."

"Darling, where will we stay?" Reginia wondered. She had seen nothing but small shanties.

"I made friends with Jim Wade during my travels back and forth. We'll stay at his home. He has a large plantation a few miles east of San Augustine and we are more than welcome to stay and let the livestock rest. His wife Betty is very nice. You'll enjoy visiting with her and they have six children for Alex and Sarah to play with. This will be a nice rest before we travel across the Old Spanish Trail to our plantation."

"That sounds wonderful, William. I'll be glad to meet some people that have lived here for a while. Betty can tell me what Texas is like." She squeezed his hand as she always did to let him know she would support his decisions.

They traveled until mid-afternoon. William pulled the horses to a stop and pointed off to the left. "Reginia, look." She looked and saw the lane leading toward a two-story house on the hill. "That's the Wade

Plantation." It was a large home with a circular porch. "What a beautiful sight," Reginia thought. William reined the horses down the lane.

"I hope they won't mind having us." Reginia was eager to have a bed to sleep in and enthusiastic smiles to welcome them. "I'll be glad to have a hot cup of tea and a nice warm bath."

"Don't worry. Betty and Jim are looking forward to meeting you."

As they neared the house, the front door swung open and there stood Betty. She was very attractive, tall and slender with dark hair and a smile as big as the Mississippi River. Her arms waved in the air, welcoming the Wilde family in. Reginia felt so welcome and knew they would be friends. Betty rushed to greet them as William pulled the horses to a stop at the front porch.

"William, how are you? Did you have a good trip?" Betty beamed as she spoke. William had told them so much about his family and now the day had come to finally meet them.

"We're fine and we had a very good trip. Betty, I would like for you to meet my family." He pointed to Reginia. "This is my wife, Reginia, my daughter, Sarah, and my son, Alex."

"I am so glad to meet you, Reginia, Sarah, and Alex." Betty motioned for their house slave Brick to come to the wagons. "Come into the house. I have tea brewing and afterward you can freshen up." Betty turned her attention back to William. "I'll have Brick show your slaves where to put the wagons and livestock." Turning toward Reginia, she smiled. "Come now, I know you must be ready to get off that wagon."

"Oh, you just don't know how good that sounds, Betty," Reginia responded as William climbed from the wagon and helped her and the children down. "I'm so pleased to meet you. William has spoken so fondly of you and Jim."

Betty hugged each of them with a warm welcome. She then instructed Brick to take the wagons to the barn and to put the cattle in the north pasture and put the horses in the pens by the barn. She told him to let William's slaves quarter with their slaves.

"Come in and rest, I know you are tired from your trip." Betty's children suddenly appeared at the front door to see the visitors. The sight of new faces to play with excited all the children. They ran toward each other with gaiety. Reginia marveled at the energy the young ones had.

"My children don't look too weary, do they. I think resting is not on their minds." She giggled as the children ran off to play. Reginia examined the house as they walked toward the front door. It was a large white wood-frame home. The white paint had become worn and bare in spots. She wondered if her home would look the same. Life in Texas was certainly not as sophisticated as in the States. Betty opened the front door and Reginia walked in. Reginia looked about in awe at the furnishings. Beautiful rugs covered the wood floors, and the furnishings were elegant. She knew Betty must have excellent taste. Life was hard in Texas in the early days, and the slaves were busy working the fields and clearing land. The slaves obviously did not have time for painting the house or barns. Betty directed them into the parlor. The tea poured from elegant silver pots into fine china cups.

"Your home is very nice, Betty."

"Thank you. Jim brought everything from our home in North Carolina. He has worked very hard to make this plantation a success. Things are finally coming together, and this summer he is going to repaint the house and the barns. Soon, our plantation will be as beautiful as our old home."

"When will Jim be in?" William asked.

"He's in the field. They're planting the cotton. He should be in before dark."

They continued drinking the tea and visiting. Betty knew Reginia wanted to clean up. "Reginia, I have a hot bath waiting for you, if you are ready?"

"I would absolutely love that, thank you." Betty took Reginia upstairs to the guest room while William took a walk about the grounds and to the barn to check on his horses. Betsy, a house slave, waited in the bedroom to assist Reginia with her bath. Life was hard on the frontier but some things remained the same.

Hospitality and family love still existed. Reginia's worries were beginning to leave. Reginia undressed with the help of Betsy. She slid into the hot, soothing tub of water. As Betsy scrubbed her back, she felt as if she could just fall asleep right there. It had been weeks since she had bathed in a tub. It seemed like months. Betsy had a pot of hot water waiting over the fire in the fireplace. She poured it into the tub. Reginia sighed and sank lower into the water, letting it cover her entire body.

Betty was in the kitchen checking the dinner preparations. She had given orders for roast chicken, buttered yams, fresh greens, and a berry cobbler. The aroma filled the house. Betty had the dining table set with her fine china and crystal. The spring flowers were blooming and she had picked beautiful blue ones for the centerpiece. She enjoyed entertaining their friends and travelers.

Jim had been one of the first settlers in the area. His intention of acquiring a large tract of land had led him to this area. He owned thousands of acres and many slaves. The land produced large amounts of cotton, corn, and grains. News of Jim's success spread throughout the area and into the States. Jim and William shared the same ideas concerning planting and the new frontier. Both men had attended college and had great ambitions. This was the basis for a strong bond of friendship that would last a lifetime.

William stood on the hill by the main barn, which Jim had built directly behind the house for easy access to the carriages and horses. He gazed out across the fields of cotton, his thoughts on his own plantation. William looked about the hills knowing Ransom would have his fields planted by the time they arrived home. William looked down the hill to see Jim approaching on his horse.

"Jim," William yelled, waving as his friend neared. Jim waved and kicked his horse into a gallop. It took only seconds for Jim to reach the top of the hill. He pulled the horse to a quick stop and dismounted quickly. "William. It's good to see you." The two men shook hands. Each had a firm handshake.

Jim Wade was five feet ten in stature and stout as a bull. His red hair and freckles accented his bright blue eyes. Jim always had a smile, but everyone knew not to ever make this man angry. He was fearless and could hold his own in a fight. Unlike William, Jim dressed more casually, wearing only a shirt, with the top button unbuttoned, and his pants tucked neatly in his riding boots.

"You've been busy. The place looks great and you have a lot of cotton planted I see."

"Yeah, the weather has been good to us this year. I think this will be my best year. I bought fifty more slaves so I can do more planting. You know, there are some wild cattle around here. During the winter, we rounded up more than two hundred heads. I plan to increase my cattle operation. I believe there will be a future in the cattle business."

"You think so?" William wasn't sure about the cattle business.

"Yep, I do. More people will move in and the market for beef should increase."

"You may be right. That is something to think about. For now, I'm just concentrating on my cotton crop. The land along the Brazos produces well. It should. It's rich and fertile. I'm glad I located near San Felipe. The capital should attract business and I wanted to be near the politics of this new land. I have a friend on the Brazos farther south. His name is Joe Bell and he's involved with Austin."

"Yeah, I met Joe about four years ago, with Stephen Austin. He issued land grants when the Mexicans imprisoned Stephen. He's a fine man and has a large plantation in Columbia, I hear."

"Yes, he does. I plan to make a trip to see him when I get the family settled."

"I'm glad you're here, William. Let's go to the house. I'm anxious to meet your family." The two men walked to the house, passing the children running and playing tag in the yard. William felt pleased at the sight of his children laughing and having so much fun. William stopped the children briefly to make formal introductions and continued on to the house. They entered the house and found the ladies in the parlor. They were in an intense conversation and did not see the men walk in.

"Look at those two, Jim, I don't know which one can talk the most."

"They don't even know we're here. Betty has longed for a good friend in Texas. I think she has found her." They walked into the parlor and the ladies looked startled. They could not believe the men had come in unnoticed.

"For goodness sakes, Jim, how long have you two been there?" Betty exclaimed.

"Long enough to see you two have plenty to talk about."

"Jim, this is my wife Reginia," William said.

"I'm pleased to meet you, Reginia. I hope your trip was a good one." Jim's vivacious voice made Reginia smile.

"Yes, it was a good one, and I am very pleased to meet you, Jim. William has told me much about your plantation and I'm looking forward to seeing all of it."

"I'm glad to hear that. Tomorrow, we'll take the carriage and I'll show you and William the place."

"Oh, that would be wonderful. But, if you don't mind, I would love to ride my horse. I haven't ridden him since we left Natchez." Reginia had developed excellent horsemanship at a young age. She loved horses. William had bought her a beautiful black thoroughbred to bring to Texas. Reginia only rode him a couple of times and was anxious to be on his back again, and riding the fields delighted Jim and Betty, for they both loved to ride too.

"Dinner will be ready in about an hour," Betty interrupted. "Why don't you men freshen up before we eat."

"That sounds good, Betty. Did you have Betsy draw our bath?" Jim knew she had. She always had everything ready for Jim when he came in from the fields.

"Yes, dear. You get cleaned up and I'll get the children in and washed up."

The two men departed. William was ready for a hot bath and a good dinner. Betty called the children in and had them wash their hands and faces. The children had fast become friends. Their laughter filled the house as they ran in. Betty's daughter Mary and Sarah Wilde were the same age. They giggled and visited nonstop. Her son Jackson was a year older than Alex Wilde but the two had also become friends. They seemed to get along so well. Alex was tall for his age and was the same size as Jackson.

Dinner was on the table when the men came downstairs. They all gathered around the table as Jim said a prayer of thanksgiving for the meal and their friends. They seated themselves at the table. Reginia and William were so grateful to have such friends as the Wades.

"The dinner looks delicious, Betty. Reginia and I appreciate your hospitality."

"Thank you, William. We're so happy to have you and your family with us."

Everyone ate heartily. The children asked to leave the table for more fun and games. Jim told them they could play until an hour before bedtime. He knew it would take the children an hour just to clean the grime from their bodies. Reginia and Betty escaped to the parlor for more talk and the men retired to the large back porch for cigars. The night was cool and clear. William felt comfortable as he sat in the rocker. "Jim, I can hardly believe I have my family in Texas. I believe the stars are even brighter here." He laughed.

"They probably are." Jim grinned. "I know you're anxious to get to your new home."

"Indeed, I am. I was going to stay for a couple of weeks, but I believe I'll leave at the end of the week. Seeing your fields being planted and the work you're doing has made me long to see what Ransom has accomplished," William explained.

"I don't blame you. I'm sure Ransom has done a fine job and you'll see a change when you get there. He should have started planting by now."

"We cleared more land, while I was building the house. Reginia will be surprised. The home is very large. Some of the Mexicans helped. It is made of clay bricks the Mexicans call "adobe;" even the large columns are adobe. It has a large porch on the front and back. The clay bricks were used on the floor of the porches. I had a balcony built on the back porch. It overlooks the fields and the creek. We built a glass observatory on the top level. You can see for miles up there. It allows the sun to shine to the bottom floor. The house has large windows. Reginia loves the sunlight. I swear I took all year to build that house. It looks like a grand Southern plantation home covered with white stucco."

"It sounds beautiful. I bet Reginia is excited," Jim stated.

"She has no idea. I want to surprise her. I even had a bathing room built near the bedrooms. It has a fireplace to heat the water and warm the room. This move was not easy for her. I know that. Reginia did not make one complaint. It is going to be hard starting over in this new land. I wanted our home to have all, if not more, of the comforts of our home in Natchez."

Jim smiled. "Well, it sounds like she will have a pleasant surprise."

The men talked for a while longer until William realized the sounds of the children had disappeared. "I think the children have fallen asleep."

"I think you're right. We should get the ladies and retire ourselves. I know you and Reginia must be exhausted."

William nodded. "Yes, we are."

The men interrupted the ladies' conversation and insisted they should get a good night's sleep. "Betty, we must retire for the evening. Reginia is tired and you need your rest so you can continue your talking tomorrow," William stated, with a smile on his face.

Jim laughed as he took Betty by the arm and showed William and Reginia to their bedroom. "We'll see you in the morning. I'm looking forward to our ride."

"Thank you, Jim, so are we." Reginia was wide awake with excitement. She wondered how she could possibly sleep.

William undressed quickly and climbed into bed. He watched as Reginia slipped into her white gown, with her long auburn curls hanging loose and free. He thought she had the most beautiful hair. She turned, catching William admiring her, and smiled, thinking how wonderful it was to be there with her husband. She went quickly to the bed and curled in beside him. He took her curls in his hands and pulled her gently for a kiss. His gentle strength excited Reginia. She looked into his eyes, stroking his face and neck. "William, I love you so much." He held her close, stroking her gently and kissing her softly all over her body. Their passion turned into lovemaking that left them breathless.

Afterward, Reginia lay limp, thankful to have a man that could excite her so much, after so many years of marriage. She felt fulfilled and easily drifted off to sleep. William watched her lying there peacefully. He could hardly believe the great devotion they felt for each other. He thought how blessed he was to have this lady in his life. William soon fell asleep, thinking of the tenderness they had shared.

CHAPTER
THREE

Morning light streaked through the slightly parted drapes of the guest room. Reginia awoke, rested and full of energy. She could hardly wait to ride her black thoroughbred and see the Texas plantation. She rolled over to William, nibbling softly on his ear. "Wake up, my darling." She continued nibbling his ear teasingly. William pretended to sleep, for he loved her little touches in the morning. "Darling, wake up. We have a lot to do today. We're going riding." She continued stroking and caressing him. William rolled over suddenly and grabbed her, rolling her about the bed. "William, quit that; you are going to wake everyone in the house."

"They are awake. I want to play with you." He continued rolling and hugging her. He held Reginia down and dared her to move. She playfully gave in. "I love you, Reginia Wilde."

"And I love you, William Wilde." The hugging and kissing continued until the aroma of the coffee and bacon overwhelmed Reginia. "Something smells good. We'd better dress and get downstairs."

"Oh, Reginia, must we," William pleaded.

"I'm starving. Now get up."

"Well, if you insist. But you might have more fun here." William smiled.

"I'm sure I would," Reginia replied, "but too much exercise on an empty stomach cannot be good for you."

Reginia bounced out of the bed and began dressing for the day. William beheld her slim figure with great appreciation. She looked the same as the day they'd married. There were no signs she had ever given birth to his two children.

"Hurry, William, I want to have breakfast and ride my horse," Reginia eagerly insisted.

William reluctantly arose and dressed.

Jim and Betty were in the sitting room having coffee. Jim saw William and Reginia and offered them a cup. "Come in and have some coffee." The morning sunlight filled the room. Reginia looked about in awe at the space with its big windows overlooking the hillside, which glistened with morning dew.

"I would love coffee, thank you." Reginia glowed with anticipation of her first ride in the new frontier.

"Did you sleep well?" Betty questioned.

"Oh yes, Betty. We were very comfortable." Reginia, with a slight blush to her smiling face, turned her head to William and winked.

"The children ate. They were eager to go outside to play. Jim gave them permission to eat without us. I hope you don't mind."

"That's fine," William replied. "What time do you want to go for the ride, Jim?"

"I thought we would leave after breakfast."

"Great. We're ready." William smiled.

They went into the dining room for breakfast. Biscuits, jams, eggs, bacon, and gravy filled the buffet. After eating, they headed for the barn to mount their horses for the morning ride.

The morning air was crisp and cool, making an excellent day for the ride. They arrived at the barn finding the horses saddled and ready to go. All eyes fell on the beautiful black gelding.

Reginia was so proud of him. The black thoroughbred was tall and had powerful muscles, with a long neck and hip. His big eyes showed intelligence and good nature. The big gelding impressed Jim. "Reginia, this is a mighty fine horse. What do you call him?"

"I call him Jet, because he's jet-black. Jim, he's also fast and can jump anything. I just love him." She was ready and eager to gallop across the fields. Reginia walked to Jet and mounted. She looked at ease and graceful in the saddle.

The others mounted their horses and they headed down the hill. Reginia was a true horsewoman. She controlled the big gelding with gentle hands, maneuvering him wherever she wanted to go.

Betty approached Reginia and asked if she would like to gallop down the trail. Reginia kicked Jet into a gallop and off the two ladies rode. They ran for a while jumping logs along the way. Reginia loved the fresh air blowing in her face; she felt very serene when she was riding her horse.

"This is splendid, Reginia. I love to ride, especially when the mornings are cool. I hope we can do this again," Betty spoke as she galloped her horse alongside Reginia.

"Oh, let's do. I would love nothing better. Maybe we can ride every morning. The weather is delightful and maybe we could ride early and watch the sunrise." Reginia continued galloping Jet alongside Betty, thinking how fortunate they were to have made friends with Betty and Jim. They all had so much in common.

The men were busy inspecting the planting when the ladies returned. Jim wanted to show William and Reginia the rest of the plantation and the cattle. The four rode all morning. It was noon before they returned back to the house.

"I enjoyed the ride very much. You have a beautiful place," Reginia said with pleasure in her voice.

"Thank you," Jim replied. "You and Betty really seemed to have fun. Betty loves to ride and her friends do not share the same enthusiasm. I'm glad you're here to ride with her."

"We're going for a morning ride each day they're here, if the weather permits," Betty responded.

They walked in the front door to find Betsy waiting for them with her warm smile. "I have lunch ready. The children played all morning and wore themselves out. I brought them in and fed them. Now they are upstairs taking a good nap."

"Thank you, Betsy." Betty knew she could always depend on Betsy. "Let us wash our hands and we'll be in the dining room for lunch."

After lunch, the men settled in the drawing room and the ladies retired for a nap. Jim wanted to show William the layout of the plantation and his future plans for planting and cattle. Jim had acquired six thousand acres and had only three thousand in production. Jim pulled his drawings from the desk and began showing them to William. Jim's plans for planting more cotton impressed William. Jim was near the Sabine River where shipping the cotton was easy. He also wanted to purchase more cattle. Jim had a vision of a future for the beef market. William found his ideas concerning Texas interesting and wanted to know more.

"William, Texas is growing. More and more families are moving in. Families with money are coming and developing the land. There is gossip among the Mexicans that the Mexican government wants to stop further immigration of Americans. I fear this may be true. The Mexicans had no success developing Texas until Austin came in. Progress has been made and I do not want to see it stopped."

"Have you talked to other settlers about this?"

"Yes, in fact, you and I can ride into San Augustine tomorrow. There is going to be a meeting concerning this matter at Tom Buckley's home. In 1826, we set up the Fredonian Republic; however, it caused much resentment and was short-lived. I feel if we had more Americans behind us, this would have succeeded."

"I'm anxious to go. We must be prepared if the Mexicans attempt to do this." William knew about the short-lived Fredonian Republic, but he was not sure if Austin knew of the Mexicans' plans to stop immigration of the Americans. "Is Austin aware of this?"

"I'm not sure. As I said, this is only gossip we've heard."

"I would prefer Reginia not know what the meeting is about until we are sure the Mexicans are going to do something. She would only worry and that would do no good for my family."

The men continued talking and making plans for the next day. They shared their ideas for the new frontier. William was glad his land was near San Felipe de Austin. This was the settlement's capital and he wanted involvement in the discussions that would affect the new land. If, indeed, the Mexicans were becoming hostile, he wanted to know. He had become friendly with a couple of Mexicans in the area and hoped to renew the friendship upon his return. The Indians were not terribly aggressive in the area where William purchased land. That was one reason he had not moved to Columbia with his friend Joe Bell. The Indians were warlike in that area, the west and the north regions. William wanted the safest location for his family.

The ladies awoke and joined the men for afternoon tea and biscuits. Betty knew Reginia always had cakes or sweets with her tea, so she explained to Reginia that obtaining sugar, fruits, and spices was difficult. They were able to purchase them at the river dock at only certain times of the year and they were very expensive. Reginia was discovering things were different but she could live with the adjustments. She was so comfortable and felt so peaceful at the Wade Plantation.

The next morning, William and Jim rode into San Augustine for the meeting, while the ladies went for another ride. It took the men thirty minutes at a gallop to reach the Buckley home. Tom Buckley greeted them at the door. There were ten other men at the Buckley home. They discussed the possibilities of the Mexicans refusing more immigration and what the Americans could do about this. The likelihood of hostilities troubled the men. William would speak to Austin and the others when he got to his home. The meeting lasted until mid-afternoon. The men rode swiftly home. Jim wanted to speak with his overseer about clearing more land.

The week went quickly. William was especially eager to get home. He wanted to see the progress on his own plantation and wanted to see Austin about the Mexicans. Jim had the wagons brought to the house the night before they were to leave and the cattle brought into the holding pens in preparation for the departure. They had gone to bed early that night. William wanted his family fresh for the early morning departure. Reginia snuggled close to William that night, with her hand lying across his large chest. Thoughts of reaching their new home soon filled her with excitement. Texas was not so bad. After all, she had found new friendship with the Wades.

FOUR

Morning came quickly. There was a light fog as Reginia looked from the window. She thought how wonderful it had been that week with Betty and her family. She hoped they would be able to visit again.

After breakfast, they were ready to leave. There was some sadness at leaving. Reginia hugged Betty and Jim goodbye, urging them to please come for a visit. Everyone said goodbye and William thanked them warmly for their hospitality. Jim helped Reginia onto the wagon and she took her place beside her husband. The wagons traveled slowly down the lane, with Reginia and the children waving all the way. Reginia squeezed William's arm. "This has been a good week. I will miss them terribly. I do hope they will come to visit us." The wagons turned off the lane and onto the trail west across Texas. William told Reginia they would be at their new home within three weeks. She could hardly wait. She could not believe she was almost there. They were on the last leg of the trip.

The trip was going well as they stopped in Nacogdoches for supplies. The town was small with shanties and log homes. One home in particular was nice. It was a large home built of wood with several chimneys. A wealthy merchant by the name of Stone had built the house. He supplied the area with goods and even opened his home to the neighboring women and children as a refuge from the Indian raids. The people were friendly and gracious. Reginia was discovering a special kindred spirit among the Texans and found herself included in the feeling of being a Texas pioneer.

The Wildes headed west with their wagons full of supplies. The wilderness amazed Reginia. The land was pretty with high rolling hills and lush green grass. Years of settlers and Mexicans traveling across Texas had worn the road. Looking ahead, the old trail seemed to disappear into a dark cloud. "What is that, William?" Reginia gasped. The darkness spread as far as she could see in every direction.

"That's the Big Thicket." William grinned with unconcern. "That's what they call this area. The trail goes through the middle of it. We'll travel a day and a half through it."

Reginia just stared ahead at the tall pines towering high across the hills. As they traveled into the great thicket, the trees blinded the bright sky. The brush was thick under the trees and the road quickly disappeared in the darkness. Only faint rays of sunlight glistened through the brush. An uncomfortable feeling came across Reginia. Her mind imagined wild animals and Indians lurking about. The thought of spending the night in the thicket sent chills up her spine. William reassured her that all would be fine, but she did not believe it.

While traveling, Reginia spent the days reading with the children and teaching them lessons. However, this day she could not see for the darkness and had to postpone their schooling until they were out of the thicket.

William came to a small clearing by a creek that evening and decided to make camp. He had the slaves circle the wagons. Reginia knew William was taking precautions against the dangers of the thicket. She insisted the children sleep in the wagon with them. It was after midnight when crashes of thunder and bolts of lightning awoke them. Reginia awakened startled with her brown eyes open wide and screamed to William. He reached over and grabbed her, trying to calm her.

The children awoke, frightened. They jumped immediately into their parents' arms. Reginia realized it was only a storm and calmed herself for the children's sake. Inside, Reginia was nervous. She did not mind storms; in fact, she enjoyed them in the safety of her home, but she did not enjoy this storm in the thicket. The wind blew fiercely, and the air became very cool. William thought it was late in the season for this cold air. The children shivered from the cold, as Reginia covered them with more blankets. Out of the dark, they heard Samuel and Big Bo.

"Master Wilde, Master Wilde," they called with urgency in their voice. William put his head out of the wagon to see if something was wrong. Indeed, something was wrong. The cattle had spooked and run away. The storm was too bad to hunt for the cattle. William instructed the slaves to secure the horses tightly and get back in their wagons for shelter. They would gather the cattle during daylight. William knew they would never be able to see the cattle at night.

The next morning, William had the horses saddled and with the slaves he went in search for his cattle. There had been a lot of rain overnight and the creek was filled with water. The ground had become muddy and slippery. Noon passed and William had still not returned.

Reginia worried about William. She ran to Laudie. "Laudie, stay with the children. I'm going to get Jet and try to find Master William. I fear something dreadful has happened."

Laudie put her hands on her hips and sternly snapped back, "Missus, you ain't doin' no such a thing. All we need is you goin' and gettin' yourself lost or hurt. Master William would have my hide if I was to lettin' you leave."

Reginia put her head on Laudie's shoulder. "Oh, Laudie, I'm so worried. I just want William to come back. Those darn cows aren't worth this."

"It's gonna be all right. Master William will be back soon. Don't you worry your pretty little self no more."

Finally, about four o'clock that evening, a weary William returned. They had searched all day and rounded up most of the cows. Only a few had escaped.

Reginia ran to him and hugged him tightly. "Oh, William. I've worried all afternoon."

"Reginia, I'm fine. Just a little muddy. Everything is going to be all right. The cattle are rounded up and tomorrow we'll be on our way."

That night, the air was still cold. A big fire was burning in the center of the circle of wagons. They sat around the fire with Samuel and Laudie. William told Reginia and the children about the day of adventure rounding up the cattle, before turning in for the night.

Samuel heated large rocks on the fire. He placed the rocks in a bucket and put the bucket in the wagon for his master. William placed it under the blanket by Sarah. William wanted the wagon as warm as possible—for Sarah had developed a chill from the cold damp air.

Morning came and the Wildes continued their journey. They crossed the country slowly with few mishaps. Until one day, while crossing a rock-filled creek, the wagon flipped; Reginia, Laudie, and Alex ran quickly to retrieve the goods that had fallen out of it. The wheel broke loose, but fortunately, William had brought extra ones along. They camped along the river that night.

Sarah remained in the wagon. For she was still running a fever and was not well. Reginia prayed her chill would not turn into pneumonia. She washed her with cool cloths and tried to keep her fever down. She hoped to reach a settlement soon. Only a few of the settlements had a doctor and she was hoping the next settlement would be one of them. The few settlements in Texas were not much, mainly a shanty or two and often just tents. Traveling in the wagon was not good for Sarah, but Reginia knew they could not stop.

The trip took longer than expected. Sarah was not improving and Reginia became very concerned. One month after they had left the Wades' home, they reached the Grosse Plantation. William knocked on the door of the magnificent home. He asked to speak with the master of the house. Mr. Grosse, an older yet dignified gentleman, came to the door and William introduced himself. He told Mr. Grosse that he and his family were traveling to their plantation, when his daughter became ill. Mr. Grosse graciously opened his home to them. He told William he had a doctor that lived on his plantation. Reginia felt relief as they removed Sarah from the wagon and into the doctor's hands. The doctor informed William that Sarah was too ill to move. He told them it would be a week before Sarah should travel. Her lungs sounded bad and he feared she was near pneumonia. Mr. Grosse insisted that William leave Reginia and Sarah with him and his wife. William felt discouraged, but he knew he needed to get his slaves and livestock to his plantation. They were so close to home. William agreed with Mr. Grosse and after thanking him he left, taking Alex with him.

It was mid-week when they reached the plantation. William missed Reginia and worried about Sarah. He hoped she would be well enough to travel when he returned for them. Ransom welcomed William and was eager to show him the planted fields. William and Ransom talked late into the evening. William wanted to know everything that had happened while he was away.

The next week went fast for William. Samuel and Laudie oversaw cleaning and placing the rugs and furnishings in the house. Laudie, determined to have the house in order for Reginia's arrival, worked night and day. The beautiful fields amazed William. He could see the cotton showing in the early stages and the grass was green and abundant. The wild flowers filled the fields. He could not wait to get his family home. He would leave the next morning for the Grosse Plantation.

illiam, Samuel, and Big Bo traveled the trail to the Grosse Plantation. The fear of an Indian attack prevented the settlers from traveling alone. Mr. Grosse was sitting on the front porch when William arrived. He walked sadly toward William, extending his hand to him. A terrible feeling arose in William's stomach. He knew by the look on Mr. Grosse's face that something was wrong.

"Where is Reginia, where is Sarah, what has happened?" William questioned with panic in his voice.

"Doctor Fields did all he could . . ."

William interrupted Mr. Grosse abruptly. "Where is Reginia and my daughter?" Panic was taking over William. Fear was mounting inside him as he stared at Mr. Grosse.

"William, sit here on the porch for a moment. I will explain everything."

William did not want to sit down; he wanted his wife and daughter. He tried to rush through the front door; but Mr. Grosse grabbed his arm and stopped him. "William, you must get a hold of yourself and listen to me first. Reginia is upstairs in a great deal of pain. You must be strong." William stood staring at him. He could not believe any of this was happening. He feared what Mr. Grosse was going to tell him and he did not want to hear it. "Yesterday morning, Sarah took a turn for the worse."

"Man. Can't you see, I just want my wife and daughter." William screamed with anger and pain. At this point, Samuel had stepped down from the carriage and was standing by his master and friend.

"Master Wilde, listen to Mr. Grosse. Missus Reginia, she needs you, she needs you to be strong." The gentleness of Samuel's voice calmed him.

William stood trembling with his eyes fixed on Mr. Grosse, beckoning to hear the very words he feared. Mr. Grosse placed his hands firmly on William's shoulder, giving William the support he knew he would need.

"I wish I could give you good news, but I cannot. Your daughter passed on late in the night."

There was a brief moment of total silence as William absorbed the unbearable reality. He stood slumped shouldered, his hands shaking, not saying a word.

"Master, are you all right?" Samuel questioned. Samuel loved Sarah and could not believe she had died. He held his master, his friend, by the arm. Suddenly, William wailed with sorrow. He could not control his emotions. He crumbled to the floor of the porch, tears streaming from his eyes. William doubled over with his head touching his knees. Samuel could not believe his master's reaction. William was a strong man, emotionally and physically. He handled everything with such strength. Samuel had never seen Master William like this. As Samuel watched his friend tormented with pain, he realized the love of family was the strongest bond on earth and to lose one member was to lose a part of yourself.

Samuel and Mr. Grosse gently pulled William to his feet. "Sit in the rocker for a while, William."

Mr. Grosse continued to console William. Samuel stayed by his master. Tears came in his eyes as he watched with sorrow. Samuel swallowed hard to prevent the tears from falling from his own eyes. He had been with his master when Ms. Sarah was born. Samuel had never seen a man so proud. Samuel felt frustrated and wanted to do something, but there was nothing that he could do.

William took a deep breath and pulled himself together. He wiped the tears from his eyes and focused his mind on Reginia, knowing she would need to rely on his strength to get through this terrible tragedy. He stood up and shook his head as if trying to shake the pain from his mind.

William looked at Mr. Grosse. "Show me to my wife."

Mr. Grosse nodded sympathetically and led William into the house and up the stairs to the guest room. William paused, sick with grief, then opened the door. He saw Reginia kneeling on the floor with her body draped over the bed, sobbing deeply.

"My God in Heaven," William murmured to himself. He could not believe his eyes. She was holding on to Sarah. He did not realize Reginia was still with the child. He forced himself toward his dead daughter and Reginia. He could not bear to look at Sarah; he kept his eyes on Reginia as he touched his wife's shoulder. She did not look up, although she knew it was William touching her; she knew her husband's touch. She slowly raised her head. She looked at William, her body and mind in complete shock and her eyes swollen and red. William slowly lifted Reginia's arms off Sarah and pulled her tight in his arms. Not a word passed their lips. Reginia began sobbing again and pressing so hard against William that she caused his body to sway. With closed eyes, fighting his own tears, he held her tighter, saying her name softly, over and over.

A few minutes passed and William opened his eyes. He saw Sarah. Her little body was stiff and blue. He could not bear seeing his beautiful, innocent child cold and all alone. He became furious, blaming himself for his daughter's death. If only he had stayed in Natchez with all its comforts, this would not have happened. Why did he bring his family to this wilderness? What was wrong with him, thinking he could provide safety for his family in this godforsaken land? Did his ambitions kill his precious Sarah? Would Reginia ever forgive him? William could not control his thoughts. Guilt overwhelmed him. He squeezed Reginia, hoping to get strength from her. She had no strength to give.

William had to get out of that room. He turned Reginia toward the door and gently took her into the hallway. He closed the door behind them and sat on a settee in the hallway. They held each other for a long while. Reginia had stopped sobbing, but tears still fell from her eyes as she looked at William. She put her hand on his cheek. "William, we have lost our baby. She is with the Lord." William, fighting the knots in his throat and the tears that were clouding his eyes, could not speak. If he spoke, the tears would fall. He could not break down in front of Reginia. She wrapped her arms around his neck and held on as if she were losing him too.

William took Reginia down the stairs and into the parlor with Mrs. Grosse. He wanted to talk to Mr. Grosse before leaving. William, determined to take Sarah home to bury her, told Mr. Grosse he knew he would have to travel day and night. Mr. Grosse agreed. He would have done the same thing if this were his child. Samuel wrapped Sarah in blankets and tied them securely with twine. He carried her little body out of the house and laid her in the back of the carriage.

William thanked Mr. Grosse and Dr. Fields for all their efforts. He then took Reginia to the carriage. Reginia wanted to be with Sarah, so the two of them climbed into the carriage by their daughter. Reginia sat by Sarah, holding her little body, as if to say, "It is all right, your mother is here." William put his arm around Reginia and placed his head on her shoulder. He felt so tired and drained; he just wanted to be home. Samuel slapped the reins on the horse's back and headed down the lane for home.

The trip seemed to take forever to William. They traveled all night and reached the plantation about noon the next day. Reginia still sat holding her little girl; she had not noticed the new home and the new surroundings. That was the last thing on Reginia's mind. Her mind was blank and she moved as if in a daze. Samuel helped them from the carriage and started to lift little Sarah's body. William stopped him. William wanted to carry Sarah's body into the house. This was his little girl and he wanted no one else lifting her. He carefully lifted Sarah's body and carried her into the library, laying her small body on the reading table. William instructed Samuel to tell Laudie and the other slaves of the death of Sarah. He asked Big Bo to build a coffin to place Sarah in. They would bury her in the back of the house under the large oak tree. The two slaves left, with heavy hearts, to tend to their duties.

Samuel told Laudie the sad news and she bolted for her Master and Missus. She entered the library and walked to William and Reginia, placing her arms around their waists. No one said a word. Tears fell from Laudie's eyes.

"We've lost our little angel, Laudie." William spoke as he patted her shoulder.

"Yes, sir, our little angel . . . she's with our Lord now. He'll take good care o' her."

William turned to Reginia. "Darling, let Laudie take you upstairs. We need a dress for Sarah." He faced Laudie and whispered, "She's in a bad way, Laudie. She needs your help."

Laudie nodded. "Come along, Missus. Let Laudie help you."

Laudie took Reginia upstairs to Sarah's room, to select a dress for the burial. Reginia walked into the room. She became alert to her surroundings. It was a beautiful room; a room filled with all of Sarah's toys and personal belongings. "Who fixed the room?" Reginia asked.

"Why, Samuel and I did, Missus. We worked real hard. We wanted that house ready for your return."

Reginia gently squeezed Laudie's arm as she moved to pick up the doll that lay on the bed. She held the doll at arm's length, staring at it briefly then caressed it to her breast. She turned slowly, gazing at each item that Sarah had once held in her own hands. Sarah would never see her new room, nor would she grow into a beautiful young lady. Reginia began to cry softly.

Laudie held her Missus, comforting her. Big tears fell from Laudie's eyes. She loved little Sarah and had cared for her since the day she was born. Reginia held on to Laudie as she selected the dress. "Laudie, please . . . would you prepare our Sarah for burial?" Laudie nodded yes. Reginia stayed in Sarah's room as Laudie departed. She sat on the four-poster bed, crying. Holding the child's doll, she wondered how life could go on without Sarah.

William was busy searching for Alex. He found him playing in a field by the barn. William set Alex down and explained as best he could what had happened. Alex had many questions for William. Alex was young and was not sure where his sister was. William sat with Alex for a long while in the field, answering his questions. Sarah was with Jesus in Heaven. Alex finally accepted this; he just could not understand where Heaven was.

That evening, as William, Reginia, and Alex sat in the library with Sarah, the slaves with lanterns in hand gathered at the front door. They came to pay their respects. They sang their gospel songs and mourned the death of their little Missus. William heard the singing and took Reginia and Alex to the front porch. What a beautiful sight was before them. The lanterns lit the area like moonbeams as the slaves sang "Swing Low Sweet Chariot." It appeared every slave had come to offer their sympathy. The respect and love the slaves exhibited touched William and Reginia deep in their hearts.

The next morning, the family, friends, and slaves gathered for the burial of little Sarah. Reginia had faith in her Lord and trusted Sarah was now in His care. William stood over the little wooden box expressing words of love and faith taken from the Bible. Reginia, with tears in her eyes, stooped to pick the orange and blue wildflowers that were blooming in the field. She tossed them gently over the box. Alex studied his mother's actions. He reached for some flowers, picked a few, and tossed them on his sister's casket. The burial was complete. William took Alex's and Reginia's hands and walked slowly to the house while Big Bo and a helper covered Sarah's little coffin with the freshly dug earth.

CHAPTER
SIX

William sat on the front porch of his home continuing to blame himself for his daughter's death. He worried about Reginia. Grief had taken a toll on her. She had eaten very little and had become weak. William had to do something to get Reginia out of that bedroom for her sake and Alex's. Alex missed his mother's love and attention and could not understand why she would not see him. William had a deliberate mission as he walked in the house and up the stairs to their bedroom. He was bringing Reginia down those stairs, even if he had to carry her down. He walked into their bedroom and to the bed with a firm state of mind. He lifted her and looked directly into her eyes.

"You must get out of this bed, Reginia." His voice was gentle yet firm. "Lying in this bed grieving over our daughter does you no good. You're making yourself sick. Laudie tells me that every morning you get sick when you try to eat. Reginia, you're being very selfish. You have a son who needs you very much and you have shown him no attention or love since Sarah's death. Now, I'm going to help you up. Fancy has a hot bath ready for you and I want you to bathe and dress in something beautiful. When you're finished, I want you downstairs to eat lunch with Alex and me."

"William, I cannot," she uttered as she clung to his arm.

"You can, and you will." He pulled her up and lifted her from the bed. She was limber in his arms as he carried her to the bathing room, where Fancy waited with her hot bath. "Fancy will help you." He took her chin in his hand, lifting her head, and made her look at him. "I'm going to leave you now and you had better be in the dining room in thirty minutes or I will come get you and carry you down." He smiled tenderly at her, trying to lift her spirits, before leaving the room to find Alex.

William and Alex sat waiting patiently at the dining table for Reginia. The door into the dining room swung open and there stood Reginia, with Fancy at her side. "Look at Missus Reginia, ain't she beautiful?" Fancy beamed with happiness to have her Missus up and about again.

"Yes, indeed she is, Fancy, indeed she is." William beamed with pride as he looked at his beautiful Reginia. William arose from the table and went to Reginia, placing her arm in his and seated her at the table by him.

Alex sat across from his mother. He looked at her with his big smile. Suddenly Reginia felt a warm tingle throughout her body. She got up from her chair and walked to her son. She reached for him, pulling his body up toward her and hugging him with all her might. Alex was so glad to be near his mother. His arms were around her waist holding her tightly. Reginia felt alive and felt love in her heart for the first time in many weeks. She pushed Alex back a little and looked into his eyes. "I love you very much, my son, and I don't think I realized how much I missed you until now. Please forgive me for not being there for you when you needed me the most." Her voice pleaded for forgiveness.

"I love you, Mother. I'm glad you're eating lunch with Father and me." Excitement filled Alex. She hugged him again. She thought how fortunate she was to have Alex. She then realized her life had to go on, even if it meant without Sarah. She returned to her chair and ate a hearty lunch with her family.

Afterward, Reginia asked William to show her the house. She'd been in a state of shock when she had arrived and hadn't noticed anything. She remembered seeing nothing but her four bedroom walls. William and Alex proudly escorted Reginia throughout their home. The house had a parlor, dining room, morning room, and library.

William had built the library with many shelves to hold Reginia's books. She loved to read and had collected the books throughout her life. The entry hall was very large. It went through the middle of the house from front to rear. A wide staircase in the middle of the entry hall ascended twelve feet to the next floor. They went up the wide staircase to the second floor where there were four bedrooms and a bathing room. Every room in the house had a fireplace. They passed Sarah's room. William had the door closed. He knew it was too soon for Reginia to enter their daughter's bedroom.

Alex, so proud of his room, urged his mother to see it first. He opened his door and took one step inside. He turned to her and teasingly bowed his body, motioning for her to enter as if ushering a queen into his room. She smiled at Alex and entered the room. Alex was so cute and full of wit. He made her realize how precious life was and how much she had to be grateful for. His room was charming. William brought all of Alex's furniture and wooden toys from Natchez. They fit in the new room perfectly. Large doors with fixed glass opened onto the back balcony. The west window allowed the sunlight to fill the room with brightness. Alex took his mother by the hand and led her through the doors and onto the balcony. She put her arms around him as they looked across the meadows of flowers. She held him close as she caught sight of the mound of dirt where her daughter lay buried. She was so thankful to have Alex. She must now be strong for him. "Alex, you and I will plant flowers on Sarah's grave. Maybe we can get Big Bo to build a cross and put a fence around it. Would you help me do this?"

"Yes, Mother, I would, and that would be nice to do for Sarah."

Reginia knew she should be positive for Alex. He did not fully understand death. "You know, Alex, Sarah is in Heaven with Jesus and He is taking good care of her."

"Oh, I know. Father told me all about Heaven. I think that is where I shall go someday. It sounds like a lot of fun."

"Yes, it is." Reginia looked at William and smiled.

Alex felt great with his mother back with him. She had seen his room and now he was ready to go play. "Father, is it all right if I go play? Mother has seen my room and you can show her the rest of the house."

William looked at Reginia and she winked at him with approval. "I think that is a good idea, son. You go play and have a good time." William was glad to see Alex happy again.

Alex rushed downstairs and out the back door to the slave quarters. William gave him permission to play with the Negro children. William didn't know, but during the week, Alex had made friends with Batha's boy, Ben, who was the same age. Alex missed playing with Sarah and was very lonely. While wandering in the field one day, Alex saw Ben and asked him to play. They had met each day in the field, playing for hours.

William turned to Reginia. "My darling, I have a surprise for you."

"A surprise? I can't imagine what more there could be."

William placed Reginia's arm in his and took her down the hall to a small winding staircase. Reginia looked up the stairs. She smiled as the light shone down on her face from the third floor. "Oh, William, you built an observatory. Why, only a few homes in the South have this." She skipped up the stairs to the balcony. Windows went completely around the small room, and a bench curved around the room under the windows. The entire rounded ceiling was a dome of glass, divided only by the framework. Reginia stood in amazement. "This entire room is glass. William, I can hardly believe this home . . . a bathing room and an observatory. No wonder you were gone for a year." She turned around slowly. "I love this room, I can see for miles and the view is magnificent."

The fields of wildflowers and oak trees took her breath away. She took William's hand and squeezed it gently. "William, I can see why you love this country." Together, they stood, hand in hand, looking across the fields. Their eyes caught sight of Alex and Ben running toward the creek. Their hearts became gladdened at the sight of Alex running and having fun with a friend. William stood silently watching Alex, recalling memories of himself and Samuel at a young age and what Samuel's friendship had meant to him. Reginia stood quietly enjoying the pleasures of the afternoon, and for a brief moment she forgot her sorrows.

Reginia asked William to show her the outside of the house. In her mind, she was seeing the home for the first time. William took Reginia outside. As she looked at the adobe house, her eyes focused toward the large square columns. William had the house and columns painted white with black painted shutters framing the windows. William explained to Reginia how the Mexicans taught them to make the adobe house. The outside adobe walls served also as the inside walls.

William had all the inside walls painted white. The ceilings were wood and he had them whitewashed, except in the library where the wooden bookshelves and ceiling had oil rubbed on the wood to preserve it. The oil brought out the natural grains of the wood, leaving a rich glistening effect.

Reginia walked away from the house and turned to see it from a distance. She thought it was beautiful. She walked slowly around the house admiring the design. She reached the back of the house. She paused, letting her eyes capture every detail. The porch was across the entire length of the back, as in the front but with a balcony. Wide stairs descended from the balcony. Split-wood shingles, soaked with oil, covered the roof. The house was an adobe Southern plantation-style home, unusual but elegant, a mixture of Mexican and American design. She thought it was perfect. William stood by her. He felt pleased to see the smile on Reginia's face. She looked to her right and saw a log building with a fireplace. It was about ten feet away and appeared connected to the main house.

"What is that building, William?"

"That's the one-room house I built and lived in when I first came to Texas. When we began building the main house, I decided to use it as the kitchen. I had it connected to the house with a hallway that opens directly into the dining room."

"William, this home is very comfortable. I think we will be happy here." Reginia knew the wait in Mississippi for her husband, while he had improved the land, had been a good idea. She walked over to William and put her arms around his neck. They stood embracing. Reginia never wanted separation from her husband again. This was home, and she wanted it to be for the rest of her days.

The afternoon was beautiful. The sun was shining warmly and the south breeze was refreshing as they sat on the front porch. Laudie brought tea for William and Reginia. Reginia sipped her tea, thinking how different life was in Texas. There was neither a school nor a church.

She would tutor Alex. She thought of Sarah and how quickly she learned. Reginia missed Sarah but was thankful for the wonderful memories of her. She shook her head to remove the lingering thoughts of Sarah.

Reginia wanted to know about William's plans for the plantation. The settlers could only plant a certain amount of land and had to ranch the remainder. William told of his plans to purchase much more land and build his herd of cattle. He also wanted to raise fine thoroughbreds. With the purchase of more land, he could plant more cotton. Reginia marveled at her husband's business mind. She reached for his hand, squeezing it, to let him know he had her full support.

That evening William, Reginia, and Alex had their first supper, together as a family, in the new home. Laudie prepared a delicious supper for them. Reginia felt at home. Throughout dinner, she thought more about the absence of a school and church in the area. She wondered if there would ever be enough families in the area to even require a school and church. There were other plantations, but they were all far away, at least half a day's trip by carriage.

The three sat in the parlor after supper. Alex told of his day's adventures with Ben. Reginia and William laughed at his wit-filled stories. Alex began to tire and yawn. William told them they must retire for the evening. He was taking them on a ride over the plantation early the next morning. The thought of riding excited Alex and Reginia as they hurried off to bed. Reginia tucked Alex into his bed, staying by his side as he said his prayers. She kissed Alex good night and departed for her bedroom.

William lay in the bed waiting for her. She removed her clothes and slid into the bed beside her husband. His warm body felt good next to her. He wrapped his arms around her, pulling her close to him. He was glad to have his wife next to him again. He kissed her gently, over and over. He could not seem to get enough of her. The passion built between them as they caressed one another under the sheets. They made love for a long while. After the lovemaking, William held Reginia in his arms whispering in her ear of the deep love he felt for her. Reginia felt safe for the first time in months as she drifted off to sleep in William's arms.

SEVEN

When Reginia awoke the next morning, she smelled the aroma of coffee and bacon. She became nauseated. She could not understand why. Had she made herself that sick over the death of her daughter? She told William she would have to wait a while for the ride. William and Alex ate breakfast and afterward they left for the barn. Big Bo had the horses saddled and waiting for them when they arrived. Big Bo helped Alex on his pony that William had given to him on his last birthday. Father and son rode their horses back to the house, side by side, with William leading Jet. Samuel came from the house and held the horses while William went for Reginia. Reginia's nausea had passed and she was ready to ride. They mounted their horses and rode toward the fields.

The beauty of the land continually amazed Reginia. They rode through fields shaded by large oak and pecan trees. The fields were lush green and the wildflowers were in full bloom. The morning sun cast a red glow over the land.

William pulled the reins, bringing his horse to a stop. "Stop your horses. Look at the sky, Reginia. It's such a bright red. It makes the ground glow like the color of your and Sarah's hair."

"It does, doesn't it?" Reginia replied.

"Auburn," William said aloud as an idea crossed his mind. "I will name the plantation Auburn. It will always remind us of little Sarah's long red curls."

"I love that name. How about you, Alex?"

"Yes, Mother. That's a beautiful name. Sarah would have liked it too."

They continued their ride through Auburn. They rode through the herds of cattle, spooking an occasional deer along the way. Reginia saw the beautiful plowed ground ahead. The slaves were busy clearing the rows of young weeds that were beginning to grow. The land impressed her. She imagined that someday the new plantation would be larger and more productive than River Bend. She became thrilled to be living in Texas. She was a part of a new frontier. Pride filled Reginia. She realized at that moment that she and William were part of creating a strong and great country.

They rode until after noon. William stopped by a small creek under a large oak tree. Laudie had prepared a picnic lunch for them of fried chicken and biscuits. The three of them had built up quite an appetite. Reginia spread a blanket on the ground as William brought out the food. They ate, then relaxed on the blanket. Alex ran to the creek to skip rocks across the water. Reginia and William delighted as they watched their son full of joy.

"William, I am beginning to feel an inner peace I never thought I would feel again." Reginia sighed. Her voice filled with satisfaction as she spoke. William saw a glow in Reginia's face as she lay resting her head on his shoulder. Alex returned filled with energy. They picked up the blanket and picnic supplies and rode for home.

Weeks passed quickly. The morning sickness continued for Reginia, accompanied by cramps. Reginia recognized the symptoms. She informed Laudie that she may be pregnant, but asked her not to say anything to William and Alex until she was sure. She hid her morning sickness from William, waiting until William left for the fields each morning before rising. Laudie tended to Reginia with special care, taking breakfast to Reginia in bed and sharing in her excitement of the possible pregnancy. Soon, the morning sickness faded and Reginia felt fine. Her eyes sparkled and her cheeks were the color of pink roses.

"Missus Reginia, you just glow. Just like a mother with child. I think you best tell Master William."

"I will, Laudie. I will tell him tonight after Alex goes to bed."

That night, after she tucked Alex in bed, Reginia joined William on the front porch. The July night was warm and clear, with the stars shining. William sat pointing out the constellations the stars formed. He told Reginia about the cotton and that they would be shipping it to the South soon. The crop was plentiful and William told of the great amount of money the cotton would bring. He continued talking. Reginia felt her nerves tingling with excitement. She wanted to tell him she was pregnant, but words would not come to her lips. She sat trying to listen to William, nervously tapping her nails on the arm of her rocker.

"Reginia, what is wrong? You seem preoccupied with your thoughts."

"I have to tell you something," she said nervously.

"What's wrong, my darling? Has something happened?" He could not understand her nervousness. Reginia sat still. William took her hand in his. "Darling, you can tell me anything, you know that." She stirred in her rocker. She decided to just let the words out. She was about to explode with the good news.

"William, I have wonderful news to tell you." She had his full attention with his hazel eyes fixed on her. "William, I'm going to bear you another child."

He sat in amazement. His heart raced rapidly with excitement. He got up from his rocker and knelt at her feet. Putting his arms around her waist, he placed his head gently on her stomach, caressing her. He stroked her curls and face tenderly. "This is wonderful. You are wonderful. I can hardly believe we are having another child." He thrust his head back, looking to the stars, and sighed with joy. "When? When do you think you are due?"

"I think I must be three months into my pregnancy and should give birth sometime in January." He was still kneeling with his head in her lap. She moved her fingers slowly through his hair and onto his neck. "I am sure I conceived while we were visiting the Wades. I did not want to tell you until I was sure."

"I'm a very happy man," he said with sincerity as he stood and lifted her to him. They held each other for a long while, looking toward the heavens. "I thank God for this blessing, Reginia."

"Yes, we'll have this child and more. I want a large family to help fill this new land. Our great love shall pass on through many generations, William." They stood in the moonlight, holding each other, grateful for this blessing.

The last week of July brought a pleasant surprise. The Rileys had finally arrived. Joseph had received a grant of land across the creek on the north side of William's property. The year before, he had built a modest one-story wooden home on a rise just north of Best Creek.

William rode to their home the afternoon of their arrival. He was glad to see his friend. After exchanging greetings, William informed them of the loss of Sarah. Martha and Joseph were deeply saddened by the news. William explained what had happened and that they were doing fine now and moving forward with their lives.

"Joseph, you haven't unpacked yet and it's getting late in the day. Why don't you and your family come home with me? We'll have supper and you can stay the night with us. That will give your slaves time to put your house in order." Joseph appreciated the offer. He gathered his family and left with William for Auburn.

Reginia rejoiced at the sight of their friends. She now had a neighbor nearby. Martha Riley had grown up in Natchez and had been a dear friend of Reginia's since childhood. Joseph and Martha had only one son, Jacob, whom they called Jake. Jake was a year older than Alex, but the two had been friends in Natchez and Alex was glad to have him spend the night.

The two couples stayed up that night talking of Texas and their future plans. Joseph told of their trip to Texas. They had to fight Indians along the way and lost a wagon crossing the Sabine River. Midnight was near when the four finally went to bed.

The summer months passed quickly. Martha came frequently every week to visit Reginia. Reginia's pregnancy excited her. Martha was unable to conceive due to complications during the birth of Jake. She was so happy to be a part of the birth of Reginia's child. William had shipped the cotton, and the pecan trees began dropping their fruit. Alex, Jake, and Ben played and picked pecans daily. Laudie cracked the pecans the children and the slaves brought her and used them for cooking. She had an abundance of the fruit and put many of them away for use during the holidays. Reginia was showing now and William beamed proudly as he rubbed her enlarged tummy, as if he were stroking the child itself.

One November day, Vasquez and Lopez, two Mexicans whom William befriended, stopped by Auburn to speak with him. They sat in the parlor discussing the increasing disputes between the colonists and the Mexican officials. The two men liked and respected William. William tried to be fair to everyone. He listened carefully as his friends spoke. William knew the settlers disagreed with many of the laws governing the colonization. A major sticking point in the laws for the Anglo settlers was that slavery was prohibited. To avoid the law, the slave owners called their slaves indentured servants. The Americans seemed arrogant and determined to have their own way. Also, many Anglos were crossing the border and squatting on vacant land. Lopez warned that these actions by the colonists were making the Mexican officials very uneasy and that it would only lead to the ending of further immigration by the next year.

William felt no personal threat from his friends, but he could hear the hostility in their voices as they spoke. He did not agree with the Mexican laws, but he never let his visitors know this. He did not want to place his family in the way of danger. He shook their hands as they left and assured them of the friendship they had come to know. William did not tell Reginia of the talk. He would not do this until he had no other choice. She would only worry about the safety of her family and they were in no danger at this time.

Thanksgiving and Christmas came. The Wildes and the Rileys spent both holidays together, feasting on wild turkey and all the trimmings. Reginia loved the holidays but regretted having to explain to Alex that there would be no fine gifts that year. Instead, she promised him that he could go with his father to cut the Christmas tree! Though not yet common practice in Texas, Reginia so enjoyed the traditional Wilde family tree-trimming event William's parents had brought with them to

Natchez. Christmas Eve morn found Alex waiting eagerly at the front door. William insisted breakfast came first, and then the two would take the buckboard into the woods to cut the seven-foot full and lush cedar tree that William had spotted back in the summer. Meanwhile, Reginia gleefully ordered the corn to be popped and strung, busying herself by gathering from the attic the German ornaments given to William's mother and passed on to William. She trusted no one to handle the prized ornaments. Reginia exclaimed with excitement as William and Alex carried the tree inside. All gathered around singing Christmas carols as the decorations were hung. The Rileys felt blessed to be a part of this tradition, gleefully clapping as they admired the creation of the fully adorned Christmas tree. The house was quiet as William told the story of the birth of Christ. After Alex had gone to bed, Reginia brought in a stocking she had made for him. She'd filled it with fruit that William had purchased at the nearby Brazos landing, a dock for riverboats. Christmas was special that year of 1829. The two families were thankful for their friendship, the new land, and their prosperity.

CHAPTER
EIGHT

January of 1830 blew in with a chill. Every fireplace was blazing with a fire. Reginia grew uncomfortable with her enlarged belly. She anticipated the day of her child's birth. She was ready. She couldn't believe the nine months since that April night at the Wades' home had passed so quickly. William had summoned Dr. Fields. Mr. Grosse urged Dr. Fields to stay with the Wildes that January. Reginia was thankful to have Dr. Fields available for the birth of her child. Joseph had taken ill and Dr. Fields rode horseback every day across the fields and creek to the Rileys'.

William regretted Joseph's illness, although mild, for William was leaving for a meeting with Stephen Austin and some other men and Joseph was to ride with him. The stories of the hostilities between the Mexicans and the Americans were becoming frequent. The Mexicans wanted to stop more Americans from entering Texas. Reginia begged William not to go. She now feared the Mexicans. William and Joseph had informed their wives of the hostile Mexicans, for their wives' own safety. William's two friends Vasquez and Lopez were no longer coming by. William feared the opposition had turned his two friends against him. He left for San Felipe, but promised he would return within the week.

The week passed slowly for Reginia and she did not see Martha, due to Joseph's feeling ill. She visited with Dr. Fields whenever he returned from the Rileys'. News was good about Joseph; he was doing much better by the end of the week. William returned and Reginia was glad to see her husband. She had begun to feel cramps and knew she would bear her child soon.

The wind howled and the rain fell hard on the thirtieth of January. William sat in the library working on his books and plans for the new year. William wanted to purchase more land that year. The lightning bolted across the Texas sky and thunder rumbled continually. William could not believe this storm. It had been raining for three days. Suddenly, Laudie pushed open the big doors into the library.

"Master Wilde, Missus Reginia is having her baby. Hurry, Master, Hurry." Laudie was out of breath from running down the stairs. William jumped from his chair and rushed past Laudie up the stairs, rushing to Reginia. Samuel stopped him at the door.

"Master, Doctor Fields asks that you wait outside the bedroom. He says it won't be long." Indeed, the doctor was right. Before William could respond to Samuel, the cry from the newborn rang through the hallway. William hesitated for a second, looking at Samuel as if he could not believe what he heard. He quickly gained his senses and threw the door open. He saw Reginia first. She looked weary but she wore a beautiful smile. William walked slowly to the doctor, who was holding the child.

"Well, come in, William, and see your little boy. He's a big one."

William stood very still as the doctor placed the infant in his arms. William took the child tenderly, as if he feared he would break the tiny baby boy, and walked to Reginia. William was proud and beamed with delight. He sat down slowly on the bed beside her and laid the baby on her breast, cautiously placing his arms around them for an embrace.

"I love you, I love you both," William spoke softly as he lifted his head and kissed Reginia softly on her lips.

"I love you, my darling." Reginia had tears in her eyes. She thought the child was a gift from God. The little boy could never replace Sarah, but he could fill the void in their lives. He was a special child. Dr. Fields took the infant and handed him to Laudie to clean. William stayed with Reginia the remainder of the day.

Samuel found Alex and told him of the good news. Alex beamed with joy. Samuel took Alex to the bathing room where Laudie was cleaning the child. Laudie had Alex sit in the chair and placed the infant in his arms. Alex didn't know how to hold the small baby. Laudie helped him by telling him to keep his hands under the baby's head. Alex loved the baby.

"What is his name, Laudie?"

"Your folks haven't named him, Master Alex."

"He needs a name. I want to see my mother."

Laudie and Alex walked to Reginia's bedroom, with the child in Laudie's arms. Laudie knocked on the door softly. She did not want to wake Missus Reginia if she were napping. William opened the door and greeted Alex with a hug. William took the baby and Alex ran to his mother. Reginia opened her arms as Alex cuddled next to her for a hug.

"What should we name the baby, Mother?" Alex questioned with great enthusiasm.

"Your father and I would like to name him John William Wilde. What do you think of that name?"

"That name is fine. But isn't that Father's name?" Alex quizzed. "Why would they give my brother the same name?" he wondered.

Reginia smiled at Alex and explained, "Yes, that is your father's name. You are named for your grandfather, and your brother will be named for your father. This is done to carry on a family name through generations. It is an honor to have a child named after a father or grandfather. We will call him John."

Alex understood. Laudie brought their supper to them in the bedroom. Reginia sat up in the bed as Laudie placed the tray over her lap. She served Master Wilde and Master Alex at the small round table in the comer of the bedroom. The three ate, enjoying the meal and viewing little John in his cradle.

The next morning, as the rain continued to fall, there was loud knocking at the door. Samuel answered the door to find rain-soaked Joseph Riley standing cold and shivering. Samuel welcomed Joseph in quickly.

"Mister Riley, come in out of the rain. Let me take your coat and hat and I will get Master Wilde for you." Samuel left to get William.

Laudie walked into the foyer to see who had come so early in the morning through all the rain.

"Mister Riley, my goodness, this is an awful morning to be out. Why, you're barely over your sickness." She showed him into the parlor by the fire to warm himself.

"Thank you, Laudie. How is Missus Reginia doing?"

"Oh, Mister Riley, Missus Reginia has had herself a grand baby boy. Why, that young'un's gonna grows up to be somethin' special. He came yesterday, with the lightnin' a flashin' and the thunder a crashin'. He's a mighty fine boy, and Missus Reginia . . . well, she's doin' just fine."

William entered the room and Joseph extended his hand with congratulations. "Joseph, what are you doing out in this weather? Is something the matter?" William had concern in his voice. No one would travel in this weather if all were fine.

"William, one of the slaves came to me this morning to inform me of the river. It is rising fast and he said it is near full. The creek between us is flooding as we speak. I had to swim my horse across it to get here."

"Let me get a coat and we'll ride to the river. We'll have to cross Best Creek. Do you know if it is flooding?"

"No, it's full, though. If the rain continues, we should move the cattle from the bottom land."

"Yes, we should." William got his long coat and hat. Samuel went for his master's horse. When he returned with the horse, the two men mounted and rode for the river.

William returned to the house about two o'clock. Joseph had ridden on home. William wanted to see Reginia, but she was napping. The news of the flood would have to wait. He would not disturb his beautiful wife. He went to Samuel to tell him to begin preparing for a possible flood.

"Samuel, get Doctor Fields and Ransom and have them come to the library," William said with urgency in his voice. Samuel departed quickly. He could tell this was important by the way his master spoke. Within a few minutes, Samuel returned with Dr. Fields and Ransom. The two men walked into the library with Samuel behind them.

"William, what's wrong?" Dr. Fields questioned. The men could see the concern in William's face.

"Close the door, Samuel." William did not want others to hear what he had to say. He wanted no cause for alarm. Samuel closed the door and stood silently, listening to his master. "I rode to the river with Joseph. The river is near cresting. Best Creek had begun to go out of its banks by the time we were returning. It's just too dangerous for you to return to the Grosse Plantation, Doctor Fields. Please stay until it's safe to travel."

"Thank you, William. Surely it will stop raining soon. Do you think the river will flood?"

"I don't know for sure, but it looks that way. Ransom, have Big Bo get some men and move the cattle to the east pasture just south of the house. I want them on high ground, out of the way of flooding waters. Tell all the slaves to prepare for the flood, just in case. Have them bring the wagons to the barn."

Samuel and Ransom were walking out the door, when William stopped them. "Ransom, be sure to have Big Bo put Jet in the barn with Alex's and my horses. Reginia would have my neck if something happened to that animal." He laughed but was sincere with his request. "Samuel, have the field slaves remain in their quarters after everything is secure."

"Yes, sir. I will take care of everything, don't worry." Samuel left to obey his master. "William, is there anything I can do to help?" Dr. Fields offered.

"If you would just check on Reginia and the baby, please." William didn't want anything to happen to Reginia and little John. The weather was so damp and cold. He feared they would get a chill. William left the library for his bedroom. He wanted to speak with Reginia about the possibility of flooding.

Several days passed before the rains ceased. The clouds still hid the sun. The creeks were flooding and the Brazos was out of its banks. William had not heard from Joseph and could not get to his house due to the creeks' flooding. He wondered if his friend was all right. His home was high, but he had cattle in the low lands too. William and Dr. Fields rode horseback toward Best Creek. The ground was soggy as the horses sank to their ankles in the mud. They hadn't even reached Best Creek when they saw the fields covered with water. William rode until the water reached the belly of his horse. He knew they could go no farther. William knew this was a great flood. It was about five miles from his house to the Brazos. All the bottom land had surely flooded. The two men turned and headed for home. William rode to the southeast pasture to check his cattle. They were fine. He wanted to get home in case it rained more.

When William returned to the house, Reginia was nursing John. She was sitting in the chair by her bedroom fireplace. The damp cold air had made a chill in the house. Reginia had a blanket about her and the child. William opened the door and peeked inside.

"Come in, William."

William walked to her. He kissed her on her forehead. "And what do we have here?"

"We have a hungry young man. He'll be a big one if his appetite continues like this."

William laughed. He admired Reginia's high spirits. She always found humor, even in the midst of the cold weather and flooding.

"What has the river done?" she asked.

"We couldn't reach the river. Best Creek is flooding and the water has backed up not far from the house. I fear the river is flooding also."

"It won't reach the house, will it?" She suddenly had concern in her voice.

"Oh, no. We' re too high. It would have to be a world flood to reach our house." He laughed. William moved to sit by the fireplace. "Darling, I would like to talk to you about something. The weather is bad and nothing can be done outside. I think it's time to clear Sarah's room of her belongings." He continued talking, connecting his sentences so Reginia would not interrupt. "It has been long enough. We will put her things in the attic and prepare the room for John. I will have Laudie stay in the room with him until he is old enough to stay by himself." William hoped she would agree.

"I think that is a good idea. Have Fancy and Batha pack her things. Samuel can carry them to the attic." She looked down at the infant nursing at her breast. "We have John, now, and we shall care for him and love him, as we did our precious little Sarah." She bowed her head and kissed the infant on his head. Reginia's response shocked William. But then, why should he be, he thought to himself, as he watched her kiss the child. She was the strongest lady he had ever known.

William had Fancy and Batha working in the bedroom. They packed all of Sarah's possessions and Samuel moved them to the attic. The girls cleaned the room all day. They cleaned the windows, woodwork, floors, and furniture and took the drapes and bedspread and beat them with a broom to shake the dust out. By that afternoon, the room was clean and smelled fresh.

Alex found his old rocking horse in the attic and had Samuel put it in his little brother's new room. Samuel did as he wished and returned to the attic to find Alex rummaging through more toys. Reginia had insisted they bring the children's baby clothes and toddler toys with them on the move to Texas.

William joined Alex and Samuel in the attic. Alex asked if they could take the toys downstairs. William agreed. He had thought it was silly of Reginia to want to haul all the toys and baby clothes to Texas, but now he was glad she had insisted upon it. He had Samuel take the trunk full of toys and clothes to the girls for cleaning.

There was laughter and cheer coming from the baby's room. Reginia's curiosity got the best of her. She carefully got out of bed and walked to the door. She opened the door slightly and peeked around the corner and down the hall toward the bedroom. They were rushing back and forth to the baby's room with hands full. She could see them bustling about with Alex, taking toys into the room. Reginia smiled, as she turned and went back to her bed to rest.

That afternoon, Alex came for his mother. "Mother, can I take you to John's room? You must see it. We have fixed it for him and it is so cute." He burst with excitement.

Reginia put her robe and slippers on and walked down the hall with Alex to the baby's room. Alex opened the door for his mother. Reginia walked in and looked about. Samuel had built a fire in the fireplace, which warmed the room. They had placed the toys about selectively and put the baby's crib near the fireplace.

Alex pointed to the corner of the room. "Look, Mother, at what I gave John," he said proudly. Reginia turned her head and saw the old black rocking horse, with brown mane and tail. It was in wonderful condition. The paint still looked new. Reginia had forgotten that they had brought it to Texas.

"Oh, Alex." Her voice was soft as she walked to the rocking horse. She ran her hands over the horse slowly, thinking back to the days when Alex had ridden it. She smiled as she thought how he would make the horse rock back and forth as fast as the little rocker could rock. She turned to Alex and put her hand on his shoulder and squeezed slightly. "This is a wonderful gift for your brother. You are so sweet. John's lucky to have you for his brother."

Laudie entered the room with John and placed him in his crib. Reginia looked at Laudie with appreciation as Laudie turned to leave. Reginia and Alex sat in the room for a while, Reginia in the rocker and Alex on the rug by the fireplace. They spoke softly as John slept in his crib.

All was well and there had been no rain for three days. The creeks' flood waters had gone down and Reginia had recovered from the birth of John. Dr. Fields bid them farewell and headed home.

Not long after Dr. Fields left, the Rileys came knocking at the Wildes' front door. The sight of their friends thrilled Reginia. She came down the stairs and joined them in the parlor. Laudie brought John into the parlor for Martha and Joseph to see.

"Reginia, he's beautiful. May I hold him?"

"Of course you can, Martha."

Martha took Little John and sat in the rocker moving back and forth until John fell asleep in her arms. She gazed at the infant's beautiful face. She enjoyed holding a baby once again.

Alex and Jake went outside and William and Joseph decided to ride to the river. William told Reginia they would be back soon, and if it were too muddy then they would not try to cross the land.

William, Joseph, Ransom, and Big Bo rode horseback down the hill and through the mud to Best Creek. The ground still had water standing as they neared the flowing creek. They swam their horses across and sloshed through the muddy fields toward the river. They reached the farmland and, with shocked looks on their faces, pulled their horses to a stop. The bottom farmland was a river of mud. Some of the storage barns had crumbled and some had washed away with the rushing water. Strips of wood from barns along the river covered the area. Trees and large limbs lay broken across the fields. The flood and high winds from the storm had ravaged the land.

William could not believe the destruction. Never had he witnessed such a flood. It would take his slaves months to have the ground ready for planting the cotton and by then it would be too late. William was sick as he scanned the soupy soil. It was a mud bog as far as the eye could see. The men rode back to the house discussing plans of rebuilding and preparing the land for the spring planting. The river had washed away years of hard work.

William visited with other plantation owners in the area. They had all suffered their share of losses. One home near the riverbank had water damage up to eight feet deep. Mud caked the floors and snakes crawled freely in the abandoned house. William felt relieved to have built his home far from the river.

The slaves worked into mid-summer clearing and preparing the land for the next year's planting. William sat one day on his horse watching the slaves working and prayed there would never be such a flood again.

William's first year in Texas with his family had been rough. In addition to the flood and the death of Sarah, the Mexican government had stopped all immigration of Americans to Texas.

William sat in the library, with his boots propped upon his desk, thinking about the troubled times. He was thankful he was wealthy, for the flood had hurt others financially and he was able to loan money and send supplies to those in need of help. He felt relieved that Joseph had had enough money and slaves to get his land in shape. Everyone had suffered that year, not just his family. He straightened up in his chair, put his feet on the floor, and gazed through the open door. There was John crawling about the foyer floor with Laudie at his heels. He smiled to himself. Yes, they had suffered tremendously, but in John, he saw a miracle.

NINE

The next three years passed swiftly. Reginia gave birth to Mary Catherine on July 6, 1832, and became pregnant again in the spring of 1833. The cotton crops were good for William and the other planters along the Brazos. The planters needed a boat landing to ship the crops rather than haul the cotton cross-country. William had the perfect location on his river property and volunteered to build the dock. The slaves finished the landing within the month, just in time for the first boat arrival. All the neighbors gathered with picnic lunches to celebrate. Welcoming the boats became the custom. Reginia took the children to greet the boats as often as possible. The boat captains brought fabric, ribbon, fruit, among other supplies, and an occasional letter from their family in Mississippi. It wasn't much, but after being in Texas for several years, it became an eager expectation in their lives.

The disputes between the Mexicans and the Americans increased. The settlers planned a meeting to draft a second constitution for the Texans to be held in San Felipe in the early spring of 1833. Many of the Texas men, including Jim Wade and the men from Nacogdoches, planned to attend.

Reginia sat in her favorite rocker on the front porch. The spring air softly blew through her auburn hair as she watched John play with Katie, the nickname given to Mary Catherine. Katie was walking now and trying desperately to keep up with John. Reginia spotted a covered wagon approaching. She never imagined it would be the Wades. As the wagon drew nearer, she saw Betty. She could not believe her eyes. She hurried to them with open arms.

"I can't believe you're here." She hugged Betty with a smile from cheek to cheek. "I didn't write. Jim wanted to surprise you and William. I hope you don't mind."

"Mind? I am thrilled. This is a wonderful surprise."

Reginia reached for Jim. "William rode to the fields with Ransom," Reginia explained while hugging him. "He will be thrilled to see you. We wondered if you would come for the convention."

Laudie entered the parlor. She tossed her hands in the air and landed them on her full cheeks. "Why, goodness me. Ain't this a nice surprise."

"How are you, Laudie?" Jim asked, remembering Laudie with her jolly ways and her stern voice.

"Well, sir, I'm just fine, just fine."

"Laudie, would you get us some tea." She looked at Betty and Jim. "I know you must be thirsty."

Laudie left to prepare the tea. Jim told of their trip. The Indians raided their camp one night and one of the men, Mr. Buckley, took an arrow, killing him. "We had to bury him by the trail. We were caught off guard. The Indians usually don't attack when there are so many together." Betty's hands shook while discussing the raid. Reginia could not believe how near she had come to losing her friends. They visited and drank the tea Laudie served them. Reginia told them about the death of Sarah and all about John and Katie. They had a great deal to catch up on. William returned to find his friends. He visited for a while with Jim and the ladies, but was anxious to talk to Jim in private. William wanted to learn Jim's feelings about the convention and asked Jim to go into the library with him. Reginia was glad to be alone with Betty. She wanted to know all that had happened over the past few years.

Reginia showed Betty the grounds and house before taking Betty up to the observatory for a grand survey of the fields. Betty thought the observatory was beautiful. She could not believe the view. She could see the rolling fields for miles! Reginia told Betty how she enjoyed sitting in the observatory pondering the life they created in Texas. It was peaceful in the observatory. The two ladies shared their secret thoughts and discussed the children. Betty told Reginia they wanted to send Jackson to the East for schooling. The thought of an education in the East appealed to Reginia. She told Betty about her time spent tutoring Alex. He was extremely intelligent. She wanted to speak with William about sending Alex to the East with Jackson. She desired an education for all her children, just as she and William had had. Betty was thrilled with the idea.

Reginia was glad to have her friend with her. She just couldn't share her thoughts with anyone, like she could with Betty. Betty and Jim would stay for a week. The men would be in San Felipe for four of the days and that would give them time to catch up on all that had happened in their lives.

The first night the men were gone, the two ladies sat up half the night visiting. The children went to bed not long after supper and the house was quiet. The two, absorbed in conversation, sat in the drawing room sipping their tea. Reginia told Betty of her deep sorrow at the loss of Sarah. It was the first time Reginia had spoken openly to anyone of her pain over Sarah. Betty consoled Reginia as Reginia spoke of her profound regrets. She told Betty how wonderful William had been during this time, and how he cared for her.

"William came to me and demanded I get up and live my life," Reginia continued. "I don't know what I would do without William. He's my reason for living."

"You and William have something special between you. Jim and I have both noticed this. The gentle way you caress William's hand and the way his eyes sparkle when he looks into your eyes. Why, it delights my heart to see two people in love as you are."

"We are blessed and I know this. I still quiver all over at his touch and we have been married for years. Our passion seems to grow with time." She blushed at such a disclosure of her life.

"You're blushing," Betty replied sweetly, with a giggle. "I think it's refreshing to hear that such affection exists. Jim and I are comfortable in our marriage and we love each other a great deal, but somehow we've allowed that spark to disappear."

Reginia appreciated her friend listening to her. She hugged Betty. "Thank you for being my friend. I have truly missed having someone I could talk to about my innermost thoughts." The two sat talking until they became utterly exhausted.

The next morning, Reginia had Big Bo bring the carriage and take her and Betty for a ride about the plantation. Betty favored the bottom land and thought Auburn was beautiful. Reginia told her about the great flood with all its destruction. Betty could not imagine that type of flooding and the work it must have created. William had built up a large herd of cattle and Reginia proudly showed them off along with all the thoroughbred horses William had raised. Betty saw a beautiful two-year-old sorrel filly and wanted to know if the filly could be purchased. William did not sell his horses but Reginia told her she would ask.

Martha came by one day to visit and Reginia delighted in having her two closest friends in her home. Alex and Jake spent all day with Ben at the creek fishing. The ladies talked of the convention and the new constitution. They spoke of the relief they felt at the promise of a peaceful life on the Texas frontier. Things would be better. The possibility of resuming American immigration and the hope of settlements filled their imaginations. Alex and Jake returned flaunting a string of catfish. Reginia wanted them to spend the night and have fried fish, but Martha insisted on leaving. She wanted to get to her house before dark. The ladies hugged one another goodbye as the boys walked to the carriage bragging about their catch.

That evening, just as they sat for supper, someone knocked rapidly on the front door. Samuel opened the door to find one of Joseph's slaves standing panicked and out of breath. He could barely speak. Reginia felt something was wrong and excused herself from the table.

"What is it, Samuel?" Reginia asked at the sight of the black man.

"He is one of Mister Riley's slaves."

The slave spoke rapidly and his words slurred together. Hysteria gripped him. Reginia could not understand anything but the words "Missus Martha."

"Stop. Take a deep breath and speak slowly. What has happened to Missus Martha?" Reginia spoke with firmness in her voice, for she felt something terrible had happened to her friend.

The slave took a deep breath. "Missus, we was in the fields a workin' when we heard the gunshots and screams. Indians streaked with paint came. Master Jake and Missus Martha . . . "

"For goodness sakes, get on with it, what did they do? Are they alive?" Reginia questioned, fearing the worst.

"Yes, Ma'am, they alive. But they're hurt mighty bad. Master Jake has taken an arrow and they beat poor Missus Martha mostly to death. We took rifles and ran them Indians off. We need help, please come, quick."

"Samuel, get Mister Hall and have him bring all the slaves to the house, with rifles. On your way back, bring the carriage. Hurry, Samuel, hurry." Reginia told Betty she was going to Martha's home and what had happened. "Please come, Betty. I'll need your help. We'll take Ransom and some slaves and I'll have our other slaves surround the house for safety. Samuel will stay here to make sure everything is safe for the children."

"Missus Reginia, you have no business goin' off in your condition," Laudie interrupted with her stern voice. "What if you get hurt and what about that child you carry?"

"Hush up, Laudie. Take care of the children. I'll be back soon."

"She's right, Reginia. Stay here and let me go," Betty whispered as they walked to the front door.

"Martha may be bad off and she'll need me. I have to go."

Ransom came with the carriage and fifty slaves on horseback, with rifles. The ladies got into the carriage and headed for the Rileys' house, as Samuel instructed the other slaves to surround the big house. The horses galloped as they pulled the carriage toward the Rileys'. Reginia held on tight to the side of the carriage. They would be there quickly at this speed. Reginia thought only of Martha and Jake, not giving a thought to the danger that could be waiting. Anger built inside Reginia at the thought of the Indians doing harm to Martha and Jake. The Indians in their area exhibited little hostility. They were more of a nuisance, always begging to trade. She could not imagine what had happened. She thought they would never get there, when suddenly they faced the small lane leading to the house.

"Missus Wilde, when we get there, I want you and Missus Wade to wait in the carriage while the slaves and I check the house," Ransom spoke with unshaken wisdom. Reginia did not dispute him.

They reached the house and Ransom took some men in with him to make sure the Indians were gone. He returned quickly for the two ladies. He had the slaves surround the house and ushered the ladies indoors. Reginia was horrified at the sight inside. The house was ransacked. Several slaves lay dead on the blood-soaked floor. Fear for her friend and fury at the savagery of the Indians raged inside her as she walked rapidly to Martha's bedroom. She flung the door open to see a Negro woman bending over Martha. Reginia rushed to Martha with Betty at her heals.

"Martha. Martha can you hear me?" Reginia took Martha's hand in hers as she spoke.

"She won't wake up. She's been that way since we found her. Master Jake, he's hurt bad. He has an arrow in his shoulder." The woman spoke with tears in her eyes and fear in her voice.

"Get the arrow out of his shoulder, right now." Reginia ordered.

"I can't do that, I just can't." The woman began to cry hysterically and Reginia began to get very upset with her. Betty walked to the woman and took her by the arm.

"Come with me. We'll take care of Jake." Betty realized Reginia was in no mood to argue with a slave, but she had pity on the young Negro woman, for she was scared half out of her mind. Betty asked Big Bo to help her. She worked with the arrow until she was able to pull it from Jake's shoulder. The boy screamed. Betty cleaned and bandaged the shoulder as best she could. Jake lay weak and speechless. The only words he spoke were in concern for his mother. Betty assured him she would be all right and sat by him until he fell asleep. She left Bo at his side and went to help Reginia.

Reginia was busy with Martha, cleaning her wounds. Martha was beaten, bruised, and cut. Her dress was torn and soiled. Reginia feared the Indians had assaulted her dear friend. The thought of her friend having been brutalized sickened her. She removed Martha's clothing and discovered a deep pool of blood under her. Her leg was severely cut. Reginia asked Betty to help clean and bandage Martha. She had slashes all over her body from the Indians' knives. Reginia knew Martha fought hard for her life and her son and if it had not been for the slaves, the Indians would have scalped them.

Reginia stayed with Martha trying to wake her, but Martha lay unconscious from a blow to her head. She continued talking to her lifeless friend. She prayed for a miracle, for she knew Martha needed the Lord's help. She went to Jake, who lay sleeping. As her eyes gazed upon the young lad, she marveled at how he and Alex had grown into such fine young men. She was thankful the arrow had not killed him. Her only worry was infection.

Betty and Reginia walked into the foyer to Ransom. Ransom had had their slaves move the dead bodies and begin to straighten the house. Suddenly, out of the dark, they heard screams.

"Where is that coming from?" Reginia asked of Ransom.

"It sounds like the slave quarters, down by the barns." Rifles began firing and the screams grew loud. "It sounds like those savages are back. Bo! Come here, hurry," Ransom yelled. Bo ran into the foyer. "Take some men and go help Mister Riley's slaves. Kill every one of those savage Indians. Do you hear me?" Ransom had the rest of the Wildes' slaves come in the house and stand guard at every window. "Reginia, help me. We'll move Jake into the room with Missus Riley."

Reginia and Betty rushed to help move Jake. Ransom woke Jake and told him they were moving him to his mother's room for safety. Reginia carried the blankets and the pillow and tucked him in by his mother. She and Betty sat in the chairs by the fireplace, watching the windows for any signs of Indians. Ransom left the room to secure the front door tightly. Reginia saw a rifle against the wall and retrieved it. The rifle was loaded. She sat down in the chair placing it across her lap. She could hear nothing but the blasts of guns and the loud screams of the Indians. The noise was deafening. She wanted to close her eyes and have this terrible nightmare end. She had heard of Indian raids, but never experienced one. She could not imagine why the Indians were so riled.

Reginia's thoughts flew through her mind. She wondered if their Negro slaves were being harmed, or worse, killed. The ladies sat motionless. A wooden door led to the outside from Martha's bedroom. Reginia's eyes left the window briefly as she glanced toward the door. It was not locked! With rifle in hand, she stood quickly. Startled by Reginia's swift movement, Betty jumped. At the same time, the door knob turned. Reginia froze and raised the rifle. She pressed it firmly against her shoulder and fixed her eyes on the door. It burst open revealing a brown barbarian with streaks of paint covering his weathered face. Reginia stood firm. The Indian hesitated before lunging at Reginia with a knife. She squeezed the trigger with grit, hitting the Indian directly between the eyes. He fell motionless on the floor. Reginia ran past the dead Indian to the door and slammed it shut, bolting it as it closed. Betty sat in shock. Her body trembled. Suddenly, Ransom ran into the room finding the dead Indian on the floor.

"I shot him. I killed him." Reginia didn't hesitate. She had passed the point of fear and only anger and the determination to survive were left inside her. Ransom dragged the dead Indian out of the room. Reginia stood staring at the savage. She found her heart filled with hatred for the first time. The gunshots stopped. Reginia sighed with relief. All was quiet. She stood listening to the stillness. She heard the pounding of hooves across the ground. "Was it the Negroes or the Indians," she questioned herself. As they approached the house, she got her answer. The bloodcurdling screams of the Indians began again. She loaded the rifle and handed a pistol she had found to Betty. "Shoot any Indian you see," she shouted to Betty. Reginia scooted to the window and broke the glass. She raised the rifle and fired at the Indians. Reginia saw the slaves running their horses in behind the Indians, firing their rifles as they rode. Ransom and the slaves in the house were killing many. After minutes of gunfire and arrows shooting through the house, silence again reigned. Reginia went to Betty to comfort her. Betty could not believe how brave Reginia was.

Ransom came into the room. "They are all dead, Missus Wilde. We took them by surprise. They didn't know we were here."

"Are any of the slaves hurt?" Reginia responded with great concern.

"A couple were injured, but nothing serious."

"Good. Have the injured cared for and then bury the Indians. I don't want any signs of them left. Ransom, what made the Indians commit this violent action?" Reginia could not believe what had taken place.

"They appear to be Karankawas or Apaches, but I can't be sure. In either case, they're far from their home. Both tribes are known for their barbaric nature and they resent the settlement of the white man. What caused this attack is beyond me. Something set them off, that is for sure."

Ransom left to do what Reginia wanted. The courage and strength of the beautiful lady surprised and impressed him. The men worked late into the night burying the small band of twenty-five Indians.

Reginia sat down on the chair and drew a deep breath and released it slowly, as if trying to ease the tension that had built up inside her. She glanced to the bed where Martha lay unconscious. Jake had moved himself to the bed and was holding his mother. Reginia raised herself and walked to Jake. She put her arms around him and told him with full confidence that the Indians were all dead. Reginia, Ransom, Betty, and the Negroes stayed overnight. Ransom slept on the sofa while the ladies slept in Jake's room. Jake would not leave his mother's side. Big Bo took the slaves and slept in the quarters with the Rileys' slaves.

Morning came quickly. Reginia was glad. She did not rest well and was ready to get on with the day. She sent Ransom home with the slaves. "Ransom, I want you to take the slaves home. Leave Bo here. Have Samuel bring Fancy and Batha. I want them to get this house cleaned and in order before Mister Riley returns. I want Laudie to stay home and tend to the children. Tell Alex what has happened and that I want him to stay near John and Katie. Tell him I will return this evening."

Reginia had to move quickly to get the house prepared for Joseph's return. The men were to return from San Felipe late that day. She hoped William and Jim would stop at Joseph's on the way home.

Reginia sent Big Bo to the quarters to get one of the slaves to cook at the main house. She wanted Jake to eat and they were hungry as well. Within the hour, Samuel pulled the carriage to a stop at the front door of the Rileys'. Reginia went to the door and had them come inside. She gave the instructions for the cleanup. Samuel and the girls went to work, eager to help their Missus Reginia. They worked all day cleaning the floors and the furnishings. Reginia directed the placement of the furniture. Reginia and Betty cared for Jake and Martha. They cleaned their wounds and put fresh bandages on them. Martha still lay unconscious, as Reginia continued talking to her, trying to wake her.

Later that afternoon, as Reginia sat by Martha, she noticed a slight quivering movement from Martha's eyelids. Reginia took Martha's hands and began talking firmly to her. "Wake up, Martha. Wake up. Jake needs you. Wake up. Do you hear me! The Indians are dead. I'm here with you. Wake up!" Reginia was determined to wake her friend.

Martha's eyes cracked open. Reginia spoke with excitement. "Wake up, Martha. It's Reginia. I'm here with you and Jake is fine, you're fine. Wake up," she insisted. Betty heard Reginia and came into the room.

Martha slowly opened her eyes. Her eyes glared vacantly. She gripped Reginia's hand with what little strength she had. Her voice was weak and soft as she spoke to Reginia.

"Reginia, I can hear you. I cannot see. I cannot see." Her small voice was stricken with panic.

"Martha, you have taken a blow to your head. You will be fine." Reginia wondered if Martha remembered what had happened the night before.

Martha waited a few minutes before she responded. Tears welled in her eyes. "It was terrible. Where is Jake?" Martha tried to speak but it was difficult with the tears and the pain she was in.

"He is fine. He is in his room." Reginia asked Betty to get Jake and help him to his mother's side. "Do not try to talk, Martha. Just rest. I will be right here and Betty will bring Jake to you."

Betty brought Jake into the room. He walked to his mother's side. "Mother, I'm here and I'm fine." Martha opened her eyes. Things were still a blur but she could see the image of her son.

She reached for him with her frail arm. He clung to her hand, reassuring her that he was fine. She stared at him until her eyes began to focus. Reginia was filled with relief when Martha regained her sight. Martha held Jake's hand, thankful to be alive. She asked Jake to go back to his room. She could see her son was still too weak to be up. Betty helped Jake back to his room. Martha took Reginia's hand. "Reginia, my dear Reginia. You are good to come here and take care of Jake and me. Where is Joseph?" Martha was apparently confused about the day.

"The men are safe. Remember, they went to the San Felipe Convention? They will be home this afternoon."

Martha looked puzzled at first and then her face became distorted with fear. "The Indians came. I thought they were friendly—I went outside. Their faces, oh, their faces were ugly, painted with streaks of colors."

"You shouldn't talk about it right now. Try to rest." Reginia could see Martha was shaken at the memory of what had happened.

"No, you don't understand. The two big ones grabbed me. I fought, but it was no use. They beat me and threw me to the ground." Tears filled her eyes as she spoke. "I heard screams from the house. I kicked and bit one on the hand. He kicked me in my stomach." She paused, the tears streaming down her battered face.

Reginia held her and embraced her tenderly, fighting her own tears. "Please, Martha. Don't talk about it now."

"I must. You have to know what happened before Joseph returns." Reginia held her friend's hands as she told her story. Her voice was weak as she described the attack. "They took turns having their way with me. The pain was unbearable. I fainted several times. They got off me and went to the house. I struggled to my feet and grabbed one right at the door. I was afraid for Jake. I saw Pearlie, a house slave, lying on the floor. She was in a pool of blood. I felt a knife cutting my skin as I tried to stop him. I grabbed him in the groin. He fell to the floor and his knife went into my leg. I remember he pulled it, slashing my leg open. He kicked me over and over in my head until I guess I passed out. I don't know what happened after that. I'm afraid Joseph will not want my love anymore . . . I feel soiled." She bowed her head as tears streamed from her eyes.

"You are a brave lady. You fought for yourself and Jake. Joseph will love you even more. Do not worry over such matters. Joseph will only be glad that you are alive to love him the rest of his days." Reginia could not bear the thought of a man losing interest in his wife for such a reason.

"What happened to Jake? He looks weak, and what is that bandage on his shoulder for?"

"He took an arrow. It was in the shoulder. He'll be fine. He just needs rest," Reginia explained.

"And Pearlie and Lillie, are they all right?"

"They're both dead, Martha. I'm sorry." Reginia felt the tears in her eyes. She hugged Martha and promised everything would be fine. Martha was not to worry over anything. She stayed with Martha until she fell asleep.

Reginia went to the kitchen to get some soup that had been made for lunch. She wanted Martha to eat something for her strength. She instructed the girls to prepare a big supper for the Rileys. She knew Joseph would need a good meal after his journey and she wanted Jake and Martha to try to eat something hearty. She took the soup and bread to Martha. She had to wake her up. Reginia thought it was best that Martha took only short naps. She knew with a head injury it was not good to sleep too long at a time. She had Martha eat the soup and bread. Martha stayed awake for a while. Reginia talked of pleasant times and nursed Martha's wounds. Betty helped with the instructions to the slaves. Reginia was thankful for Betty. Betty was a true friend. She placed her own life in danger to assist Reginia. Reginia would be forever grateful.

Late that afternoon, as Martha and Jake rested, Reginia and Betty went to the front porch to sit, each holding a small glass of Joseph's brandy that Reginia had poured. The afternoon was sunny and the air was mildly cool.

"I just had to get out of the house and get some fresh air. I think the brandy is just what we needed for our nerves." Reginia was exhausted as she sipped her brandy. "I cannot believe this has happened. I only hope Martha and Jake completely recover. I'm worried about Martha."

"I know. She has been through a great deal. Joseph is going to be devastated by this. Is he a strong man?"

"Yes, he is. He will be glad his family is alive and will do all he can for them." The ladies continued sipping the brandy and discussing the events of the night before. The Texas frontier was showing all its ugliness. Reginia wondered how much they would have to suffer before this country would be civilized.

Reginia and Betty were serving supper to Martha and Jake when the men returned from the convention. They had no clue of the massacre the night before. Reginia heard the men approaching and rushed to the door.

"Reginia, what are you doing here this late?" William was totally surprised to see his wife.

"Come into the house. Jim, please come in too. Betty is here." Reginia was strong in her voice, her soft eyes were hardened by the terrible events. William knew something was wrong when he looked into her eyes. The men dismounted and entered the front door. William walked to Reginia and embraced her. His heart told him something horrible had happened. Everything was clean and in place, but Joseph noticed items were missing, including the foyer rug. The rug was blood soaked from Pearlie's wounds and had been removed.

"What's going on? Where are Martha and Jake?" Joseph could not imagine what was happening. He never suspected an Indian raid.

"They are fine, please sit down and let me tell you what has happened." Reginia was determined to tell Joseph what had happened before he saw Martha battered and swollen. They sat in the parlor listening to Reginia tell of the raid, the fight and the death of Joseph's house slaves. She told in detail of Martha's bruises and wounds and of Jake taking the arrow. She told the men everything but the one thing Martha feared most. She would not tell Joseph of the rape. That would be Martha's decision. Joseph went directly to Martha.

"William, I would like to leave Fancy here for a few days. At least until Joseph gets another house staff," Reginia said.

"That is fine." He hugged Reginia tightly. "I am glad you are safe and well. You are awfully brave to have come. You should have left that for Ransom and the men."

"I had to come for Martha and Jake, they needed caring for." She paused and hugged her husband. Suddenly she felt weak. She no longer had to be the strong one, for William was home. She held on to him tightly. Her head was on his shoulder as she spoke to him.

"I'm awfully glad you are home. It has been difficult seeing my friend hurting, and seeing our son's best friend lying in that bed weak and drained from seeing his mother assaulted. I can hardly bare to think about it."

William was proud of Reginia. She was a remarkable person and he was glad she was his. He could see her exhaustion. He left her in the parlor with Jim and Betty and went to see Joseph. He was at the bed holding Martha. William told Joseph of the plans to leave Fancy. He told Joseph they would leave him with his family but that he and Reginia would return the next day to help. He shook Joseph's hand and hugged him. Joseph was grateful to have such a friendship as they had in William and Reginia. William got his slaves and helped the ladies and Batha in the carriage. Samuel drove the carriage and they headed for home. Reginia and Betty were glad to be going home.

CHAPTER
TEN

It was dusk before they arrived home. Laudie and the children greeted them at the front door. Laudie hugged Reginia tightly.

"Oh, my Missus Reginia, I'm glad to see you safe at home. Lardy, lardy, my heart is just happy all over!" Laudie was trembling with relief and her body jiggled with joy. "Supper is almost ready. I cooked late so you could eat with your family."

"Thank you, Laudie. I'm glad to be home." Reginia continued to hold her precious children. She was tired. "I would like a hot bath, Laudie, and I am sure Missus Wade would too." She looked to Betty, who was nodding her head.

"I knew you would, Missus Reginia. I have water heating over the fire right now!" Laudie was pleased to have guessed her Mistress's wishes.

Reginia and Betty left for their bath. William and Jim took the children into the drawing room to visit. William wanted to visit with Alex and John. Katie curled in her father's lap and snuggled against him while he talked to the boys. Alex was thirteen years old and a handsome young man. He was tall for his age, and his features were becoming more manly in appearance. William listened to Alex talk, with his recently acquired deep voice, and realized he didn't have a young boy in Alex any longer. Jim told William of their plans to send Jackson to school in the East.

William thought it was a wonderful idea and wanted to talk to Reginia about sending Alex with Jackson to school. As William sat listening to Alex, he knew the boy was mature enough to go away to school. He could hardly wait to talk to Reginia about his idea.

The ladies entered the drawing room refreshed and clean. William and Jim both left their seats to hug their wives. They were fortunate men and they knew it. Laudie prepared a beautiful table with roast chicken, potatoes, beans, corn, and biscuits, and a delicious cobbler for dessert. They were all famished and ate to their hearts' content. After dinner, Alex asked to be excused. He wanted to finish reading a novel. Reginia tucked John and Katie in their beds and returned to visit with Jim and Betty.

"Honey, I want to talk to you about something." William smiled meaningfully to Reginia as he spoke. "It concerns Alex and school."

"Oh, yes, William, I want to talk to you too."

William interrupted her quickly before she could give her idea on the subject. "I would like to send Alex to school in Boston alongside Jackson. He will get a good education and preparation for college."

"I cannot believe this! This is exactly what I wanted to talk to you about!" Reginia hugged William and kissed him sweetly on his lips. "I want the children to have an education, and Alex would love to go with Jackson. He would not be as lonely if he had his friend."

Betty and Jim were thrilled. They talked for a while making plans to send the boys the following September to Boston. Jim and William told their wives about the convention and the new constitution they proposed to Mexico. The Texans called for repeal of the law of April 6, 1830, banning settlement of citizens of foreign countries lying adjacent to the Mexican territory. They also demanded separation from Coahuila. Stephen Austin would be leaving to take the constitution to the Mexican leaders. By the time the conversation about the convention ended, they were all exhausted and retired for the evening.

As Reginia prepared for bed, she posed a question to William: "My darling, we have many thoroughbreds now, and I was wondering if I could give one to Betty as a gift? She is such a dear friend and risked her life to help me with Martha and Jake. I took her to see the horses and she just fell in love with one of your two-year-old fillies. Could I please give it to her?" Reginia pleaded with her little-girl smile and batted her big brown eyes softly as she spoke to William. He could never resist her charm.

"I think that can be arranged," he said with a smile. He was totally under her influence. How could he resist her charm, especially after her bravery and dedication to her friends?

Reginia rushed to the bed and hugged and kissed William. "Thank you, my love. Thank you. I will surprise her tomorrow with the filly." Reginia curled into her husband's arms and fell sound asleep.

Jim and Betty stayed one more day with William and Reginia. After breakfast, they took the carriage to the Rileys'. Reginia helped clean and put new bandages on Martha and Jake. Martha was doing much better but the knife wound to her leg was swollen and did not look good. Reginia cleaned it thoroughly and put the medicine that she had found in Martha's cupboard on it. She wanted to have Dr. Fields come and tend to Martha and Jake. She talked to Joseph and he agreed to send for him. Reginia promised Martha she would come every day to see her. Martha smiled and squeezed Reginia's hand with appreciation. She was very weak and had lost a lot of blood. Reginia knew it would be weeks before Martha would be up and about. The two couples left for home.

"William, before we go to the house could we see the horses, please?" Reginia wanted to surprise Betty with the filly.

"Do you think Betty and Jim want to ride all the way to the pasture, Reginia," William teased.

"Why sure they do, don't you?" she asked of Jim and Betty.

Betty was excited to see the filly again, hoping William would sell her to them. "Oh, yes we would. I want Jim to see the gorgeous sorrel filly. She is just lovely, Jim. She is a bright sorrel with a white blaze on her face and four white stockings, and her mane and tail look like flaxen silk."

"She sounds beautiful. I would love to see her." Jim had no idea what the ladies were up to and Betty had no idea the filly would be a gift.

They arrived at the pasture and Betty hurried Jim to see the filly. She was very excited. The filly was as beautiful as Betty described. The filly had a long hip and neck with a tiny head and big eyes.

"Isn't she magnificent!" Betty just loved the filly. She whispered in Jim's ear. "Can I ask William to sell me the filly? I want her badly."

Jim told her yes and to try to make a deal with William for the purchase. Jim knew the filly would not be cheap, but he could not refuse Betty.

"William, I really love the filly and would love to have her. Would you consider selling her to me. I will pay whatever you ask." Betty was eager to have the filly.

"My dear Betty, you don't tell the seller you will pay him anything. You make an offer and bargain from there," Jim teased Betty. Betty never purchased anything other than goods for the house and felt silly. She blushed at the thought of appearing ridiculous.

"That is true. I may ask a small fortune for the filly and you would have to pay it." William joined Jim in the fun of teasing Betty, who was very serious. "Honestly, I must think this over. This is the best filly I have and I am not sure I want to part with her."

Betty was disappointed as they left for the house. William dropped the ladies and Jim at the house and told them he would take the carriage to the barn and would return shortly. Reginia was a little disturbed with William. She wanted him to give her friend the filly, but she would not argue with him in front of company. When he returned she would speak with him in private.

Reginia took Jim and Betty in for tea. Lunch would be served quickly. William was at the barn for over an hour. Reginia became concerned. He knew they were hungry and were ready to eat.

Finally, William entered the house. He insisted they come outside. Reginia wanted to eat lunch first, but William insisted. The three of them followed William out the front door. There stood Big Bo holding the beautiful, freshly groomed filly.

"Betty, you are a dear friend. I want you to have this filly as a gift from Reginia and me."

"I can't believe you want to give her to me," Betty stated shyly. "This filly is well bred, beautiful and much too expensive to give away. William, I can't . . . "

"Nonsense," he interrupted. "Reginia wants you to have the filly and so do I."

Betty embraced Reginia and William, then went immediately to the filly. She rubbed her hands across her wide back and down her sides. Betty was proud of her. She could not wait to get her home. Jim shook William's hand, thanking him. "I'm certainly glad you gave her that filly," Jim teased. "I was afraid if you agreed to sell her, I would be going home a broke man!" The two men laughed as they walked into the house.

After lunch, Reginia wanted to take a nap. The pregnancy and all the activity tired her. While Reginia napped, Betty, Jim, and William went to the barn. Betty wanted to see the filly again. William had a slave named Buck that broke his horses. Buck was a thin black man and had a way with the horses. He could break the young horses quickly with his gentle hands. Buck had been riding the two-year-old for a couple of months and William wanted Betty to see her filly ridden. William instructed Buck to saddle the filly and ride her in the pen. Buck walked, trotted, and galloped the filly. When he stopped the filly, she almost sat down! He spun her one way and then another on her hocks. Betty was impressed with the way the filly handled herself. She was light in her mouth and on her feet. The filly responded to Buck's every request without balking. Buck took her out of the pen and galloped her across the open field. Betty thought the filly was breathtaking as she glided across the field with her head stretched straight out in front. The filly had a gentle spirit and Betty was eager to ride her.

When Buck returned, she asked William if she could ride. "She is your filly, you can do whatever you like with her," William replied with a teasing tone to his voice. "Just ride with caution. She is just green broke," he added seriously. Betty rode the filly in the pen for a while and then headed across the field with her at a gallop. The filly floated across the ground and Betty thought it was like riding on a cloud. The filly was smooth to ride. She returned to the barn and handed the filly to Buck.

She went to William and hugged his neck, telling him how much she appreciated her gift, for the filly was even finer than she had imagined.

The next morning, the Wades were ready to leave for San Augustine. Goodbyes were exchanged, along with hugs. Reginia was sad to see her friend leave, but she would see her again next year when they took Alex and Jackson to school. The two couples made plans to meet at Betty and Jim's and leave from there with the boys. Reginia and Betty both wanted to take them to Boston, stopping in Natchez to visit Reginia and William's family. For Reginia and William had never seen Ben's children. It would be a wonderful trip. Reginia could hardly wait for the next year to pass. She was ready for civilization! Reginia and William watched their friends as they left Auburn, with the filly trotting behind their wagon. Reginia stood holding William's hand with her squeeze of appreciation and love.

CHAPTER

ELEVEN

A few months later, Mr. Grosse sent his overseer with a message to William. William invited the man in for coffee and read the message.

Dear William,

I am sending you this message to inform you of Stephen Austin. He has been imprisoned. I fear this will cause discontentment among the settlers and will create further hostility. I understand Joe Bell will handle many of the affairs from his home in Columbia. I will keep you informed.

Sincerely, Jarred Grosse

William could not believe the Mexicans would put Stephen in prison. He was furious. Mr. Grosse's overseer returned home after his coffee. William went for Reginia to inform her of Stephen's misfortune and the misfortune for all of them. Reginia was upstairs in the observatory looking across the fields. She loved the fall for the simple reason that the trees had lost their leaves and she could see for miles. Reginia saw the stranger ride away on the horse. She wondered who he was as she sat on the bench feeling totally at peace, thinking about her friend Martha. Martha was recovering nicely and Jake was doing fine.

It concerned Reginia that Martha had not told Joseph of the rape. She knew this ate away at Martha and Reginia felt Martha would be much better off if she would just tell her husband the truth. Reginia could not imagine keeping anything from William, especially something like that. She heard William's footsteps coming up the stairs to the observatory. She turned her head to greet him.

"Hello, darling. Who was that man that just rode off?" Reginia questioned William as he walked in and sat by her.

"That was the overseer for the Grosse Plantation. He brought me a message from Mr. Grosse. I have bad news. Stephen Austin has been imprisoned by the Mexicans." William's voice held deep concern as he told Reginia about the message.

"What will happen, William? Are we safe or not?" Reginia was concerned, but she exhibited no fear. She was becoming used to the upheavals on the frontier. William reassured her of their safety. He did tell her he feared an outbreak of hostility between the Americans and the Mexicans. The worst thing he feared would be battle between the two nationalities. They talked for a long time about the possibilities that could occur. Maybe they would release Stephen. Their prayers were with their friend and leader.

Time seemed to move slowly, especially to Reginia. She was large with her pregnancy, and very uncomfortable. The boats did not come as often due to the Mexicans' interference.

Thanksgiving and Christmas passed. Martha was well and came to visit Reginia often. Reginia was still concerned that Martha would not tell Joseph. This secret kept Martha from being as happy and jolly as she used to be. She was always serious. Joseph attributed her change to the attack itself and the loss of their house slaves. Reginia talked to her repeatedly about telling Joseph the truth, but she could not convince her. The secret brought Martha and Reginia closer as friends. For Reginia was the only one Martha could talk to about the rape. Martha told Reginia that she could not bring herself to make love to Joseph. The rape and the terrible scars on her leg prevented her from doing so. Reginia could not believe Martha's reactions and her stubbornness in not telling Joseph. Reginia hated seeing Martha tormented.

January 14, 1834, was a cool clear day. It was simply beautiful. Reginia walked about the grounds of the house with John and Katie. She took them to Sarah's grave and placed fresh holly, loaded with red berries, on her grave. She told them stories of their older sister and how she had gone to visit Jesus in Heaven. She still missed little Sarah, even after all the years. She held her two children and felt blessed to have them. The child within her kicked. She put John's and Katie's little hands on her stomach.

"Feel the baby kick." Reginia smiled. The baby kicked four times in a row. The children giggled out loud, as they felt the little punches from their mother's stomach. "Our baby is ready to come out and play!" Reginia hoped this was true, and that the baby did want out real soon. She felt like a stuffed bird, ready to pop! Reginia hoped if she walked enough, maybe the baby would come.

She kept herself busy until late afternoon. She began to cramp, but not often. She went to the outdoor john. She was surprised to find blood on her underclothes. Startled by the blood, she came out screaming for help. Laudie was on the back porch and heard the screams. She ran to Reginia and helped her into the house.

"I can't make it up the stairs, Laudie." Reginia felt weak from the cramping. She stood bent at the waist holding her large stomach. "Laudie, get blankets and fix a place on the rug." Reginia thought the firmness of the floor would feel good to her aching back.

Laudie rushed to prepare a bed on the floor of the drawing room. She put the folded blankets on the big rug in front of the fireplace. Reginia lay down on the pallet and the warmth from the fireplace soothed her. Laudie put a pillow under her head and covered her with another blanket. When she had Reginia comfortable she went to Samuel, who was in the kitchen. "Get Master William. Missus Reginia is a havin' her baby!" They both ran from the kitchen, Samuel after William and Laudie to tend to her Missus. Laudie put water on the fire to boil and grabbed fresh towels.

Reginia called to Laudie, "Laudie, get Missus Martha, get her quickly." Reginia's pains were more frequent now and she knew the baby would come soon and she worried there was trouble because of the blood.

Laudie left the room looking for someone to get Mrs. Martha. Just as she entered the foyer, she heard a knock on the door. "Oh, thank ya, Lord, thank ya, Lord," Laudie said out loud to herself. She was sending whoever was at the door to get Mrs. Martha. She didn't care who it was. Laudie ran to the door and opened it to find Ransom. She did not ask him what he needed or anything else, she just exclaimed with her stern, excited voice, "Fetch Missus Martha, quickly. Missus Reginia is a havin' her baby and there may be troubles!"

Ransom asked no questions. "Okay, Laudie, I'll be back with Missus Riley real soon, don't you worry!" He ran to his horse. Ransom jumped on the horse's back and galloped all the way to the Rileys'.

Samuel brought William to the house. William rushed to Reginia's side. She was in great pain. She didn't know what was wrong. "I can't lose this baby, William!" she cried.

"You won't lose the baby, I promise." He sat on the floor beside her, holding her hands, consoling her, as her pains gripped her insides. They seemed to be only about five minutes apart. William was worried.

"Master William, I needs to get her ready to have that baby. Missus Martha ain't here yet and I don't know if this child is a gonna wait for her or not." Laudie had delivered her share of Negro babies and was sure the child had not turned properly to come out. "Now, you go on out of this room and let me tend to Missus Reginia and I needs Batha in here to help me."

William kissed Reginia and reassured her that all would be fine. He left the room and went for Batha, who was waiting eagerly outside the drawing-room door.

Just as William took a seat in the foyer, Martha and Ransom entered the house. "I came quickly, William. Is Reginia okay?"

"No, there was blood and she's cramping bad. Laudie says the baby's breech."

"Don't worry, I know what to do." Martha spoke with such confidence that it helped William to relax a bit. "Joseph and Jake will be along shortly. I rode my horse with Ransom and Joseph's bringing the carriage. She placed her hands on his shoulder and told him again that Reginia would be fine. She went into the drawing room to find Reginia prepared to give birth.

"Missus Martha, am I glads to see you! This baby won't turn and Missus Reginia, she's ready! Her water's done broke!"

Martha looked at Reginia lying on the floor. She knelt close to her, taking her hand, and whispered in her ear. "I'm here for you as you were for me. I'm going to deliver a fine baby for you, don't you worry. I helped old Doc Richards do this several times back in Natchez."

Reginia was relieved to see Martha. She took a deep breath for the next pain and released with a scream. "Here, Laudie, let me try to turn the baby." Martha knelt on the floor between Reginia's legs. "Bend your knees, Reginia, and spread your legs farther apart." Martha guided her legs to the position she wanted. "Do not push, Reginia, until I tell you to." Martha gently put her small hand inside Reginia. She felt the baby's shoulder. It was sideways. Martha worked gently to turn the baby. Reginia screamed from the pain. "It's all right, Reginia, I turned the baby, it's ready to come."

The contractions were coming constantly. Martha told Reginia to push and she did. Laudie stood anxiously, with towels, scissors, and hot water. Reginia screamed as she pushed. Martha could see the head. "Push, Reginia, push!" Reginia pushed as hard as her weak body could. Martha was busy guiding the baby into the world. There he was. Reginia heard the baby's cry. "You have a healthy, and I do mean healthy, baby boy!" He was big, at least nine pounds. "This is this biggest baby I have ever seen!" Martha laughed for the first time since the Indian attack. She cut the cord and wrapped the baby in a clean blanket. She held the infant close for Reginia to see.

"Let me hold him, Martha." Martha placed the baby in Reginia's arms. Reginia held the baby boy, admiring his beauty. He looked half grown! Reginia was glad to have him; she smiled and softly giggled through her pain and exhaustion.

Laudie brought William in to Reginia. He was a proud father, for the fifth time. He embraced his wife and newborn. They admired their son for a few minutes before giving him to Laudie.

Samuel had a big fire roaring in the bathing-room fireplace and warmed the water for Laudie to clean the child. William went out of the room while Martha and Batha cleaned Reginia. Reginia had torn herself very little in the delivery. Martha was relieved. If Alex had been this size, he would have ripped Reginia terribly. Reginia was tired and she just wanted to sleep. Martha told her she could take a nap, but when Joseph got there, she was going to have the men move her to her bedroom. Reginia didn't want to move anywhere, but she was too exhausted to argue.

Joseph and Jake had arrived, unbeknownst to Martha, while she was delivering the baby. Martha left Reginia's side and walked into the foyer, where she found her family waiting. Joseph was pleased to see the big smile on her face. She explained to Joseph and William about the complications of the delivery but that Reginia would be just fine after a good rest. She told the men they needed to carry Reginia upstairs to the bedroom, for it was too cool for her to stay on the floor of the drawing room. Alex and Jake ran up the stairs to see the baby. Alex was glad to have another baby brother. The two men went with Martha to move Reginia upstairs. William, with his strong body, needed no help carrying his wife. He lifted Reginia as if she were a baby herself and carried her gently up the stairs. He tucked her in the bed and held her for a while.

Reginia fell asleep in her husband's arms. William sat looking at the beautiful strong lady in his arms and thought how fortunate he was. She took each hardship without a complaint. He wanted life to be easier for his family, but the frontier was still untamed and he didn't know what more he could do. It would take years before Texas would be developed like the Southern States were. He only hoped they would live long enough to see it happen.

William entered the parlor to find Joseph and Martha sitting on the sofa side by side. Joseph had his arm around her shoulders and they were laughing and enjoying one another for the first time since the Indians raided their home. William insisted they spend the night. It was too late for them to travel home. Martha and Joseph enjoyed the pleasures of lovemaking that night. Martha felt a deep closeness to Joseph as she lay in his arms. The fear of telling her husband the truth of the Indians' assault left her mind. She decided she must tell him the truth and she would just as soon as they got home.

The next morning, Martha told Reginia goodbye and told Reginia of her plan to tell Joseph the truth about the rape. It pleased Reginia to see Martha happy and back to her old self after months of anguish. Martha and Joseph left for home with Jake riding her horse. Martha could hardly wait to get home. She felt good about finally relieving herself of the guilt and shame of the rape. She realized her husband would stand by her and understand the pain and humiliation she suffered. Things were looking upward for her as they traveled to their home.

CHAPTER
TWELVE

When they arrived home, Martha asked Jake to take the horse and carriage to the barn. She wanted to be alone with Joseph when she told him the truth about the attack. She asked Joseph into the parlor and explained she had something very important to tell him. Joseph could not imagine what it could be, but his wife was happy and he never dreamed of the horrors she was about to tell him. They sat on the sofa and Martha took her husband's hands in hers and looked directly into his eyes.

"I love you, Joseph, and I must tell you the truth about something that occurred during the raid. Please don't say anything until I've finished telling you." Her hands trembled and she feared if Joseph interrupted she might not tell him everything. "I've suffered much grief and humiliation. I wasn't going to tell you, but I can't go on living a lie."

Joseph sat listening to Martha, clinging to every word she spoke, totally unprepared for what he would hear. "The Indians came and we thought they were wanting to trade. I walked outside to find their faces covered in streaks of paint. Their faces were angry and cold. It frightened me to the point to where I stood still for a moment in disbelief." Tears formed in her eyes as she recalled the horrifying afternoon. She could no longer look in Joseph's eyes. She held his hands firmly as she looked out the windows. "I turned to run for the house and felt the hands of an Indian grab me by my hair. He jerked me back. I struggled to free myself, but he was too strong. I felt a second Indian grab my waist and they threw me to the ground." She paused briefly, wiping the tears from her eyes. Joseph thought this was when they must have beaten her. He waited patiently while Martha pulled her thoughts together, not saying a word, as she had requested. "They hit me and kicked me about the ground until I was weak and then . . . " She paused, and after taking a deep breath, she blurted the words "they raped me."

Joseph sat staring. The words "rape, rape, rape" kept running through his mind. He visualized the Indian with his wife and not just one but two. He could not sit there any longer. His mind could not accept what he was hearing. He pulled his hands free from Martha's grip. He stood in disbelief. His eyes were cold and distant. Martha was in shock. What had she done? Her worst fear had come true. Her beloved Joseph did not understand and her stomach tightened in a big knot. Joseph turned and walked from the room. Martha, sickened by his response and panic-stricken, leaped from the sofa and ran after him. The tears streamed down her face as she ran trying to explain. Joseph stopped her dead in her tracks at the front door.

"Stop, Martha." The tone of his voice, cold and without feelings, was foreign to Martha's ears. She stopped and began pleading with him to understand. This was not her fault, she had done all she could to prevent the rape. "I can't listen to another word. Do not follow me, I can't bear to see you right now." Joseph turned and walked toward the fields. Martha did not know what to do. She became ill, her stomach filled with a burning sensation. She hurried outside as she felt the burning sensation spread from her stomach to her throat. She heaved over and over. She sat on the ground and buried her head in her skirt sobbing from the depths of her soul. Would Joseph ever understand? Would he hate her? What was she to do? Questions echoed in her mind. She sat on the ground, unaware of her surroundings.

"Mother, are you all right?" Jake questioned as he approached, bewildered by his mother's behavior. He saw the vomit by his mother and asked her again. "Mother, are you all right? Are you sick?" He grew very concerned.

Martha lifted her head slowly in a daze and in a complete state of confusion. She responded slowly. "I'm fine, Jake. I just became ill and sick to my stomach. I'll be all right. Why don't you go visit Alex today and fish or something?" Jake lifted his mother and helped her in the house. Bewildered why she wanted him to go see Alex, since they had just returned from there, he wasn't going to argue with her request. He loved to fish with Alex. He thought he would leave quickly before his mother had a chance to change her mind. Jake would never know what disturbed his mother so deeply.

Several weeks passed. Martha remained in her room, in bed. Joseph would not see her, he slept on the sofa at night, explaining to Jake that his mother had a fever and he did not want to disturb her. Jake believed his father, for why would his parents lie to him? Joseph became more bitter with each passing day. Martha could not bear the pain and void in her life. She had to talk to Reginia. By now, she thought, Reginia should be fine from the delivery of her child. She desperately needed to talk to someone. She dressed herself for the ride to Reginia's house.

Martha arrived at the Wildes' home, knocking desperately at the door. Laudie answered the door. "Why, Missus Riley, it's good to see ya. Where's you been? I thought ya would've been here to see that fine young'un before now."

"I wanted to give Missus Reginia time to recover, that's all, Laudie." She followed Laudie into the drawing room where Reginia sat in the rocker holding the baby. "Hello, Reginia, how are you feeling? Let me see that big boy." Martha tried to be nonchalant to hide her feelings of despair. She did not want Laudie and Reginia to suspect something was wrong.

"I'm fine and look at my baby boy. He's such a good baby. We named him Thaddeus James. We call him Thad." Reginia thought her friend looked different, perhaps distant in her thoughts. "Laudie, take Thad upstairs to bed and let me visit with Martha." Reginia could see her friend had visited for a reason other than seeing her baby. Laudie took the child and left the room. "Sit by me, Martha. I've missed our visits." Reginia had truly missed her dear friend and was glad to see her. "William told me that you and Joseph looked like two love birds when you left that morning. Where have the two of you been? Jake came to see Alex and told me you've had a fever." Reginia continued visiting with Martha, realizing Martha's mind was elsewhere. "Martha, what's troubling you. Do you still feel bad?"

Martha hung her head. She could not hold in her feelings any longer. She broke into tears. Reginia didn't know what to think! She left her rocker and put her arms around Martha. She held her friend, until she stopped sobbing.

"Martha, I'm here. Tell me what is wrong? I can't stand to see you troubled." Reginia felt helpless and didn't know how to comfort Martha.

"I told him," Martha spoke softly through the tears, with her head buried in Reginia's shoulder.

"Who did you tell? And what did you tell?" Reginia felt totally confused by Martha's behavior, for she never thought Martha would tell Joseph the truth.

"I told Joseph. I told him about the Indians attacking me." She sobbed clinging to Reginia. Reginia was confused, as she held Martha, comforting as best she could. Reginia could not imagine why telling the truth to Joseph was upsetting to Martha. She took Martha by her shoulders and looked into her eyes. Reginia saw fear and pain in Martha, unlike ever before.

"Martha, please talk to me, tell me what happened."

"He hates me. He hasn't spoken to me in two weeks."

"Honey, he doesn't hate you. He just needs time to absorb this terrible thing that happened to you." Reginia responded with sympathy.

"You don't know, Reginia. He is cold and uncaring. He will not come to the bed at night. He says he can't look at me. I can't endure Joseph ignoring me this way. I don't know what to do. I feel dead inside. Help me, Reginia, please help me."

Reginia thought for a moment. What could she do? She had an idea. "Martha, let me have William speak to Joseph."

"No, oh no, I don't want William to know!" She panicked at the thought of another man knowing what had happened to her.

"Listen to me, Martha, I can't understand Joseph's behavior, but I do know my husband and I know he would never judge me harshly, nor would he judge you. William would be my greatest support, if this had happened to me. He could hate the Indians but never me. Please, let me tell him. He can make Joseph come to his senses, I know he can."

Martha finally agreed. She even had hopes that Joseph would again love her. Reginia had tea served and the two ladies visited for hours. By the time Martha left, she felt much better. She was glad she had visited with Reginia and told her what happened.

That evening, when Reginia and William had gone to bed, Reginia told him about her visit with Martha and the problems between her and Joseph. William could not believe Joseph's response. William told Reginia he would go to Joseph the next morning and talk to him. Reginia was grateful to have such an understanding husband. She hugged and kissed William, telling him of her great appreciation and love for him.

The next morning William left to see Joseph. Joseph was at the barn saddling his horse when William arrived. "William, what are you doing here this early in the morning? I was just going to the fields to check on the work that needs to be done for planting. Would you like to ride with me?" William agreed. He told Joseph he needed to talk to him. The two men rode off for the fields.

"Joseph, I need to talk to you. Reginia and I have some concerns about Martha." William was a strong man with strong ideas. He was not a man to beat around the bush. He went directly to his concern. "You and Martha have been good friends for a long time. Reginia informed me last night that you cannot live with the fact that your wife was raped by Indians."

"Martha had no business discussing our problems with Reginia." Joseph puffed with angry pride.

"Damn, Joseph, she had to talk to someone. Reginia is her best friend. You weren't there for her. What's wrong with you?" William was firm in his belief that Joseph should stand beside Martha, not push her away.

"You don't understand a thing, William. Two filthy Indians had their way with my wife!" He shouted at William, overwhelmed with anger.

"They were savages. Martha didn't take part in that willingly. There was nothing she could do. She's lucky to be alive. Hell, you're lucky she's alive." William was angry or, at the very least, disappointed in Joseph's refusal to listen to the facts. William tried to talk to Joseph, but Joseph did not want to hear the truth about his actions. He was too proud to admit to his own weakness. He kicked his horse into a run and left William behind. Joseph ran the horse out of William's sight, trying to block the vision of the assault on Martha from his mind.

William returned home and gave Reginia the disappointing news. Reginia was angry with Joseph's stubbornness. He would not listen to William; he would not listen to anyone. She decided to give Joseph a few days to think over what William told him, before going to visit Martha. She did not want to appear as an interfering friend. Reginia was certain that Joseph would think about his actions and go to Martha with an apology and show her the love and support she needed. Joseph wasn't unreasonable. He was bound to understand the pain he was causing Martha.

That night, as Reginia and William sat in the drawing room, reading their books, a thought flashed through Reginia's mind. What if Joseph responded coldly to Martha because he felt guilty? She told William of her suspicion. William agreed. He had known Joseph most of his life and knew Joseph to be a kind and good man. This behavior was unlike him. William thought for a moment. "Reginia, honey, I think you may be absolutely correct. For only guilt could cause Joseph to act this way. We'll go see them the day after tomorrow. For if you are right, there is no need for Joseph to carry a burden of guilt and I think I can make him understand that. I would go tomorrow but I have some matters to tend to." William felt relieved. He knew his wife was probably right. He was anxious to speak to Joseph.

The next day, as William and his family sat at the dining table eating lunch, Jake came running in. He saw them in the dining room and entered, out of breath. "What is wrong, son?" William asked.

"I just need to talk to Alex. May I speak with him, sir?"

"Father, may I be excused?" Alex was curious and wanted to see what Jake wanted.

"Yes, Alex, go ahead."

The two boys went outside for a while. Alex came back into the dining room and asked to speak with his father. William followed his son to the library. Alex informed his father of his conversation with Jake.

"Jake says his parents had a terrible argument. He's very upset, Father. His mother screamed at his father and his father just turned and walked to the barn. Missus Riley ran to the barn after him, but she couldn't stop him. He left on his horse and Jake doesn't know where he is. He said his mother won't leave the barn, she just sits there staring at the loft. She won't even talk to Jake. Jake said it was like she didn't even realize he was with her. Jake's real scared, Father. Please, won't you go to the Rileys' house and find Mister Riley?"

"Yes, son, I will. Let me get your mother and we'll both go. Take Jake into the dining room and fix him something to eat. We'll be back as quick as we can."

William and Reginia left for the Rileys', never expecting anything like what they found. William pulled the carriage to a stop at the front of the house. Anna, the new house slave, came running. "Missus Martha, she's in the barn." She turned to William. "They had a terrible fight, you just gotta do somethin', Mister Wilde. You just gotta get that poor lady to come back to tha house." Anna was obviously shaken by the argument. William realized it must have been a terrible argument for her to tell him this. Reginia was very upset. She had to get to Martha.

"Take me to the barn, William. I'll get Martha and take her to our house until Joseph comes to his senses," Reginia spoke firmly. For when she made up her mind to do something, she did it. William jumped in the carriage and took Reginia to the barn.

"Get Martha and take her home. I'll get one of Joseph's horses and find him. I'll talk some sense into him. They'll be back together in no time, don't worry." William knew if he talked to Joseph and if it was guilt that had created this problem, he could solve it. William helped Reginia from the carriage and went to the pen for a horse.

Reginia opened the barn door and walked in. She looked all over the barn but there was no one there. She looked in the empty stalls and by the saddles. She became nervous. Where was her friend? She started up the ladder to the hayloft. As she grabbed the ladder, pulling herself up higher, her eyes glanced upward. She stopped. She closed her eyes. She didn't believe what she saw. Fear filled her as she slowly opened her eyes.

"William! William!" she screamed at the top of her lungs. She was petrified and could not move. William heard her screams of panic. He ran in the barn as fast as he could. He saw Reginia on the ladder just pointing with her finger toward the rafters. He looked and saw Martha hanging by the neck from a rope tied to one of the rafters. Reginia climbed the ladder with William at her heels. She was horrified. None of this made any sense at all. How could her friend do such a thing? William climbed on the hay and with his knife cut the rope, gently lowering Martha to the floor.

Reginia grabbed her and began screaming at her. "Martha, open your eyes. Open your eyes right now. Do you hear me?" Martha's body lay limp in Reginia's arms. "Martha, this is Reginia, open your eyes and talk to me. I promise you, everything will be all right." Reginia's eyes filled with tears. She began to sob, embracing the dear friend she had come to love. William pulled Reginia up and turning her toward himself, he pulled her to him and held her tightly. She cried as she spoke, her body trembling from the sight of Martha dead before her eyes. "Why would she do this . . . take her own life?" She buried her head in William's chest.

"Reginia, let me take you to the house. I must find Joseph." Reginia looked up at William. "He will never be able to live with this, and poor Jake . . . he loves his mother with all his heart."

"Darling, this is a time we must cling to our faith. I don't know how they will get through this, but they will with God's help."

William took Reginia to the Rileys' house and told Anna what had happened. Reginia was in a state of shock. Anna shed tears for her Missus. She brought tea to Reginia and tried to comfort her. William had two of Joseph's slaves take Martha into the house and lay her on the bed. He instructed them to use the bedroom door, thus Reginia would not see her. William then left on horseback to find Joseph.

It was an hour before William found Joseph. He was sitting under a big tree by the creek. He looked up at William. He was glad to see William. He was ready to talk to someone. He began talking uncontrollably, not stopping to take a breath. William could not get a word in edgewise. "William, I don't know why you are here but I'm glad you are. I can't stand this any longer. I feel the attack on my family is my entire fault. Martha and Jake would have been fine, if only I had been home . . . none of this would have happened. I have been awful to her. She didn't deserve the treatment I've given her. I walked out on her this morning. She's been in such pain. I'm ashamed. I'm extremely ashamed." Joseph hung his head, his voice cracking and his throat choking from fighting his tears. "I cherish her. I can't go on like this. Will she forgive me for not being there to protect her from those savages?"

William didn't know what to say. Blame was a terrible thing. It had killed an innocent lady. If only he had come that morning to speak with Joseph. He stopped himself as he began to think: "I won't take on this terrible burden of blame and allow it to destroy me as it has Joseph and Martha." He told Joseph to get on his horse. He wanted him to go back to the house. William wanted him home before he told him of his tragic loss.

As they rode back to the house, Joseph spilled his innermost thoughts to William. William listened to Joseph and his plans for him and Martha. He babbled on and on about his love for her. Joseph was like a new man after releasing the blame he had harbored. William was torn inside. Why did this have to happen? William dreaded telling Joseph. It was going to kill him. He had to get him home. He knew Joseph was going to collapse.

As they approached the house, William stopped him. He would tell him about Martha outside, under the privacy of the old oak tree. "What is it, William? I really want to get to Martha."

"Get off your horse, Joseph, I have to tell you something." The two men dismounted. "Something has happened, something horrible," William spoke softly.

"What has happened?" Joseph had no idea it would concern Martha.

William put his hand on Joseph's shoulder. "Martha's dead, Joseph."

Joseph just looked at William. He was outraged. "What do you mean, 'Martha is dead'? What kind of sick joke is this, William?" Joseph did not want to believe William, but in his heart, he knew William would never joke about something like that. William tried to talk but Joseph cut him off short and turned for the house. William put his arm on his shoulder and tried to stop him.

"Get your hands off me," Joseph declared. "I have to get Martha." Joseph walked faster and faster toward the house. "Martha is dead" echoed through his mind over and over. He felt delirious. His friend would not lie to him. He began to run. He ran into the house calling her name, expecting her to come to him. He ran into every room calling her. Reginia tried to reach out to him, but he was oblivious to her presence. William came in behind him, shaken by his friend's grief. He grabbed Reginia. It was too much. They held on to each other, each crying tears of sorrow. Joseph thrust the bedroom door open, calling out for Martha. He saw her body on the bed. He ran to her and grabbed her body, burying his head in her chest. "Martha, I knew you were here. I knew you were." Joseph was losing his mind. He would not accept her death. He would not let go. William tried to get Joseph off Martha, but Joseph would not let go of her.

"Martha's gone, Joseph. Come on. She's gone, let her go." He pleaded with Joseph. Joseph held his wife and began to scream violently.

"No! No! No!" Joseph cried furiously.

William pulled him to his feet and walked him into the parlor. Joseph was limp with the horror of losing Martha. He slumped over William's shoulder. William set him down with Reginia and went for the brandy. Reginia and William placed their own sorrows aside and tried to comfort Joseph. The man was out of his mind with anguish. Never had Reginia seen such grief. William knew why Joseph was bitter. The guilt had taken complete control of Joseph. He knew Joseph blamed himself for his wife's assaults and now, worse, he blamed himself for her death. How would his dear friend ever recover?

Reginia stayed with Joseph while William went after Jake. William wanted to bring Jake home before telling him. The news of his mother's death would be a terrible shock. The carriage bounced across the bumpy road as William urged the horse to gallop faster. Jake was with Alex in the drawing room. He had been confiding in Alex about the troubles he sensed between his mother and father. William walked into the room to get Jake, trying to hide the sorrow within himself. "Jake, come with me and I'll take you to your home."

"Why, I can ride home by myself, Mister Wilde." Jake thought it was strange that William wanted to take him home. He rode to visit Alex all the time, ever since they were small children. Jake looked at William and thought he looked worried about something. "Where's Missus Wilde? Is she with my mother?"

"Yes, Jake. She is with your mother and father," William answered without batting an eye. He knew it was not a lie, he just didn't tell Jake the entire truth. It was for Jake's own good, he rationalized.

Jake was not a child anymore. He knew something wasn't right. "Mister Wilde, something's wrong. Won't you please tell me? I want to know." He spoke like an adult, with his newly acquired deep voice.

William looked at the boys. They were young but both were very mature and he knew he could not keep the truth from Jake. Jake knew something was wrong. William felt he should tell him. He thought it might be better to tell him with Alex nearby for support and asked Alex to wait in the foyer. William escorted Alex to the door and returned to Jake. He placed his hand on Jake's shoulder. "Sit down, son, and I'll tell you the truth." William sat down by Jake on the sofa and put his arm around the boy. "Your mother has been terribly troubled since the Indians attacked your home. You know this, I'm sure." Jake nodded his head. "She could not recover from the attack. She tried, but it consumed her mind. I feel it caused her to actually lose her mind. She loved you and your father very much, I want you to always know this." Jake sat staring at William. His heart told him something terrible had happened. Tears began to fill his eyes. William embraced him. "Your mother could not deal with the pain any longer. She just wanted peace. I'm sorry, Jake. I'm direly sorry." Jake slumped against William's shoulder in tears. William held him tightly.

"She's dead, isn't she?" Jake said softly through his tears.

"Yes, son, she is." William held Jake while the boy sobbed. Jake cried for the longest time. William held him, assuring him that he and

Alex were there for him. William began to explain to Jake the deep sorrow his father was feeling. "Your father will need your support, as you will need his. You must be strong, Jake. This is what your mother would want. Remember how she loved you and she will always be with you in spirit."

William left Jake to get Alex. He wanted Jake to have a little time to himself to sort everything out in his mind. William told Alex about Martha's death and asked him to go in to be with Jake. "When he's ready, Alex, you and I will take him home." Alex went in to be with his friend, shocked himself by the news.

The two boys stayed in the drawing room for an hour before William went for them. William entered and was pleased by the boys' maturity. Jake was calm as he sat listening to Alex talk. William asked Jake if he was ready to go home. Jake stood up erect and spoke very boldly. "Yes, sir, I'm ready. I must get home to be with my father. I know he needs me." Jake turned to Alex and asked him to please ride home with them. William didn't know what Alex had said but he knew it was helpful. As the boys walked from the room, William squeezed Alex's shoulder and looked at him with pride and approval. His son had handled a very tough situation like a man, and it showed.

William and Alex took Jake home. Jake spoke of his father and the help he would need from him. Jake had prepared his mind to take on a big job. He was ready. They reached the house and Jake went directly to his father. Joseph broke into tears at the sight of Jake. Jake grabbed his father and hugged him, promising his father that he would help him and that his mother would want them both to be strong and continue with their lives.

Reginia and Anna had Martha prepared for her burial. They put the most beautiful dress in Martha's armoire on her and had two slaves put her body in the parlor. Joseph was in a state of shock. Jake took his father to his room to rest. He asked if Alex could stay overnight with him. Jake didn't want to be alone. His father was exhausted and fell fast asleep. William agreed and he and Reginia left for home.

The next morning, William and Reginia rode to Joseph's for the burial. They buried Martha under a large oak tree among the wildflowers. Joseph fell to the ground from grief. William felt sorrow for his friend. He could not imagine his life without Reginia. He helped Joseph to his feet and took him to his home. Joseph was distraught, he only wanted to be left alone, and even Jake could not reach him. The Wildes stayed, most of the day, with Joseph and Jake.

That afternoon, William talked to Joseph and told him he could not blame himself and that he needed to be strong for his son. Joseph was a good man and knew William was right. "William, I won't easily forgive myself, but I must take care of Jake. I will be all right, we'll both be all right. I don't want you and Reginia to worry about us. I'll do what's best for my son. Just give me some time." Joseph embraced his friend and went for Jake. William felt better and could take his family home with the reassurance that Joseph would not reject Jake.

CHAPTER
THIRTEEN

M onths passed and Joseph and Jake were doing better. Jake worked hard helping his father. Reginia missed her friend and thought of her often. There were only a few other women nearby, but Reginia knew them only casually. She had not become as close to any of them as she was with Martha. Time was nearing for them to send Alex to school. Reginia could not wait to see Betty.

May was a month away. Alex spent every day with Jake. The two boys would miss each other while Alex was away. William spent April preparing Ransom for work details and getting his books in order for their summer trip.

William wanted to make a trip to Harrisburg for goods for the trip and for the plantation. It was a three-day trip to the town. Harrisburg was located on the big bayou that emptied into the Gulf of Mexico. He took Big Bo and several other slaves with wagons. William loaded the wagons with supplies and visited the local merchants.

The Mexicans were becoming more hostile and the Americans were becoming rebellious against the leadership of President Santa Anna. He was corrupt and had turned the Mexican government into a dictatorship. The Americans were enraged by the imprisonment of Stephen Austin. William feared the possibility of war. He totally supported the new country, yet he saw no way it could develop under the rule of Santa Anna.

William returned home a week later, disillusioned by the passiveness of other American settlers he met in Harrisburg.

The last week of April was spent preparing for the trip. Alex was filled with excitement. He spent his last day with Ben and Jake sharing his excitement and dreams of his future with them. He would miss his family but going to school with Jackson was like a big adventure. He was unfamiliar with civilization as his mother knew it. She had told him stories of the grand lifestyle and the large cities in the East. Alex had wonderful memories of his home in Natchez too. He could hardly wait to leave. Reginia gave final instructions to Laudie and Samuel while William covered every detail with Ransom. Reginia was taking Fancy to help with the younger children and William selected the slaves that would drive the wagons. By the end of the month, everything was prepared for the journey.

When May the first finally arrived, the cool damp air refreshed the Wilde family as they arose bright and early for their trip. Enthusiastic chatter filled the room as the family gathered for breakfast. They would be leaving Auburn at daylight. Reginia ate quickly, excusing herself to give her final instructions to the house servants. She could not wait to see the sun peak through the windows.

The sun rose and the sky was beautiful, crisp, and clear. William gathered his family and they boarded the wagons. Laudie, Samuel, and Ransom stood on the porch waving farewell as the wagons pulled down the lane. Reginia and the children waved vigorously. Reginia stared fondly at the big home until it disappeared with distance. She had grown to love her home, in spite of all the hardships and losses they suffered. It was her home and it was her children's home. As thrilled as she was to return to Natchez and Boston, she knew she would be equally excited to return to Auburn. They planned to be gone almost a year. She suddenly realized how she would miss the Texas plantation.

A week later, they arrived at the Wades' home in San Augustine. Reginia sighed with relief at the sight of Betty and Jim. The difficult part of the trip was over. She was amazed at how beautiful the place appeared. The paint was fresh and Betty's gardens were beautiful. Jim had his wagons in the front yard, loaded and ready to leave. They would rest that night and leave early the next morning.

After dinner, Jim, Betty, William, and Reginia shared stories about their lives growing up in the South and their times spent in the East. Excitement gripped the children as none of them had ever experienced the fine lifestyles described to them by their parents. Their young minds could barely conceive such grandeur.

The next day, the two families departed for Natchez. They traveled several weeks, stopping along the way at plantations to rest. The children's eyes became large with wonder as they approached the great Mississippi River. The children were captivated by its size. Large boats waited to take the travelers across. They could see the town of Natchez as they boarded the boat. Reginia could not wait to see her family. The four had not seen their families in five years. The Wades' family lived north of Natchez and the Wildes' lived south. They would part ways for one month and meet again in Natchez on the first of July for the trip to Boston. They were to travel to Savannah, where they would board a ship to Boston. They planned to be in Boston for two months, before returning to Natchez for the winter.

The two families said their goodbyes and headed for their families' homes. William turned the wagons down the lane to the old plantation. How grand it was! The large oaks lined the lane to the big home. Childhood memories flooded Alex's mind. He could not wait to see his uncle Ben and aunt Elizabeth and wondered what his cousins looked like for he was so young the last time he had seen them.

Ben, outside when the wagons reached the house, rushed to greet his family. Ben raised his arms just in time to grab Alex as he jumped from the wagon. William helped Reginia and the other children from the wagon and turned to his brother, embracing him. Elizabeth ran from the house and straight to Reginia, throwing her arms around her and gripping tightly. Elizabeth loved Reginia and had missed having her nearby. Reginia introduced them to their younger children and followed Ben into the house. Reginia gazed about the foyer and into the parlor. The old house was beautiful. She felt good to see that Elizabeth had kept it furnished so elegantly. William and Reginia visited with Ben and Elizabeth for a while before dinner while the children became familiar with their cousins.

After dinner, Ben took them into the drawing room to visit. William told them about Texas and all the hardships that they suffered. Ben and Elizabeth could not understand why they stayed and wanted them to return home to live.

"Oh, we couldn't do that," William told him emphatically. "Texas will be a great country someday. The land is rich and I and my family will be a part of its greatness. There are hardships to conquer in any new country. Texas is beautiful, I could never leave it."

Reginia just listened. She wasn't sure Texas would see its greatness in their lifetime, but it was their home and she would be with her husband, no matter what.

It was late when William and Reginia retired to their old bedroom. Elizabeth and Ben followed, for Elizabeth wanted to see Reginia's face when she opened the door, as Elizabeth had had the bedroom furnished just as Reginia had. They opened the door and Reginia gasped with surprise.

"Why, look, William, it looks exactly the same!" The bedroom was beautiful. Reginia could not believe it. "Elizabeth, I can't believe you replaced everything as I had it."

"We missed you very much. I wanted something of the house to remind us of you." Elizabeth knew that someday William would bring his family home for a visit. She hoped seeing the room would tempt them to stay. Reginia turned to Elizabeth and hugged her. She appreciated Elizabeth's efforts.

The month passed quickly. Reginia spent time visiting her parents, siblings, and friends. A large party was given for William and Reginia. Alex enjoyed visiting his childhood friends, but found himself taken by the beauty of Jacqueline Exavier. Her family was from the delta area near Natchez. Mr. Exavier and William were longtime friends. Alex had played with Jacqueline and her brother Robert when they were small. Jacqueline had grown into a striking young lady. Her flawless olive skin accentuated her long dark hair and vibrant green eyes. Her figure was developed, and, like Alex, she was mature for her age. Alex could not stop thinking about her.

They spent most of their days together riding their horses to a small brook, sitting under the large tree for hours, talking about their lives and school. Jacqueline would be attending school in the East not far from Alex. The two made plans to meet in Boston. He was smitten and knew he was in love. William and Reginia were tickled at their son's first love. They never imagined it would be a love such as theirs.

CHAPTER

FOURTEEN

The first of July came quickly, and the Wildes met the Wades to continue their trip via Savannah where they would board a ship onward to Boston. Alex was filled with excitement at the thoughts of Jacqueline being near him. He thought of her always, telling Jackson in detail of her beauty. Jackson could not wait to meet her. Reginia and William listened to their son, realizing he was becoming a young man and his interest in girls had begun. Reginia saddened with the thought of her son becoming a young man. Her little boy was gone forever. She held on to her younger children, as if she would never let them grow older.

As the ship pulled into the Boston harbor, Reginia and Betty rushed to see the sight. It had been many years since Reginia had been there, and memories of her youthful years captivated her thoughts. As a young girl, she had been sent to live with family in Boston, benefiting from an education while there. The harbor had changed. It was larger, with new buildings. A rush of excitement filled them as they set their feet on land. They could not wait to get settled in the hotel and see the town. The next few days were spent enrolling Jackson and Alex in school and getting them settled. Betty and Reginia called on friends from their childhood and the two couples attended social functions and the theater. The couples took in all the sights over the next month.

The ladies spent many days shopping. The dresses, hats, and shoes were beautiful. Reginia purchased a beautiful dark blue satin gown and robe. Teasingly, she told Betty she would save it until the last night. The men spent time taking care of business. William and Jim talked with the businessmen and told them of Texas and the progress they had made with their plantations. The boys loved Boston. There was much for them to see and do. The thrill of being in the civilized world made them wonder why their fathers ever wanted to move to Texas!

The last night in Boston was spent with all the children. They had a fine dinner and walk through the town, for the last time. The street lanterns cast a soft glow on the buildings and cobblestone streets. Carriages passed as the two families strolled along. Reginia wanted this moment to last forever. The night was beautiful, the air was cool, and the sky lit brightly by the stars and the moon. But most of all, they were safe. Reginia had forgotten what it felt like to feel safe. She was happy with the thought of Alex in this environment, if only she could give this to her other children.

They walked the boys to their living quarters and returned to the hotel. They packed their belongings for the trip back to Natchez and prepared for bed. Reginia tucked the children into bed in the adjoining suite and returned to their room, closing the door behind her. William lay waiting for her in the big brass bed. She paused in front of the bed and gently pulled the pins from her hair, letting the long curls fall gently on her shoulders.

William thought she was beautiful in the dark satin. He stood up and walked to her, kissing her gently. Her head tilted back as he kissed her neck and shoulder. She felt her skin quiver at his touch. William ran his fingers slowly over her body, down each perfect curve. She became more beautiful with each passing year. He lifted her in his arms and placed her on the bed. The passion between them had grown strong over the years. William could never get enough of Reginia. They made love for what seemed like hours. They held each other tightly, exchanging their vows of love for one another, until they fell asleep.

Early the next morning, they bid farewell to Alex and Jackson and boarded the ship for Savannah. They were all ready to return to

Natchez. William wanted to buy ships for transporting cotton from Texas, Louisiana, and Mississippi. He wanted to talk to Ben, whose help he would need. William could see there was money to be made in this business. He would tie the Gulf ports into the East with more ships. The Atlantic ports were busy with ships transporting goods and people across the ocean. Savannah and New Orleans were major ports and the need for supplies and transportation in the South was in demand. Many large rivers fed the Gulf and shipping would be easy.

The trip back to Natchez went well. The fall weather was warm and the travel had been comfortable and without problems. William wanted to spend a week in Natchez before going on to Texas. This would give them time to visit their families and rest. Reginia begged William to spend the winter with Ben and Elizabeth. She feared the weather would turn cold and she didn't want the children to become ill as Sarah had. Thad was still too small to travel in the cold, she begged, until William, smiling at his wife's persistence, agreed to stay.

Reginia wanted to spend the holidays with their entire family one last time. William knew Ransom would take good care of everything, and if Ben agreed to be partners in the shipping business, he needed time to make all the arrangements to get the ships and the captains and crews. Betty and Jim were glad. They had planned to spend the winter with their families and wanted the Wildes with them on the trip back to Texas.

William spoke with Ben about the shipping business. Ben became very interested. He wanted to go to New Orleans and make plans to open the main company there. William agreed. New Orleans was not far from Natchez and the ships could dock and leave easily. Ben's good friend Josh Strong lived in New Orleans. He was intelligent and had been schooled at Harvard. His family had been in the shipping business, but hard times had hit and he was left broke. Ben told William he thought Josh would be a good man to run the new business. The two men made plans and left for New Orleans that week.

William and Ben spent several weeks in New Orleans, purchasing a building on the waterfront and speaking with Josh. Josh was eager to have a job with steady pay, especially in a business he knew much about.

He guided William and Ben in their endeavor. William was impressed with the knowledge and honesty Josh displayed. He felt very sure the business adventure would pay off in time. They sent Josh to Savannah to purchase the ships. They would meet again in December to make further plans. William wanted everything in place before the cotton was picked. Josh began his journey to purchase ships and William and Ben returned to Natchez.

Thanksgiving was special on the big plantation. The house was full with William and Reginia's families. The children played and the adults visited and enjoyed the holiday. Singing and gaiety filled the house. Reginia's mother played the piano and her father played the banjo while the others sang. William and Reginia loved their family and wished they could always be together. This was an extraordinary time in their lives, and they had much to be thankful for.

William and Ben left again for New Orleans, both anxious to see Josh. They spent two weeks with Josh. The ships would be in New Orleans by March. Josh purchased four ships and hired the captains and crews while in Savannah. William and Ben put most of their money into the business. They prayed for a good cotton crop and a successful business.

The two men shopped for Christmas gifts for their families. Times were good for the Wildes and money was plentiful. William thought the money was there for the taking. The two men concluded their business and returned to Natchez.

FIFTEEN

Christmas was only a few weeks away. The ladies were busy decorating for the holiday. They made stockings and ornaments for the tree and spent time rejoicing in all their blessings. All the family gathered and friends came by often. There were many social gatherings during the month.

Ben and William wanted to have a big ball on New Year's Eve. The ladies made plans for the gala event. Reginia was excited about the holidays, but she thought of Joseph and Jake all alone. She hoped they had overcome the death of Martha and shared the holidays with friends. She thought of Martha frequently and how tragic and unnecessary her death was.

The week before Christmas, they received a letter from Alex. He was having a wonderful time at school. The schoolwork was challenging and he was studying hard. He saw Jacqueline on the weekends. She stayed with friends in Boston. The letter consisted mainly of stories of Jacqueline. Jackson was doing well and spent a lot of his time with Alex and Jacqueline. Alex would be spending the holidays with Jacqueline and her friends in Boston. Reginia was glad to receive the letter as she missed Alex greatly. She spoke with William about the letter. She was concerned about Alex spending so much time with Jacqueline. William reassured her that Alex's infatuation with Jacqueline would pass. This was his first girlfriend and he was merely excited. William told Reginia there would be many more girls in their son's life, and she had better get used to it!

Christmas Eve came. All the families were together again. Mrs. Stuart played the piano while the others sang Christmas carols. Ben and William had brought a large cedar into the foyer for the family to decorate. The children took the ornaments and decorated each branch. Reginia and Elizabeth placed small thin candles on the tree when the decorations were all in place. All the men worked quickly to light the candles. The light from the candles on the tree was the only light in the foyer. Thad, almost one year old, was fascinated by the tree all aglow. He clapped his hands with excitement. Reginia loved watching John and Katie. She felt the children, with their candor and expectations, lent a certain kind of magic to Christmas.

The children were put to bed early. All the toys were placed under the tree and the stockings were filled with fruit. Each would get a toy. John and Katie didn't know what it was like to have more than fruit. Reginia thought how wonderful it was to be able to have real gifts to give. There were real advantages of living near a large port and city.

Christmas morning came early for the adults. The children awoke shortly after 5:00 a.m., screaming with excitement as they rushed down the stairs. John and Katie were amazed at the sight. Never had they seen so many toys. John had received a wooden train set and Katie had found a beautiful doll under the tree. The stockings were filled with fruit, nuts, and candy. Reginia watched the children, her heart filled with glee. She thought of Alex and wondered if he was enjoying his Christmas. William walked to Reginia and gave her the Christmas gift he had purchased for her while in Boston. Her eyes lit up at the sight of the small rectangular box. She opened her gift carefully, enjoying each moment. As she lifted the top, her mouth opened and she gasped. Every eye in the room fell on Reginia. Inside the box was an exquisite diamond-and-emerald necklace with matching earrings!

Reginia held them up gently, allowing the necklace to rest over the palm of her hand, holding the earrings ever so carefully by her fingertips. Everyone admired the jewels.

CHAPTER FIFTEEN

"Darling, I bought these, with Jim's help, while in Boston. I hope you like them," William said proudly.

"Like them? I love them! They are beautiful. I can't believe this." Reginia put the earrings on and draped the necklace around her neck. "Please, clasp the necklace," she spoke softly to William. William moved her long hair out of the way. Reginia was still in her gown and robe. Her robe was deep green velvet. The necklace looked beautiful against her creamy white skin and deep auburn hair.

Reginia's mother walked to her to admire her necklace. "Honey, that necklace is beautiful. It just looks beautiful with your robe, I can't wait to see it when you are dressed!" Everyone laughed with agreement.

Reginia had a gift for William. She had bought him gold cufflinks while in Boston. They were engraved with his initials. He was thrilled with his gift. Christmas was wonderful that year, just as Reginia had imagined it would be.

Everyone finished opening their gifts, then headed for the dining room. The buffet was filled with dishes of eggs, bacon, biscuits, jams, and potatoes. Everyone sat down to eat. The children were eager to return to their toys. After breakfast, everyone went to their rooms to dress for the day. The day was warm and clear and the children played all day.

That evening, before dinner, they gathered around the piano for more singing. It was a joyous occasion for all. Afterward, they sat down for the traditional turkey dinner. William sat at the head of the long dining table. This would be the last time he would have that privilege. He gave a toast of thankfulness and good wishes. Reginia looked at her husband affectionately, thankful for him and the love they shared for one another.

The week ended with the great New Year's Eve Ball. The weather could not have been better. Everyone from Natchez and the delta area attended to bring in the new year, 1835. Reginia was glad to see Betty and Jim. They recollected the grand parties that had been held in the big home and visited with all their friends. They danced to the music and laughed all night. "What a great event," they all thought. The gowns flowed to the floor, in a variety of colors and fabrics. Reginia was clearly the most beautiful. Her jewels sparkled against her skin with her low-cut gown. Her hair was pinned up with soft curls accenting her earrings. William was proud of his wife. He was still amazed at how this beautiful lady with great poise and etiquette could also be humble and strong. He looked at her and thought how she belonged in a world of gaiety and friendly surroundings, rather than Texas. He thought, briefly, how selfish he was to take her from her good life to the uncivilized wilderness. He walked to Reginia, took her hand proudly, and asked her to dance. He held her close as they danced, knowing all the other men wished they had what he did!

The winter passed quickly. William and Ben made another trip to New Orleans on business. Josh was doing an excellent job, making arrangements with the plantation owners for shipping their cotton. William met Dr. Tom Bradley while on his trip to New Orleans. The doctor, in his early thirties, was intrigued by the talk of Texas. He had longed to move to the new frontier. William offered to take him and his family with them. William told him he would build him a house and pay him a salary if he wanted to go. William thought how thrilled Reginia would be to have a doctor at Auburn. There was no doctor for the settlers in his area. Tom agreed eagerly. He would meet William the first of March for the departure to Texas.

Reginia kept herself busy, visiting with family and friends. She wrote a letter to Alex each month they were there. She knew getting letters out of Texas was difficult. She began to think of Texas and Auburn. She was sad to leave Natchez but she was becoming eager to get home. However, she had no idea of the hostilities and friction that had grown bitter between the Mexicans and the Americans.

CHAPTER

SIXTEEN

The first of March came and the Wildes, Wades, and Dr. Bradley and his family left for Texas. Reginia was glad to have the Bradleys traveling with them. Tom and his wife, Maggie, were sociable and well educated. Reginia and Betty quickly befriended Maggie. Maggie was near the same age as they, exhibiting grace and strong will—characteristics needed to survive in Texas. The ladies enjoyed hours of conversation as they traveled through Louisiana to San Augustine.

They arrived the first week of April. Jim and Betty wanted them to stay for Easter. Reginia wanted to stay. The holidays were lonely in Texas and she did not want to be on the trail for the holiday. William agreed. He was never happier about the decision to stay over, for they awoke Easter morning to bitter freezing weather.

Rain had fallen the night before and had turned to ice. The children were excited to see the icicles hanging everywhere. They wanted to pick them and lick the ice. Betty, Reginia, and Maggie bundled the children warmly with coats, gloves, and caps and sent them out to play. William could not believe the weather. Never had he seen this kind of weather so late in the year. Jim became concerned for his freshly planted crops and the damage the ice storm would cause. William wondered if it had frozen in his area. His crops would be destroyed, creating a financial difficulty. A couple of days later, warm weather returned and the Wildes headed for home.

Reginia hated this part of the trip. She would be glad to be home. It had been a wonderful year. One she would never forget. She could hardly conceive how fast the time went by. Reginia thought about the differences in the way of living between the States, especially in the East, and in Texas. The States offered safety and everyday conveniences. Her only consolation was her pride of being a part of this new frontier. She hoped for so much. It would be years before her younger children would be ready for schooling in the East. She wanted a school and church badly. She wanted civilization!

The wagons pulled down the lane to the Texas plantation late in the afternoon and Reginia felt her heart leap with joy. She saw the big house peek through the trees and any feeling of regret left her. She was home. The Bradleys, after traveling through wilderness, thought Auburn to be a welcomed sight. Maggie and Tom were excited to be a part of this new frontier. They had not experienced the hardships the Texas frontier had to offer and were eager to make their new home here.

Laudie and Samuel opened the front door and hurried to greet their master and his family. William helped his wife and children from the wagon as Laudie embraced them all with generous hugs. The Wildes had been truly missed on the plantation. The Bradleys were introduced to all the house slaves and taken to the guest room to rest. William eagerly asked Samuel about the freeze and was glad to hear they had had no ice nor freezing temperatures. He wanted to see Ransom immediately and sent Samuel for him. William wanted to introduce Ransom to the Bradleys and tell him of the plan to build them a house. William also wanted to know everything that had taken place at Auburn for the last year.

Ransom met with William in the library, and William told him of the Bradleys and that he wanted him to get a few slaves and start building the house. He laid the drawings of the house before Ransom. The house would be built a short distance from the main house. He went over each detail with Ransom, instructing him in the construction of the home. William wanted the Bradleys to have a comfortable home to live in and to provide them with as much safety as possible.

After they had finished the discussion about the doctor's house, William listened to all the news from Ransom concerning the plantation. Ransom had much more to tell, to William's surprise. "I have some other news for you, Mister Wilde. Mister Riley married the widow Johnson."

"You mean he married Golda Johnson?" William was shocked. The Johnsons came with the original families to Texas and their property adjoined Joseph's on the north side. Mr. Johnson died from a fever and Golda, half her husband's age, stayed and ran the farm. They were far from wealthy and Golda was basically plain in her looks and dress, but she was a good, hard-working woman.

"Yes, sir. He married her in January. She invited them for Christmas, and I guess she was Mister Riley's Christmas present!" The two men chuckled. Ransom smiled warmly as he became more serious. "Mister Riley needed a woman, sir. I think the death of Missus Martha really devastated him. He seemed very lonely. Missus Golda has been good for him and Jake. He is happy again and Jake is very fond of her."

"Well, I'm glad to hear that. I can't wait to tell Reginia the good news. Ransom, I want you to stay for dinner and meet the Bradleys. He's a good doctor and we're fortunate to have them."

Laudie prepared a special dinner and everyone enjoyed an evening of fine food and conversation. Fancy was glad to be home. She told Laudie and Samuel all about her trip. William and Reginia had brought gifts for Samuel, Laudie, Batha, Ransom, and Big Bo. They had new material, thread, and buttons for clothing to give to all the slaves. Reginia had bought Laudie a beautiful dress and a new apron. Laudie was proud. She wore her new apron that evening while serving the dinner.

Laudie was beginning to age. Reginia and William noticed the difference in her the minute they saw her. Laudie's hair was mostly gray and her movements were much slower. Reginia was concerned about Laudie's workload and spoke to William about bringing in another house girl and letting Laudie limit her work to overseeing the girls. William thought it was a good idea. He would speak to Samuel about getting another girl for the house.

The next morning, Ransom had the carriage ready and took the Bradleys on a tour of the plantation and showed them where their home would be built. William and Reginia spoke to Samuel about finding a new house girl. Reginia wanted this done with finesse. She did not want to hurt Laudie's feelings. Samuel told them about a girl that worked in the house for Mister Barbeaux. The Barbeauxs were settlers that lived about five miles south of them. William had only met them on a few occasions. The Barbeauxs were very mean to their slaves. They beat them for any reason. Samuel told them the girl was a hard worker and was well bred. Mr. Barbeaux had purchased her in New Orleans and treated her very badly. Samuel asked William to try to buy her. "Master, she's a beautiful woman, about thirty or maybe a little younger. Her master takes his way with her and then beats her. She can read and write, Missus Reginia, and would be a great help to you."

"Okay, Samuel. Let Missus Reginia and I discuss the matter. I will talk to you more about this later. Samuel, let me ask you something. How do you know about her?" William was a bit puzzled about Samuel's knowledge of the woman.

"Well, Mister Barbeaux came by one day to see you about something and had her with him. When he went off with Mister Ransom, I visited with her. Her face was bruised and she told me about herself and her life with the Barbeauxs. I promised her I would never speak of the matter to anyone. She fears him greatly."

William hated to hear of such treatment and agreed to speak to the man. Samuel left William and Reginia, so that the couple could discuss the purchase. Reginia was sickened by the thought of cruelty to slaves. She knew some plantation owners were this way, but she was firmly set against it. "The slaves are valuable possessions. Why would anyone do harm to his or her own assets? This would only lower the slave's value. Moreover, the slaves are human beings too," Reginia thought to herself.

"William, I would like to see about purchasing this woman. She sounds like she would be good to have in the house and would appreciate a good home. You know Laudie, she would take her in like a bird with a broken wing."

"Yes, indeed she would. This slave girl might be the perfect one to buy. I think Samuel sounds a bit more interested than he says. I've never heard him speak so fondly of any other woman before! We will take the horses and ride to the Barbeauxs first thing in the morning. I'm glad he came by while we were gone. We won't look suspicious with our plan, when we come calling." William chuckled.

William told Samuel to have the horses saddled and at the house after breakfast. They were going to call on the Barbeauxs. Samuel's face beamed with a delighted smile. William then knew for sure that Samuel had a fondness for the woman.

CHAPTER
SEVENTEEN

Morning brought a bright clear sky. After breakfast, Reginia and William mounted their horses for the ride to the Barbeauxs'. Reginia was glad to be riding Jet again. Oh, how she had missed her wonderful steed. She filled her lungs with the clean, crisp air as they galloped across the fields. They reached the Barbeauxs' and Reginia was impressed. The large one-story wooden house was immaculate and the fields were beautiful. Reginia and William tied the horses to the hitching rail and walked up the steps to the large porch.

William knocked on the door. A beautiful, light-skinned Negro woman answered the door, with all the manners of an aristocrat. Her hair was dark and wavy rather than the black curly hair the Negroes generally had. She wore her hair pinned up in a fashionable manner. She barely showed any African features. Her soft voice had a Creole accent. William asked to see Mr. Barbeaux. She asked them into the foyer while she went for her master. Reginia looked at William and whispered, "Darling, she is truly beautiful and I do believe she is a mulatto. It is no wonder that Samuel was taken by her!" Reginia was impressed with the woman's manners. Her posture was flawless as she held her shoulders erect and walked gracefully from the room. She was petite with a beautiful figure. Reginia could not understand how anyone could mistreat such a person! Her thoughts were interrupted, as Mr. Barbeaux entered the room. He was a man of medium height and good looks, but he exuded arrogance. She noticed his eyes were cold and unfeeling. He shook William's hand as William introduced him to Reginia.

"Reginia, this is Don Barbeaux. This is my wife, Reginia." William introduced them and noticed the man eyed his wife up and down while taking her hand and kissing it. Jealousy overwhelmed William, as the man seemed taken by Reginia's beauty.

"I'm pleased to meet you," Reginia replied as she pulled her hand free from his touch, thinking that he seemed full of conceit.

Don asked them into the parlor. He called for his wife. She was striking in her looks, but terribly shy. Reginia wondered if he beat her too. She always looked at her husband before speaking, as if needing permission to speak. Reginia believed in being submissive to one's husband, but this was too much! William explained to Don that Samuel had told him he had come by while they were gone. Don began telling him why he wanted to see him.

"I had been to Harrisburg for goods and saw a good friend, Sam Houston. The Americans are fed up with Santa Anna and the Mexicans. Santa Anna is president now and acts more like a dictator. They have yet to release Stephen Austin. Sam told me there is talk of a war to free Texas from Mexico. The Americans are sick and tired of the Mexican laws. Sam, James Fannin, and others were sending word to the States for help."

"I cannot believe they will go against the Mexicans. But I am glad to think we may one day be a free country. What can I do?" William was eager to help in any way.

They continued talking about Texas and their freedom. Reginia hated to think of war. She was glad Alex was gone and could not be involved. They had chatted for quite a while when the beautiful slave woman entered with tea. Don snapped at her sharply, as if he had become dissatisfied with her. She continued serving them, with her head held in confidence. He commented very negatively about her when she left the room.

"She is an arrogant wench. She thinks she is too good because she can read and write. I got her when she was a teenager. I taught her manners and allowed her to learn and be educated. That was my first mistake! I bought her fine clothes and treated her like a member of this family and her arrogance is what I get in return," he spoke with resentment.

His wife lowered her head as if ashamed by his actions. They had no idea what had really brought William and Reginia to their home. William took this opportunity to approach him about the slave. "Is she a good worker?" William asked without appearing suspicious.

"Oh, yes. A good whipping keeps her in line. I'm just tired of dealing with her," he sneered. Don had obviously become bored with her.

"We have an old slave that can't keep up with her work. We want to let her oversee the house slaves. I need a new house girl to assume her responsibilities. Would you be interested in selling her?" William made it sound as if the woman would receive demeaning work around the house.

"I will sell her and any slave for a price." Don talked as if he were speaking of one of his animals. This infuriated Reginia, but she kept her feelings hidden and smiled at him, as if in agreement.

"How much would you want for her?" William asked. He thought of Samuel. The two slaves were a lot alike. Both had a high-class demeanor, fashionable to their masters, rarely seen in the black folks. He was eager to buy her and give her a good life.

"I would have to have seven hundred and fifty dollars for her," Barbeaux said smugly. William agreed to the price. Reginia took William's hand and squeezed gently with her approval.

"Well, you have yourself a deal. I'll go tell her to get her things and she can leave today with you. I'll get her, right now." For some reason, he was eager to be rid of her. Don went to the kitchen where he found her, all alone, tending to chores. He grabbed her by her arm and swung her around to face him. She stared off as if in another place. He ran his hands over her body thrusting himself hard against her. Her body tensed from his actions. He reached out and punched her stomach. She flinched with pain. "You get rid of that seed growing in you. Do you understand me?" He smirked. "Go and get your things together, wench. I just sold you to Mister Wilde. You're going to see your life here wasn't as bad as you thought. You won't get to wear fancy clothes and you'll be doing menial labor. Now go." He slapped her on her rear as she left to pack. He straightened his jacket and pants and changed his callous look to his arrogant smile and returned to the parlor. "She's getting her things together. I told her to be quick about it. Would you like some lunch before you leave?"

"No, thank you. We better get home. I have things I must attend to." William was not prepared to take the woman with him, but he did not want to leave her there one more day. "I didn't come prepared to buy a slave," William laughed, while hiding the truth. "If you'll let me borrow a horse for her to ride home on, I'll send my house man tomorrow with your horse and the money."

"Oh, that's fine. I'm just glad to be rid of her. I hope this will teach her a lesson and she loses that pomposity of hers." Don was smug. He thought he was really hurting the poor woman. "By the way, her name is Rogette."

Reginia was thrilled. She could not understand why Don was eager to be rid of her. She thought maybe he had become bored with her and took the opportunity to make money with her. Rogette's bags were tied across the horse and they mounted and rode home. Rogette didn't utter a word and never looked back. She didn't know what kind of situation awaited her, she was just grateful to her Creator for delivering her from that house. On the way home, William and Reginia told Rogette about Auburn and Laudie. The tension began to leave Rogette's face as she listened to her new master and mistress.

The three rode to the front of the big home. Samuel came through the door and, to his surprise, there was Rogette. William saw the delight in Samuel's eyes.

"Samuel, we have new help for the house. Why don't you help her from her horse and show her to her quarters?" William smiled as he gave Samuel the directions, which pleased Samuel immensely. Samuel rushed to help Rogette as William helped Reginia from her horse. William and Reginia went into the house and immediately summoned Laudie into the library. William wanted to inform Laudie of Rogette's arrival and of their plans for her before Laudie met Rogette.

"Laudie, Missus Reginia and I have something to talk to you about. You have been a loyal slave and friend to this family. You practically raised me, for goodness sakes," William explained as Laudie smiled in agreement. "We wish to make life easier for you, Laudie, and take some of the household burdens from Missus Reginia. We want you to be head of the house girls and the functions of the house. You did a splendid job of caring for the house while we were gone and we want to reward you."

"Oh, Master Wilde, thanks ya, but who would tends to my chores?" Laudie couldn't imagine anyone capable of replacing herself.

"We have a surprise for you. I bought a young woman from Mister Barbeaux. Her name is Rogette. She worked well running the house. He wanted rid of her, so we bought her and brought her home. Samuel has taken her to her quarters. She has had a hard time of it and I would like for you to care for her and teach her how you want her to do your chores. Now, go to her and in a couple of days let me know what you think of her." William hoped for the best as Laudie left to meet this woman called Rogette. She didn't know what to think, but she would do whatever Master Wilde wished. She loved him as if he were her own son.

The weeks passed quickly. Laudie tried her best to find something Rogette could not do. Everything Rogette did was to perfection and she could do everything. Her cooking was superb and the family loved her Creole-style meals. Laudie couldn't help but like the young woman. Her beauty and ability to work was pleasing to Laudie. Laudie found her beautiful, kind, generous, and humble with a deep pride within herself. Reginia enjoyed Rogette too. Rogette was intelligent and spoke with refined English. The French accent seemed to make her exotic. Rogette often spoke French, which she learned from Mr. Barbeaux, for amusement. Reginia longed to learn the language and Rogette obliged by teaching her one hour each evening, after her chores were completed. Everyone was clearly accepting Rogette as a part of the family, especially Samuel. Samuel took her for long walks in the evenings and introduced her proudly to the other slaves. Samuel thought her voice was magnificent as she sang the soulful hymns at night with the other slaves. He found himself falling in love for the first time.

Joseph brought Golda and Jake to visit William and Reginia. He was proud to introduce his new bride. It was clear that Joseph was a new man and happy again. Golda certainly wasn't as pretty as Martha had been, but Reginia liked her. Golda was hardened by the work she had done, but was kind to Joseph and Jake. She had a deep religious conviction, which Reginia appreciated. Golda and Reginia spent the day getting to know one another. Golda had common sense and a true frontier spirit. She loved to ride the horses. Reginia was glad to have someone to ride with. They introduced the Rileys to Dr. Tom Bradley and Maggie. Maggie and Golda became instant friends. They each had two children about the same age. Reginia was glad to have three ladies close by to visit with.

June came and the spring showers were still prevailing. The river was full of water and boats were coming up the Brazos, docking at Wilde Landing, with goods and mail. William received his first letter from Ben, who wrote of the big ships that had been purchased. They would be in Harrisburg the first of September to gather the cotton for shipping. William was thrilled. He would go to Harrisburg and make all the arrangements.

Joe Bell was on the boat. William was glad to see his old friend. Joe came from his home in Columbia, up the Brazos, to visit William. He wanted to go to Harrisburg with William. The discontent of the settlers grew. William wanted to meet with Sam Houston. His friend Jim Bowie, from New Orleans, was there and he wanted to see him too. Jim was wild and free-spirited, but Joe had always liked the man. William invited Joe to spend the night and leave with him the next day. Joe was a man of great integrity and intelligence. He had been instrumental in the secretarial details and issuing land grants for Stephen Austin while the capital was in Columbia. He had been influential among the settlers.

The two men traveled to Harrisburg. William made business arrangements to ship the cotton to the southern port of Savannah. The two men spent several days talking to Sam, Jim, and others about the Mexicans. The Texas colonists' anger and frustration soared, due to the overbearing attitude of the Mexican government toward them. Many were ready to fight. Joe told them to wait. He wanted no harm to come to his dear friend Stephen. They listened to Joe with respect. William and Joe parted, each traveling to their respective homes. They said goodbye, knowing war would be inevitable.

William returned home with the good and bad news for Reginia. He told her about how large the ships were and that they came with many goods and would deliver cotton to the East. Reginia was proud of her husband. William had confidence that the ships would be a valuable asset to Texas and the other Gulf States. If all went as planned, William and Ben would have more money than they ever thought possible. William was a man ahead of his time. He had great visions for Texas, which included separation from Mexico. He shared his thoughts with Reginia. She hated the thought of war and her husband being in it. She knew he would fight for his country. She didn't want to lose him to the war he thought was inevitable.

CHAPTER

EIGHTEEN

A great heat wave covered the Texas countryside that summer. Everyone on the plantation, including the slaves, stayed out of the heat during the middle of the day. The slaves worked from daylight until noon and from three o'clock until dark. Reginia napped every day, with Batha fanning her as she rested. Every evening, Rogette taught Reginia French. Reginia caught on to the language quickly. She enjoyed Rogette's company. She was the most stylish black woman Reginia had ever known. Rogette would brush Reginia's hair and curl it beautifully. Reginia felt close to the exotic beauty. Rogette was gaining weight, but Reginia thought it was due to her being content with her new home. One hot evening, Laudie knocked on Reginia's door.

"Missus Reginia, it's me, Laudie. Can I speaks with you, please?" Laudie spoke unusually softly. Reginia could tell something disturbed the old woman.

"Why, certainly. Come in, Laudie. What is troubling you?"

"This ain't my place to tell you, but I can't help it. You just gotta know. I knows you will know what to do."

"What is it, Laudie?" Reginia could not imagine what troubled Laudie so.

"It's Rogette."

"What is wrong with Rogette? Has she taken ill?" Reginia's concern grew. "Tell me, Laudie."

"Well, Rogette, she's with child. But that ain't the half of it. It's the child of that terrible Mister Barbeaux. He was a terrible master. He abused her somethin' awful, Missus Reginia. He told her to get rid of that baby, but she won't do it. Thanks the Lord. That poor baby. And that ain't all. Samuel, he's gone and fallin' in love with Rogette. She loves him too. He wants to take her as his wife. Can you imagine that? Our Samuel, finally done gone and fell in love!" By now, Laudie was speaking in her usual stern matter-of-fact tone. She did not give Reginia a chance to say anything.

Reginia just sat nodding her head, surprised by Rogette's pregnancy. She realized now why Don wanted rid of her so fast!

"Well," continued Laudie. "Rogette won't marry Samuel, 'cause she's shamed by her condition. She told me everything. That poor child is torn up inside. She don't know what to do. What should she do, Missus Reginia? Won't you speak with her? She fears that terrible man will find out she didn't get rid of the baby."

"She has nothing to fear, Laudie. That man will never set foot on this property. He is a disgusting man and William feels about him as I do. Bring her here to me, Laudie. You and I will talk to her. Oh, Laudie, how far along is she?"

"Oh, Missus Reginia, she's already seven months along, she thinks! Let me get her. I'll be right back."

Laudie returned quickly with Rogette at her side. Rogette was embarrassed and hung her head. "Come in, both of you. Rogette, lift your head. You have nothing to be ashamed of." Reginia was sympathetic and her words were soft and gentle as she spoke. "Tell me what troubles you, Rogette."

Rogette started to speak, but tears filled her eyes. Reginia gave her a handkerchief and urged her to tell her story. Rogette cleared her throat and began telling Reginia her terrible secret. "Master Barbeaux bought me as a young girl. He had a grand home in New Orleans and took me there to live. He was very nice in the beginning. He groomed me and taught me. I trusted him. He treated me like a daughter instead of a slave girl. Missus

Barbeaux was quiet, I rarely saw her. I had no idea, at that time, how he mistreated her. When I was sixteen, he moved her into another bedroom. I would hear her cry at night. I now think he beat her. Shortly after he moved her, he came to my room one night. It was very late and he smelled of whiskey." She paused. The terrible memories were hard to talk about. Reginia walked to her and hugged her. Laudie's eyes filled with tears as she listened to the young woman. Rogette lifted her head to Reginia. "I am sorry. I want to tell you, but I don't want you to think bad of me."

"I could never think bad of you, Rogette. We love you. This is not your fault. You must understand that." Reginia could not believe anyone could behave so badly to another human being, especially a young child. Rogette continued her story, glad to finally rid herself of the dark secrets within herself.

"As I was saying," she continued, shaken by the sinister ways of Don Barbeaux. "He came into my room. I was already in bed. He told me to stand. I had no idea what he wanted. I thought that maybe something was wrong with Missus Barbeaux. He came to me and pulled me close to him. I just stood there. He ran his hands over me. I pulled back, but he grabbed my hair and jerked me against him. He started kissing me all over and ran his hands up my nightgown. He ripped it over my head and threw it on the floor. I was in shock and scared. He threw me on the bed. I closed my eyes. I was scared to death. The next thing I knew, he was on me. It hurt so bad, I could hardly stand the pain. I think I just passed out. He was gone when I woke up." Rogette was crying as she spoke of the horrifying nightmare she was reliving for the first time in twelve years. "He returned every night. I hated him from then on. We moved to Texas. I wanted to run away, but there was nowhere to run. He beat me often, as he did Missus Barbeaux. He was tiring of me. I was getting too old. He wants the young girls. I told him I was with child. He slapped me and threatened me if I did not get rid of it. I cannot do that. This is my baby. I thank the Lord every day for you and Master Wilde. My baby would be dead if it were not for you."

Reginia held her tightly. She felt sick with the thought of Don Barbeaux committing such actions. "Everything will be all right. You'll have your child. Tell me of your feelings for Samuel."

"Oh, he is the most wonderful man I have ever known. He is gentle and understanding. I fear he will hate me, because I carry another man's child."

"Do you love Samuel?" Reginia knew Samuel would understand. "He will only love you more. Samuel is a good man. He will take care of you and your child, if you let him."

"I love him very much. I just do not want to hurt him."

"You won't. Trust me. Tell him the truth. You are a fine person. Samuel has waited a long time for someone such as you. You could only make him happy. You must go to him. Just tell him the truth. You will be glad you did." Reginia hugged her and Rogette embraced her, thanking her for listening to her and caring for her much.

Before her nerves could fail her, Rogette left Reginia and Laudie and went to Samuel. She spent hours with him. She told him everything. Samuel listened patiently. He wanted to kill Barbeaux. He held Rogette, reassuring her of his love for her. He asked her to be his wife in the sight of God. He promised to love her child as if the baby were his own. The slaves were not allowed a legal marriage. They performed ceremonies to unite one another by jumping across a stick or broom. A celebration of singing and food among the slaves followed.

Samuel went to William the next morning as a friend. He wanted to share his news with the best friend he had and that was William. William was happy for Samuel. William told him he wanted him to betroth Rogette on the front lawn. William would have a hog butchered and they would have a grand party. William told Reginia of the wedding plans. She was excited. It was a warm July night when the two slaves married. The large hog cooked slowly all day over the fire. Laudie helped prepare all the food. Joseph and Golda came and allowed some of their slaves, who were friends with Samuel, to attend. The lanterns lit the sky as all the slaves gathered on the front lawn. Dr. Bradley and Maggie joined William, Reginia, Golda, and Joseph as they watched the couple. It was a tradition among the Negroes to jump a broom held at each end by friends. Laudie and Big Bo held the broom as the two jumped. The broom was held low for Rogette, who could not jump easily in her condition! William, Tom, and Joseph took the ladies into the house and Laudie brought them plates full of food to eat. When they had finished eating, they went to the porch to sit and watch the celebration. The slaves sang and danced until midnight. Samuel was happier than William had ever seen him. William was glad to see his friend with a family of his own at last.

The cotton was high and full that August. The spring rains had made the cotton produce well. William and Reginia rode their horses to look at the fields. The fields were white with cotton blooms. Reginia thought it was a beautiful sight. The slaves were picking the cotton and singing as they picked. William was reminded of his days in Natchez. He saw great success ahead for Texas. William talked to Reginia all the way home about the shipping business. He was excited to make his first trip with the cotton to Harrisburg.

NINETEEN

The warm weather continued through September. William prepared for his trip to Harrisburg the first week of the month. Many of the plantation owners agreed to ship their cotton with William. The ships would leave Harrisburg and return to New Orleans to load cotton from the Mississippi delta. From there, they would travel to Savannah to sell the cotton. Ben planned to come with the ships. He wanted to visit William and see the Texas plantation before returning to New Orleans. The ships would be in Harrisburg for several weeks. That would give Ben a few days to visit at Auburn.

The wagonloads of cotton departed for the port. It was a three-day trip to Harrisburg. William arrived to find the two ships docked and Ben and Josh waiting happily. The three men discussed business ideas for hours. Wagonloads of cotton arrived all evening and every day over the next two weeks. Josh stayed in Harrisburg to supervise the loading of the ships, while William took Ben to Auburn.

Reginia greeted William and Ben at the front door. How glad she was to see them both. Ben was impressed with the large plantation and the big home. Laudie came running to give her Master Ben a big hug. She missed the young man that she had cared for as a boy.

"Oh, Master Ben! You just looks fine. Real fine!" Laudie exploded with excitement.

Ben continued hugging the old slave vigorously. "It's good to see you, Laudie! How has Texas been treating you?"

"Oh, Master Ben, it's a big country, kinda wild, but it's become home. It ain't Natchez, that's for sure. But I'm happy here with Master William and our Missus Reginia."

"That's good. Laudie, I brought you a present." He pulled a small box from his pocket and handed it to her.

"Oh, you shouldn't have done that, Master Ben." Laudie blushed as she took the small box. It pleased her that Ben had thought of her. She opened the box and found a beautiful cameo pin. "Master Ben! Oh, Master Ben! Thanks you, so much!" She was surprised. She had admired the cameo pin that Ben and William's mother wore when they were young boys and always wanted one. She couldn't believe Ben remembered that. It was a beautiful cameo. She pinned it on her dress and hugged Master Ben again. Laudie would proudly wear that cameo every day for the rest of her life. "Well, I'm gonna fix you a fine supper, Master Ben, for this." She strutted off wearing the cameo to show to the girls.

Ben was pleased with Laudie's reaction to the pin. The three laughed happily with Laudie. Ben wanted to see Samuel, Big Bo, and Ransom. William told him about Rogette and Samuel and about Joseph and Golda. Ben could not believe Samuel had finally taken a wife. William took Ben to visit the slaves and the Bradleys. Reginia planned a big lunch the next day, inviting the Rileys and the Bradleys.

The next morning, Ben and William rode about the plantation. Ben thought the country was beautiful. William showed him the boat landing and the cotton fields. Ben could not imagine all the work that had been done. The plantation was beautiful and the land was rich.

They rode back to the house for lunch with their friends. Ben was thrilled to be in the great new land he had heard much about. Tom kept himself busy caring for the settlers in the area and Maggie assisted him with his doctoring. Ben was glad to hear there were many people. Tom was a caring man and showed no partiality to race, when it came to medicine. He treated the slaves as well as the whites. Joseph wanted William and Ben to come for coffee and to see his place, the next day. Ben kept a full schedule, seeing everything he could in his short visit.

The next four days passed quickly and the two men returned to Harrisburg. The ships were loaded and ready to depart for New Orleans. William bid Josh and Ben farewell and returned home. He was pleased with the early success of the new business and could not wait to tell Reginia. He returned to an empty house. He called out Reginia's name from the foyer. He could not imagine where they were. Fancy came running to the balcony of the foyer, filled with excitement.

"Master William, Rogette, she is havin' her baby! Doctor Bradley, Missus Reginia, Laudie . . . well, sir, theys all at Rogette's side! They left me here to tends to the childrens."

William walked out the back door and across the lawn to the small shotgun-style house that Samuel lived in. These houses were long and narrow, befitting the name, shotgun. Samuel sat on the small porch nervously. Samuel leaped to his feet at the sight of William. He feared William would be upset to find Reginia at the slave quarters. "Master, I told Missus Reginia she should not be here. She wouldn't listen to me." Samuel's voice was apologetic as he spoke.

"Don't worry, Samuel, Missus Reginia has her own mind. Even I could not have stopped her from being here!" William laughed and walked to the porch with Samuel and the two sat down on the small bench. "So, you are about to be a father. How about that!"

"Master, you and Missus Reginia are good to us. I—"

William interrupted Samuel. "Nonsense. You are my slave, this is a fact, but Samuel, you are also a dear friend. You have been my friend since we were young lads." William was very sincere about his feelings. Samuel had been with him all their lives. He felt as close to Samuel as he did to anyone. Samuel molded himself after William, educating himself as best he could, and dressing well. William bought his slave's clothes and furnished Samuel with fine shirts and pants. Samuel had the sophistication of a European butler. The two men sat on the porch reminiscing about their childhood.

Suddenly, they heard the cry of the newborn baby. Reginia came to the door for Samuel, who was already on his feet heading into the house. She was surprised to see William. She hugged him proudly. "My darling, when did you return?"

"About an hour ago. I've been keeping Samuel company."

"William, you should see Rogette's baby! She is a little girl and she is as white as snow! I am happy for Rogette, but I fear the news of the white slave child will spread across the area. Barbeaux will be furious." William promised her that she had nothing to fear. He would never allow anything to happen to Rogette and Samuel's child. This was a promise William kept forever.

The slaves gathered that evening to see the new child. Their eyes opened wide at the sight of the white baby girl. Samuel explained, without shame, that a white man had attacked his wife. He told them he was raising the infant as his child and he asked them to not discuss her birth with other plantation slaves. They all agreed. The slaves resented white men that took advantage of the slave women.

CHAPTER

TWENTY

William would never forget October 10, 1835. A traveler from Gonzales stopped at Auburn to rest before traveling on to Harrisburg. William greeted the stranger at the door. He informed William of the battle between the colonists and the Mexicans on October the second. The Mexicans had tried to take back the brass cannon that they had given the settlers in 1831 to fight off the Indians. The settlers refused. A flag had been made by two ladies, he told William. It had a white background centered with a black replica of the cannon and emblazoned with the taunting words "Come and Take It." The gentleman laughed as he told William, "The Mexicans came to take it, but one shot from the cannon and they all hightailed it back to where they came from!"

While the man rested his horse, he spoke more with William. The two men agreed something should be done to free Texas from Mexico. They did not think much of the Mexican army and were not worried about what the Mexicans might do. The man had biscuits and coffee before leaving. He thanked William for his hospitality and went on his way.

The year was coming to a close. The holidays were festive in Texas that year for the Wildes. The house filled with friends, laughing and singing. The Bradleys and the Rileys and their children had joined them for the celebrating of Christmas and the new year. Reginia was glad Ben and Jake were still friends. The only young boy that was Jake's age lived near San Felipe. Rogette's little girl was growing. Her brown hair hung in soft curls. Her big brown eyes were beautiful. Samuel and Rogette were proud of their little girl. Rogette named her Belle. In French it meant fair and beautiful, which the little girl certainly was. John, Katie, and Thad were also growing quickly. For the time being, things were quiet on the plantation.

One crisp February morning, a buckboard wagon pulled up the lane to the Wildes' home. Samuel was outside and recognized the man sitting by the slave driving the horses. It was Barbeaux! He ran to Rogette and told her to take Belle and go to their quarters. He went to William and told him that Barbeaux was coming up the lane. William wondered what the man could possibly want this early in the day. William went to the front of the house to see Don Barbeaux, a man William cared little for. Barbeaux had his slave stop the wagon by William.

"Barbeaux, what can I do for you this morning?" William questioned him without inviting him to come inside. This was rude for a Southern gentleman, but William did not care.

"I've got a slave in the back of the wagon I need Doctor Bradley to look at. He tried to pretend to be sick so he would not have to work. I taught him a lesson about lying. I almost killed him!" Barbeaux laughed sarcastically, as he told William what he had done. William walked to the back of the buckboard, while Barbeaux continued talking. "Hell, I can't let the Nigger die. I paid a thousand dollars for that slave!"

The words rang in William's head. He was filled with hatred for Barbeaux as he looked in the wagon at the black man. The poor man lay unconscious. William pulled the blanket off the slave and was horrified at the sight. Barbeaux had whipped him repeatedly, tearing deep gashes in his back. Most of the skin was gone, leaving muscle exposed. William wanted to rip Barbeaux's head off. "My God, man! It is a miracle this slave is alive. Pull the wagon over to Tom's house. I will meet you there."

William rushed to Tom and told him to care for the slave. Tom could not believe this terrible sight and he knew the only reason Barbeaux even brought him to be cared for, was due to the money Barbeaux had invested in him.

William was repulsed at the sight of the arrogant and cruel man. Rogette was right when she said Barbeaux was evil. William truly believed this. How could anyone be so inhuman? It would take months of care before this slave would totally recover. William was overwhelmed with sympathy for the slave.

Tom felt the slave's forehead. He was burning with fever. Tom looked at Barbeaux with disgust. Tom was sharp-tongued when provoked and he cared nothing at all for Barbeaux. "You crazy fool," he told Barbeaux. "This slave didn't lie to you. He is very sick and thanks to your beating, he probably will not live. If he does, he won't be worth a plugged nickel!" Tom had the slave taken to the small office he had built beside his home.

Barbeaux kicked the ground and looked at William. "If I had thought the damn slave would die I would have put him in a hole and not bothered bringing him here!" Barbeaux was not angry with himself for beating the slave. He acted like it was the slave's fault for the injuries.

William just stared coldly at Barbeaux. He did not want to hear another word from him. William blurted out at him without even thinking: "I'll buy the slave from you. I will give you one hundred dollars and that is all. He will probably never be able to do hard labor again." William did not want the slave to return. He knew he would be beaten to death if he was unable to do hard work again. William wanted a bill of sale for the slave, therefore Barbeaux could not return to claim him.

"You will give me one hundred dollars for that ripped-up piece of meat?" Barbeaux thought William was a fool to pay anything for the slave. He eagerly accepted William's offer. Barbeaux followed William to the house and signed the bill of sale that William drew up. William sent Barbeaux on his way without offering him anything to drink. William hated Barbeaux and wanted him off his property.

Tom kept the slave and cared for him until he gained consciousness. He then moved him to the slave quarters where the black women cared for him. Tom went to the slave daily, dressing the man's wounds. The grateful slave told Tom it was worth the beating to get away from Barbeaux's wrath!

Late in February, William received word that there was to be a convention at Washington on the Brazos. The colonists were meeting to adopt a declaration of independence on the second of March. William prepared himself for travel. He and Joseph would travel with other settlers in the area. It was a time of excitement among the colonists. They wanted freedom from Mexico and they were bound and determined to get it.

CHAPTER
TWENTY-ONE

March 2, 1836, was an invigorating day for the Texas colonists as they gathered together at Washington on the Brazos. Only the elected delegates from each municipality in Texas convened in the unfinished wood-frame building. A dozen poorly constructed shanties and only one noticeable street made up the small town. The town had been cut out of the woods, stumps still standing. Food and lodging were scant, but the convention would be held.

William, a delegate from his area, took a covered wagon, supplies, and a couple of slaves for the journey to the convention. He spent his nights under the shelter of the wagon, thankful he brought supplies and food. The Texans wanted to adopt a constitution modeled after that of the United States. Texas declared independence from Mexico and wrote the new constitution, establishing the Republic of Texas. The men organized an interim government while the forces of General Santa Anna laid siege to the Alamo. One hundred and eighty Americans lost their lives at the Alamo. Santa Anna moved his troops toward the convention, massacring James Fannin and over three hundred Texas prisoners. On March 17, the delegates, the townspeople, and other colonists received news that Sam Houston's strategy was to retreat. Those in the path of Santa Anna and his army desperately packed up and moved out to safety. The headlong expedition to safety became known as the Runaway Scrape.

William rushed home to his family. Fear had gripped everyone at Auburn, for Santa Anna had passed nearby and had camped southeast of Auburn. William and Joseph wanted to join Sam Houston and his men, to fight against Santa Anna and his army. Reginia begged William not to go, but her begging was to no avail. William would fight for the new country and freedom, even if it meant his death. The two men departed to join the ranks of Sam Houston. "Remember the Alamo" and "Remember Goliad" became the Texas war cries.

Santa Anna had stormed Harrisburg, burning it to the ground, by the time William and Joseph reached Sam Houston and his men. Sam was a big man with determination and great skill at fighting battles. Sam and about nine hundred men retreated to the coast cutting Santa Anna off from his only means of escape. Before dawn, on April 21, Sam Houston and his men surrounded Santa Anna's army while they slept in a field east of Harrisburg. Houston ordered the attack. The Texans surged forward shouting, "Remember the Alamo! Remember Goliad!" Within minutes, it was over and Santa Anna was defeated.

Nine Texans lay dead and thirty-four wounded that morning of April 21. However, Santa Anna was missing. Sam and his men hunted all night and finally found him the next day. William rode with Sam and a few men to take Santa Anna to Columbia, where he was held prisoner for five months in the home of a Texas doctor. William celebrated with his longtime friend Joe Bell and other settlers in Columbia. It was a glorious victory for the colonists. With the defeat of Santa Anna, Texas had won its independence.

William returned to the open arms of Reginia. The war was over; they were a free country! Celebration occurred across the land. William invited all the neighboring colonists and the settlers along the Brazos for a day of celebration. Many gathered on the lawn at Auburn. Two calves and two hogs cooked over hot coals. Everyone brought vegetables and desserts. Music filled the air as the men twirled the ladies about the wooden floor William had had the slaves build for the event. Sam Houston attended the celebration. He was a national hero. The people loved him and wanted him for their president. Joe Bell had traveled with his wife up the Brazos to attend the gala event. William, Joe, and Sam discussed the presidency in the privacy of William's library. William and Joe backed the people in wanting Sam to be the first president of Texas.

There was much to be done for the new Republic. The small postal service that had opened in San Felipe the year before had already gone into debt. The Texans wanted the untamed Indians run out of the areas they ravaged. Sam kept an open mind to the idea of presidency as the men discussed possibilities for the future of Texas.

The summer passed and the slaves picked the cotton. That September, Sam Houston was inaugurated as President of Texas, at Joe's hometown of Columbia. Eventually, the Texas Rangers were formed to run the Indians out of Texas. The next year found William very busy. He purchased several thousand acres and bought more slaves. He farmed many acres of cotton and built his own cotton gin. The shipping business had grown, with ships coming into Columbia to pick up the cotton taken down the Brazos. Ships came frequently with goods from overseas and from the East. Ben and Elizabeth came to visit occasionally.

Times were easier with the influx of more settlers. They came from the States and overseas, each possessing different skills. There were blacksmiths, teachers, preachers, doctors, and businessmen, to name a few, that came to Texas. Reginia could see that the pioneering efforts and sufferings of the Americans were not in vain.

Reginia talked to William and had him build a church and school for the children in the area. Reginia devoted her time to teaching the children. Sundays were a day of worship and rest for the people, as they gathered in the small church. They often brought picnic lunches and enjoyed the day together with fellowship and games for the children. Reginia enjoyed her life on the frontier, but she missed Alex. Alex had been away at school for four years. He would graduate soon and Reginia wanted him home. William made arrangements for Alex and Jackson to take a ship to Savannah, where they would board one of William's ships. The boys would be home that spring of 1838. Betty and Jim came each year to visit. Reginia wrote to Betty and told her of the arrangements to bring the boys home. She asked them to come for a visit when the boys arrived.

Reginia filled with excitement at the thought of having Alex home again. He was seventeen years old now. She wondered how he looked and how he would feel about being back home.

CHAPTER
TWENTY-TWO

Reginia continued teaching the children, riding Jet back and forth to the school. The horse was getting older and Reginia knew she would have to retire him soon. How she loved him. She selected a young two-year-old filly to replace him the next year. The filly was beautiful. She was a deep blood bay color with black legs and white socks. She had a beautiful white blaze in her face. The trainer would ride the filly for one year before Reginia took her. Reginia planned to turn the black steed she loved so much out to pasture the next spring, when the grass was deep and the weather was warm. John and Katie rode their horses to school with Reginia. William had given John his old gelding to ride and Katie rode the old pony that Alex had grown up riding. The children rode well. Katie was already five years old. She reminded Reginia so much of Sarah. She was free-spirited like Sarah and loved the outdoors and riding her pony. John and Katie were both smart and learned quickly. Little Thad would soon be four. He was already rebellious and a handful to raise. Laudie cared for the young boy as she had all the others.

Laudie was very old now. She was determined to oversee the house, although Rogette, Fancy, and Batha needed little if any advice on what to do. Laudie could no longer climb the stairs. She was arthritic and her old bones were brittle. Reginia would not have Laudie doing chores, but Laudie insisted she must do something. She would sit in the kitchen and would give directions to the house slaves, demanding perfection from them.

After Christmas of 1837, Laudie took ill. Rogette tended to Laudie, giving her special care. Reginia went to the quarters to see Laudie every day. She took a rocker and put it on the porch of the small dwelling for Laudie. On warm days, Laudie would sit in the rocker and watch the children play. Reginia knit her a shawl to wrap around her shoulders. Laudie was grateful for the kindness of her Missus and gingerly wrapped herself in her shawl. Many times, Rogette would take Belle and visit with Reginia and Laudie.

Belle was two years old and running about the lawn. She was a beautiful child. Rogette had made her little dresses from material Reginia gave her. Laudie loved the visits and would ask Rogette and Reginia to converse in French. She loved to listen to the foreign language.

The first of May arrived. Reginia counted the days to the return of Alex. He would be home in two weeks. Reginia had the house spring-cleaned and the lawn manicured. She spent each moment preparing the home for Alex's return. A few days before Alex returned, Laudie became very ill. Laudie knew she was dying. She asked for Missus Reginia. Rogette went for Reginia and the two rushed to Laudie's side. "Missus Reginia, I knows I'm a dying. But I ain't gonna die before Master Alex comes home." Her voice was weak, as she struggled to speak.

Reginia took her frail, wrinkled hand and held it. "Laudie, you aren't going to die. I won't hear such talk. Master William is going to come see you in a while and I will bring the children, if you like." Reginia fought the tears as she could see Laudie would not be with them much longer.

"Missus Reginia, I want Rogette to have my broach when I die. Please give it to her. She's been like the daughter I never had." Laudie had never married and had children. She had been a mother to everyone. She cared for the Wilde children for two generations and for many a slave child. With her gentle nature, Rogette had captured Laudie's heart. Due to Rogette's cruel mistreatment in the past, Laudie had always felt sorry for her and wanted to do something special for her.

Reginia knelt by Laudie's bed and put her head gently on the feeble woman's lap. "I promise I will give Rogette the broach." Reginia was touched by Laudie's love and sincerity. The old slave placed her hand on Reginia's back and patted her softly.

Jim and Betty arrived the week before the boys would be home. Alex and Jackson finally arrived at the Wilde Landing. William, Reginia, Jim, and Betty waited patiently on the dock while the boys got off the boat. Reginia could not believe her eyes. They were no longer boys. They were young men! She grabbed Alex and hugged him for the longest. She stepped back a step to look at him closely. He was so tall. Her eyes searched upward to look into his. He was six feet three inches and well built. She put her hand on his cheek, softly stroking her finger down his face. "My sweet Alex, you shave." She looked bewildered. Alex just laughed with his deep voice and hugged her.

"Mother, what did you expect. I am eighteen after all!"

They all said their hellos and left for the house. Reginia had a million questions for Alex. She wanted to know all about their schooling and Boston. Jackson and Alex were both well dressed with excellent manners. Alex was especially handsome and debonair. She expected to see her young, carefree son, but those days had passed. He had grown into a fine young man. Reginia was so proud of him. William told Alex the sad news about Laudie. Reginia had written many letters over the years to Alex, keeping him informed of the changes at Auburn and in Texas. He was aware of everything but Laudie's illness.

As soon as they got to the house, Alex greeted his brothers and sister. The young children did not recognize Alex, of course, for he had changed tremendously. "It is me. Your brother Alex. Has it been so long you don't remember me," he teased. The children were filled with delight. They ran and grabbed him, almost knocking him to his knees. Samuel, with luggage in hand, grinned at the children. He was glad to have Master Alex home. He took the boys' trunks to the guest room.

Alex could not wait to see Laudie. He urged his father and family to go see her. Alex walked through the door into the dimly lit house and paused at the sight of his beloved slave. He never imagined her to be so frail . . . old. Laudie took one look at Alex and extended her hand beckoning him to come closer. Alex went to her side and gave her a gentle hug. Laudie began to weep softly. He pulled out his handkerchief and wiped the tears from her eyes. "Master Alex," Laudie spoke softly and with great effort. She had very little strength left. "I been a waitin' for you. The angels, they been callin' for me, but I told 'em I couldn' leave without seein' my sweet Master Alex," she gasped.

"Well, I'm here, Laudie. I'm so glad to see you." He hugged her again. Reginia's eyes filled with tears to see Laudie so ill. William walked over to Laudie.

"He's made a fine young man, hasn't he, Laudie? Stand up, Alex. Let Laudie see how tall you are." Alex stood by his father never letting go of the old woman's hand. He was taller than William.

"Yes, sir, he's a fine 'un. He's taller than you, Master!" Her voice raised a pitch higher as she struggled to laugh. "Stays awhile and tell me how you's been, Master Alex. Let me listen to you talk."

Alex stayed and talked to Laudie for almost two hours. He told her everything about Boston, his school, and most of all, Jacqueline. Laudie loved listening to Alex's stories. He talked to her until she fell asleep. He tucked her frail body under the covers and went back to the main house. Later that night, sometime after supper, Samuel came running into the parlor, where they all sat visiting. "Master Wilde, pardon my intrusion. I have bad news." Samuel tried to be strong, but inside he was suffering the loss of his dear friend, who was like a second mother to him. The whole room was silent and every eye focused on Samuel. "Old Laudie has passed away in her sleep." Tears fell from Reginia's eyes. Samuel turned his attention to Alex. "If it weren't for you, Master Alex, we would not have Laudie as long as we did. She wouldn't go until she got to see you. She surely loved you, Master."

Alex smiled and hung his head, grateful he had seen her one more time. Samuel turned to William. "We will prepare her for burial and lay her to rest tomorrow afternoon. Master William, all the slaves want to see her and pay their last respects, sir."

"That's fine, Samuel. Of course, we will be at her funeral too." Samuel left to help Rogette prepare Laudie for burial.

Alex left his chair and sat by his mother. He stretched his long arm around her shoulders, comforting her. Alex maintained his charm and wit. He began telling stories about Laudie and how she would run after him when he misbehaved. His mind was filled with enjoyable stories of her. "I remember one time when Father had punished me for sneaking cookies out of the jar before dinner. Father made me sit in the kitchen and stare at the cookie jar all day and not touch one of them. Well . . . Father had to go to town that day and after lunch Laudie took pity on me. She sent me out to play with Ben, who had come into the kitchen and had sat, quiet as a mouse, staring at me, staring at that old cookie jar." Alex laughed remembering how silly they must have looked. He took a deep breath, raised the pitch of his voice, and mimicked the words exactly as Laudie had spoken them. "It just ain't right to make a child sit there and stare at them cookies all day without havin' none. Why, this is upsettin' me worse than it is you, Master Alex. You scat now, but you best be back in this kitchen before dinnertime. And don't you breathe a word of this, or I'll skin you alive!" He paused. "Well . . . Ben and I went fishin' and caught a bucket full of catfish. We took them back to Laudie before Father returned. Boy, did she get riled up." He returned to his mimicking voice. "Now, Master Alex, what do ya expect me to do with those fish? I guess you want me to fry them up for dinner. And just who should I say caught them?"

Everyone laughed. "She was so mad at us. She took those fish, huffing and puffing." It wasn't long before he had his mother and father laughing and reminiscing of their lives with Laudie. She had truly been an inspiration in all their lives, and now she was at peace with her Creator.

Betty and Jim left early the next morning to return home with Jackson. They wanted to leave before the funeral. It was a time of mourning at Auburn and Jim wanted to give the Wildes time alone to grieve the death of Laudie. Jackson told his family of Alex's plans to return to the East. Jim knew the Wildes would want uninterrupted time with their son.

William gave all the slaves time to pay their last respects to Laudie. He gave instructions to Ransom that they would not work that day.

They, too, needed a day to mourn the death of Laudie. William also did this out of respect for her. Laudie had been a big part of his family's life for as long as he could remember. Reginia had gone to Laudie before they put her in the wooden coffin. There was the broach pinned to her dress. Reginia shed tears of sorrow as she carefully removed the pin. Reginia took one last look at Laudie. She gazed at the old slave lying still and peaceful. "Goodbye, my dear Laudie. I will miss you." Reginia hung her head with sorrow, yet grateful to have had Laudie in her life.

After lunch, William took his family with all the slaves to bury Laudie. Rogette led them in soulful hymns. Reginia wept and sang with Rogette and the slaves as they sang "Swing Low Sweet Chariot." The slaves chanted and waved their arms to and fro with the rhythm of the song. William spoke the words from the twenty-third Psalm and continued on with words of respect. "We bury a great woman today. A woman of loyalty and courage. She has loved us all and we have loved her. She is now with our Father in Heaven. For this I am sure of." He said the Lord's prayer and then knelt and picked a handful of dirt and sprinkled it over her coffin. He did not say another word. He fought back the tears, for his feelings of loss had overwhelmed him.

William turned to his family. He took Reginia by the arm and walked slowly to the house with his family behind them. After everyone had left, Big Bo and the other slaves covered her wooden coffin with dirt.

Reginia walked beside William, slightly leaning against his arm. She suddenly remembered the broach. She stopped William and looked anxiously into his eyes. "William, Laudie wanted me to give her broach to Rogette. I almost forgot. I must go to her now."

William nodded in agreement. Reginia rushed to catch Rogette. She asked her to walk to the other side of the lawn where she could speak with her in private. Rogette followed Reginia, curious at what her mistress wanted. Reginia sat on the grass, with her hand patting the ground, motioning for Rogette to join her. "Sit down by me, Rogette."

Rogette carefully tucked her skirt and sat down by her Missus. Reginia opened her hand and exposed the beautiful broach.

"Missus Reginia, that is Laudie's broach. I pinned it on her dress myself. Why did you take it?" Rogette could not believe Reginia would take Laudie's prized possession. She was completely puzzled by Reginia's actions.

"Laudie asked me to get the broach after she died and give it to someone she loved dearly. I promised her I would. This broach meant a lot to Laudie and she wanted the one most like a daughter to her to have it." Reginia opened her hand with the broach in it and passed it to Rogette.

"Me? She wanted me to have it?"

"Yes, Rogette, she loved you. You were very special to her. Your kindness and your gentleness moved Laudie's heart. Wear the broach proudly. Someday you can give the broach to Belle and tell her of the special one that gave it to you."

Rogette took the broach and held it in her hand over her heart. "I will cherish it forever." Reginia took the broach and pinned it on Rogette's dress. Reginia stood with Rogette at her side. Reginia hugged her and sent her on her way, to join Samuel.

It was a sad day on the plantation. Everyone would miss Laudie. Reginia joined her family on the porch of the big house. William was visiting with Alex about his plans for him. Alex sat quietly, listening to his father. The last thing Alex wanted to do was to stay in Texas. His heart was with Jacqueline. He had his own plans. He wanted to continue his studies at Harvard the next fall and, after graduating, live in Boston. Alex knew exactly what he wanted, but how would he tell his father?

Reginia watched Alex, sitting with his head hung down, as his father spoke. She knew her son and she knew something was bothering him. "What is wrong, Alex?"

William looked at Alex. He noticed for the first time that Alex's attention was not on him. Reginia asked Alex again what was troubling him. Alex had to tell them. He didn't want to disappoint his father, but he wanted to fulfill his own dreams, with his own family.

"Father, Mother, I would like to talk to you about something." William listened to his son, who talked with such maturity. "I don't want you to be disappointed, but I have plans for myself that I wanted to talk to you about while I was home."

William was intrigued by his son's manner of speaking. "And, what are these plans you want to speak to us about, Alex?"

"I want to attend Harvard next fall and study law." He looked at his father for approval, before continuing. "And . . . I want to live in Boston after graduation."

William was proud that Alex wanted to attend Harvard but he felt very disappointed that Alex did not want to return to Auburn after completing his studies. He would not allow his son to see his disillusionment. "I am proud that you want to continue your education, Alex, but are you sure you want to remain in Boston after you graduate? This is a big decision. I think you need to give it more thought."

"I have thought it over, Father. I love Boston and I have made many friends there. I enjoy the city and all it has to offer. I wake up excited with the thought of practicing law or having my own business. I know this disappoints you, but I am not interested in living on the plantation. I can appreciate you and Mother wanting to challenge the wilderness, but honestly, I prefer the civilized States. I want to do more with my life, Father. I want to mark my place in this world."

William listened carefully to Alex. He was disappointed, but he respected his son and only wanted the best for him. "This is your life, son, and you must live it to your own expectations. Everyone thought I had lost my mind when I moved to Texas. I wanted a challenge just as you do and I longed for a new frontier. This is your frontier, Alex. I will help you all I can. But . . . " William smiled. "If you ever want to come home, you know you are welcome." William stood up and hugged his son like a man. "Now, when do you have to leave, my son?"

"I will leave in July. I want to go to New Orleans and take a boat to Natchez. I will stay with Uncle Ben for a while, before leaving for school." Alex was determined to see Jacqueline.

"Alex, why do you want to go to Natchez? Can't you stay with us a little longer?" Reginia questioned him. She wanted her son as long as possible and could not understand why he would go to Ben's instead of staying home with them.

"Mother, I have a friend. A close friend." Alex did not know how to tell them of his affections for Jacqueline.

Reginia looked at her son and smiled. "A friend? Could this friend be Jacqueline Exavier?" she teased.

"Yes. You know me so well!" Alex grinned. He was relieved to finally get to tell them about Jacqueline. He reached for his mother and hugged her. He slowly dropped his arms and took a step backward. He didn't know how to tell them what he wanted and just blurted out the words "I'm in love with her, and we want to marry when I finish school. Whew, I said it. I can't believe it. Well, what do you think?" Alex was all smiles. He had told them of his plans. Maybe not elegantly but he had told them. He rubbed his sweat-filled palms together staring directly at them in anticipation of their response.

William and Reginia looked at one another. Their son was a determined young man and they realized Alex had given the matter a great deal of thought. They were proud of him and welcomed the idea of having such a lovely girl in the family. "I want to hear more about your plans with Jacqueline." Reginia wanted to know every detail. They sat on the porch for hours, listening to Alex speak of Jacqueline and their plans.

Alex spent the month at home with his family. He loved his little brothers and sister and wanted to know them well before he left. William spent hours with Alex discussing his business ventures. Alex was very interested in the shipping business and questioned his father in great detail about the operation of the business. William was impressed with his son's intelligence and answered each question with pride. Jake came occasionally to visit. The two had matured and grown in different directions. They spent time together fishing and discussing their plans. Jake wanted to run his own plantation and Alex wanted to be involved in the politics of the States and be in his own business. He told Jake about the shipping business and his interest in it. Maybe, someday, he could be partners with his father and uncle.

Time flew and it was soon time for Alex to leave. Reginia was saddened by his departure. She thought of her own parents and how they must have been sad when she left with William for Texas. The fact that Alex would be in a safe and civilized world relieved her mind!

The morning Alex was to leave, Reginia had a large breakfast prepared. Everyone was quiet at the table. The trunks were placed in the carriage. The entire family went to the dock to see Alex off. Samuel, Rogette, and the other house slaves waved goodbye as Big Bo slapped the reins on the horse. The carriage traveled down the lane through the plantation to the river. John sat by his brother, hugging him all the way.

The steamer docked at the Wilde Landing. Reginia walked slowly to Alex. Her arms extended to him. "Take care of yourself. We will all miss you." She put her arms around his broad shoulder and hugged him tightly. She placed her hands on the back of his neck, gently pulling his head down so she could whisper in his ear. "I love you, Alex."

"And I love you, Mother." He hugged her firmly. Alex loved his family and wondered if he had made the right decision, for he knew he would miss them terribly. He had three years at Harvard to decide. If it did not work as he planned, he could always come home.

Alex turned to his father and embraced him. "Take care of Mother. I don't want her to worry about me." He grabbed John and gave him a big bear hug. "You are the oldest son at home, now. Take care of Katie and Thad and don't let them get into trouble."

"I'll take care of them, don't you worry about that, Alex." Alex smiled at John's seriousness. He shook John's hand and the young boy beamed with delight.

Alex knelt and put Katie on one knee and Thad on the other. He held them close to him in a three-way hug. "I love you kids. Mind our parents and I will see you again. Soon . . . " He hugged them tighter. "I promise." Their little arms clung around his neck.

Alex boarded the steamer with Big Bo at his heels carrying Alex's trunk. The Wildes stood on the dock waving to Alex as the boat headed down the Brazos for Columbia. Alex would board a waiting ship for New Orleans and then on to Jacqueline. He was sad to leave his family, as he waved farewell. Thoughts of Jacqueline entered his mind. He could not wait to see her. He was on his way to starting his own life! He suddenly filled with excitement as the boat paddled down the river.

CHAPTER
TWENTY-THREE

Texas was developing, as the United States recognized the independence of the country. Settlers wanted to be a part of the great new land. A new town was built to replace the burned town of Harrisburg. The Texans were proud of their new president, Sam Houston. The new town was named Houston, after their president and hero. The capital of Texas moved there. William traveled to Houston frequently, taking Reginia with him on occasions. Reginia enjoyed visiting with the ladies while William tended to business and the politics of Texas. William loaned money and did what he could to help improve Texas. He and Sam became close, sharing the same ideas for the great country. Stephen Austin died not long after he was defeated for presidency, by Sam, but Austin's ideas for Texas had not died. Austin wanted Texas to be made up of people who could help the country develop. He wanted people with integrity and high morals, with work skills and ethics. Austin did not want heathens and outlaws in Texas. Sam and the colonists wanted the same things for their country.

The newspaper and the postal service in San Felipe continued to grow in debt and the mail carriers were given land for pay. Many things had to be achieved. The new Republic had few assets but had much land. Land was given to the veterans of the Revolution and used to lure more families to Texas. However, the land could not pay for everything and the debt grew. Many of the colonists had a hard time surviving. Texas soon became a reluctant Republic and sought annexation from the United States.

Everything was changing for William and Reginia. They lost their dear friend Joe Bell in 1838, and they traveled to Columbia for the funeral. His son Thaddeus had been one of the first white children born in Texas, among the original three hundred colonists. He was sixteen and as regal as his father. Reginia could not believe how their children had grown and all the changes that had taken place since she had first arrived at Auburn. Time seemed to have passed too quickly. Horse races had become a large part of the Texas frontier and Joe had been a big part of that, along with the politics of the land. He had fine thoroughbreds and had conducted many horse races in Columbia. Everyone came from miles around to the funeral to give their last respects to Joe. He was one man the Texans would never forget!

William and Reginia returned home. Houston was becoming a leading outlet for cotton, lumber, and sugar produced in the surrounding areas. Regular steamboat services were offered to the Gulf. This helped William and his shipping business. Hundreds of settlers came to Houston and the surrounding areas. William and Ben purchased a ship for the transportation of people to New Orleans and Savannah. Packet boats were crossing the Atlantic in two weeks, making regular voyages to Liverpool twice a month. With the influx of more people, Reginia became more socially active. She entertained often, opening her beautiful home to friends. She had teas for the ladies and gala events for all the holidays. Many of Reginia's friends did not have grand homes and Reginia wanted them all to share in the pleasures that she could offer. Money was pouring in for William. He amassed a fortune with his cotton, sugar, and shipping business. Life was easier for the Wildes.

In 1839, the capital of Texas was moved to Austin and remained in Austin until 1842. The Cherokee Indians were expelled from the area. William did not want to see the capital moved. Houston continued to grow with businesses and new trade. William did not enter into the politics in Austin. He concentrated on his business. The school grew and Reginia looked for a school teacher to take her responsibilities. A settlement grew south of Auburn. A young couple by the name of Huffinan moved in. Georgia Huffinan was well educated and Reginia convinced her to teach in the small school. Georgia loved children and took the job eagerly. She taught the children for many years before retiring. Reginia kept busy with her friends, helping William and assisting Georgia occasionally.

The holidays passed quickly with the arrival of the new year of 1840. The years seem to fly as Reginia found herself near forty years of age. John would be ten, Katie eight, and little Thad would be six. She could hardly believe it! She thought of Alex often, wondering how he was. She wrote to Alex each month, and she received letters from him frequently, reading them aloud to the family. He would graduate from Harvard the next year. Her oldest son would begin his life.

She thought of his youthful years on the plantation. She never dreamed Alex would want to live his life so far from home. She now realized how hard it must have been for her parents to give her their blessings when she left with William for the unsettled frontier. She found comfort in knowing that Alex was in a civilized world; one without danger and despair.

Very little changed that year. Reginia and Golda kept busy with local women quilting blankets and crocheting sweaters and knitting socks. It was more of a social gathering than anything. Tom and Maggie were busy caring for the settlers. Life in the frontier was settling down. Many of the Indians were gone. The ones left in the area were friendly and traded with the settlers. Reginia had grown accustomed to the lifestyle she had led for over a decade. William was steadfast in his business ventures.

Reginia and William had grown deeply in love over the years. They depended on each other for the comforts of love and friendship. They were an inspiration to all that knew them. They were both very active in the needs of the community. Reginia had a way with people. She could encourage them when times were bad and would always be available when needed. William was a fair man with good judgment. He was considered a true gentleman and very respected. Each month during the spring, horse races were held. This was an exciting event for the people. William had many fine horses and won frequently. The settlers came dressed elegantly for the affair. The wealthy women wore fine dresses and hats. This was a time of social gathering for the rich. Reginia loved the horses and cheered for any that won!

The shipping business was growing by leaps and bounds. Josh purchased more ships and engaged in shipping goods to and from England. Ben and Elizabeth came each year to visit, as did Jim and Betty. That year, the clipper ship came into being. Reginia wanted to travel to the East and visit Alex and take the clipper to England. She had never been to Europe and wanted to go badly. William promised her he would take her the spring of 1841. They could see Alex graduate and go on to Liverpool. She was excited, anticipating the day of departure.

CHAPTER

TWENTY-FOUR

The winter of 1840 raged with yellow fever. Many were sick and dying. Tom and Maggie worked from morning until late at night. William kept his family in the house, not allowing them near anyone. He would not lose another member of his family. Reginia kept busy inside supervising the cleaning of the house. She sorted old clothes and toys to pass her time. She gave to the slaves what she did not keep. The days wore on her nerves. She wanted the fever to end and she felt remorse because she could not help the sick.

Rogette came running into the house one day. The weather was freezing as she stood shivering before Reginia.

"Many of the slaves have taken ill, Missus Reginia. Samuel and I have done all we can. We need more blankets and Doctor Bradley is gone tending to some folks south of here. I don't know what to do."

Reginia could not stand by and watch as their loyal slaves suffered from the fever. She went upstairs and gathered all the spare blankets and went with Rogette to the quarters. The fever spread quickly. She and Rogette passed out the blankets. Samuel entered the quarters and found Reginia. He scolded her for disobeying his master. "You shouldn't be here. Master William does not want you out of the house and exposed to this fever. You have no business down here!"

Reginia ignored Samuel's concern. She could not find Big Bo. She was afraid he had taken ill. "Where is Bo?" she asked Samuel with great concern.

"Bo is sick, Missus Reginia. He is in his quarters."

"Come with me, Samuel. We must tend to him."

Reginia entered the one-room shanty and found Bo lying in the bed. His wife stood by him. Reginia took cool, wet rags and placed them on his forehead. Bo needed to eat. Rogette had prepared a huge iron pot of chicken soup for the slaves. She sent Samuel for soup to give to Bo. Reginia tended to the slaves every day for a week until Tom returned. She retrieved medicine from Tom's office and administered it to all the ailing. William could not stop her. She had a mission. The fact that these people were black slaves made no difference to her. They were humans and needed her help. Rogette worked by her side every moment, amazed at the goodness and strength of her mistress. Reginia begged William to go to Houston to get more medicine.

William hated leaving his family, but he knew that without more medicine, many would die—possibly his own family! He left hastily for Houston. The slaves moaned with pain. The wails could be heard all through the slave quarters. Reginia entered each shanty, without hesitation, caring for each one. The slaves that weren't ill helped vigorously.

William returned home to find Tom and Maggie at his house. "Reginia is upstairs," Tom said without alarm. He did not want to startle William. William interrupted Tom and handed Tom the medicine and told him of the spreading epidemic. Tom knew all too well about the fever. "I've treated many of our friends and neighbors. Rebecca Norris and all her children died during the week. Pete is taking it hard. He's ill but he will recover." Tom paused. He hated to tell William about Reginia. She had become ill the night before with a high fever and fell into a state of unconsciousness. "William, I must tell you something. It is Reginia . . . she has taken the fever."

William bolted for the stairs, but Tom grabbed his arm and stopped him. His voice was soft yet stern. "Listen to me. She is not awake and her fever is high. I need to give her this medicine and you don't need to be near her. You will take a chance of getting the fever too."

The fever had claimed many lives. William felt helpless. He wanted to hear no more. He glanced at Tom, his eyes tired and bloodshot from lack of sleep. At that moment, William didn't care if he got the fever or not. He just had to see Reginia. He rushed up the stairs with Tom behind him. William found her sleeping and could only stare in fear. Her eyes had dark circles that looked deep against her white skin. She appeared frail as she lay unconscious. Reginia had not eaten much while helping the slaves and had lost weight. William sat in the chair by her side. Tom gave her the medicine and placed cool towels on her head. He glanced at William who looked exhausted and consumed with worry.

"William, I am going to stay here. You look tired. Why don't you get some rest? There is nothing you can do for Reginia right now. And she needs you to be strong."

"I want to be alone with my wife." William would not look away from Reginia and there was no way he would leave her side.

"William, you have to get some sleep," Tom persisted.

"Get out! Do you hear me! I want to be alone with her. I will get rest when I choose to get rest!"

Tom shook his head. William, tired and overcome with panic, did not think rationally. Tom knew he might react the same if it were Maggie. "William, I will be outside the door if you need me."

William nodded. He picked up Reginia's slender hand. His eyes filled with tears. He loved this wonderful lady and admired her generous spirit but her generous spirit had caused this to happen to her. He could not help wondering what he would do if he lost her. He held her hand, pressing it gently against his cheek. "I love you. Can you hear me, my darling? Please wake up." He raised his head toward the ceiling. "Please, Lord, let her live. She is my life. Don't let her die. I beg You, take my life, but spare her, oh Lord. Spare her." He slumped across Reginia, burying his head on her belly. Tears filled his eyes. His voice quivered as he pleaded, "Wake up and be well. Wake up, my Reginia."

Reginia lay unconscious all night. The next morning, she awoke with William still at her side. He had fallen asleep in the big chair. "Wake up, darling," she struggled to speak, her voice weak from exhaustion and fever. William opened his eyes and bent over her hugging her gently. He summoned Fancy to bring Dr. Bradley.

William sat on the edge of the bed gently stroking her face. "You are going to be fine. I promise. I will take care of you."

"William," her voice cracked. "I love you." Her eyes closed and again she was unconscious.

"Fancy, where in the hell are you? Where is Tom?" William bellowed. Filled with agony, William rushed to get help. Tom heard his screams and ran past Fancy, meeting William at the bedroom door.

"What is it? Fancy said Reginia awoke."

"She did for a brief moment and then drifted off. Do something, Tom. I can't lose her. Please help her."

"If she woke up, that may be a good sign." Tom walked to her and felt her head. It was still hot. He gave her more medicine and placed fresh cool towels on her head. Fancy watched from the door, afraid to get close to the fever. "William, I don't know what else to do. She is in God's hands. All I can do is give her this medicine and pray the fever breaks."

"Master William, whats will we do if our Missus—"

William stopped Fancy short. "Hush up, Fancy. Don't you worry. Missus Reginia will be fine. Why, I promised her she would be." William trembled from exhaustion

"Yes, sir, Master William," Fancy responded in an obedient tone.

Tom worried about William. "You need to eat something. Fancy, bring Master William something to eat." He turned to William. "And you . . . I want you to get some rest. I am not asking, either. I am telling you."

Fancy departed and returned within minutes with a tray of biscuits and bacon. "You needs to eat somethin', Master William. I brought you some breakfast. I'm gonna have a hot tub of water waitin' just for you. You eats your breakfast, take a good bath, and get to bed. Why, you look as bad as she do! And our Missus Reginia, she don't needs you to be sick." Fancy had picked up all the stern traits from Laudie.

William didn't argue. After he ate, he went over by Reginia. "I will be in the room next to you. I am going to rest and then I will be back."

He kissed Reginia on her forehead as if she were awake and could hear his words.

Fancy cared for the children, keeping them in the house and away from the fever. John understood his mother was sick and helped entertain Katie and Thad, who did not understand and constantly wanted their mother. For three days, Reginia remained unconscious. Fancy brought each meal to William, who stayed continually by Reginia's side. The third morning, Reginia awoke. William, still by her side in the chair, had fallen asleep with his head on the edge of the bed. Her arms weak, she reached for him and fondly stroked his face.

"You're awake." He smiled. "I can't believe it. You're awake." He touched her cheek and then her forehead. "Your fever is gone. Reginia, you're going to be fine." William was ecstatic. He reached over and kissed her cheek. "Let me get Tom. I will be right back." He rushed from the room to see John playing with Katie and Thad. "Children"—he paused—"your mother is better. She is going to be fine."

John jumped to his feet. "Can we see her now?"

"Not just yet. I must get Doctor Bradley."

"Can I get him, Father? I will hurry." John wanted to do something to help. After all, he was the oldest son in the house, now.

William smiled with approval. "That would be fine. Hurry and bring Doctor Tom back here quickly." John ran all the way to Tom's house with the good news.

Tom and Maggie followed John back to the house. John ran all the way back, beckoning them to hurry. Tom entered the bedroom and had a pleasing surprise. Reginia was propped up on her pillow with a faint smile on her face. He felt her for fever, but the fever had gone. He pulled out his stethoscope from his bag and listened to her lungs. They were clear. "You are a lucky lady, I must say."

It was hard for Reginia to speak as she muttered softly, "I couldn't die, I had William's strength to carry me."

"That is for sure. He hasn't left your side. It is a miracle he isn't sick himself. Reginia, you are very weak. I need you to try to eat. I will have Fancy bring you some chicken broth. Please drink it. I want you to get your strength back." Tom had Fancy feed Reginia the chicken broth every two hours for several days, before giving her a heavier diet. The children came often to visit their mother. They would lie in bed by her, while she told them stories.

It was a month before Reginia had gained all her strength and was totally recovered. Reginia and William lay in bed talking about all they had been through. He looked at her and smiled. "She looks beautiful," he thought. Her eyes were bright and the dark circles had disappeared. They lay in each other's arms, grateful to have one another. Reginia felt the passion build inside her as William kissed her. They made love with intense passion. The two had grown to know each other's most intimate desires over the years. "How wonderful it is to love each other as we do," William thought as he embraced his wife.

The holidays were grim that year. The fever had taken so many of their friends. More graves filled the Texas plains. Reginia was thankful they had escaped the fever. William lost fifty slaves to the fever and many friends suffered the loss of their loved ones. It was a terrible time of grief in Texas. Reginia could not wait until spring. She was eager to leave for her trip to see Alex and travel abroad.

CHAPTER
TWENTY-FIVE

Alex had been busy the last two years in Boston. He attended Harvard and with the money his father sent, he invested in a shipping business. In the evenings after school, he went to the business to work. He put every dime his father sent him into the business. Within a year, he was a full partner. Alex had a brilliant mind for business. His success at a young age was the talk of Boston. He purchased a large home on Beacon Hill and with Jacqueline's help decorated it beautifully. Alex hired a house staff, including a butler. The blacks were free agents in the North and Alex accepted the fact and paid them for their services. He did not agree with the freedom of the blacks but he wanted no problems with Northerners.

Jacqueline lived in a boarding house in Boston and worked for a lawyer, keeping his records. The legal profession and the politics of Boston intrigued her, but women were currently excluded from taking the bar exam to become a lawyer. Jacqueline was outspoken in her beliefs, which was rare for the women of Boston. Alex loved her bravery in speaking her mind. She was beautiful and intelligent. The men listened to her, if for no other reason than to view such a gorgeous lady. Alex and Jacqueline spent as much time together as possible. Their love grew deeply. Alex wanted to marry her after graduation. Many people in Boston admired Alex and Jacqueline and invited them to all the grand social affairs.

Alex and Jacqueline planned to marry the spring of 1841, while his parents were visiting. Jacqueline invited her parents to come early. They wanted to surprise the Wildes with the announcement of marriage and the success Alex had achieved.

William took his family, along with Fancy, for the trip that April. They would make one stop in New Orleans for William to purchase more slaves. He took Ransom with them. Ransom would return home with slaves to begin planting. Fancy was excited to go to England, but was fearful of crossing the ocean! She imagined large serpents. Reginia reassured her there were no such serpents, but Fancy was determined to believe there were.

The ship pulled into the Boston harbor with Alex waiting. Reginia was thrilled to see her oldest son, who was now twenty-one years old and extremely handsome. Jacqueline stood by his side. The two made a beautiful couple. Alex was as handsome as she was beautiful. Alex and Jacqueline greeted his family with warm embraces and kisses. Alex lifted his mother and whirled her about, teasingly.

"Alex, put me down!" His strength amazed her as he turned around and around with her as if she were a little doll. Alex put her down and bowed to her as if she were a queen. William and Jacqueline laughed at Alex. Alex was still full of his wit and charm. Reginia blushed as the other passengers burst into laughter.

"Alex, son, you are such a tease. Will you never outgrow this!" Reginia scolded, but inside she loved his charm and affection.

A beautiful carriage awaited them. Alex took them to his home on Beacon Hill. William and Reginia were surprised to see the large home. They looked at one another with confusion in their eyes. Alex had several surprises awaiting them.

"Who do you live with, Alex?" Reginia was sure he lived with a college friend.

"This is my home, Mother," Alex replied proudly.

"Your home?" William exclaimed with added confusion. "How can you afford such a home?"

"Come inside and I will tell you and Mother all about my life the past couple of years."

William and Reginia could scarcely wait to hear his explanation. They wondered what in the world he had been up to. The Exaviers came to greet them as they were getting out of the carriage. Reginia and William were surprised to see them and greeted them eagerly. A tall black man followed the Exaviers from the house and began taking the luggage inside. Alex stopped his butler, Jasper, and introduced him to his family. He had hired Jasper, who had fled the South through the underground system, a few months prior to his family's arrival. They entered the beautiful home where Alex's housekeeper and cook had tea waiting. William and Reginia were amazed by Alex's wealth. Jasper took Fancy and the children upstairs, while the adults entered the parlor.

William could not wait to hear Alex's explanation of his wealth. Alex sat down by Jacqueline, taking her hand as he spoke. "Mother, Father, I know you are surprised, as I wanted you to be. I hope you will be proud of what I have to tell you." Alex continued his story, telling of his investments, and how he had acquired his wealth. William beamed with pride as his son told him he had invested in the shipping business. "I may not be as wealthy as you, Father, but I will be someday," Alex joked. "I want to talk to you about becoming a partner with you and Uncle Ben."

"Can you afford us, Alex?" William teased him.

"Yes, sir, if you ask a fair price, that is," Alex came back with his own wit. "But, we can talk about business later. I have more news for you." Alex squeezed Jacqueline's hand as he proudly told them his biggest surprise. "Jacqueline and I will be married this Saturday. All the plans have been made. I hope you will be happy for us."

William and Reginia were ecstatic. They both went to Alex and Jacqueline, hugging them and giving them their blessings. Reginia hugged Jacqueline's parents, Antoinette and Frank. Reginia could not believe that in just three days, her son would be married. How quickly, indeed, the very night after his graduation!

The next two days found Reginia and Antoinette shopping the stores of Boston. Reginia and Antoinette purchased new dresses for the graduation and the wedding. They were excited about the wedding. It was to be a grand event. The ceremony would take place in the old yet still beautiful Christ Church. Alex planned a great reception ball afterward at his home. Alex had Jasper escort Fancy and the children about Boston, showing them the town he was so proud to live in. Alex, William, and Frank spent their time with business. Alex was proud to show them his shipping business and introduced them to his partners and other businessmen in Boston.

That Friday, they all attended Alex's graduation and later feasted on a delicious seafood dinner provided by Alex in his home. Other friends and fellow graduates attended. Toasts were made to and by Alex. It was a night of celebration and enjoyment for the families. The commemoration of the graduation and the marriage was in every toast.

Reginia beamed with pride. Alex had made arrangements to take Jacqueline abroad for their honeymoon. He announced the news of their planned trip to Europe late that evening. William and Reginia were thrilled that the young couple would be traveling with them to England. They would all board the ship early Monday morning. Everyone drank, laughed, and visited until after midnight.

Saturday morning came quickly. Everyone was up and about making last-minute preparations. The reception would be held on the back lawn following the wedding at three o'clock. The lawn was beautifully manicured with large shrubs and flowers. Tables were placed and covered with fine linens to hold the food and wine. Alex had a small orchestra arranged to play for dancing. Reginia was impressed with the detail Alex and Jacqueline had given to their wedding. It was a custom for the parents to provide such a wedding, but the two wanted to plan and give their own wedding.

Antoinette and Reginia helped Jacqueline dress for the wedding. The white wedding gown was beautiful. Antoinette had insisted on buying her daughter's dress. It was made of satin and lace and hung to the floor elegantly with petticoats holding it out full. Jacqueline looked like an angel in her dress. Pearl buttons closed the lace sleeves and the back of the dress. Reginia gave her a string of beautiful pearls to wear around her neck. Tears fell from Antoinette's eyes as she looked at her beautiful daughter. The carriage waited downstairs to take the ladies to the church. The men and children had been taken ahead of time. The ladies entered the carriage and traveled the cobblestone street to the church. Jacqueline held her mother's hand as the horse-drawn carriage moved toward the church. This was the last time Jacqueline would be with her mother as a single lady. Jacqueline became nervous as the carriage pulled up to the church. Frank waited at the door to escort his daughter down the aisle to marriage. Frank was proud to give her to Alex. He thought highly of Alex and his family. In Frank's mind, his daughter could not have done better!

Ushers escorted the two mothers to their places in the church. Reginia sat close to William holding his hand. The church was filled with friends of Alex's and Jacqueline's. Their friends were Boston's elite. Lawyers, businessmen, politicians, novelists, philosophers, and doctors attended. Alex and his partner and dear friend, Asa Rhome, stood at the altar waiting for Jacqueline to enter. The organ played as Jacqueline's bridesmaid, Joanna Crump, walked the aisle. There was a pause in the music. Suddenly, Jacqueline and her father appeared. Alex could not believe his eyes. Jacqueline looked exquisite. She did indeed look like an angel. Her green eyes sparkled at the sight of Alex. Frank gave his daughter's hand to Alex and took his place by his wife. Antoinette and Reginia both shed tears of happiness.

The couple exchanged their vows and the preacher pronounced them man and wife. Alex lifted the veil from Jacqueline's face and kissed her tenderly. The crowd applauded loudly. The wedding was beautiful. Afterward, everyone parted for the reception. It was a gala event. The laughter, dancing, and drinking continued all evening.

Alex and Jacqueline stood in the back lawn under the stars and the bright full moon. All the guests were gone and their families were tucked away in their rooms fast asleep. Alex gazed into Jacqueline's eyes. How they sparkled in the moonlight. Her beauty mesmerized him. He kissed her passionately and swept her into his arms. Quivers of delight swept through Jacqueline as her strong and loving husband carried her up the stairs to their bedroom. She was very nervous as she slipped into her beautiful gown for bed. She stood behind the dressing screen nervously wondering what making love would be like. She and Alex had waited patiently for this moment. They had reached great peaks of affection in the past but refrained from indulging in sexual intimacy. Alex waited in the room adorned in his satin robe. Jacqueline came from behind the ornate screen. Alex stood and looked at her. She had a full figure and the gown exposed every perfect curve of her body. He filled with desire just by looking at her. He walked to her and took her in his arms. "I love you, Jacqueline," he said softly.

"And I love you, Alex, with all my heart." Her heart beat rapidly. This was the moment they had both waited anxiously for. Alex kissed her on her mouth and down her soft neck. He lifted her and carried her to the bed placing her gently on the soft mattress. He lay carefully over her body, as if she were a china doll and he would break her. His hands were caressing and stroking every inch of her. Jacqueline gasped as his subtle strength aroused her. They spent an hour with gentle foreplay, exploring and touching each other lovingly, before consummating their marriage. Jacqueline lay in Alex's arms feeling totally fulfilled. She spoke softly to Alex as he held her in his arms. "I am Jacqueline Wilde, Missus Alexander Wilde," she said proudly. He kissed her long and hard. They were filled with long-awaited passion.

Alex and Jacqueline slept late the next morning. Antoinette and Reginia had a beautiful brunch prepared for them and took it upstairs on a large tray. They set it by the door and knocked vigorously to wake them. The two ladies hurried back down the stairs, like two children, so they would not be seen. Alex opened the door to find the tray filled with food and fruit. He smiled as he took it to the bed. "I think we can attribute this to our mothers," he said playfully. They were starving. They ate everything, before returning to their newly found pleasure of lovemaking.

Alex and Jacqueline joined their families sometime after twelve. They visited with the Exaviers and the Wildes all afternoon. They had a late lunch on the back porch and continued visiting, while Fancy and Jasper entertained the children on the lawn. William and Frank each handed the young couple sealed envelopes that read "Congratulations" on the front. Alex and Jacqueline each took an envelope and opened it. Each contained ten thousand dollars! They looked at one another with surprise. They could not believe their parents had given them such an extravagant amount of money. Frank was as wealthy as William and they both wanted the best for their children.

"We want you to invest this wisely for the future," William explained to Alex. "You and Asa are good friends and you will remain good friends easily, if you are not partners. We wish you would consider buying Asa's part of the company and work alone. Ben and I will do all our business with you, and with the business you already have, you will make yourself and Jacqueline a fortune." Alex never imagined owning the company without Asa. He thanked them for the money and agreed to think the matter over. Alex wanted to talk to Jacqueline in private before coming to a decision. "The money and the decision of what to do with it is strictly up to you and Jacqueline." Frank nodded his head in agreement. The Exaviers left for Natchez the next morning, as the Wilde families departed for England.

Two weeks later, the Wildes were in England, shopping and sightseeing. Alex and Jacqueline spent hours alone seeing the old city, with its beautiful buildings. Reginia, William, and the children, tended to by Fancy, toured the area. Reginia and William left Alex and Jacqueline to themselves. This was their honeymoon and the last thing they needed was their family tagging along. Reginia was thankful that Alex had found a love in Jacqueline equivalent to her and William's.

The families traveled, by ship then carriage, to Strasbourg in eastern France. They were intrigued by the castles and the history of the old country they passed on the way. The buildings in the towns were very old. Jacqueline's ancestors were from this old city and Alex took her to the cemetery where her great-grandparents were buried.

After a month, they all returned to Liverpool. Jacqueline found herself pondering thoughts of yesteryear and what her life would have been like if her grandparents had not emigrated to the States. William and Alex took time to visit the shipping companies in Liverpool, while Reginia and Jacqueline went on a shopping spree. The time passed all too quickly, and it was time to return home. The trip abroad had been delightful.

William and Alex made business connections that would soon make them some of the wealthiest men in America. They would sell cotton and sugar to the English, as much as their ships could hold.

The trip back to Boston was a good one. Fancy was glad to be off the water. She was sure the dolphins were sea serpents of the deep and would swallow them up! William and Reginia spent several days with Alex and Jacqueline before leaving for Texas. Alex and Jacqueline agreed that Alex should offer Asa the money to buy him out of the business. They valued Asa's friendship and this would only be an offer. The decision would be left up to Asa. Alex went to Asa when they returned and proposed the offer. Asa was thrilled, to Alex's surprise. Asa was ten years older than Alex and was interested in politics. He wanted to run for the senate but did not know how his time would allow it. Alex's offer gave Asa the opportunity he longed for. The deal was made and both men were happy. They sealed the agreement with a handshake and the two would be friends until their dying day.

Alex went home to share the good news with his family. William was proud of Alex's decision and happy for Asa. This was the beginning of an empire for the Wilde family. The Wildes spent two more days with Alex and Jacqueline before boarding the ship for Savannah. Reginia would miss her son and daughter-in-law, but she was eager to return home. She enjoyed Boston with all its splendor, but her heart and mind were now a part of the big frontier. She had the true pioneer spirit and longed to return to the beautiful plantation and the friends who shared the same feelings for Texas.

William and his family arrived home that August. The weather was hot and steamy. Rogette and Samuel waited at the dock with the carriage. Reginia was glad to put her feet on the Texas soil. She reached down and picked up some dirt and held it tightly in her hand. She held her hand high in the air and let the dirt fall to the ground. "Texas soil, there is none finer in the whole world," she exclaimed with pride. William smiled at her as he lifted her in his arms and placed her in the carriage. He, too, was glad to be home on Texas soil.

They rode in the carriage, passing the fields white with cotton, to their home. Rogette wanted to know all about England. Fancy told stories of the sea serpents. They all laughed. Reginia had bought fine clothes for Rogette, Samuel, and Belle while in France. She could not wait to give the gifts to them. She had purchased fine colognes and would give some to Batha.

Texas was growing in people and in debt. Sam Houston was voted in as President again. The Texans tried to occupy New Mexico but failed. The country was struggling as a government, but William's business was growing. He visited with Sam about the economy problems. The postal service was still a great concern. The public debt had grown into the millions. Sam felt the future development of Texas would be greater under the United States. William agreed to visit with his friends about the concerns for Texas and annexation by the United States.

CHAPTER

TWENTY-SIX

Alex had been busy establishing himself as a brilliant businessman. He was greatly respected by his peers. Jacqueline had become pregnant while on their honeymoon. Alex hovered over her with endless attention, giving her whatever she wanted. Jacqueline enjoyed his thoughtfulness, but only wanted a healthy baby. She hoped for a son for Alex. The two were excited to be parents, waiting with great anticipation for the birth of their child. Alex wrote his mother of the good news. William and Reginia were thrilled and would not miss the bringing forth of their first grandchild. They planned to leave for Boston the day after Christmas, leaving the children at home with Rogette and Samuel. Reginia wrote and told Alex they would be coming. He was thrilled to have his parents with them for the very special occasion.

Jacqueline decorated the baby's room with great care. Alex had carpenters cut a door from their room into the adjoining room, which Jacqueline was converting into the nursery. The nursery was large with a big fireplace. Jacqueline planned to have many children. She wanted a large family to fill the house. Alex wanted to hire a nurse to care for the child. Jacqueline agreed, and began interviewing prospective nurses. It was late January of 1842 when they found the perfect person to nurse their child. The woman was Mildred Cook. She was forty years of age and had never married. She was plain and plump, but her warm smile lit her rosy cheeks as she spoke. She came highly recommended by friends in Boston. Mildred was a delight and had worked for a local doctor for years. She had tired of the demands placed on her working with the busy doctor and decided to care for children in the home. Jacqueline was thrilled to have her. She wasn't due until March. That was fine with Mildred. She would move into the home in February. Jacqueline was relieved. If she had any problems, Mildred would be great to have near.

William and Reginia arrived in Boston the last week of February. The town was covered with fresh snow. Reginia delighted at the sight. Alex met his parents at the dock and took them to his home. Reginia and William were thrilled to see their son and Jacqueline. Jacqueline waited at home for them to arrive. She was extremely large with child and very uncomfortable. She rushed to the door to greet them as they came up the steps to the house. She hugged Reginia and William. William hugged his daughter-in-law and rubbed his hand across her protruding belly.

"William, for goodness sakes!" Reginia blushed with embarrassment at her husband's gesture.

"Hey, that is my grandson in there!" he replied with pride.

"It's all right, Missus Wilde. I just want to know how he knows it is a grandson?" Jacqueline responded, as she smiled and welcomed them inside.

Alex introduced his parents to Mildred. Reginia was pleased with the woman's charm and knowledge of medicine. They visited for a while that evening, exchanging information about the last year. Jacqueline tired early. Her child was kicking and causing her discomfort and cramping.

The next week found Jacqueline in bed. She was miserable and the cramps continued. The doctor visited daily. He told them the child would come at any time. Mildred slept in the nursery by Jacqueline and Alex's room. It was March 10 when Jacqueline went into labor. Mildred stayed at her side while Alex sent Jasper for the doctor. Pacing the floor, Alex trembled from excitement. Mildred sent him out of the room as she prepared Jacqueline for delivery. Jacqueline wanted Reginia with her. Reginia held Jacqueline's hand as Jacqueline screamed with pain. Jasper returned with the doctor and showed him to Jacqueline's room. William took Alex by the arm and set him on a chair in the hallway.

William reassured Alex that all would be fine. "I've been through this many times, Alex. Trust me when I tell you all will be fine. We didn't have the luxury of modern medicine, either." William put his arm around his son, giving Alex added reassurance.

Alex could hear the faint cries of his wife. He could not bear the thought of her suffering. The cries continued for hours. "What is happening, Father? I must see Jacqueline." Alex was beginning to panic over the length of time it was taking.

"Childbirth isn't easy, Alex, but Jacqueline is strong and she will be fine."

About the time Alex could no longer stand the intense waiting, the doctor emerged from the room.

"Alex, you have a big baby boy, and I do mean a big one!"

"I told you it would be my grandson, didn't I!" William jumped with joy.

Alex ran into the room to finally be with his wife and new son. Mildred cleaned the infant and placed him in Jacqueline's arms. Mildred and Reginia left the room to give the new parents time to be alone with their child. Alex put his arm around Jacqueline's neck and kissed her tenderly. He looked at his son. He was large, weighing over eight pounds. He was a bald baby with big blue eyes.

"I don't know who he looks like," Alex said seriously.

"Well, he certainly has no hair. Maybe he looks like you will in about twenty years!" Jacqueline teased Alex.

Alex hugged her and laughed. His tension was gone. His wife felt good but weak. "This is to be expected," Alex thought. He was glad everything had gone well, as his father had told him it would. He stayed with Jacqueline for about an hour. The doctor came in and told him Jacqueline needed to rest. Mildred took the child to the nursery and Alex went downstairs with his parents. They ate an early supper and Alex excused himself for the evening. He took a tray of food to Jacqueline and stayed by her the rest of the night. He watched lovingly as she nursed the infant. They discussed naming the boy. Alex wanted to name him William, after his father, the man he admired most. Jacqueline agreed happily. They would tell his parents the next morning.

Meanwhile, Reginia took William by the hand. "Darling, let's put on our coats and go for a walk. I want to walk in the snow. The lanterns light the streets of Beacon Hill so brilliantly."

William got their coats and held Reginia's coat open while she put her arms into it. He put his coat on and extended his arm to her. "After you, Grandma," he laughed as he guided her to the door.

They walked up and down the streets. The snow glistened from the lanterns and the bright moonlight. Reginia felt very romantic as they strolled the streets. She felt fulfilled. She thought of the wonderful marriage she had and the wonderful marriage Alex had. The thought of being a grandmother was very rewarding to her. They were on their way back to Alex's home when the door of one of the houses opened.

"Mister and Missus Wilde!" They turned to see who was calling them. It was Asa. He and his wife had bought a home near Alex. "What are you doing out on a cold night like this? Come inside and have some tea."

Reginia and William entered the home. The warmth from the fireplace felt good. They visited with Asa and his wife, Caroline, for almost two hours. Asa didn't know Jacqueline had given birth. William told them Alex planned to put an announcement of the birth in the newspaper and that he would visit Asa the next day, to tell him in person. It was nearly ten o'clock before Reginia and William left the company of Asa and his wife.

Reginia loved walking in the crisp air, kicking the snow gently as they walked home. "I feel wonderful," she exclaimed with high spirits.

"I would say you feel a bit frisky, myself." William grabbed Reginia and twirled her around, kissing her very deliberately on her soft full lips.

"William," she said with a soft, seductive voice. "We are grand-parents, for goodness sakes!" Her arms draped gently around his neck.

"Well, we're not 'old' grandparents." His voice deepened as he stretched the word "old." "I have a lot of spunk left in me. How about you?" He teased and kissed her again.

"I have a whole lot of spunk left in me, I'll just have to show you!" She bolted from his arms and ran to the house with William running behind her. They felt like two young lovers in the night. They entered the house and William picked her up quickly and started up the stairs. "Be quiet, William. You'll wake the kids," she fussed at him, while the passion built inside her.

"I think by the looks of our grandchild, the kids know all about what we are doing," he whispered with his own seductive voice.

The next morning, after breakfast, Alex asked them to join him and Jacqueline in the bedroom. Alex was anxious to tell them the baby's name. William and Reginia were eager to see their grandson and followed Alex to the bedroom. Jacqueline had just finished nursing the baby and sat upright in the bed holding the sleeping infant. She greeted them warmly as they entered the room. "Come in and see your grandson. He is the sweetest baby. He never cries. He is so happy and content."

"He is a happy child," Alex agreed, looking at his son with love and pride in his eyes. "And I will make sure he is always a happy child." Alex stroked the baby's forehead tenderly, reflecting on the love his parents had showed him growing up as a child. Reginia and William stood smiling at the baby, and it pleased them to see the love the young parents had for the infant. Alex told them that he and Jacqueline had named the baby. "We named him John William Wilde. We will call him Will, if this is all right with you, Father?"

William beamed with surprise. Reginia squeezed her husband's hand with her sign of approval. "All right? Why, I am honored." William walked to Jacqueline. She held the baby up to him to hold. He took him in his arms and held him proudly. "You will be a great man, just like your father, one day."

A feeling of warmth filled Alex, hearing his father's words. Everyone was pleased with the naming of the infant. Alex wanted to put an announcement in the newspaper and check on his business. He asked William to go with him. They would stop by Asa's on the way back home.

Five days passed before Jacqueline braved the stairs. She was still very sore from the delivery of baby Will. She was glad to be out of the bedroom. The air turned warm, melting the snow. She sat in the sunroom looking across the lawn. Reginia sat with her visiting all morning. Jacqueline loved Reginia and was grateful she came to be with her. The Exaviers would come later. Antoinette had taken ill and could not travel at the time of the birth.

William and Alex spent most of the days at Alex's office taking care of business and making future plans of expanding the shipping business. Reginia enjoyed her days with Jacqueline and baby Will. Friends came frequently bearing gifts for little Will. April came all too quickly, as William and Reginia hugged their family goodbye. William told Alex he would have to bring his family to Texas for a visit. Alex agreed. He would love for Jacqueline to see Auburn.

Reginia and William returned home to their younger children. They were anxious to hear about their little nephew. Reginia carried two daguerreotypes that Alex had made—one showing Will, and the other of himself and Jacqueline holding their infant. The children were thrilled. Reginia bought a beautiful doll for Katie, a wooden soldier for Thad, and new clothes for John.

Sam Houston came to visit William. He spoke of his work to have Texas annexed by the United States. William worked in agreement with Sam the next two years, talking to many about Texas and of annexing the country to the United States. The Texas debt continued to grow, reaching near eight million dollars by the year 1844. The Texans knew something had to be done. Other problems had occurred. In 1842, the Mexicans raided San Antonio, and Washington on the Brazos became the capital again. There were disputes over the land between Mexico and Texas. In 1844, a convention voted for annexation and a state constitution was adopted. The proposed annexation brought a bitter fight in the United States over the question of slavery.

William was firmly rooted in his ideas of slavery. The plantations needed the slaves. Alex wrote to his father informing him of many of the Northerners' views concerning the slavery issues. The majority of the Northerners were against slavery and resented the fact that the Southerners allowed the blacks to be held in bondage. Alex kept his ideas to himself, refusing to take part in the argument. He was shrewd.

His concern was his shipping business, he could not afford to make enemies on either side. His hard work made him and his family very wealthy. The talk of abolishing slavery would not get in his way. He held to his neutral position.

Texas as an independent republic was coming to an end. It would only be a matter of time before the country became the twenty-eighth state of the Union. William knew the only way Texas could prosper would be as a State; for the debt was too severe and Texas needed the Union to survive.

CHAPTER
TWENTY-SEVEN

On December 29, 1845, Texas was admitted to the Union, following great efforts by Sam Houston and Anson Jones, the newly elected President of the Republic of Texas. Sam Houston had refused a general's commission but had decided to serve as senator for the new State. A wave of immigration followed the annexation, doubling the population of Texas. The stability afforded by the annexation and Texas's liberal land policies were irresistible to the immigrants. The large state kept its public land and reserved the right to divide into no more than five states.

Annexation brought on the Mexican War, which was over a boundary dispute between Mexico and the United States in the southern region of Texas. The Union troops filed into south Texas in 1846 to fight the Mexicans over the boundary dispute.

John was now sixteen years old, and tall and handsome like his brother Alex. That was the only thing they had in common. John was uninterested in the shipping business. He loved the big plantation and spent his days after school with Ransom. He wanted to learn all he could about the farming and cattle business. He dreamed of operating Auburn one day. He knew Alex would never return to the plantation to live. He was now next in line to work with his father. He had a great love for the horses and cattle. His life was on the frontier and he never wanted to leave.

One hot May afternoon, John rode his favorite thoroughbred to the creek for a swim. He stripped of his clothes and dove into the warm water. Upon emerging from the water, he heard a scream. He turned his head to see who it was. A dark-haired girl was submerged in the water, with only her head showing.

"Close your eyes!" the girl shrieked at him. "I've nothing on and I'm getting out to dress. Please, turn your head, while I get out."

John turned his head. "Okay, I can't see you now." The girl hurried from the water and ran behind a tree, where her clothes lay on the ground. "What are you doing down here?" John asked, as he continued talking to the unfamiliar girl. "What is your name and where do you live?" John was full of questions for the dark-haired girl. "Are you dressed?"

"Yes, I am," she replied as she walked to the edge of the water.

"Well, don't just stand their staring at me. Turn your head while I get out and dress." John wanted out of the water, for his curiosity had the best of him. John got out of the creek and dressed quickly. He walked to the tree where the girl stood shyly. "Who are you?" John asked again.

"I'm Josie Barbeaux. I live south of here. I ride here sometimes to swim. I have to go. My father would skin me alive, if he knew I was here." The girl sounded fearful.

"Don't go," John pleaded. He had heard scarcely anything of the Barbeauxs, but he had no idea they had a daughter. The young girl intrigued John. He couldn't believe he had never seen her.

"I must go. Promise you won't tell anyone you saw me, not anyone," she begged nervously.

"I promise." John wanted to see her again. He talked quickly as Josie leaped on her horse to ride away. He called to her as she turned her horse to leave. "When will you come back?"

"Tomorrow at two o'clock," she hollered as the horse galloped away.

"I'm John Wilde! I will see you then!" His voice rang across the field to her. She never looked back, she merely raised her arm and waved a sign of agreement. John rode his horse across the fields to find

Ransom. He couldn't wait for the next day and the visit with the dark-haired girl.

John found Ransom in the fields, watching the slaves work the ground. He rode quickly to the man. "Ransom, how are you today?" John spoke with enthusiasm.

"I'm fine, John. How are you?" Ransom replied, noticing the broad smile on the boy's face. "What are you up to? You sure have a big grin on your face."

"Oh, nothing, nothing at all. I want to ask you a question." John was curious about the Barbeaux family.

"Well, fire away," Ransom responded quickly. He figured John had more questions about the plantation.

"Who are the Barbeauxs? Tell me about them," John blurted.

"The Barbeauxs?" Ransom was taken off guard by John's request. "Why do you want to know about them?" Ransom knew the story about Belle and feared John had somehow discovered the truth about the young girl's heritage.

"No particular reason. I heard talk of them today and wondered why we didn't know them. They live so close and all." John tried to be discreet. He would not mention meeting Josie. He would keep her secret.

"Well, there's not much to tell. To my understanding, Don Barbeaux is a Frenchman from New Orleans. He moved to Texas not long after your parents. He's a miserable fellow. No one care's much for him. He beats his slaves half to death. That's how Rogette came to be bought." Ransom continued talking, telling the story of how his father came to buy Rogette and the suffering she had endured while she was a slave of Barbeaux's. He omitted telling him about Belle. "I understand he is cruel to his wife. They never socialize with the other people in the area. I hear tell he is also a gambler and frequently visits New Orleans for his pleasures. I know one thing, your father has no use for the man."

Ransom explained about the man to the best of his knowledge. John was satisfied with the answers. This explained a lot why John had never met the girl. He imagined her locked away in a room most of her life. John told Ransom not to mention the conversation to his father. "If

Father dislikes Barbeaux, the man must be real bad," John thought. For his father liked everyone and everyone liked his father.

John had a hard time concentrating on his studies the next day at school. He heard very little his teacher, Ms. Georgia, had to say. He could not wait to see the mysterious girl again. Ransom's talk about the Barbeauxs had only roused John's curiosity. After school, John galloped his horse across the fields to the creek. Katie wanted to ride with John but he told her no. He could not let Katie see Josie Barbeaux, and sent her home with Thad.

Katie was fourteen now and had little use for her twelve-year-old brother. Furious with John, Katie rode her horse home, running him all the way. Her long auburn curls were blowing in the breeze. She could not understand why she couldn't go with John.

Thad was cute as a button with his dark red hair and freckles. His bright blue eyes sparkled mischievously. He didn't care that his sister went home by herself. He didn't want her with him, anyway. He wanted to play with his friends from school. The young lad was wild as a March hare! He loved the excitement of danger and feared absolutely nothing. He would climb the tallest tree and jump down, just to see if he could make it without hurting himself! Reginia did have her hands full with the little daredevil.

John arrived at the creek to find Josie sitting under the big oak tree. He leaped from his horse and rushed to her side. He was anxious to know all about her. John asked her many questions, but Josie told him very little. Only that she lived on a plantation and was taught by a tutor her father had brought from New Orleans. She spoke French as well as English.

John loved the French language. He had heard his mother and Rogette speak it frequently. He had picked up a few words of French, from his mother, and spoke them to Josie. She laughed at his frontier drawl and tried to teach him the correct way to accent. The two giggled as John attempted the correct pronunciation. Josie was well dressed and seemed friendly enough to John. He couldn't imagine that she had such a disliked father. The two visited for over an hour, when Josie suddenly had to part company. She promised to return the next day. John could not wait!

John and Josie met almost every day that summer, swimming and lazing about under the big oak tree. They only missed seeing one another if it rained. They were the same age and became best of friends. John was loyal to his friendship with Josie and kept their meetings a secret. Josie became more comfortable with John and found it easy to express herself. He was a great listener, allured by her every word. She had never had anyone she could talk to; actually, she had never had a friend.

It was a hot July afternoon when Josie came running on her horse to meet John. She was crying and her face was red and bruised. She jumped from her horse and flung her arms around John, crying. John didn't know what to think. He insisted on knowing what was wrong with her. She could not hold her feelings inside any longer. She finally had someone she could confide in. She told John about her cruel father and his terrible temper. He never allowed her or her mother to leave the plantation. Her mother was a recluse and a broken woman, she explained. Josie escaped to the creek every day while her father rode the fields. John held his dear friend, consoling her as she spoke. Her father had beaten her mother severely that day. Josie had tried to stop him, but he had grabbed her, hitting her in the face with his fist. John filled with anger. No wonder his father disliked this man! He could not imagine such treatment from a parent.

Time passed quickly that day, and Josie had to hurry home. John begged her not to go. He offered his home as a safe haven. She feared her father too much to leave with John. She assured him she would be all right and sped home. John was miserable. There was no one he could talk to. John rode through the herd of cattle. His thoughts were on Josie. He hoped she would be at the creek the next day.

John went each day to the secret meeting place, but seven days passed and there was still no Josie. He worried about her and missed his friend. He decided if she was not there the next day, he would speak to his father about her. He rode his horse quickly to the creek, the next day. There sat Josie. Her eyes were swollen with tears.

"Where have you been?" John questioned as he rushed to her side.

"My father, I hate him!" She exploded into more tears. John held her tightly as she cried on his shoulder, her body trembling against his.

She raised her head and looked desperately into his eyes. "He came back to the house early the last time I was with you and saw me riding from this direction. He was furious. He began slapping and cursing me. Mother tried to help me, but he turned on her. She was already weak from his beating her earlier. He grabbed an iron from the fireplace and, John, he hit her over and over. I tried to stop him, but he hit me so hard that I fainted. When I came to, my mother was lying face down in a pool of blood. I grabbed her, she wasn't breathing. I screamed!" Her voice cracked and tears welled in her eyes. "He killed my mother!" John sat in total disbelief. He held her closely while she spoke with tears falling from her eyes. "He heard my scream and came in the room. He grabbed me and forced me upstairs in my bedroom, locking the door. I couldn't get out. I heard him tell two slaves to bury her. He would not allow me to see her. I don't think he even watched them bury her! He finally let me out of my room. He threatened to kill me too, if I ever left home again." Anger filled her voice. She stood up and pointed to the horse. "Well, I left that plantation and I'm never going back. See that bag on my saddle? I'm running away. I don't know where I'll go. I'm just going to ride until I'm far away!"

"Josie, I can't let you do that. Come to my house. My father would never let him near you. I never told you, but my father despises your father. You'll be safe there." John spoke with a promise in his voice.

"I can't do that, John. It would only cause problems for your family."

"No, it won't." John hugged her tightly. "My father will handle everything. You'll see. Now come on. Get on your horse. We're going to my house, right now!" He spoke with such authority, that Josie did not argue. She got on her horse and rode with John to his house. John did not know how he would tell his parents, but he was not worried. His parents were the most understanding people he knew.

Reginia sat on the front porch, as the two young people rode up. She wondered where in the world John had found this young beauty, as she looked at the dark-haired girl. John got off his horse and helped Josie down. He took her to meet his mother. He was almost glad it was his mother they saw first. He felt Josie would be more at ease meeting her first. Reginia watched the girl as she walked toward the house. The girl appeared to be distraught. "Where did she come from?" Reginia wondered. It was not like John to pick up strangers!

John approached his mother, with Josie shyly at his side. "Mother, I want you to meet my best friend."

Reginia thought to herself, "Best friend? Where has John been keeping her?"

John continued speaking. "This is Josie Barbeaux."

The word Barbeaux sent quivers through Reginia. "How did he meet this girl?" she wondered. Reginia composed her feelings before speaking. There has to be a good explanation. "John is too responsible to have been going to that man's plantation," she thought to herself.

Reginia responded with an uncertain tone to her voice. "I'm pleased to meet you, I'm sure. How did you and John meet?" Reginia asked inquisitively, anxious to hear an explanation of this friendship.

John pulled two rockers by his mother's and they sat down. John told his mother how they had met and had become such close friends. He then told her the story about Josie and her mother. Reginia filled with sorrow for the young girl, and hatred for Don Barbeaux. Josie sat, with her head hung down, as John spoke.

Rogette came out of the house and saw Josie. She looked at the girl, who had grown up to be a beautiful young lady, and recognized her immediately. Josie looked up and saw Rogette standing there. Josie became overwhelmed with gladness at the sight of Rogette, who had cared for her so lovingly when she was small. Josie leaped from her rocker and threw her arms around Rogette. "I didn't know what happened to you. You just disappeared and Father wouldn't tell me where you were!" Josie cried tears of joy at finding her Rogette. Rogette hugged the girl tenderly.

"How did you get here, my child?" Rogette asked of her.

"I've left home. Father"—she paused—"killed Mother." Josie felt safe in Rogette's arms.

"John, take Josie into the house and show her to the guest room. I want to speak to your father." Reginia would not let harm come to the poor girl, but she wanted to speak with Rogette first. She had questions that she needed answered.

John felt relieved by his mother's decision. He gladly escorted Josie to the guest room. Reginia waited until the two were out of sight before speaking with Rogette. Rogette explained the mistreatment by Barbeaux of his daughter. She had been very young when Rogette had last seen her. She had not mentioned the girl, out of fear of Barbeaux. His private life was his own and he would have killed anyone who spoke about it, especially a slave. Reginia understood. She went to William and told him what happened. William was enraged. "The thought of that man sickens me. He needs a whip laid across him!" William shouted.

Reginia took his hand. "Calm yourself, darling. I feel the same way, but this fury won't do any good."

"You're right, of course." He smiled. "But we have to do something to help his daughter. She deserves much better."

They agreed to allow Josie to live with them. She was sixteen and could live wherever she wanted. There would be nothing Barbeaux could do.

TWENTY-EIGHT

Barbeaux did not bother looking for his daughter. He figured she had run away. If the frontier did not kill her, he imagined she would leave Texas. It was good riddance as far as Barbeaux was concerned. He brought a whore from New Orleans to live with him; Josie would have only been in the way of his wild drunken evenings. He took the woman everywhere he went, sporting her on his arm, as if she were a prize heifer. She stood by him while he gambled and drank in the saloons of New Orleans. Barbeaux felt free at last from the holds of a wife and daughter.

Josie was superbly educated. Her tutor had taught her well. Reginia delighted in the young girl, speaking French with her often. Josie moved into the bedroom with Katie. They became close friends. Josie enjoyed having a girlfriend for the first time. Josie was too advanced in her studies for the small school. She stayed home with Reginia during the day. John finished school but did not want to attend college. Reginia was disappointed, but John was determined to learn all he could about farming and raising cattle. He worked with Ransom every day and studied the bookkeeping of the plantation at night with his father. William was glad to have John so interested. He proudly taught his son the "ins and outs" of the plantation.

Two years passed by quickly. John assumed more responsibilities at Auburn. He was intelligent with the books and William had turned over a lot of that responsibility to John. Katie finished her schooling with Ms. Georgia. John had become busy with the plantation and had little time to spend with Josie, which was all right, because Josie and Katie had become very close. The two girls spent long hours sharing intimate thoughts about their lives and plans for the future. Josie didn't know just what she wanted, but Katie knew exactly what she desired! She wanted to marry a handsome, good man and have many children and live in Texas. She wanted to be just like her mother!

Thad was fourteen and into everything but what he was supposed to be! His best friend, Mark Mathis, was just like him. The two boys would rather sleep under the stars than in the comfort of their home. They skipped school and fished the days away. They built a raft from logs and cruised lazily up and down Best Creek. William scolded the boy and tried punishing him. William's efforts were futile. His rebellious son was determined to do what he wanted. Thad had no interest in school, Auburn, or the shipping business. His idol was the late Davey Crockett, who had died at the Alamo. Thad had heard great stories about the frontiersman and wanted to be just like him. Thad was not a bad child. He just loved to explore and seek adventures in the wilderness. He even trapped a raccoon and skinned it, sporting a coonskin hat wherever he went!

William needed to go to Boston to meet Alex on business. Reginia was thrilled to go. She missed Alex, who now had three children; Will, Sarah, he had named after his sister, and Alex Jr. Reginia's parents were both dead. She thought how she had missed seeing them. She would not let that happen to her and Alex.

She went with William every time he went to Boston, which was each year in the spring. John did not want to go to Boston that spring and neither did Thad. So, William and Reginia took Katie and Josie and left for Boston.

Alex and Jacqueline waited for them at the Boston dock. They were pleased to meet Josie. Reginia had written so much about her. The children ran from the house as soon as the carriage pulled up.

"Grandmother, Grandfather!" they yelled with glee as they ran to greet them with hugs and kisses. Will was six years old, and Sarah was five, with little Alex three years of age. Reginia hugged each of them.

"My, haven't you all grown this last year! I don't have a baby anymore." She grinned as she gently pinched little Alex's soft cheek.

Mildred came to the door to greet them. She continued to work for Alex and Jacqueline. Jacqueline had grown very fond of Mildred. Mildred cared for the children with love and was excellent with them. She played with the children, read to them, and took them outside teaching them about the wildlife and nature. Jacqueline wanted her to stay with them until the children were all in their teens.

Josie and Katie spent time exploring Boston, shopping and watching the ships go in and out at the dock. Josie was reserved, while Katie was outgoing. By the end of the first week, the two girls had met many of the young people, thanks to Katie! Josie with her exotic French looks and Katie with her deep auburn curls attracted the eyes of the young Boston boys.

Over the years, William and Reginia had met and become friendly with many people from Boston. Alex planned a grand ball for his parents' return. People gathered at the large home and danced to the music of an orchestra. The ladies were adorned in fine gowns. Reginia had bought Katie and Josie new dresses and pinned their hair in fashionable curls. The two girls were beautiful. Reginia proudly admired them. Katie and Josie knew many in the young crowd that night. The two graced the dance floor all night, as the boys stood in line to waltz with them. Reginia and William danced, while watching Katie, who seemed to have grown up all too soon, glide about the dance floor.

There were many grand affairs that spring in Boston. The girls had so much fun dancing and visiting with the younger set. Asa's youngest son, Asa Rhome III, developed a fancy for Katie. The seventeen-year-old lad followed her about asking to dance with her each chance he got. He spent his days at Alex's visiting the girls. Katie thought he was so cute and spent hours whispering about him to Josie.

One afternoon, just before they were to depart for Texas, Katie and Asa sat on the bench in Alex's back lawn. Asa listened to Katie tell her stories about Texas. Asa was fascinated by the frontier. He longed to see the new state. He could listen to Katie for hours. Her long auburn curls hung softly about her face. He couldn't resist touching them. He ran his hand down the curls, very carefully. Katie liked him touching her hair. Asa, taken by her beauty, quickly kissed her on the lips. His action surprised Katie. She had not been kissed by a boy, except by John or Alex, and that was in a brotherly way. For the first time in her life, she had nothing to say!

"I hope I didn't offend you," Asa said cautiously.

"Why, of course not, you silly boy!" Katie responded curtly, while batting her eyes at him. She did not want him to think she had never been kissed before. She was sixteen, after all! Actually, she would have enjoyed his kissing her again. Katie relished her newfound feelings.

"I'm going to miss you, Katie Wilde." Asa squeezed her hand and continued holding it as they visited on the lawn.

Asa left for home and Katie rushed to Josie. She told Josie every detail about Asa holding her hand and kissing her. Katie was so excited, tossing her head as she spoke. The two girls giggled and told stories all evening. Josie was eighteen and had never been kissed. She was so reserved. Josie wanted to be kissed by the perfect man. One she could love all her life.

The month in Boston passed too fast for Katie and Josie. Neither girl was ready to leave the splendor of Boston and their new friends. The sun shone through the window of the room in which Katie and Josie slept, waking them up. They looked at each other with disappointment. It was the morning of departure. The two girls dressed and prepared to join the family downstairs. Alex and William sat chatting in the parlor. There was a knock at the door.

"I wonder who that could be so early in the morning," Alex asked aloud as he walked to the door. Alex opened the door and to his surprise there stood Asa. "My goodness, Asa, what can I do for you?"

"May I see Katie, please. I just want to tell her goodbye." Asa had to see her before she left.

"I think I can arrange that. Come in while I get her." Alex turned to get his sister. He passed his father, who was going after coffee, and winked at him cockily. "It is Asa to see our little Katie!" he laughed.

William just walked on to the dining room, with a grin on his face. "Oh, how these kids are growing up," he said out loud to himself, while shaking his head. He thought about the situation. Asa was a good boy, however, William was glad he lived so far away. This was one boy he would not have to worry about courting his daughter! He wasn't ready to see his little Katie interested in boys.

Katie ran to see Asa. Reginia stopped her at the landing of the stairs. "Where are you off to in such a rush."

"Asa is here to see me!"

"My dear, never run to a man. You just glide into the room. Let them know it's their pleasure to see you, not yours to see them." Reginia spoke slowly and elegantly to set the mood for Katie.

"Okay, Mother." Katie lifted her head, held her shoulders straight, and walked slowly down the stairs as if she had no care in the world. Reginia watched her daughter and giggled at her seriousness.

Asa watched spellbound, as Katie descended the stairs. He asked her to come to the front porch. They walked outside and Asa closed the door behind them. Reginia and Alex stood on the landing watching the two as they disappeared out the door.

"Wow, this must be a serious matter. What do you think, Mother?" Alex remarked teasingly, putting his arm around his mother. The two laughed and Reginia returned to finish her packing.

"I wanted to see you one last time, Katie. I enjoyed every day with you." Asa was nervous. He had had girlfriends before, but none had captivated his attention like Katie.

"I enjoyed my time with you too," Katie said self-consciously. She tilted her head downward, half blushing with the unfamiliar feeling she felt inside herself.

"I brought you something, to remember our time together." Asa pulled a necklace from his pocket. It was a gold chain with a charm dangling on it. The charm was a golden horse. "I know how you love horses. I hope you like it." He held the chain before her eyes.

"Oh, my, it's beautiful. I love it. Thank you, Asa." She turned allowing him to put it around her neck. Asa reached around her from the back and lowered the necklace softly about her neck. Katie brushed her hair aside so he could clasp the necklace. She turned around, finding herself very close to Asa. They stared into each other's eyes.

"May I kiss you, Katie?" Asa asked bravely, fearing she would say no.

"Yes," Katie responded softly and, to her own surprise, without hesitation.

Asa took her by the shoulders and pulled her gently to him, kissing her softly on her lips. Katie closed her eyes, enjoying the moment. She would never forget Asa. Asa could only stay for a short while. He told her he would visit her in Texas someday. Katie made him promise to come. Asa kissed her once more before leaving. She stood on the porch waving to Asa until he was out of sight. Katie reached to her neck for the charm, holding it gently in her hand. Enchanted by Asa, she quivered with excitement as she proceeded into the house. This had certainly been her best trip to Boston!

The Wildes returned to Auburn. The cotton was growing as they crossed the fields to the house. John was at home when his family arrived. He had longed to see his family and especially Josie. He missed his friend more than he thought possible. He greeted his family and Josie with warm hugs of affection. Josie had missed John too.

That night, after dinner, William and his family relaxed in the drawing room. John had news for his father. "Mister Houston came by while you were gone."

"Oh, really. What was on his mind? Did he say?"

"Yes. In fact, he stayed overnight. It seems the immigrants that have moved in are having trouble, especially those settling in the central section of Texas. Too many have moved in and food and jobs are scarce. The Indians are giving the surveyors problems too. Mister Houston said the Indians call the surveying instruments 'the things that stole the land.' The Rangers have their hands full with the Indians. Anyway, I think he just wanted to talk to you and get some ideas on how to help the situation."

William thought a moment. "Well, there may be something we can do. I will have to talk to Sam and see what he has on his mind."

"I feel we are very fortunate," Reginia said with a sigh. "We have plenty of food and success. It has to be hard for these people that have come here with no money and are trying to forge a new life. The promise of land, religious freedom, and a free country must have looked like the 'land of milk and honey' to them. I thought it was hard for us, but we had the security of wealth. I hope we can do something to help make their dreams possible."

William went to bed with his mind wondering about the immigrants. He could barely sleep, tossing and turning all night. He wanted to help and would find a way. He was proud of his state and wanted every person living in it to be proud too.

CHAPTER

TWENTY-NINE

The next day, William left to see Sam. He promised Reginia he would return within the next two weeks. Sam was in Houston and William thought it would be good to talk to him and the other businessmen who could possibly help.

John and Josie mounted their horses and rode for the creek. They swam in the warm water, playfully dunking and splashing one another. After the swim, they lay under the oak tree, as they always had with John listening to Josie. She told him all about her trip to Boston and the shopping trips and all the balls with fine orchestras. John thought Josie seemed overly excited when telling about waltzing with the young men. The thought of Josie dancing with another young man roused a feeling of jealousy in John. He suddenly found himself wishing he had gone to Boston. Josie had missed their time together at the creek and so had John. They promised each other to meet every day and swim in the creek and share their thoughts under the old oak tree.

The two kept their promise to one another. Every day, for the rest of the summer, they went to the creek. The cotton was being picked that September, as the two hurried off to the creek. It was hot for that time of the year and John talked Josie into a swim. An hour of frolicking in the creek left them exhausted. Josie ran to the old tree and fell limp on the ground. "Whew, I'm out of breath," she hollered to him. John got out of the creek and joined her under the oak, leaving his shirt hanging in the tree. John was almost nineteen years of age and very handsome. Hard work had made his muscles ripple. His physique caught Josie off guard. "Why haven't I noticed his good looks before," she wondered.

She lay in her slip, her hair and body wet from the swim. Her slip clung to her, showing her beautiful full figure. John looked at the lovely girl beside him. Suddenly, their friendly laughter and talk ceased. They each saw something in one another that they had never noticed before. They lay speechless, staring into each other's eyes. John looked at her figure with adoration and back into her eyes, as Josie ran her fingers slowly across John's muscular chest. They never uttered a word. Although they had swum many times together, it was as if they were seeing each other for the first time. Josie looked at John with her soft brown eyes. John wanted to kiss her badly. He wanted her in his life forever. The love of his life was right beside him, all this time! She wanted him to hold her. They had come to know each other well and seemed to know what the other wanted. Without saying a word, John took her into his arms and kissed her softly. Josie put her arms around him and looked lovingly into his eyes, letting him know she wanted him to kiss her again. She had waited for the perfect man and now she had him. John could not resist the beauty by his side. They kissed passionately, over and over. Suddenly, Josie pulled away.

"John," Josie spoke softly, as if out of breath from the desire raging inside her. She felt guilty. She was sure her feelings were sinful.

John interrupted, "Don't say anything, Josie. Don't be afraid of me, I would never hurt you." He pulled her close without any resistance from her. He loved the way her body fit perfectly next to his. "I love you, Josie. I want you with me always. We will go no further with our love, until we are married."

She looked into his eyes with surprise. "Until we are married? You would marry me, John?"

"Yes, I want to marry you," he said with certainty.

She kissed him tenderly. "I love you, John. Yes, oh yes, I'll marry you."

John was thrilled. The two lay in each other's arms, making plans for their future.

It was late in the evening before the two came back to the house. Dinner was already on the table. They rushed in and took their places at the long table. They could hardly eat for looking into each other's eyes. Both had smiles that appeared peculiar to William. Reginia thought nothing of them. She knew they were friends and went riding together, often coming in late. William could see something was different. He recognized the look of love in John. It reminded him of himself the first time he had made love to Reginia. He knew that look of serious love all too well. William only hoped they had not gone too far with their obvious passion.

After supper, William asked John into the library. He closed the doors and asked John to sit down. "Son, I see a look in your eyes, which appears to be love." William was always direct. He never believed in beating around the bush. "You and Josie could not take your eyes off each other tonight. Why don't you tell me what is going on between the two of you?"

John was very much like his father, strong willed and direct. He answered his father honestly. "I love Josie and she loves me. We want to get married."

"You're awfully young to be thinking of marriage. Don't you think?"

"Father, I'm only a year younger than you were when you and Mother married," John replied emphatically.

William thought a moment before responding. "You're right, John. I was young and I remember having this same conversation with my father." William laughed at his own foolishness. "How will you care for your Josie, if you two marry?"

"I would like to work for you, Father. Ransom has his hands full with all the planting. Let me take care of the cattle end of your business. I've learned a lot from Ransom. I would do a good job for you."

William was proud of his son. He knew John would do a good job. Ransom spoke frequently about how much John knew about the workings of the plantation, and William had seen firsthand how good his son was with the books. It pleased William to have both his older sons interested in his business.

"Let me ask you something. How quickly do you plan to marry Josie?"

"As soon as possible." John wanted her for his wife now!

William could not believe his son's urgency. "Son, you haven't gotten Josie in trouble have you?"

"Father! Of course not. I love her; I would never take advantage of her feelings. She would never allow that, anyway. Josie is wonderful. I just want to get on with my life and I want her in it." John felt insulted by his father's question and William realized it.

"I'm sorry, John. I should've never asked you such a personal question. Josie's a fine young lady and your mother and I'll be proud to have her as a daughter-in-law. We've come to love her very much. Your mother will be thrilled. You two marry as soon as you like. The two of you can live here. This house is certainly big enough for two families." He walked to John and hugged him with affection and approval. "I tell you what I'll do. I'll give you the cattle business. It'll be yours to run. I have more money than I can possibly spend. It's only fair. I helped Alex get started in the shipping business and I'll help you get started in yours. No son of mine will ever do without."

John was thrilled. He thanked his father and hugged him with great appreciation. "There's something else I'd like to speak to you about. I heard from Sam. We're going to send a ship filled with supplies to Matagorda. From there, wagons will take the supplies to the settlers. The steamers can't get up the river; it's just too low. I plan to go to Houston and meet Sam. There is a group of us that are buying the supplies. What I'd like is for you to go with me. What do you think?" William asked.

"Father, I'd like to go. Just let me know when."

"I told Sam we'd meet him at the end of the week in Houston. We should be gone about three weeks."

"Three weeks?" John questioned.

"Is that a problem, John?"

"No," he murmured. His mind was on Josie and three weeks was a long time. "No, Father, that's fine. It's just that I must tell Josie about our plans."

He hurried to tell Josie the news of his father's agreement to the wedding and the plans to go to Houston. Josie was not eager for John to leave for three weeks, but she knew it was for a good cause and many people needed help. She admired him for his choice to go. Josie put her arms around John and the two embraced. They sat up half the night making plans for the wedding. They wanted to marry in October, before the cold winter came.

Reginia was thrilled by the news, but this meant a lot of work for them with William and John away. They had only four weeks to prepare for the wedding. The first thing she had to do was place an announcement in the newspaper, inviting all their friends to the wedding.

Reginia went to the attic and opened the old trunk. Inside was her wedding dress. It was still beautiful and in perfect condition. She held it up, recalling her own wedding. She took the dress downstairs and showed it to Josie. Josie thought it was the most beautiful gown she had ever seen. "Josie, why don't you try this dress on. I'd be honored if you'd wear it on your wedding day." Josie was ecstatic. She rushed to her bedroom to try it on, with Reginia directly behind her. The gown fit perfectly, except that the length needed about two more inches. Reginia said not to worry. She had beautiful lace she could sew on the bottom of the dress to extend the length. Josie looked into the long oval mirror. The dress looked beautiful against her deep olive skin. Katie entered the room and gasped with admiration of the dress on Josie.

"You look simply gorgeous, my dear!" She laughed with pleasure as she skipped across the room with delight. "You're going to be my sister soon. I'm so happy. Imagine old John, sneaking up and catching your affections. How about that brother of mine!" Katie was such a character. She had the same charm and wit that Alex had. "Mother, your dress looks wonderful on Josie. Are you going to let me wear it when I get married?"

"Of course you can wear it," Reginia teased. "Provided the dress lasts that long!"

"Well, you act as if I am going to be old and haggard by the time I marry. I tell you true, I will be married by the time I am twenty!" Reginia and the girls laughed and enjoyed every minute of planning the grand wedding.

William and John rushed through their meetings. The people in Houston were willing to do what they could to help. The ship was loaded with supplies. Sam wanted to go with the ship and onward with the wagons into the central part of Texas. He was a Texas hero and everyone loved him. His presence would give settlers hope. William felt satisfied. He knew he had done all he could do. It would be hard for many settlers, but everyone was willing to work together to make Texas a great state.

CHAPTER

THIRTY

It was the week before the wedding when the two men returned to Auburn. Josie ran to greet John. She and Reginia had worked hard making all the plans. William was impressed with what all the women had accomplished. It would be a fine wedding and they were all eagerly awaiting the day.

That evening, William told Reginia about his trip. "I sent supplies I purchased in Houston, on the ship, enough to get the settlers through the winter. It cost a lot of money, but, darling, I felt it was worth it. Many live in houses that are nothing but shanties and are in such despair and destitution. The thought of children suffering along with their parents breaks my heart. I had to do something."

"I know." Reginia took his hand. "I'm proud of you. What good is all our money if we can't help others in need. I forget sometimes how hard it can be. It seems as though we've come very far in the development of this part of Texas, when west of here it's still full of danger and hardships." Reginia hugged William, thankful for her generous husband.

The wedding announcement was in the paper the week before the marriage. Don Barbeaux sat in his dining room, drinking his brandy and reading the paper. He spotted the wedding announcement. He raged in his drunkenness. Why, Josie was right there under his nose! He thought she was dead or far away. He would not tolerate such actions by his daughter. He felt humiliated. He would go after her and take her home. Barbeaux sent his slave for the carriage. He called to the woman he kept.

The carriage pulled to the front of the house. He hurried to meet it, climbing into the front seat and pushing the slave aside. "Get out the way, nigger. You aren't goin' on this trip." Barbeaux's woman had not come from her room. Her slow response angered him. "Get out here. We have to go for a ride. I've some business to tend to with William Wilde," he slurred.

"Where'd you say we're going?" the mistress questioned as she walked through the front door.

"Never you mind," he shouted. "Just get in the carriage."

The woman climbed into the carriage. Barbeaux cracked the whip across the horses' backs, making them bolt into a run. He carried a bottle of whiskey. Taking large gulps, he whipped and screamed at his horses all the way to Auburn.

William and John were in the library, going over the cattle books, when suddenly they heard the loud thud of hooves coming up the lane. The men rushed outside to see who it was.

"Damn, it is Don Barbeaux." William's voice filled with hatred. John glared at Barbeaux, the man he had heard so much about. He hated Barbeaux without ever having laid an eye on him. Reginia came running when she heard the horses. She saw it was Barbeaux and sent Josie quickly to her room. Instead, Josie ran upstairs to the observatory and stared down at her father. Barbeaux was drunk with whiskey. The woman at his side looked like the barroom prostitute that she had once been. The woman dressed cheaply and wore bright red lipstick and rouge. Reginia looked at her and Don with disgust.

"I came for my daughter!" he bellowed from the carriage.

"You can't have her! She's going to be my wife," John screamed back at the man.

Rogette heard the familiar voice and ran for Belle, who was now approaching thirteen years old. She hid the girl in the house. Barbeaux stumbled from his carriage, cursing as he hit the ground. His appearance repulsed John. Barbeaux got to his feet. His eyes glanced upward and spotted Josie watching from the observatory. He shook his finger at John as he approached the two men.

"I see the little wench. I'm going to get her and you'll not stop me." Barbeaux hurtled himself forward. John stepped in front of Barbeaux, stopping him dead in his tracks. The fact that Barbeaux referred to Josie as a wench enraged John even more.

"You're not going anywhere, except back in that carriage and off our land," John spoke firmly with no fear in his voice. He wanted Barbeaux to make the first move, so he could give him the beating he deserved. Barbeaux reached for John's shoulder and attempted to shove him out of the way. John swung at him with a tight fist, hitting Barbeaux in his left jaw. John's strength hurled Barbeaux backward. John lunged at Barbeaux, beating him repeatedly with his fists. Barbeaux's face was full of blood. William grabbed John and pulled him off Barbeaux, who lay crumpled on the ground. Barbeaux was half-unconscious from the beating. The woman screamed curses from the carriage. John could care less about Barbeaux and his whore. He kicked Barbeaux in the groin, as hard as he could. Barbeaux doubled over in pain, as he tried to get up off the ground. John backed off.

"Now, get up and get off our land. If I ever see your face again, I'll kill you. Do you hear me? I'll kill you!" John turned his attention to the woman. "Get him out of here. Now!" He screamed the order at Barbeaux's woman. She jumped from the carriage, with fear in her eyes, and helped Barbeaux into the carriage. He slumped over, beaten and broken. She whipped the horses into a gallop.

Josie rushed down the stairs thrusting herself into John's arms. For the first time in her life, Josie had no fear of her father. John held her tightly. "He'll never be back. You'll never have to face him again," John spoke reassuringly.

William looked at his son, proudly. John had done what William had always longed to do: beat the hell out of Barbeaux! William put his arm around Reginia and the four of them walked into the house.

Rogette was in the house with Belle. Belle wondered who the stranger was and why he had acted that way. Rogette explained as best she could to her young daughter, without telling Belle too much. Rogette never wanted Belle to know that Barbeaux was her real father.

The last few days before the wedding were spent on last-minute preparations. William had friends with instruments to play music for dancing. The wedding would not be as elegant as Alex and Jacqueline's, but it would be the grandest wedding the Texas frontier had seen!

The wedding day arrived. The home and lawn filled with friends. Many came all the way from Houston and Columbia. Jim and Betty came to spend several days with the Wildes. William had two hogs and a large steer turning on long thin irons over hot coals in the ground. Samuel and Rogette, dressed in their finest clothes, greeted the guests and seated them in chairs, placed on the lawn. Long tables were filled with food. William had a wooden floor built for dancing on the lawn and sprinkled sawdust on it to make it slick for dancing. A beautiful arbor, which was covered with honeysuckle, would be the site for the wedding vows. Chairs were placed in rows, with an aisle down the middle, for a perfect view of the couple.

John paced nervously at the foot of the stairs, while Reginia and Katie helped Josie dress. Reginia pinned Josie's hair in loose, flowing curls. Josie looked divine! The music played and the people talked about the grandeur of the wedding. Reginia came down the stairs and took her place in the arranged chairs, John took his place under the arbor, and Thad stood proudly as John's best man. Suddenly, Josie appeared at the landing of the stairs. Katie walked in front of her, as William took Josie's arm. William would give Josie away, standing in place of her father. William was proud to escort his son's beautiful bride-to-be down the aisle.

Two trumpets played an uplifting wedding march as Katie, the maid of honor, walked down the grassy aisle to the arbor. Katie led the way in front of her dearest friend, Josie, and her father.

William beamed with pride as he gave John Josie's hand. Reginia shed tears of joy. How wonderful it was to have John marry Josie. The Wilde family loved Josie and were glad to have her legally bound to them! Their friends jumped and clapped their hands loudly as the minister pronounced them man and wife. John took Josie and kissed her passionately, lifting her in his strong arms as he turned about! Their friends clapped even louder, with the whistles from the men piercing the sunny sky. The behavior was rambunctious, but, after all, this was the wild Texas frontier!

The party lasted until late in the evening. Everyone feasted on the food and drank the wine and whiskey. Dancing on the wooden dance floor was a treat for all. John and Josie danced gaily to the waltzes. Every eye was on the handsome couple as John and Josie flowed about the floor with great ease and affection. John and Josie were young, yet mature beyond their years. They each knew exactly what they wanted from life. This was a new beginning for Josie, as far as she was concerned. Josie's past was finally behind her. A breeze of new life flowed through her body. Her face shined with happiness and love.

John and Josie were leaving for Savannah to honeymoon. Josie loved the elegant South and longed to visit the beautiful city on the Atlantic. The Brazos was low and the boats could not travel to the Wilde Landing. They would have to travel to Houston and board a steamer for the Gulf. William made arrangements for them to take one of his ships to and from Savannah. They would be gone a month. Josie could hardly wait. She longed to be alone with John and lay by his side all through the night.

The party was long into the evening when Josie gathered her bouquet of flowers and threw them in the air to the waiting maidens. Katie caught the bouquet and held it close, jumping for joy. "I will be married next!" she screamed with delight.

John took the garter from Josie's leg. The young single men formed a line to catch the garter. They teased one another, with pushes and shoves. John tossed the garter high in the air. They all ran to catch it, but it flew to the side and landed in the unexpected hands of Thad. Thad jumped and threw the garter high and away from himself. "Someone else take the darn thing, I don't want it! No woman is going to trap me!" The free-spirited Thad wanted no part of marriage. Everyone laughed at Thad and his apparent fear of the garter.

Belle stood by quietly, all during the wedding, watching all the white folks dancing and singing and having a merry time. She looked down at her hands that showed no trace of black blood in her. "Why, I am as white as these folks," she murmured to herself. Belle did not fit into the black man's world and wasn't accepted by the whites. She hated slavery, even at her young age. Rogette had educated her daughter well. Belle was intelligent, speaking English and French fluently. She was pretty and as graceful as her mother. She looked white and wanted to be accepted as white. Belle loved Samuel, but she began thinking that he could not possibly be her real father. If he was her real father, then why was she not dark?

John danced one last dance with Josie. Many people were still dancing and celebrating with the Wilde family. William, Tom Bradley, Joseph Riley, and Jim Wade offered toasts to the new couple all through the night. John took Josie by the hand and led her to the front door of the house. He stopped the music to make a brief speech. Friends and family gathered around them. John thanked them for coming and instructed them to continue celebrating and to have a good time. He swiftly lifted his bride in his arms and carried her into the house, while everyone clapped and cheered them on. The men whistled and shouted hoorays for John. Josie blushed with embarrassment as John carried her away!

William shouted, "On with the music, everyone dance and have a good time!"

John carried Josie up the stairs. She had her head on his shoulder, kissing his neck softly. He took her into his bedroom and closed the door with a kick of his heel. He looked into her eyes. "I love you, Josie Wilde." Her soft brown eyes sparkled with delight as the words "Josie Wilde" filled her ears. She loved the new name. She was proud to finally be a Wilde! They kissed passionately. John slowly let her down, turning her around, and began unbuttoning her wedding dress. He kissed her gently down the back with each open button. Still standing behind her, he slowly removed the dress from her shoulders, continuing to kiss each shoulder and down each arm, as the gown fell to the floor. John turned Josie toward him, kissing her neck and face. His lips searched for her lips as he kissed her gently. John had waited patiently for this moment with Josie and wanted to savor every part of her beautiful body. He carefully lifted her in his arms and kissed her, as he carried her to his bed.

CHAPTER
THIRTY-ONE

Everyone slept late that morning, except John and Josie. They dressed and walked the field by the house at sunrise. They were thrilled to be husband and wife. They lay in each other's arms, in the middle of the field, and watched the sun rise over the eastern sky. John kissed her tenderly in the morning light. Josie let her fingers wander across his muscular body as their bodies lay intertwined, in the grassy field.

John and Josie returned to the house to find their families and a few friends who had stayed over having a big breakfast. Reginia looked up with surprise as John and Josie entered the dining room. John and Josie were radiant with broad smiles on their faces. "My goodness, where have you two been? I thought you would sleep in this morning," Reginia exclaimed.

"We went for a walk and watched the sun rise," John said with a gleam in his eyes, as he grabbed Josie's hand, holding it tightly. John and Josie sat down and ate breakfast before preparing to leave on their honeymoon.

Rogette prepared a basket of food for Josie and John to take with them on their journey to Houston. She filled the basket with fried chicken, biscuits, and a bottle of fine wine. Big Bo would drive the carriage for Josie and John. William, Reginia, Katie, Thad, the Wades, and a few other friends stood on the porch with Rogette and Samuel in the rear waving goodbye to the newlyweds as the carriage pulled away.

John and Josie arrived at the great port of Savannah, located on the beautiful Savannah River. William made arrangements for his friend Alan Sharpe, who was also in the shipping business, to pick them up and take them to the hotel. Alan and his wife, Karly, entertained John and Josie, giving a grand ball in their honor and taking them on steamboat excursions up the Savannah River.

John and Josie were having a wonderful honeymoon in Savannah. They visited large Southern plantations that were owned by friends of the Sharpes. Josie thought Savannah to be the most beautiful and friendliest city in the world.

The last week of the honeymoon, John and Josie received a surprise visit. There was a knock one morning on the door of the hotel room. John could not imagine who would be calling on them so early in the morning. He put his pants on and went to the door. He was shocked and delighted to find Alex and Jacqueline. "Surprise!" Alex shouted as John opened the door. John stood in amazement for a brief moment, then suddenly, John grabbed his older brother and the two embraced heartily. Josie put her robe on and rushed to greet Jacqueline.

"What are you doing here?" John asked Alex with a great happiness in his voice.

"Well, if you invite us in, I'll tell you," Alex teased.

They all entered the room and Alex told John and Josie why they were in Savannah. "Mother sent us a letter, along with a clipping of your wedding announcement. Jacqueline and I couldn't make it to your wedding, so we made plans to intrude on your honeymoon!" Alex was humorous and they all laughed with excitement.

John and Josie dressed quickly and joined Alex and Jacqueline in the lobby of the hotel. They all had lunch that day with the Sharpes. Alex and Jacqueline knew Alan and Karly well. They had become good friends through the shipping business. Alex and Jacqueline stayed the week at the Sharpes' home, visiting and entertaining John and Josie. John and Alex shared their business ideas with one an-other. Alex was glad that John had such an interest in the Texas plantation. John and Alex enjoyed their time together, getting to know one another more personally. It would be the beginning of a long and close relationship.

Meanwhile, back in Texas, another incident took place that would change the lives of John and Josie. Don Barbeaux was sick and dying. The whiskey had eaten away at his liver, leaving Barbeaux yellow-skinned and feverish. John's beating had weakened Barbeaux, but it had knocked some sense into the dying man. Barbeaux feared his own death and wanted to do one thing that was good, before he died. Barbeaux gave one thousand dollars to his kept woman and sent her back to New Orleans. He sent for a lawyer, Jacob Crowe, and had his will drawn. Barbeaux left his home, wealth, and plantation to Josie. Barbeaux had Jacob write her formal name, Josette Evonne Barbeaux-Wilde. Barbeaux had no love for anyone but himself. But he hoped his one good deed would give him peace at death. Barbeaux gave Jacob instructions to deliver his will to William Wilde upon his death. Barbeaux died alone only two days later. Jacob took the will to William, whom he knew well, and explained what had taken place. William could not believe Barbeaux's change of heart. William gave all the credit to his good Lord.

Josie and John returned from their honeymoon, with wonderful stories about their trip and the unexpected visit from Alex and Jacqueline. William and Reginia took them into the library and asked them to be seated. William told them of Barbeaux's death. Josie shed not one tear. She only felt relief.

"Your father did one good deed before he died, Josie," William told her with a small smile of satisfaction on his face. He handed Josie the envelope containing Barbeaux's will. Josie opened the envelope and read the paper, never expecting to read anything like this from her father. She finished reading the will, with no expression on her face, and without saying a word, she handed the will to John to read.

John looked to Josie. "What do you think of this, Josie?" John asked as he finished reading over the document. He did not know how Josie felt about receiving her father's gift. Josie, still surprised by the will, shrugged her shoulders. She did not know how she felt.

William began to speak and told them the story of Barbeaux's death and everything Jacob Crowe had told him. "I think he just tried to find some peace within himself before he died," William concluded.

Reginia declared her thoughts to Josie. "I think you should accept the gift from your father, Josie, if for no other reason than for yourself and your mother. You have been through a lot with his cruelty and you deserve something good from him. Take the homeplace and build from it. With your own plantation and John's cattle business, the two of you will have a grand life. I feel, also, this is a gift from our Maker. Take it and enjoy it!"

Josie looked to John for approval. He looked into her eyes and nodded his head. Josie looked at William and Reginia. Both were smiling with happiness. She was very serious as she spoke. "There's one thing we must do first." They looked at Josie with curiosity. "John, you and I must fire that terrible overseer. His name is Spark Hunter. I want him gone immediately! He treats the slaves cruelly. His whip has left scars on the backs of most of them. I'll have no more of that on my land!" She looked at John and softly smiled. "Excuse me, John. Let me say 'our' plantation!"

The next morning, Josie and John, their bags packed, joined his parents and went to their plantation. John pulled the carriage to a stop in front of the Barbeaux home. The big, white, single-story house was erected on brick columns, standing eight feet high off the ground. A large porch graced the entire house, with wide curving staircases, on each side, descending to the ground. Beautiful iron work, bought in New Orleans, adorned the porch and staircases. Under the house were several carriages. A small iron staircase led upstairs from underneath. The house was extravagant. The lawn was manicured and lined with shrubs and roses. Wide brick walks enhanced the lawn. Don Barbeaux was extravagant and it showed in the luxury of the house place! John was excited to make this their home. He had no idea of the wealth that had been bestowed upon Josie!

They were getting out of the carriage, when the deep mahogany front door opened wide. Carrie Mae, the head house slave, came running down the stairs, with arms opened wide to Josie. "Missus Josie, Missus Josie," the black woman cried. "I ain't seen you in years!" Carrie looked at John and the gold band on Josie's finger. "Oh, my goodness sakes alive, child, have you done taken yourself a husband?"

"Yes, indeed I have. Carrie this is my husband, John Wilde, and his parents Mister and Missus Wilde."

"I's pleased to meet ya. Have you and your gentleman come to stay?" She was almost pleading. Josie hugged Carrie Mae warmly.

"Yes, Carrie, we have, and things are going to be a lot different around here now," Josie reassured Carrie. "Where is Spark Hunter? I want to see him immediately."

Carrie looked relieved and replied quickly, "He's at the barn. You wants me to fetch Mister Hunter for ya, Missus Josie?"

"No, Carrie. Master John and I will go to him. Please show Mister and Missus Wilde into the house and give them some tea." John liked the sound of Josie referring to him as Master John. He suddenly felt overwhelmed with pride. He never imagined having his own plantation. This was more than he had ever dreamed of.

John and Josie walked to the big barn. Carrie took William and Reginia into the house and served them tea from a silver tea-service set. As Josie and John entered the barn, they saw Spark beating a slave. Josie, filled with anger, shouted at Spark to stop. "Get your whip off my slave!" Spark looked up in surprise. The slave moved aside quickly. Spark knew nothing of Don Barbeaux's will.

"What are you doing here?" Spark questioned.

"This is our plantation now." She looked at John, standing right beside her. John was proud of Josie for standing her ground so bravely. He would let her speak her mind to Spark. "Father left his belongings to me and the first thing I wanted was to get rid of you!" She had had enough of his brutality.

"You can't fire me," he asserted.

"I can. As a matter of fact, I just did! Now, get your things together and get off this plantation. I better never see your face here again!" She was firm and this angered Spark. He started toward Josie, and John stepped forward.

"You want some of me, Spark? Just keep coming." John had his fist raised. He would not allow anyone to disrespect his wife. Spark took one long look at the strapping young man and stepped back. "Now, you get your things and get, like my wife told you to do." John hated the looks of Spark, with his deeply set, cruel eyes and spiteful grin.

"Look, don't get me wrong. I was just doing what your pa would want. I need my job." Spark tried to recover his error in judgment, looking to Josie and back to John.

"No, I don't think we need your kind on this plantation. Now pack up and be on your way. I don't want to see you around here again," John warned Spark.

"You can't do this. I need my job. Look, I'll do whatever you want. I don't need a whip to make these niggers do what I want."

"It's too late. You'll never change. Now leave." Josie stood firm in her decision.

"You'll regret this. I've been with your father most of my life. I'll be back. You can bet on that." Spark turned and stormed off.

John and Josie watched as Spark gathered his belongings and mounted his horse. "Like I said, you're gonna regret this." Spark kicked the horse hard, and galloped down the lane off the Barbeaux plantation.

John and Josie walked back into the barn. She turned to the slave that was still kneeling in the corner of the barn. "What is your name?" Josie asked sweetly.

"My name is Bim, Ma'am," the black man replied shakily. He could not believe what had happened.

"Bim, I want you to go to your quarters and put something on your wounds. Then I want you to get all the slaves and come to the main house this evening after work. I want to tell you all that will take place here from now on." Bim left and spread the news among the other slaves about the meeting and the new mistress and master of the plantation. He gladly told them that Spark Hunter was gone!

John and Josie joined Reginia and William. William asked if everything was all right. John told him things could not be better. John and Josie told them of their plans to meet with the slaves and how they wanted to run the plantation. John expressed to his father that he would need to find an overseer, quickly. William thought a minute. He had an idea. "You know who would be excellent? Jake Riley. He works with his father and knows farming and cattle well." "That is a good idea," John thought. Joseph Riley had done well, but he was far from wealthy. He would offer the job to Jake with good pay and a home to live in.

"I will go to Jake and Joseph when we get home. I will have him come see you tomorrow." William hoped Jake would accept the offer. William and Reginia left and returned home, excited for John and Josie.

Josie took John all through the house. It was furnished magnificently. The rooms were filled with beautiful wool rugs and fine furniture. The house had three large bedrooms, a dining room, parlor, library, and a music room that housed a grand piano. Josie showed John the bedroom she had had growing up. She led him to the bedroom her father had inhabited. It still smelled of whiskey and the smoke from his cigars. She pulled back the heavy drapes and opened the double glass doors, which opened onto the porch, and let sunlight and fresh air into the room. The room had a big fireplace and beautiful wood walls. Josie wanted the big room, which faced the east, for herself and John, so the morning sun could shine on their bed as they awoke. John liked that idea. She left the doors open all week to air the room. She and John would sleep in her old bedroom until she had the big bedroom redone and clear of any remembrances of her father.

Josie and John went into the parlor. There was a large painting of Don Barbeaux hanging over the ornate fireplace. "Take it down, John." Josie wanted nothing to remind her of her father and did not want to see the painting for a moment longer. Josie's mother had decorated the house and everything in it helped Josie to feel close to her. While John took the painting down, Josie hurried to the attic with Carrie at her heels. Josie found the oil painting of her mother. The painting had been done while her mother was young and filled with love for her father. Her mother had had striking features. Her rosy cheeks and light brown hair accented her hazel eyes, which had once been bright and full of life. The frame for the painting was ornate with wood carvings. Josie dusted the frame and asked Carrie to take it to John, in the parlor. Carrie gladly did as she was asked. He hung the painting carefully, in replacement of Don Barbeaux's. Josie stood back and looked at her mother's painting. She was satisfied.

"What shall I do with this?" John asked, as he pointed to the painting of Barbeaux.

"Burn it," Josie replied emphatically. And so, the painting was burned, to fulfill her wishes.

That afternoon the slaves gathered about the Barbeaux home. The house sat on a small rise overlooking the Brazos River. Josie and John stood on the porch looking down at the many slaves who had gathered there. Josie explained who she was, for some did not realize she was Barbeaux's daughter, and told them that John would be their new master. She assured them of good treatment, and promised them that, in the future, kind words would replace harsh treatment in the running of the plantation. She promised an easier life for them. All she expected from them was loyalty and good honest work. She told them to repair the quarters and to come to Carrie with any need they had. Josie told them they would hire a new overseer, but whomever they hired would be a good man! The slaves shouted with joy. Josie looked about the lawn. The holly that lined the lawn were full of red berries.

"Never refer to the plantation as the Barbeaux plantation. From now on, it shall be called the Holly Hill plantation."

John looked at her. "Where did she get that?" he wondered. She told them to butcher a calf and celebrate. "And I want to hear you singing melodies, all the way up here!" Josie loved to hear the slaves sing, as they did every evening at Auburn. The slaves did as their mistress requested. They butchered a calf and cooked it outside, singing and celebrating until late in the night.

The weather was mildly cool that late November evening. Josie and John held each other's hands, as they sat on their porch under the warm glow of the lanterns, listening to the slaves rejoicing in their hymns. Life could not be better for them. Josie told John why she had named the plantation Holly Hill. John liked it. He thought the name had a nice ring to it. Josie and John both knew in their hearts that their new home was truly a gift from God, and they would do their best to care for the big plantation, now called Holly Hill.

CHAPTER
THIRTY-TWO

The next morning, Jake arrived, smiling broadly. He was so happy for John and Josie. He eagerly accepted John's offer to oversee Holly Hill. John and Josie took Jake to see the frame house that had been built for Spark Hunter. It was a two-bedroom, quaint wooden home. The house was painted white with dark shutters gracing the windows. The house had a small porch in front and was completely furnished. Josie was glad for one thing. Her father did want everything to look perfect and beautiful. If only he had been as perfect, as the way he wanted everything around him to be! Jake was excited with the money John offered and the house was an added thrill for Jake. "When do you want me to start work?" Jake asked with enthusiasm.

"Right now," John laughed.

"Let me ride home and get my things. I will be back before the sun sets!" The young men shook hands and Jake left to get his belongings.

John wanted to get to know some of the head slaves, so Josie left John and returned to the house to begin cleaning out the bedroom her father had used. She got Carrie and several black girls and a couple of strong black men to help move the bedroom furniture out. She had the men move all the furniture to the largest of the two bedrooms in the overseer's house. She wanted to give Jake the furnishings. She appreciated his taking the offer and wanted to do something extra nice for him. Besides, she wanted nothing in the room to remind her of her father.

Josie was busy cleaning out the bedroom, when Jacob Crowe arrived. He had finalized all the legal papers for Barbeaux and wanted to show Josie all of Barbeaux's holdings. Her inheritance was a fortune. He not only owned a bank and a fine hotel in New Orleans, but the man had two hundred thousand dollars in cash, probably acquired in his successful gambling days. Josie, in utter surprise, sat quietly for minutes. She looked to Mr. Crowe. "My goodness, I am rich! I had no idea . . . "

She jumped from her chair and bolted for the door, running quickly to John. Josie told him the wonderful news. John couldn't believe it. Why, they were as rich as his own parents, if not richer! John grabbed Josie and swung her around and around. She gripped his waist with her legs and held tight with her arms around his neck as they spun about! The two went to Mr. Crowe, who stood on the porch smiling at the pleasure he had brought them, and thanked him. Mr. Crowe wished them well and returned to Houston.

The bedroom was empty and free of any indication of Don Barbeaux's former presence. Josie had Carrie and the girls scrub the walls with soap and water to remove the stale odors of whiskey and tobacco. The walls and floor were scrubbed and polished with bee's wax. Josie gave the rug, drapes, and bedspread to Carrie for her quarters. Carrie was thrilled to have the beautiful things. The women had worked all week cleaning the room to perfection. Everything shined bright and clean.

Josie wanted to fill the room with fine furnishings, a new rug, and fabrics of bright colors. She talked John into taking her to New Orleans on a shopping expedition. Josie wanted the room finished by Christmas and she wanted to see her newly acquired hotel. John agreed. He knew Jake was capable of running Holly Hill in his absence. The two departed immediately for New Orleans.

They arrived at Josie's hotel the following week. When she introduced herself, the hotel employees went out of their way for her and John. John and Josie spent the first day with the manager of the magnificent hotel making all the arrangements Josie deemed necessary. Shopping in New Orleans was exciting for Josie and John. They bought beautiful fabrics filled with deep green and burgundy colors. John found a huge, beautiful four-poster bed with a dresser and long mirror. It had two armoires to match. Josie spotted two overstuffed chairs in the corner of a shop. They were covered in a deep green linen that matched the fabrics she had selected, perfectly. Josie had to have them. The wool rug had all the same colors as the fabric. Josie could picture how beautiful the room would be. Fine china vases were bought for the room. John and Josie bought all the Wildes lavish gifts for Christmas. Josie picked up special gifts for Jake, Carrie, Belle, Rogette, and Samuel.

Josie and John were exhausted from shopping. They had crammed their shopping into just two days. They were both eager to return home. The three days spent in New Orleans had been thrilling, as they boarded the ship with all their new belongings and headed home.

It was the second week of December when John and Josie arrived back at Houston. Jake was waiting at the dock with the wagons and slaves to carry all the fine furnishings to Holly Hill. Josie was so excited when the wagons pulled up to the big house. The slaves carried the big rug up the stairs and spread it across the center of the bedroom floor, at Josie's direction. Josie waited in the bedroom, having the slaves place all the furniture exactly where she wanted it. The large four-poster bed was centered on the wall opposite the big glass doors. The two green-covered chairs were placed on each side of the fireplace. Each piece of furniture fit in the room perfectly. She had the slaves put the big bathing tub in the corner nearest the fireplace, with a beautifully carved wooden screen from her old bedroom in front of the tub, concealing it from the rest of the room. The room was finally in order. How beautiful it looked and how fresh it smelled!

John wanted to visit with Jake, and Josie was eager to begin making the drapes and spread for the bedroom. She summoned Carrie to find women from the slave quarters that could sew well. Josie sketched drawings of how she wanted the drapes and spread made. Carrie returned with five women to sew the fine linen. The women sewed without stopping, except to eat, sleep, and relieve themselves, for five days straight. The drapes were lined with heavy burlap for warmth, and the spread was filled with cotton, backed with cotton fabric, and tacked in large squares. The drapes were hung on the big iron rod over the glass doors. The knobs on the end of the rod were ornate and accentuated the richly colored fabric. The women laid the spread on the bed. They all stood back and admired the room.

"This room's beautiful! It's just as I imagined it would look. Thank you for all your hard work." Josie exclaimed, as she hugged Carrie.

Josie led John upstairs that night after dinner. John didn't know the room was finished. She opened the door and his eyes filled with wonder. The fabrics added the finishing touch. Never had John seen such an exquisite setting. The fire burned slowly in the fireplace, adding a soft glow to the room. John hugged Josie and kissed her tenderly. He lifted her and put her gently on the big bed. Josie sank in the soft mattress as he lay down by her, slowly seducing her with his kisses. Josie felt blessed to have John's love and a life that was finally good. She lay in John's arms that night sleeping peacefully, as the fire burned slowly in the fireplace.

December 25, 1848, was clear and the air was crisp. John's family came to join him and Josie for the Christmas celebration. Carrie prepared a feast for the two families. John said grace before they ate, giving thanks to God for all He had blessed them with. Everyone ate and later exchanged gifts, as they sat around the big cedar Christmas tree. Katie and Thad marveled at their gifts from Josie and John. They gave Katie a ruby ring and Thad an original bowie knife. William and Reginia were pleased as well. William enjoyed a new smoking pipe with fine tobacco and Reginia loved her new silk gown and robe. Reginia played Christmas carols and favorite hymns on the piano while her family sang along. It reminded Reginia of the long past days in Mississippi with her own family. It was a meaningful day for Josie. This was the first happy holiday she had ever spent in the big home and 1848 had been a full and rewarding year.

CHAPTER
THIRTY-THREE

Texas continued to grow under the Union. Railroads extended through much of the eastern states, as far as Savannah. The settlers in the Houston area talked of building a railway to serve the surrounding region. William spent a great deal of his time in Houston, discussing these plans with other businessmen. The railroads were reliable transportation in the East and William could see the need for Texas to flourish as the eastern states. During the 1850s, the railroads would expand, entering Texas and the Houston area.

William expanded his planting fields, becoming one of the largest cotton planters in the area. Ransom became more than an overseer for William. With the marriage of John and Josie, William lost the prospect of having John take over the great plantation. William turned over more responsibility to Ransom as William continued spending much of his time in Houston and in New Orleans with the shipping business. Ben, Josh, and William met frequently as the business grew. They owned many ships now, and controlled most of the shipping through the Gulf. Alex had worked hard, dedicating long hours to his business. Alex was brilliant in his business endeavors and deft in his public relations. He knew how to get his way with people and the two shipping companies became known throughout the States and England.

Thad dreamed of traveling the great frontier of the North. He had no interest in being tied down to one place. There was a great land to see and he wanted to see it all. Thad heard many tales of the mountains and rushing rivers, clear and cold with an abundance of trout! He longed to be old enough to leave for his explorations.

Katie was eager to start her adult life. She longed to be in love and married as were Josie and John. She visited her brother and Josie frequently. Katie and Josie sat for hours talking about love and marriage. Katie was restless, desiring more out of life. She worked with Ms. Georgia, in the school, helping all the pupils with their studies. Katie loved the children and longed for a family of her very own.

In the spring of 1851, Katie and Thad, much to Thad's disappointment, traveled with their parents to Boston. William and Reginia wanted the children to see their brother Alex and his family. Thad had no use for the big cities, with their modern ways. Thad wanted to travel the unsettled frontiers, but William forbade him to leave at the young age of seventeen. The Wildes arrived in Boston late in May. Alex and Jacqueline had many plans for their family. Katie was eager for the party Alex was preparing for that following Saturday. She wondered about Asa. What did he look like now, and what was he doing? Reginia and William spent most of their time with their grandchildren, Will, Sarah, and little Alex.

Saturday arrived and the house was filled with food, fine wines, and an orchestra. The party was elegant. Everyone dressed in their finest. Thad reluctantly dressed up for the party. Reginia thought how handsome Thad was when he put forth an effort. The evening filled with wonderful conversations and dancing. Thad entertained everyone with his stories of the Texas frontier. The young girls from Boston were intrigued by the handsome, free-spirited Thad. He danced with all of them, discovering his ability to attract the opposite sex. He enjoyed the girls making over him and wanting his attention. Katie quickly renewed her friendship with Asa. Asa found his attraction for Katie still very much alive. Never had any girl caught his affections as had the lovely and charming Katie.

Katie and Asa spent every day together for the next two weeks. Asa was studying medicine. He talked to Katie about Texas. Katie urged him to come. Asa promised he would when he finished school. Katie assured him that she would return to Boston the next year. Asa begged her to stay in Boston with Alex and Jacqueline. Katie could not possibly leave Texas for that long a time. She loved the great state and her life there. Asa longed to see the land that Katie loved so much.

Thad walked the streets of Boston with at least two or three young girls by his side. His vanity mounted to new heights! He could not imagine why John and Alex had married with so many girls available. Thad found them all friendly and pretty in their different ways. Why, he could love them all! He decided then, that would be exactly what he would do, love them all! He would never dull his life by settling down with one woman and raising a bunch of kids!

William and Alex spent their time with the business. They traveled to Washington, DC. Millard Fillmore was the president of the United States. William and Alex supported the Whig president. Alex knew many political leaders and he and William wanted to discuss world trade and the use of their ships with President Fillmore. Fillmore worked hard to increase world trade and William wanted to be a part of this. Fillmore gave his full support to the Compromise of 1850 that Webster and Clay initiated. The compromise would allow slavery to continue in the South. The abolitionists were enraged. Fillmore thought his support would win him favor on both sides of the slavery issue. Fillmore's support of the compromise would cost him the next presidential election. William, however, was pleased with the compromise. It gave him hopes for continued success in the cotton industry. Alex and William talked with Fillmore extensively, giving him their ideas and support, and hoping for favors in return.

Katie and Asa took the carriage to the country for a picnic, one beautiful spring afternoon, just after the Wildes returned home. Katie spread the cloth on the ground as Asa retrieved the basket full of food from the carriage. They conversed all afternoon in the shade of the big tree. Asa longed to kiss Katie. They had been young teenagers when he had kissed her last. Katie still wore the necklace Asa had given her. Asa spotted the chain around her neck and pulled it up gently in his hands.

"You're still wearing the necklace I gave you," Asa spoke softly as he gazed into her eyes.

Katie blushed and lowered her eyes. "Yes, I have never taken it off."

Asa placed his forefinger under her chin and lifter her head slowly, until their eyes met. He looked into her large eyes with great affection. "Katie, do you care as much for me, as I care for you?"

Katie felt vulnerable by the question as she responded, hoping his feelings were indeed as strong as hers. "I care deeply for you, Asa. I always have."

Asa gently reached for Katie, kissing her softly. "Someday, I want to marry you, Katie. Would you be my wife?"

Katie was shocked. She spoke without giving the matter any thought. "Yes, oh, yes I will!" Asa embraced Katie and held her tightly as they made plans for their future. She relished the warm feeling she had as Asa held her. They spoke of marriage and their desires for children and a home. Asa wanted to be a doctor in Texas! Katie was thrilled beyond belief! She could not wait to tell Josie the good news. They returned to Alex's, beaming, as they told their family of their plans for marriage. William and Reginia were pleased. They liked Asa and knew he would be good to Katie. William was happy for Katie. Asa was a good man, William only wished Katie had fallen in love with someone who would be interested in the plantation.

The last night in Boston, Asa, his parents, and both Wilde families enjoyed fine dining and conversation at Alex's home. The talk at the dining table focused around the engagement of Asa and Katie. Asa would graduate in two years and his mother, Caroline, wanted them to marry in Boston. Caroline wanted a large celebration with all their friends. Reginia and William looked at Katie, then to each other. Katie had a look of disappointment on her face. Reginia did not say a word and squeezed William's hand, under the table, with a signal to allow their daughter to handle her own affairs.

Asa looked at Katie hopefully. Katie, outspoken as she was, sweetly smiled and replied with great assurance, "This is something I feel Asa and I must talk about in private."

Caroline was firmly rooted in her idea of the wedding. She assumed Katie would consent to marrying Asa in Boston. Caroline did not want Asa in Texas! Her family was prominent in the East as was her husband's. She wanted Katie and Asa to carry on the family name in Boston. Caroline continued speaking of her plans for Katie and Asa. Katie sat straight in her chair, smiling with an air of discontent. Reginia knew her daughter's strong will. She knew whatever Katie decided would be between her and Asa and no one else!

That night, after dinner, Asa and Katie went for a stroll, hand in hand. They spoke of the marriage and Asa was more than eager to move to Texas. Katie wanted to marry at Auburn. Asa did not want to disappoint his mother. She had been good to him and had supported him in all his ideas and plans. How could he disappoint her? But how could he deny Katie, the one he loved, her wishes? Asa was torn and Katie was determined. Asa hugged Katie and reassured her that he would allow her to have her wishes fulfilled. Katie threw her arms around Asa. "Thank you, this means so much to me." He was glad he had pleased Katie but doubts about his mother bothered him as he kissed her ever so tenderly.

The next morning, the Wildes boarded the ship for home. Asa hugged Katie goodbye. Their young hearts were filled with sadness by the parting. Jacqueline, Alex, and their children waved goodbye as the ship left the harbor. William and his family stopped in New Orleans and took a steamer up the river to Natchez. They spent a week visiting old friends and family. Unbeknownst to them, this would be the last trip William and Reginia would make to Natchez.

THIRTY-FOUR

The last week of June found William and his family back in Texas. A heat wave settled over the great state and the humidity added to the heat. It was smoldering hot. The slaves could only work until mid-afternoon. The Wildes arrived at the plantation to find John. He had arrived at Auburn early that morning to start the slaves working. John was giving directions to Big Bo for the work that needed to be done before mid-day. William could not imagine why John was doing this. Big Bo greeted William and his family warmly, with sadness in his eyes, before leaving for the fields.

"Father, Mother, how was your trip?" He embraced his parents and Katie. Thad put his hand out to John for a strong friendly shake.

"It was a good trip. I will tell you all about it later." William's curiosity was building. "What is going on, John? Where is Ransom?"

John hesitated. He dreaded what he had to tell his parents. "Father, a terrible thing has happened. Please, all of you come inside and I will tell you."

They all went into the house, out of the scorching heat. Rogette and Samuel greeted them and gave them cool lemonade to drink when they were all seated.

"Father, the heat has been unbearable," John continued. "Ransom was working in the barn, despite the high temperatures. Big Bo found him unconscious in the hayloft. It must have been a hundred and ten degrees up there! Bo carried him to Doctor Bradley. He cared for Ransom and did all he could. Ransom died that night. Seemed like a heat stroke. We buried Ransom last week. I have been trying to manage Auburn, until you returned." John spoke with great concern for his father. He did not know what his father would do without Ransom. Good overseers were hard to find and his father had relied on Ransom completely.

William sat staring in shock. He could not believe Ransom was gone. Ransom had been with William for over forty years. Reginia took William's hand and squeezed it gently. William grieved for Ransom.

"Father, I will come each morning and help you, until you find someone to replace Ransom. Jake is taking care of Holly Hill just fine. You need to take your time and find someone as capable of running this place as Ransom was." John was sincere and dedicated to his father.

"Father, I will help too. I don't know as much as John, but he can teach me." Thad earnestly supported John's suggestion.

William looked at his two sons proudly. He expected this offer from John, but not from Thad. William's heart filled with emotion at the sight of his sons, side by side, in this decision. Reginia squeezed his hand again to console him and to support the boys' offer. William squeezed Reginia's hand, in return. "Thank you, John, and thank you, Thad, very much. I will take you up on your offer. I would like to see Ransom's grave and pay my last respects. We must get a headstone for him."

"I have taken care of that, Father," John said as William stood up, taking Reginia by the arm.

"Take us now, to see Ransom," William implored.

John took them out the back door and toward the burial site. Ransom was buried not far from little Sarah. "We buried him here, Father, in our family section. We were actually all the family Ransom had."

"This is good, John." William stood with Reginia at his side, holding her hand, looking down at the grave of his friend and overseer. "How will I ever replace Ransom?" he wondered.

"You will. We will put out word and someone good will come. We will place a notice in the newspaper and send word into Houston,"

Reginia reassured William. Her tone revealed the inner strength she had to survive the frontier.

The summer passed with John and Thad working side by side. John taught Thad all that Ransom had taught him. In the evenings, after dinner, William taught Thad how to keep the books. Thad dedicated himself to learning and helping his father, but he did not want this to be his lifelong job! His dreams were in the mountains of the Kansas Territory, which would later become the state of Colorado.

William interviewed many men for the job of overseer. News of the abolitionists' fight to free the slaves had reached Texas. Most of William's slaves were content. They actually feared freedom. Their life at Auburn was good and they wondered what they would do if they were freed. However, many slaves were badly abused on other plantations and longed to be free. Some escaped their owner's wrath by the underground railroad to the East. William had to hire the right man, one who was good-hearted, kind, and with the knowledge of how to run a plantation. The search was a difficult one. It was the spring of 1853 before the right person arrived for the job.

Josh Strong had met Stanley Groves in New Orleans. Stanley was tall and thin and in his early thirties. He was a good and generous man with great respect among the plantation owners. He handled the slaves without the whip and with kindness. He oversaw a large plantation just outside of New Orleans and shared his ideas with Josh about longing to work on the Texas frontier. Josh told Stanley he had a friend who had lost his overseer to death. Josh told him all about the Wildes, Auburn, and his business dealings with William. Stanley was very interested in meeting William and possibly working for him. Josh agreed to write to William and tell him about Stanley. A few weeks later, Josh received a letter from William. He was eager to meet the man Josh spoke of highly. Josh told Stanley the good news and sent him immediately to meet with William.

Stanley arrived at Auburn within the month. After a brief conversation, William hired him. William trusted Josh's judgment and liked the way Stanley presented himself. John was glad to finally have someone to replace him—as was Thad. Thad was nineteen and eager to proceed with his plans to explore the mountains and rivers of the wild.

John returned home to Josie to tell her about the hiring of Stanley. She was so pleased to hear the good news and glad to have her husband home during the daylight! Josie and John still had no children, after trying so hard. Josie became fearful and wanted to speak with Dr. Bradley about her problem. Josie kept her concerns to herself, but decided to speak with Tom the next day. John wanted to take her to meet Stanley and she would speak with Tom then.

The next day, Josie and John went to his parents. John introduced her to Stanley. Josie found the man to be sincere and filled with kindness, much like Ransom. They visited over lunch; afterward, Josie slipped away to speak with Tom. She knocked at his door and Tom came immediately. "Hello, Doctor Bradley, may I speak with you?" she asked nervously.

"Why certainly. Come on in. Maggie and I just finished lunch. Have you eaten?" Tom took Josie into the parlor as he welcomed her to lunch.

"Yes, we ate with Mister and Missus Wilde. I just met Stanley. He is such a nice man. I am so glad for Mister Wilde." Josie continued making conversation.

"Have a seat young lady, and tell me what I can do for you." Tom always had an open ear and was always willing to help.

"I think I may have a problem." Josie became nervous and embarrassed. Her hands became clammy as she twisted them together rapidly. She hung her head shyly.

"Don't be nervous, Josie. Is this a personal problem or a medical problem?" he spoke with his soothing voice. He placed his arm around Josie's shoulders as he sat down by her on the sofa. "Now, it is all right. Why don't you just tell me what is wrong and maybe I can help you."

"Well," she stuttered. "I think it could be personal and medical. You see, Doctor Bradley, John and I have been married four years, almost five years"—she corrected herself—"and we still have no children."

"Oh, I see. You obviously want children, to be so concerned."

"Oh, yes we do. We have tried very hard but I am still not pregnant." Josie began to cry softly.

"Don't cry, my dear. Why don't you come into my office and I will examine you. Let me get Maggie to assist me." Tom got Maggie and the three went into his office. He checked Josie thoroughly and could find nothing physically wrong. He patted Josie on the shoulder and told her to sit up. "You look healthy as can be! You know, sometimes when you want something badly you get all tied up inside with your nerves. I bet if you did not try so hard and just relaxed, you would get pregnant very soon. You and John have been under a great deal of strain lately. Try drinking a glass of wine before you go to bed at night. The wine will relax you and you just might get pregnant!"

Maggie talked to Josie, while Josie dressed, to reassure her that everything would be all right and told Josie she would soon have a bunch of kids tracking in and out of her house! Josie laughed with relief. She thanked Maggie and Tom as she left their house. She asked them to keep her visit a secret and they agreed they would. Josie ran to the big house to see Katie. She wanted to spend time with her before going home to try the wine!

Josie ran up the stairs to find Katie in her room. The girls had visited long hours together after Katie had returned from Boston. Josie was so thrilled with the announcement of Katie's engagement. Time was nearing for the wedding. They wanted to marry that fall. Katie was determined to marry and live in Texas, near her father's plantation. Katie sat on the bed with her head down.

"What is wrong, Katie? Why do you look so sad this beautiful day?" Josie was bouncing with excitement, with the remarkable news that she could bear children.

"Oh, it is Asa. I received a letter from him and he's giving in to his mother. Now, he not only wants to marry in Boston, but he asks if I would like to live in Boston the first few years, while he practices medicine! Well, I will not! He only is asking this because of Missus Rhome. This is our life! He wanted to come to Texas to live. Why can he not stand up for our wishes!"

"Now, Katie, I am sure he will, once you let him know how strongly you want to live in Texas." Josie tried to comfort Katie with her soft voice.

"Well, it takes a man of fortitude to live in Texas, a man with guts! And he better find some, and stand up to his mother!"

Josie smiled sympathetically. She knew it would take a strong-willed man to be married to Katie, one who could stand on his own decisions. Josie wanted to ask Katie to spend the night with her and John, but she thought of the wine and her other plans with John. She decided to postpone the invitation. The girls visited for several hours before Josie and John returned home.

Josie and John sat on the front porch of their fine home sipping wine and gazing lazily into the clear, moonlit sky. There was a gentle breeze that evening, which cooled the air from the blistering heat of the day. They could hear the slaves singing hymns in the background. John pointed out the constellations to Josie, as she slowly sipped her wine. Josie reached for the decanter and poured them another glass. She wanted to ensure that she was totally relaxed by the time they went to bed.

An hour passed with easy conversation and sounds of the rhythmical songs of their slaves, still echoing in the night. Josie felt relaxed and was a bit tipsy from the wine. She reached to John and took his hand, fondling each of his fingers, purposefully. Josie, now thoroughly aroused, slowly began to seduce John. She got up from her chair and knelt before him. She slowly unbuttoned his shirt, while stretching upward and kissing his muscular chest with each motion. John was pleasantly surprised and very aroused by Josie's first attempt to initiate lovemaking! Josie continued her seduction until she and John could not resist one another any longer. He reached down and picked her up and carried her off to the bedroom, kissing her passionately all the way. They were filled with desire for one another, making love several times before falling to sleep.

John enjoyed Josie's approach to making love so much, that each evening he got the wine and took Josie by the hand to the front porch. They enjoyed the splendor of lovemaking each evening that week. The following Friday, Katie appeared on their doorstep to stay for the weekend. Katie ended their time of sipping wine on the porch! Katie was still troubled by the letter from Asa. She wanted to talk with Josie. Josie was glad Katie came to her. John listened to his sister go on and on about Asa for over an hour. "Ladies, if you will excuse me, I think I will go to bed." John excused himself politely. He had listened to all the girl talk he could stand for one evening! Katie eagerly excused John before Josie had a chance to say a word. She was eager to get into a deeper discussion with Josie about Asa and did not want John to hear what she had to say.

Josie listened patiently to Katie, as Katie tried to sort out her feelings for Asa. "You know, Josie, I'm beginning to question my love for Asa. I'm not sure this is the type of man I want to be married to for the rest of my life. I want a man who can make a solid decision and stand by it. I don't want a man who falters on every judgment. I want a man just like my father. One with his own ideas and dreams. A man who is strong. That is what I want!" Katie was abrupt. She did indeed know just what she wanted and like her father she was very strong-willed.

Josie grinned, trying to prevent herself from laughing aloud. She thought how Katie wanted all these things in a man as long the man was doing what she wanted!

Katie talked and Josie listened until midnight. Josie offered only one bit of advice. "Katie, this is the rest of your life you are talking about. You must only do what is in your heart and what will truly make you happy. We live a short while on this old earth and we must make the most of every moment. If you make a mistake, you not only hurt yourself, but you will hurt Asa too. You must marry Asa only if you love him and can accept him the way he is. Maybe, living in Boston are his true wishes."

Katie just looked at Josie. She knew this was a matter she would give a great deal of thought. "Thank you, Josie, for listening to me. Maybe I am too headstrong. But you are right and life is short." Katie tossed her curls as she got up to go to bed. She turned to Josie with a grin on her face and pointed her finger at her. "And you know what? I'm going to live my life the way I want to!"

Josie shook her head. She only hoped there was a man who could stand up to Katie.

Katie lay in bed, going over each word Josie had spoken. Josie gave her sound advice and Katie had a lot to think about. She could appreciate Asa wanting to stay in Boston, but she was sure she did not love him enough to move from Texas.

Sunday morning, John, Josie, and Katie went to church. The small church was full. They rushed to sit with William, Reginia, and Thad. The day was bright and full of the hot sun. After church, they decided to take Thad and the four of them would go for a swim and picnic at Best Creek. Thad's friend Mark wanted to go along for the swim. "The more the merrier," Katie shouted with her spunky voice. They all climbed into John's carriage and went by way of Auburn, singing and laughing all the way.

They stopped at the Wilde home so the girls could prepare a picnic lunch. Full of excitement, Katie jumped from the carriage first and ran into the house ahead of everyone else. She flung the door open as she ran into the foyer. She was not paying attention as she ran into the tall stranger who had just descended the stairway. Katie jumped back with surprise! There stood a tall, lanky, blond-haired, young man with piercing blue eyes. His skin was the color of gold. His good looks captivated Katie. "Excuse me," she exclaimed. She had no idea who the good-looking stranger was. She fumbled for her words. "Who are you and what are you doing in my house?" She shocked and embarrassed herself by her curt words. "How could I sound so rude to this perfectly handsome stranger?" she thought. She immediately apologized.

The young man, in his mid-twenties, just looked at the redheaded beauty, so full of life, and smiled. "My name is Quincy Tyler, Dr. Quincy Tyler. My uncle is Tom Bradley. I have come for a visit and the Wildes were nice enough to let me stay here. I didn't arrive until late in the evening. I am afraid I slept in and did not make it to church this morning, with Uncle Tom and Aunt Maggie." Quincy was direct with his words and spoke with elegance. She appreciated his gracious manners.

"Where are you from?" she quizzed.

"I am from Virginia, originally. I have been in New Orleans the past year practicing medicine."

John, Josie, Thad, and Mark entered the house. Katie proudly introduced Quincy. "Quincy, I would like for you to meet my brothers, John and Thad, and Thad's friend Mark Mathis. This is John's wife and my best friend, Josie. This is Doctor Quincy Tyler." Katie explained who

Quincy was and why he was visiting. The men shook hands. John was cordial and invited Quincy to go with them for the picnic and swim. The thought of cool water sounded inviting to Quincy and he gladly accepted. Katie beamed, as she took Josie to help her prepare the lunch.

The six young adults reached the creek shortly after one o'clock. The sun was high and hot. They all ran for the water, jumping in and splashing one another as if they were teenagers once again! Thad and Mark took turns swinging from the long rope, attached to an overhanging limb, into the water, while the others frolicked in the creek. Katie was such a flirt, as she used her charm she had inherited from her mother on Quincy. He found her exciting. Her fair skin sparkled in the sunlight, as the water dripped off her. Swimming had made them all hungry. John spread the blanket while Josie and Katie took the food from the basket. Katie dominated the conversations, asking Quincy many questions. He told them all about himself. He told of his life in Virginia on his family's plantation, his schooling, and his life in New Orleans. Katie batted her big eyes as she flirted with Quincy. Josie poked John and winked at him. Josie knew Katie had no thoughts of Asa that day!

"How long will you be here," Katie asked Quincy, hoping he was staying for a while.

"I will be here for the rest of the summer, at least. Uncle Tom is thinking of retiring. He and Aunt Maggie want to travel to the East and abroad. Uncle Tom made good investments and now wants to enjoy his life, so he says!" Quincy laughed, remembering the way his uncle Tom had made that statement. "Uncle Tom wants me to take over his practice. I am going to stay for a while and work with him. If 1 like Texas, I will stay, as my uncle wishes."

Katie was overjoyed. She wanted Quincy to not just like Texas, but to love it! She began telling him all the wonderful attributes of her great state. She chatted on and on about Texas, until John broke in and changed the subject. They engaged in conversation all afternoon. Thad and Mark told of their plans to explore the mountainous frontier. Katie and Quincy could not take their eyes off one another. Asa was absent from Katie's mind. She could see nothing but the golden gentleman before her.

Katie and Quincy spent hours visiting and getting to know one another over the weeks that followed. Quincy spent his days with Tom, tending to the sick. The evenings, however, were spent with Katie. Katie could not wait to speak with Josie. One Monday morning, following a Sunday swimming trip to the creek with Quincy, Katie rode to see Josie. It was mid-morning when Katie arrived. She jumped off her horse and rushed up the stairs and into the house. Carrie greeted her in the foyer. "Where is Josie?" Katie asked, excited and half out of breath.

"Missus Josie, she's on the back porch. You sure do seems like you's in a hurry, Miss Katie," Carrie responded.

"I am, Carrie. I surely am," Katie said as she rushed to find Josie. As she went on about her chores, Carrie shrugged her shoulders, giggling at the young girl's excitement. Katie went to the back porch where she found Josie darning socks for John.

"Katie, what a nice surprise. Sit down and have some lemonade with me." Josie set her darning down and poured them each a glass of lemonade from the pitcher that sat on the ornate wrought-iron table. "Well, what have you been up to? We haven't seen you in a while."

"Oh, Josie." Katie had a smile from ear to ear as she told Josie about Quincy. "Quincy is just wonderful! We have spent every evening together since we all went swimming that Sunday! He is so intelligent and warm. He is strong and handsome and knows just what he wants out of life! Oh, and that golden skin and those crystal-blue eyes just excite my very soul! He is such a man!" Katie was totally taken by Quincy. Josie became amused by Katie's intensity. Katie talked at length about Quincy, never once mentioning Asa.

"Katie, you speak of Quincy with such fondness. What about Asa?"

"Well, I've given some thought to what you advised me, concerning my life and marriage. I just do not think Asa is the man for me. He needs to marry someone who can live in Boston with him and his mother! I have already written to him and broken the engagement. And I already know what you are thinking." Katie grinned at Josie. "Quincy had nothing to do with my decision to end the engagement with Asa. Well, not directly, anyway. But I did realize, by getting to know Quincy, that there are more fish in the sea, so to speak!"

Josie laughed. She did feel that Katie had made the right decision, whether Quincy was the right man for her or not. Katie continued. "We went for a swim yesterday and sat under the big oak for hours just talking and laughing." Josie thought back to the time when she and John spent so many days doing the same. "Oh, Josie, I feel so good when I am with him and he feels the same way about me. He is going to stay and take over his uncle's practice. I am so excited! He kissed me, Josie. I felt goose bumps all up my spine! Why, goodness me! I had a flash of heat surge through me like never before! Oh, he is such a man! I am going to marry Doctor Quincy Tyler, you just wait and see!" Katie was exuberant with joy. She had never felt so strongly about anything in her life. Josie held back her laughter at the sight of Katie. Katie had such a way with words. Josie just loved Katie, with all her energy and love for life.

Katie never heard from Asa. That October, Katie did marry her Dr. Quincy Tyler. Their wedding was on a grand scale, just as John and Josie's had been. Everyone in the area came. Quincy met everyone and charmed them with his social grace. The Bradleys and Wildes were thrilled by the union of Katie and Quincy. Joseph and Golda came with their children. Jake came with his new bride. He had married a girl from Columbia he had met while on business for John. Katie was now twenty-one and glad she had waited for the right man.

Belle stood in the background watching the ladies and gentlemen dancing and enjoying the festivities. She was well into her teens and resented the freedom the whites had. Belle daydreamed for a different way of life for herself and all the slaves. She wondered what it must feel like to be able to make choices and to do what one desired. A glimmer came in her eyes as she stared at the crowd. "Somehow I am going to leave this plantation. I will be free and I am going to help my people," she said softly with determination in her voice.

The wedding ended and Katie and Quincy spent their first night together in her parents' home. They opted against leaving Auburn for a honeymoon. Tom Bradley planned to leave within the week and Quincy would have to be available to take his place. Katie did not mind. She was anxious to begin her role as Mrs. Quincy Tyler.

Tom and Maggie left on their travels, leaving their home and business to Quincy. Quincy and Katie could remain in their home, working out of Tom's small office until they returned. She assisted Quincy just as Maggie had assisted Tom. One night, as Quincy and Katie had dinner with her parents, William proposed, "Sweetheart, I have an offer for you and Quincy." Katie looked curiously at her father as he continued to speak. "I gave Alex a large sum of money upon his marriage, I gave John the cattle business for his marriage, and I want to give you something for your marriage. I know you and Quincy want a large family. So, your mother and I would like to give you land and build a house, with many bedrooms in it, for you two and all your children!" Katie and Quincy were thrilled. Quincy had no plans for farming, but a small amount of acreage would be nice for the horses and the few head of cows they needed for beef and milk.

Katie and Quincy were very grateful. William and Reginia wanted to show them the land: five hundred acres on the far southeast side of the plantation, near the church, school, and small settlement that was nearby. The next morning, they would look at the land.

That night, William showed them a drawing of the house he wanted to build them. It was beautiful. It had two stories with large porches and four bedrooms. Katie loved the house and was eager to decorate it. Reginia promised her a shopping trip to New Orleans. Katie could not wait!

Thanksgiving was a joyful time for all. William and Reginia had John, Josie, Katie, Quincy, and Jake and his wife, Trudy, along with Joseph, Golda, and their children, who were all grown, join them and Thad for the Thanksgiving feast. The day was filled with laughter and conversation.

After dinner, Thad announced his departure for the northern frontier with Mark. The two young men planned to leave the following March. William and Reginia hated to see Thad leave, but they understood his desire to explore a new frontier. William reflected on his young years and his own desire to explore and settle the Texas frontier.

Josie and John ended the day with excitement, as they shared their good news. Josie had become pregnant and was due in March. "Why, Josie, that is only four months away." Reginia was bewildered.

"I know. We didn't want to say anything until we were sure. I feared you would have guessed by my weight gain," Josie replied as she took John's hand for support.

"My goodness. I don't know how you kept this a secret. Why, I noticed that you had gained some weight. I just thought your appetite had increased." Everyone laughed.

"Seriously, I am very pleased." Reginia walked to Josie and hugged her and then turned to John with a smiling face. "So, you are going to be a father. It just seems like yesterday I was giving birth to you." Tears of joy filled her eyes as she hugged John.

William proudly hugged Josie and John. "You have made this Thanksgiving a very special occasion." Everyone took their turns congratulating the couple on the blessed event before leaving.

THIRTY-FIVE

The Brazos bottom lands experienced a mild winter that year. The new home for Katie and Quincy was near completion by the new year. The house would be ready to move into by March, before the planting season began. Everyone was excited as the arrival date for Josie's baby approached. Thad wanted to wait to see his new nephew or niece before leaving.

Reginia and William took Katie and Quincy to New Orleans in late February to buy furnishings for their new home. Josie had insisted they stay in her hotel. She had sent a letter instructing her manager to give them excellent service and not to charge them for their stay. Upon arrival at the hotel, the manager and staff greeted William and his family at the entry door. The manager seated them in the lobby and furnished them with cool drinks while the hotel slaves took the luggage to their suite. The manager assured them a pleasant stay. The exquisite suite overlooked the bay and downtown. It had a large parlor with two bedrooms. Each morning began with a large breakfast served in their parlor and the suite was promptly cleaned when the couples left for shopping.

The week in New Orleans was spent buying beautiful rugs, furnishings, and fabrics for the new house. William spent his money extravagantly on his family. Katie wanted her old bedroom furnishings for one of the bedrooms. William bought Reginia an exquisite new bedroom set for themselves. Reginia would move their old furniture into Katie's vacant room. The ladies shopped for new clothes, while Quincy and William visited with Josh and some of Quincy's friends. At night, they dined at the finest restaurants.

They spent the last evening in New Orleans with Quincy's friends, the Blackmons. The Blackmon home was beautiful with a large courtyard graced by ornate iron gates. The architecture of the house intrigued Katie. She especially liked the ironwork. The Blackmons welcomed Quincy and his family into their home and treated them to a dinner of seafood seasoned with herbs and spices. After dinner, the Blackmons had brandy served to them and their guests in the courtyard. It was unusually warm for that February evening as they sipped the brandy and engaged in conversation. The lanterns softly glowed in the moonlight reflecting against the flowers in bloom. The sweet fragrance of the honeysuckle vines filled the air as the Gulf breezes cooled the courtyard. Katie, enjoying the splendor of the setting, turned to the Blackmons. "Thank you so much for your hospitality. This has been a perfect ending to a wonderful trip. I must say our week's stay in New Orleans passed all too quickly." Reginia smiled and agreed with her daughter.

By the middle of March, Quincy and Katie were moved into their new home. It was beautiful and decorated exquisitely. Large trees surrounded the home and dotted the fields that bloomed with spring flowers. William filled the new barn with fine thoroughbreds, a beautiful carriage, and gave them fifty head of cattle and two fine bulls. He gave them five slaves. Two slaves were selected to tend the house chores and three slaves to tend to the grounds and the animals. Quincy was learning quickly how rich his father-in-law actually was. William wanted to give them chickens and hogs. Quincy declined the offer, laughing, as he explained that they usually received chickens, eggs, and pork in return for his medical services. William and Reginia had done more for them than Quincy had ever expected.

Josie was large and uncomfortable with her pregnancy. John stayed at her side. Reginia and Katie met at Josie's every day to see how she was doing. March was ending. Thad teased Josie without mercy that if she did not hurry up and have this baby he would miss his trip to the mountains! The last day of March, as Katie and Reginia sat with Josie, Josie began to cramp. Reginia sent Katie for Quincy. It was a mile ride across the fields to her house. Katie kicked her big thoroughbred and galloped all the way home. Quincy grabbed his medical bag and rushed with Katie to Josie's side.

Quincy stayed with Josie all night, as she screamed in pain. "This baby just does not want to come out," Quincy teased Josie. He patted her shoulder gently. "You have made life too easy in there for this infant." Josie struggled to smile through her discomfort. Katie assisted Quincy, while Reginia stood by holding Josie's hand. John paced the floor with William at his side, assuring John that everything would be all right. He told John of John's own birth, during the thunderstorm, and what a blessing he had been to him and Reginia.

Thad had come to the house late that evening. He brought whiskey from home and poured a good drink for John and his father.

"John, drink this whiskey. You need to relax, brother. It looks like Miz Josie is going to take her good sweet time about having my niece!" Thad teased John as John took the whiskey and swallowed it quickly. He held his glass out for another shot.

"What do you mean by 'niece'? It could be a nephew, you know," John remarked.

"No, I'm partial to young beauties. It will be a niece," Thad responded with certainty.

At four o'clock in the morning on the first day of April, after a night of pain, Josie gave birth to a baby girl. She was a beauty, with dark hair and steel blue eyes. Quincy left Josie's room to get John, who was leaning against the wall, exhausted from anxiety. William and Thad were fast asleep in chairs. "John, you have a beautiful baby girl," Quincy spoke softly. John jumped with joy. He kicked Thad with a soft thump to his limp leg, waking him from his sleep. "By George, brother, you were right! We have a baby girl!" A sleepy-eyed Thad rose to his feet, as John rushed to Josie. Thad woke his father and gave him the news.

Reginia, with tears in her eyes, greeted John with a hug as he entered the room. "My darling, you have a beautiful baby girl. I am so proud. There are three generations of Wildes in the same room, once again!" John hugged his mother and turned to Josie who had the infant tucked securely by her side. He hesitated. Reality struck him. He was a father. John walked to Josie and knelt beside her bed staring at his little baby girl. Katie and Reginia left Josie and John to be alone. John embraced his weary, perspiration-soaked Josie. Josie was exhausted, but smiled with complete delight at the sight of her little girl and husband. John held his daughter for a while before placing her in the crib. He went to the parlor to find his parents. Everyone was gone! They had found a bedroom and collapsed from their night filled with excitement and exhaustion. Thad lay on the parlor sofa. John threw a blanket over him and returned to his own bed.

The sun was just rising as John crawled into bed beside Josie, who was fast asleep. It was nearly noon when John was awakened by the whimpers of the baby. She was hungry. John changed her diaper and gave her to Josie, who began to feed her. The baby fed until she had her fill and fell fast asleep. John once again placed her in the crib and curled up in the bed next to Josie and slept until almost three in the afternoon.

Carrie had a large meal prepared for everyone. They sat at the dining table talking about the new little girl. John took a tray of food to Josie. She ate heartily. Life was good and Josie was very content. Carrie came to help Josie clean herself and put on a fresh gown. Carrie put fresh linen on the mattress and helped Josie back into the warmth of her clean bed, placing the infant in her arms. Carrie was wonderful for Josie and the baby. John entered the room. He was eager to name his daughter. Josie and John had discussed many names over the past months. The name Josie loved was John's choice, Danielle Evette Wilde. John invited his family into the bedroom and announced the name of the little girl.

Thad held Danielle with great pride. The next time he would see his niece she would be nearly ten years of age. Thad hugged Josie and shook John's hand in farewell. He would be leaving for his adventure the next day.

Reginia hugged John. "We must go too. We want to spend some time with Thad before he leaves. I feel we have gained a grandchild as we are losing a son."

"Oh, Mother. You sound as if I will never return." Thad smiled as he put his arm around Reginia. "I will be back before you know it."

William shook John's hand and congratulated him and Josie. "We really should leave now. Josie needs her rest and this is a time for you and your family."

John walked them to the front porch, thanking them for coming and wishing Thad the best on his trip. John watched as his parents' carriage traveled down the lane. He hoped Thad had a safe trip and did return home soon.

That evening, Thad, Reginia, and William sat in the parlor. Reginia wanted to know where Thad planned to go. He got a map and showed his mother the planned route. She expressed her fear of the Indians and the unknown. Thad promised her he would be careful. William smiled as he reminded Reginia that they had faced the same fears and had done just fine.

"I know. But somehow that seems different. We had slaves with us to help. Thad only has Mark," she responded.

"Would it make you feel better if I sent some of our slaves with them. I can arrange for that, immediately." William was serious. He had his own concerns for Thad's safety.

"You two just stop. I am going to be fine. Please, do not worry. Now, I must finish packing. So, if you will excuse me, I am going to do just that."

Reginia followed Thad to inspect his packing. She wanted to be sure he took plenty of warm clothes and the necessities for the trip. She had had supplies and food prepared for them, enough to last a month.

The next morning, Reginia hugged her son goodbye. It was a sad day for Reginia as Thad and Mark left for their long-awaited adventure. They were on horseback, with two pack mules. Thad wore his coonskin cap as the two young men set off for the mountains. Reginia and William stood on the porch watching them ride away.

Reginia sat down in the rocker. William turned and pulled another rocker beside her. "Do you mind if I join you?" He smiled. The two rocked as the morning sun rose high in the sky. William held Reginia's hand as they looked across the Texas fields. "Here we are,

Reginia, just like we started out, only a little older," he chuckled. "Just the two of us again."

Reginia squeezed his hand in agreement and nodded her head as she gently rocked. She felt content with life. Her children had grown into fine adults and were all living good lives. She had much to thank her Lord for. She thought of Sarah and how old she would be if she had lived. Sarah would be thirty-two years of age, had she not died. Time had flown, like a shooting star. "Reginia, what do you say we saddle our horses and take a ride, just the two of us." Reginia thought it was a wonderful idea. It had been a while since Reginia had ridden. The thought filled her with excitement.

She and William rode across the fields. Reginia, letting the wind blow her hair freely, galloped the big thoroughbred. She suddenly felt young and alive. Her petite figure still looked the same. Only the few lines about her eyes gave any sign of aging. William had wrinkles around his eyes and a few around his mouth. His hair was gray now, but his body was fit. William watched Reginia, still beautiful and elegant. How grateful he was for her. Their devotion had never died; in fact, it had grown deeper over the years. Their lives were content and fulfilled. He wanted his children to experience this same kind of love.

CHAPTER
THIRTY-SIX

Rogette and Samuel had their hands full with Belle, now eighteen years old. She was a beauty, just like her mother. Her skin was a light olive and she had not a hint of the African features. Belle continually questioned her mother about her coloring and her background. Belle was sad and never felt like she belonged anywhere. Rogette hated to see her daughter suffer, as she did. Belle read of the arguments to free the slaves. She wanted this badly. She longed to go to the East, where no one knew her, and live as a white lady. Belle had all the elegance and knowledge of a fine Southern lady. Rogette had educated her well, and Belle imitated with perfection the style and sophistication of Reginia. Belle begged to be set free. She wanted Rogette to help her escape through the underground railroad. Rogette feared misfortune would fall upon Belle and she would not help her. Belle became more determined. Rogette and Samuel decided it was time to tell Belle the truth. She was Josie's half-sister. Rogette prayed Josie would aid Belle in her travels to the East. Belle would be safe with Josie's help. She actually favored Josie in her appearance. No one would suspect she was a slave girl.

Rogette spoke with Reginia about her concerns for Belle and her intention of telling Belle the truth. Reginia loved Belle and hated to see the young girl so tormented. She tried to understand Belle's desire to live in the white world. Reginia had no idea how Josie would respond to such news. Reginia wanted nothing to disturb her son and Josie. She also realized it was not her place to make such a decision. Josie had always cared for Belle, spending time talking with her and speaking French with her, but to be her sister might be a different story! Reginia told Rogette to let her heart lead her in her decision.

The next few days, Samuel and Rogette discussed Belle's predicament. They reached the decision, after much painful deliberation, to tell Belle the truth. Samuel feared losing his daughter forever, but he trusted in the truth and knew the truth was the way of his Maker. Rogette and Samuel prayed for Belle and asked for wisdom. They called Belle into the small house and told her the truth. Rogette explained her life at Barbeaux's hands. Belle remembered, all too well, the day John beat Barbeaux. Belle was sick inside but felt relief by knowing the real truth about herself. She suddenly looked at her parents. "Why, Missus Josie is my sister!" Belle jumped up and hugged her parents and ran for the door.

"Where are you going?" Rogette rushed after her.

"I'm going to my sister. My white sister!" Belle was ecstatic. She suddenly felt white and found the world she belonged in.

"Stop, Belle. You can't just run to Missus Josie. She has no idea." Rogette filled with panic as she ran after Belle. "Stop," Rogette screamed. Belle ran all the way to the barn. Rogette could not catch her and was out of breath. She could not run any farther. "Belle, please stop. Listen to me!" Rogette watched helplessly as Belle jumped on a horse. Belle would not listen to her mother. All Belle could think about was the freedom she knew she must get. She kicked the horse, making him run all the way to Holly Hill.

Belle reached Holly Hill, full of excitement. She knocked on the door. Carrie answered. Carrie had never seen the girl before. The secret of Belle's background was well kept on the Wilde plantation. "Mays I help you?" Carrie asked.

"I'm here to see Missus Josie Wilde," Belle replied, with anticipation mounting inside her.

"Come in. I will fetch Missus Josie." Carrie ushered Belle into the foyer. Belle gazed about the fine home while she waited, dreaming of a better life in the white man's world.

Carrie went into the parlor to find Josie with Danielle. "Missus Josie, there's someone here to sees ya."

"Who is it, Carrie?" Josie asked.

"I don't know her. She's a white young lady," Carrie answered. Josie handed Danielle to Carrie to put down for a nap and went to see her visitor.

"Belle, for goodness sakes, what are you doing here? Is something wrong at the Wildes'?" Josie could not imagine Belle coming to her home. She was surprised by Carrie's description. Josie had always considered Belle a mulatto. Josie suddenly took a long look at Belle. Why, she did look white!

"I need to speak with you. I have wonderful news," Belle continued, to Josie's bewilderment.

Josie took Belle into the parlor. Belle in all her excitement, blurted out her news. "Missus Josie, you are my sister!" Belle exploded without thinking.

Josie just stared at Belle, speechless. She could not understand why Belle would say such a thing. Belle burst into the explanation of how their father took advantage of her mother. Belle told Josie the story told to her by Rogette and Samuel. Josie sat in disbelief and shock. Belle continued to press Josie for approval. Josie abruptly stopped her.

"Do not call me Missus Josie one more time," she scolded Belle. "Just sit still and do not say another word! I cannot even hear myself think!" Josie got up from her chair and walked outside. She stood on the front porch staring out across the fields. Belle sat in her chair, realizing too late that she should have listened to her mother. She cried softly to herself. Would anyone ever accept her?

Josie stood in shock, thinking of her father and how despicable he had been. Josie's mind raced with confused thoughts and questions. How could her father have done such a thing? How could she have a Negro for a sister! She felt humiliated and the old hatred for him rekindled inside her. She lowered her head and stopped her painful thoughts. The goodness in

Josie surfaced. She thought of her father's evil ways, of her mother and of Rogette. Barbeaux had hurt so many people. Josie had vowed when she took the plantation that no more injustice would take place there. If she turned her back on Belle, it would only perpetuate the evil he had committed. She thought about Belle. Belle was her father's daughter. She was Belle Barbeaux. This was not Belle's fault! Belle had not asked to be the victim of her father's depravity. She was the victim of his evils. "Belle does look white," Josie thought. Why, Belle even had some of her own features! How horrible it must have been for Belle to be white in appearance, living as a slave's child. Josie filled with sympathy for Belle. Josie would go to Belle; after all, Belle was a Barbeaux and her half-sister.

Josie entered the room and went to Belle. She took Belle's hand and sat beside her. Belle was quiet. She did not know what to expect. Josie asked her what she wanted from life. Belle did not understand the question, but she tried to answer directly. "I am as white as any white person could be and very educated. I want to go to the East, where no one knows me. I want a new life. I want a good life. I am not accepted here by the blacks or the whites. I feel lost, as if I don't belong." Josie heard the pain in Belle's voice. She thought of all the time she had spent with Belle in the past and the warm feelings she had for her.

"I will help you, Belle. Go home now, for I must tell John and we will decide how we can help. When you get home, please send Mister and Missus Wilde over here. You come back in a few days. I will have everything worked out for you." Josie was sweet and sincere. Belle rose and thanked her. Belle wanted Josie's love but would be grateful for only her help.

Josie told John the entire story. Somehow John was not surprised. He remembered when Rogette had come to live at their plantation. He was young, but he remembered the snow-white baby born to Rogette shortly after her arrival. He would support Josie in any decision she made. The Wildes came that afternoon. Josie told them of Belle's visit. She informed them of her plans to send Belle to the East. She had the full support of William and Reginia. Josie loved William and Reginia as if they were her own parents. They had an early dinner and the proud grandparents held and cooed over Danielle, before returning home.

Belle returned a few days later, as Josie had requested. John greeted Belle with a warm smile and left Josie to tell Belle her news. Josie was warm toward Belle, showing Belle the same fondness she had always shown.

"Belle, I don't know if you are fortunate or misfortunate by our father's behavior. But one thing is for sure. You are his daughter and my half-sister, therefore, as my sister, I want the best for you." Josie smiled warmly at Belle and continued, "I have made arrangements for you to receive fifty thousand dollars." Belle's mouth fell open with surprise as Josie continued, "John and I will take you to Houston to board a ship for New York. I will give you a thousand dollars for your travel. You will make a stop in New Orleans. You will stay in my hotel as my guest and sister, Belle Barbeaux." The sound Belle Barbeaux rang pleasantly in Belle's ear. She had a real last name for the first time. "The banker will give you your money. Buy yourself some fine dresses. You will have enough money to buy yourself a home and start a new life. Be wise with this money, Belle. It is enough to last you a lifetime. Remember this: education is a good thing, but if a person without wisdom gets caught in a thunderstorm, they won't know how to get out of the rain. Be wise in your decisions."

Belle hugged Josie with gratitude. "I will remember that and I can never thank you enough. Your kindness is most generous. I will guard the money and spend it wisely. I will never ask you for anything else."

"I will always be here for you, Belle. If you need help, you write to me. I only have one request. I do not want you to return."

"Never return?" Belle felt confused. How could Josie ask this of her?

"Belle, listen to me. I am not trying to hurt you. Please understand. It would be others that would cause problems. Problems I wish to avoid. Problems that you must avoid. There are cruel people. People that would make your life and our lives miserable. The fact that you have black blood would be held against you. And you can't take the chance of anyone finding out about this. This is a situation where we can't trust anyone. Only our families can know."

"I don't know if I can do this. Never see my mother and father again? You're telling me to forget my past—my people?" Every word

Belle spoke had a questionable tone. Her voice exposed the regret she felt.

"Oh, no, Belle. Don't forget your past and never forget your people." Josie put her arms around her. "After all, I am one of your people. Aren't I?"

"That isn't what I mean. My people are slaves. I wanted to do something to help them."

Josie was not sure what Belle meant by help her people. There had been talk of abolitionist in the East. This was a subject Josie did not want to engage in. She knew this would never be a topic she and Belle would agree on. For the first time, she realized that freedom was worth a lot and worth even more to a slave. "This is painful for you, I know, and maybe this is something you should think over. There is a price to pay for freedom and a larger price to pay by claiming your white heritage. I feel your pain, Belle. If only life were different. I could also have the sister I always wanted. But, the fact that you do have black blood in you must always remain a secret if you want the life you are asking for. I have Danielle and I never want her to be ridiculed by others for having an aunt with black blood. This is also a loss for Danielle. She would have loved you, Belle."

Josie truly felt regret. Her heart ached for Belle and for her own loss. "Life seems so unfair at times. I wish things could be different. Maybe someday . . . " Josie stopped short. Her mind wandered for a second with thoughts. How could things change? They would never change. The blacks were slaves. How could they ever fit in the white man's world? Maybe it is a blessing for Belle that she looks white. It all seemed too sad to Josie.

Belle hung her head. "I understand. I must go. This is my chance for freedom. I have dreamed of this all my life."

"God speed, Belle." Josie hugged Belle and sent her to pack her things and to bid farewell to Rogette and Samuel. Josie and John would leave with Belle for Houston the next day.

Rogette shed tears for Belle. She would miss her daughter greatly. Rogette was glad Belle would have a place in the world. Most of all, she would have her place in the free man's world. That thought brought great comfort to Rogette and Samuel.

Six months later, Josie received a letter from Belle. She had reached New York and had bought herself a home. It was a small, well-constructed wood-framed home with two bedrooms. Belle had purchased fine furnishings and stated that she felt very comfortable in her new home and city. She had found a job as a bookkeeper and taught French on the side. She had made friends with other young people in New York. Her new friends had never suspected she had black blood. She told of her happiness and thanked Josie again for her help. Belle did not inform Josie of her joining an abolitionist group. Belle wanted freedom for all slaves, but most of all for her mother and for Samuel.

Belle later became interested in the law of the Union. After putting herself through school, she looked forward to the day when women could become lawyers. In the meantime, she worked as an assistant to a Boston lawyer and learned all that she could. Belle had been determined to gain the respect and admiration of the white community, remembering to always make wise choices. Her beauty and intelligence, along with her sophisticated elegance, gained her that respect. Her friends adored her.

Josie told Rogette of her letter. Rogette had received a letter also. Rogette and Josie now had something very much in common. They both wanted the best for Belle.

THIRTY-SEVEN

Time passed and Danielle grew quickly. She was crawling everywhere by the holidays. Katie surprised everyone with news of her pregnancy. Everyone was happy with their lives. No one knew where Thad was, but they were sure he was somewhere in the deep wilderness!

The next five years were pleasant times in Texas for the Wilde family. John and Josie had three children, Danielle, Victoria, and Elijah. Katie and Quincy worked fast making their family. Katie was as fertile as a fine brood mare! They had four children, Jane, Quincy Jr., Splaine, and Lathe. On Sundays, after church, the families gathered at William and Reginia's home. The proud grandparents spoiled and entertained their grandchildren. During the summer, the entire clan spent time picnicking under the old oak by the creek and swimming. John and Quincy taught the youngsters how to swim. The cotton fields flourished and the shipping business grew steadily.

Thad and Mark were in the mountains of the Colorado Territory. They had built a one-room cabin out of logs, beside a mountain river. The trout were plentiful and the hunting was excellent. Indians roamed the area. Thad, with his winning ways, befriended the Ute Indians. Thad and Mark picked up the Ute language and taught the chief the English language. The Indian girls found the redheaded, rugged Thad interesting. They followed him about, rubbing his dark auburn hair, which Thad had grown long. Mark laughed and teased Thad about all his women! No matter where Thad went, the women found him irresistible. In 1857, Thad and Mark found gold in the mountain streams. Others were finding the gold too. By 1858, the Colorado gold rush was in full force. The gold rush brought many people to the Colorado Territory, then still a part of the great Kansas Territory. Thad quickly amassed a wealth of gold.

Thad and Mark were not far from a small settlement, approximately a two-day ride. Once a month, the two headed for the settlement. By 1859, the settlement, now named Denver, had a general store, newspaper, and saloons. Saturday nights were wild with drinking, gambling, and wayward women. Thad enjoyed all three! Thad thought little of his Texas home. He exhilarated at the joys of leading a wild and free-spirited life. Mark passed his time in Denver, gambling. Often, Mark would get into fights. Thad was tough as a boot and always came to Mark's rescue. Thad was not one to start a fight but he never backed away from one. Mark and Thad quickly became known for their fighting skills. No one in the area could whip either one, which earned the two young men great respect.

Late in 1859, Mark fell in love and married a Denver girl named Veronica. Mark was rich from the gold and wanted to return to Texas and make a home with his wife. The free-spirited Thad wished them well as they left for Texas when the winter ground thawed. Thad was alone for the first time. He took in a young Indian girl, whom the Utes called Little Star. She was beautiful. Her long dark hair framed her soft round face and big brown eyes that sparkled with the joy of life. Thad enjoyed Little Star, who cared for his every need, but she would never have his heart. Thad continued his trips to Denver, leaving Little Star at the small cabin. He drank, gambled, and had his way with the women in the saloon. Thad cared nothing of the outside world. He heard news of the troubles between the Northern and Southern States, but paid little attention to it. Thad never dreamed a civil war would take place!

Mark and Veronica returned to Texas. Mark proudly introduced Veronica to all his friends. They visited William and Reginia. Mark brought them up to date on Thad. Mark told them of the gold and wealth he and Thad had acquired. Reginia was thrilled to hear the stories about Thad. She longed to see her youngest son again.

Troubled times lay ahead for the United States. A long series of quarrels had erupted between the Northern and Southern States over the interpretation of the United States Constitution. The difference of opinion came primarily from economic considerations. One issue, however, overshadowed all others, the right of the federal government to prohibit slavery in the western territories. The North was against slavery and the South wanted to expand slavery to the new states. Without slavery, the small farmer would be created and the plantations would virtually be done away with. This would destroy the cotton industry, as the Southerners saw it. William kept in touch with Alex. Alex informed him of the headstrong politicians of the East and the movement by the abolitionists to free all slaves.

William was a man of great vision. He saw no way to settle the differences. Somehow, he knew there would be war, but he never imagined how devastating a war it would be!

By 1861, the Southern States had seceded from the Union. The Confederate States were formed and Jefferson Davis became the first and only president of the Confederacy. Sam Houston opposed Texas seceding from the Union. This was the first time William did not agree with his friend. He spent hours with Sam, trying to encourage the Governor to back the popular wish of the Texans to join the Confederacy. Sam would not change his mind. Sam was deposed as Governor in 1861. Texas seceded from the Union and joined the Confederate States. Sam Houston died two years later. William attended his funeral. The two men had remained friends throughout, never allowing their differences to interfere.

Abraham Lincoln was president of the Union. Fort Sumter, located in South Carolina, was owned by the federal government and occupied by Union soldiers. On April 12, 1861, despite Lincoln's attempt to maintain peace between the North and the South, and against Lincoln's vow to protect "the property and places" in the South, Charleston land batteries opened fire on Fort Sumter. The Civil War between the Confederate States and the States of the Union was on.

THIRTY-EIGHT

News of the war between the states was announced. The minister spoke of the war and the desolation that would follow. The Texans saw victory for the South States and after church they gathered to prepare plans to aid the South in war. Quincy and John were eager to face the Yanks in the fight for their beliefs, as were Jake and many of the other men. William and Reginia asked John and Quincy to stay home, but they were determined to go. No one expected the war to be more than a few short battles. John made plans to prepare for departure. He, Jake, and the others would meet at Quincy's home that very afternoon and travel to join the Confederate Army.

Josie kept quiet on the trip home. She did not want John to leave. Just before they arrived at Holly Hill, Josie broke into tears. "John, please do not go. There are plenty of men to fight the North. We need you here. What will I do without you? Jake will not even be here!"

"I have to go," John said firmly. "If everyone stayed home, as you ask of me, the Yanks would have their way. Can you conceive what would happen to the plantations? Why, there would be no slaves to work, and small farms would cover the South. Is that what you want?" John became angry with Josie and her unrealistic request. "Now, you can take care of Holly Hill until I return. Father and Mother will help you and Katie and Doctor Bradley is here to help, if you need him. The war will end quickly. The South has the North on the run. I will be home before you know it."

John picked several good horses and a pack mule for the journey. He summoned Bim to travel with him to tend to his needs. Bim welcomed the opportunity to tend to his master. John and Josie had delivered him from the pits of hell and he would go with his master anywhere! John hugged his children goodbye, commanding them to obey their mother. Josie wanted to go with John to Katie's house. "Carrie, take care of the children, I will be home before dark." Josie's voice trembled as she hugged the children and ran for her horse to ride with John to Quincy's home.

They reached Quincy's to find many families waiting to bid their husbands and fathers farewell. William and Reginia said their goodbyes, wishing them a safe journey. Josie held tight to John, kissing him with all her might. Katie hugged Quincy. Katie hated the Yanks for interfering where she felt they had no business. She just knew the South would win and Quincy would be home quickly. The men mounted their horses and waved as they left for war. Katie shouted as they rode off, "God speed, and give those Yanks a whipping they will never forget!"

"Katie, how can you be so willing to send Quincy off to war and maybe even his death!" Josie was angry and hurt by the declaration of war. Katie infuriated Josie with her eager support.

"Don't you get huffy with me, Josie Wilde. I didn't start this damn war, the Yanks did," Katie replied pompously. "How dare you not support the ideals of the South. This is our way of life. Do you want to lose everything you have? You are spoiled and selfish! That is what you are!"

Reginia interrupted Katie. She did not approve of her daughter's language. "Katie, you watch your language. You and Josie are going to need one another and there is no sense arguing over something like this."

Katie had a quick temper and strong opinions. Her mother's interruption only angered Katie more. "Mother, I meant every word I said. If Josie isn't woman enough to accept it, well, that is her own problem! As for myself, I will take care of my home and my children, while Quincy fights for our rights!" Katie, determined to stand her ground, firmly placed her hands on her hips and glared at Josie.

Josie resented Katie's attitude. Katie always had to have the last word, but Katie had gone too far this time. She had embarrassed Josie in front of all her friends and this would be something Josie would not quickly forgive her for. Reginia tried to comfort Josie, but Josie did not respond. Josie got on her horse and galloped for home, determined to show Katie that she was strong and could take care of Holly Hill, without any help from John's family.

The feud between Katie and Josie continued. Each felt too much pride to speak to the other. Reginia visited the grandchildren. The arguing between Josie and Katie disgusted her. Reginia told them both: "John and Quincy are fighting together. The last thing they need is for their wives to be at odds with each other." Katie refused to listen and Josie would roll her eyes with displeasure at the mention of Katie.

Josie worked hard managing the plantation, learning quickly how to function in the man's world. That summer, Josie shipped more cotton than ever! She dealt with the men on their level, becoming known as a hard businesswoman. She refused to take no for an answer.

William wanted to do something for his country. His age prevented him from going to war. He and Ben were asked to be agents for the Confederacy, working with the British and French. The Confederacy needed the trade overseas. William and Ben were to ensure the cotton trade with their ships. The two brothers met in New Orleans and boarded a vessel for Cuba, where they would board an English steamer.

Reginia seemed secure with the departure of William. William was brilliant and Reginia knew he could make agreements with the British and the French. Stanley stayed behind to oversee Auburn. He cared nothing for the war. He thought the war would be short-lived and he knew William needed him. With William gone, Reginia appreciated Stanley remaining at the plantation.

Each week, Stanley looked in on Katie, taking her fowl and pork for meals. Katie was indeed the spoiled one. Quincy, a doctor and not a businessman, made Katie rely on her family's wealth and the help of Stanley. Josie became further irritated with Katie's arrogance and spoiled nature. Katie had changed over the past few years. Her family's fortune had gone to her head. Katie did as she pleased, with little concern about any danger to John and Quincy. She was only concerned with herself and her personal comfort. The war became a burden to Katie. She pouted and blamed the Yanks for any misery she encountered. While Josie kept busy with her plantation and work, Katie held teas for the ladies of the area.

Josie called Tom, her head slave over the fields, to the house. She needed to go to Houston for supplies and visit with Jacob Crowe about her business in New Orleans. Josie had Tom get the wagon and go with her to Houston. On their way, they had to pass by Katie's house. Katie sat on the porch entertaining her friends with a tea. She hollered at Josie to stop. Josie had Tom pull the horses to a stop. She assumed Katie wanted to ask forgiveness for her actions against her. Josie got down from the wagon and walked to the front lawn where Katie met her. "Where are you going dressed like that?" Katie questioned, with a sneer on her face. Josie dressed in a simple dark dress, one without frills and petticoats. Josie raised an eyebrow at Katie in disapproval of her remark.

"Not that it is any of your business, but I am going to Houston for supplies and business. I do not feel this is a time for flamboyant dresses."

"You should at least dress decently. Why, you are a disgrace to the Wilde name. You look wretched!" Katie blurted sarcastically.

"Wretched! I have more than you will ever have and I will work to maintain Holly Hill in John's absence. If you had any pride whatsoever, you would do the same! Our husbands are fighting for our rights and their lives, as you sit drinking tea and gossiping with your friends. You could not even exist if it were not for your mother and her money!" Josie was sick of Katie's casual attitude toward the war and the safety of the men. She would not allow Katie to get the last word this time!

Now, Katie would have her turn to be embarrassed. She could not stand to be humiliated in front of her friends. Katie raged with anger and raised her hand, slapping Josie across the face. "Don't you ever talk to me that way!"

Josie had had enough of Katie. She grabbed her by her red hair before Katie could say another word. Josie took Katie's arm and held it tightly, twisting it behind her back. Josie pushed Katie's face into the oak tree. "You better think twice before slapping me, you spoiled brat! I am sick of you walking about with your nose stuck up in the air like some queen! You are just another person, like everyone else here. You need to grow up and accept your responsibility as the wife of a Confederate soldier! Why, Quincy could be lying dead somewhere, for all you know! You just wear your fancy dresses and your petticoats, sipping tea. You are the disgrace, not me! And it will be my husband who comes home proud of his wife, not yours! You are pathetic and disgusting!" Josie let go of Katie abruptly with a shove. Katie fell to the ground, speechless. Katie's friends stood standing on the porch in amazement at what had taken place. Josie was shaking with anger as Tom helped her in the wagon.

"Well, you sure got her told, Missus Josie," Tom laughed as he whipped the horses on.

"Yes, I did, Tom. It's about time someone did! I'm almost glad she slapped me. I would have never done that if she had not angered me so." As the wagon headed for Houston, Josie beamed with pleasure. For she had finally had the last word with Katie!

Josie and Tom arrived in Houston two days later.

She sent Tom for the supplies while she visited with Jacob. Jacob was elated to see Josie, as she entered his office. "Josie, my dear, how are you?"

"I am fine. Working hard! We had a large shipment of cotton this year. The largest ever! John would be so proud. Jacob, I need to speak with you about my affairs in New Orleans."

"Of course, Josie." Jacob could tell by speaking with Josie that she had not received word of William and Ben's capture by the Yanks. "Josie, have you heard about Mister Wilde and his brother, Ben?"

"What do you mean?" Josie had no idea what Jacob was referring to. William should be in England by now, or on his way home.

"William and Ben reached Havana on a blockade runner and boarded the British steamer Trent, bound for Europe. In mid-ocean, the Trent was overtaken by the Federal steamer San Jacinto. Mister Wilde and his brother were taken prisoners. I understand they are being held under guard in Fort Warren, at Boston Harbor."

Josie looked horrified. "Has any harm come to them?"

"No. Moreover, the British have protested to the arrest and seizure of them off their ship. The British were enraged and claim the capture was contrary to international law. It has become known as the Trent Affair. However, I hear President Lincoln and Prince Albert have been negotiating the problem to prevent the danger of war between the Union and England. The most the Yanks will do is keep them prisoners until the war ends. They can't afford to anger Britain and France anymore. I feel certain Alex is in touch with Mister Wilde."

The Trent Affair did more damage to the South than imagined. When Prince Albert discovered the reasons for the war and that the North was fighting to abolish slavery, he pulled England's support to the South and began buying cotton from other sources.

Josie felt relieved with the thought of Alex in Boston. She would tell Reginia as quickly as she returned. "Jacob, I need your advice concerning my bank and my hotel. I am considering selling the hotel and purchasing Confederate bonds. I want to do something to help our men at war. What do you think?"

"Josie, hold on to your hotel. At this point, I believe that the South will win this war. But, it is my advice that you do not buy the bonds. In truth, I suggest you sell the bank and remove your money for safekeeping."

"Sell the bank? Why should I do such a thing? It has been very profitable."

"We do not know the outcome of this war. If the South should lose this war, the bonds will be worthless. In fact, there is news that Lincoln is sending warships to blockade the southern ports. I don't know if he will succeed, but if he should, you don't need your money in the bank."

Josie could not imagine the Yanks taking the port of New Orleans, however, she trusted Jacob and would not risk losing her fortune. "Jacob, would you go with me to New Orleans and handle the sale?"

"Yes, I would be glad to help you. This is a wise move; one can't be too cautious in these times. Let's get a trunk to put the money in. You can place clothes over the money to hide it. No one must find out you are traveling with so much cash. Do you understand?"

Josie nodded. The thought of traveling with hundreds of thousands of dollars suddenly alarmed her. She would do as Jacob said. Josie wrote a letter to Reginia, telling her of William's and Ben's capture and her request to keep the children while she journeyed to New Orleans on business. She told Tom to take the supplies home and return for her in two weeks. "Go to Missus Reginia and have her get the children. Tell her I had to go to New Orleans on business. I am sending this letter to her. Be sure she gets it." She sent Tom home without her, as she departed for New Orleans with Jacob.

THIRTY-NINE

Jacob and Josie arrived in New Orleans. They met with Mr. Trundle, the manager of her bank. Josie informed him that she wanted to sell the bank. Mr. Trundle knew a rich man in New Orleans that would be eager to buy. Mr. Trundle told Josie about Constantine Branch. He owned a large plantation and spoke often of buying or building a bank. That evening, Josie, Jacob, Mr. Trundle, and Mr. Branch met for supper. They discussed the sale of the bank. Josie impressed Jacob with her business style. She dealt with the man with great self-confidence and determination. Constantine was eager to purchase, just as Trundle had said. Jacob drew up the papers; the next afternoon, the bank belonged to Mr. Branch.

Josie spent a few days with the hotel manager, reviewing the books. The hotel appeared to be doing fair. Josie took the risk of keeping it. "Surely the South will win," she thought. The hotel was still making money and she would have her cash at home in a safe place. She bundled the cash in the trunk, locking it with the key. At the hotel, she placed clothing across the top of the money for added security. No one in New Orleans knew she had removed her money, not even Mr. Branch. She made Mr. Trundle swear not to mention the transaction to Mr. Branch until after her departure. Josie and Jacob boarded the steamer for Houston.

Tom waited for Josie at the dock. He loaded all the trunks, as Josie watched. She told no one about the money, not even Reginia. Josie feared Reginia would tell Katie and the Lord only knows whom Katie would tell! They arrived home to Holly Hill two days later. The children were with Reginia. Carrie met Josie at the door. "Missus Josie, I'm so glad you's home. I worried 'bout you travelin' without Master John."

"Everything worked out fine. Jacob Crowe traveled with me. I just had to take care of some business."

"Oh, Missus Josie. I plum forgot! Old Spunky died today. He lies in the backyard. You wants me to have him buried?" Carrie knew the children would be upset over the death of the dog. Josie thought a minute. This was perfect timing for the old fellow.

"No, I will take care of Spunky. After Tom brings the trunks in, I will have him dig a hole to bury him in. I prefer to bury him myself. He has been a good and faithful dog."

Josie had Tom dig a hole by her father's grave. She would bury Spunky on top of the trunk full of money. No one would ever find the money there! Late that evening, after the slaves were in their quarters, Josie carried the trunk to the grave. She put the trunk in the hole and put Spunky on top, covering the trunk and Spunky with fresh dirt. The next day, she had Tom make a wooden cross to place at the grave. Her putting a dog to rest by her father astounded Tom.

"Missus, it ain't none of my business, but I can't believe you put that dog to lie by your father."

Josie found this amusing. "I know, Tom. It's a shame to have such a fine and faithful animal have to lie eternally by my father! Should I move old Spunky to another location?" Josie laughed at the thought of her father placed to rest with Spunky.

"No, Ma'am, I think this is a fine resting place for old Spunky!" The two laughed as they walked away.

"Missus, I think you done a fine job seein' over Holly Hill. I hears the talk to free us slaves, but I want to tell you, I remembers a day when I dreamed of bein' free. Why, Hell itself would've been better! You and Master John have been good to us. I don't know what me and my family would do withouts Holly Hill. This plantation is alls we know." Tom spoke with sincerity and concern for his future. Tom had come to find some pleasure at Holly Hill but the thoughts of freedom had not left his mind completely. It just seemed to be something he would never have.

"Thank you, Tom. I'm glad you're happy here. I don't know what this war will bring, but I do know Holly Hill will always be here. Don't you worry about anything. I have to go to Missus Reginia's and get the children. I should be back this afternoon. Please get my carriage." Josie thought for a moment about what would happen if the South lost the war. The thought terrified her. She put it out of her mind. Josie had other concerns. William and Ben were in prison and she worried constantly about John.

Josie pulled the carriage to a stop at the Wilde home. Danielle, now seven years old, and Victoria ran to greet her. Reginia walked, holding little Elijah's hand, to see Josie. Reginia was in torment over the imprisonment of William. Josie hugged her children and took them in the house with Reginia. Josie told her all the news she had concerning William and Ben. She reassured Reginia that Alex would do all he could for his father.

Alex worked faithfully trying to free his father. He dealt with the British protestors. William and Ben were treated fairly while in prison. Alex went daily to see his father and uncle Ben, taking them food and clothing.

William and Ben heard all the talk about the Federal blockade on the Southern ports. The Union soldiers were not gaining ground on the battlefield, but if the blockade was successful, it would do great harm to the Confederate Army and the South. Alex traveled to the White House to request the release of William and Ben. President Lincoln respected Alex and welcomed his visit. Alex argued his point of view well. The Union could not survive without the support of England and France. They could not afford to anger the two great countries. President Lincoln gave thought to his negotiations with Prince Albert. Lincoln knew he had made strides with Albert over the slavery issue. The release of the men might win greater favor with Prince Albert and put an end to trade between the South and England. Lincoln agreed with Alex, without revealing his reasons, and William and Ben were released from prison within three months of their capture.

Alex met his father and uncle Ben at the fort on the day of their release. The two men went with Alex to his home. William was grateful for his son's help. They made plans for their return home. William and Ben would take a train south to Savannah and board a ship for home. William could not wait to get home to Reginia. He knew she had to be worried about him. The news of the capture filled the newspapers. Many of the abolitionists seethed with anger and some became violent with the lack of progress made by the Union Army. The release of the prisoners added fuel to the already burning fire of hatred. The war tore at Alex. He had to keep his support for the South and his opinions favoring slavery to himself. His son Will believed strongly in the Northern views and went to war under the leadership of General Burnside, later joining the forces of General Sherman.

Alex took William and Ben to the train. Alex wanted his father out of the North. It was not safe for them to be in Boston with the heated tempers of the Yankees. William wanted desperately for Alex and his family to go to Texas. William feared for their safety if the South won the war, as he assumed it would. Alex would not leave. Boston was their home and he would stay. William hugged Alex goodbye. Ben moved forward to shake Alex's hand, when suddenly a man pushed Alex aside, pointing a gun in Ben's chest. Before Alex or William could move, a shot rang through the air. Ben fell limp to the ground. Officers, nearby, restrained the assailant, who later was found to be an abolitionist. William fell to his knees by Ben. "Ben, I'm here. We'll get you to the hospital. You'll be all right." Blood poured from Ben's chest turning his white shirt red. William took his jacket and placed it over the wound. He could see that Ben had taken the bullet near his heart. Alex screamed for help. Ben tried to speak, his voice weakened. William bent over him trying to hear his words.

"William, I'm dying. Take me home. I won't have my body lie in the North. Promise me, William."

William held Ben closely, whispering in his ear, "I will take you home, brother. That's a promise." Ben closed his eyes and gasped his last breath.

William grabbed Ben in his arms, rocking back and forth. Alex took his father by the shoulders. "He's gone, Father. Let him go. There is nothing we can do now."

William slowly let Ben's body down and looked up to Alex. "I promised Ben I would take him home."

"Yes, Uncle Ben should be taken home."

Soldiers carried Ben's body away. The trip was postponed yet another day. Ben's body was prepared for burial and placed in a coffin for the return trip. The Union soldiers were instructed to accompany William to the safety of the South. The next day, the grief-stricken William took Ben on his last journey home. The trip was solemn for William, as the train moved toward the Southern States. The Union soldiers did their job of protecting William, but none were friendly nor sympathetic toward his loss. The soldiers escorted William to Maryland, where he traveled safely through the South to Natchez.

William kept his promise to Ben. He and Elizabeth buried Ben in the family cemetery, on the Mississippi plantation, beside his parents. William stayed a week with Elizabeth. Ben and Elizabeth's boys were gone to war. Her daughter, Jolene, stayed with her on the plantation.

It was late November before William arrived home to Texas. The evening air blew cold and damp. William opened the door to see Reginia coming down the stairs. Reginia filled with joy at the sight of her worn and grieving husband. "My darling, my darling," she shouted as she grabbed him, gripping him around his neck. Tears of joy fell down her cheeks. She stepped back and placed her hands gently on his cheeks. "You look exhausted and cold," she remarked as she wiped the tears from her eyes.

Reginia took William's hand and walked up the stairs. She prepared a hot bath for William and scrubbed his back. As he soaked in the soothing water, he told her about the death of Ben. Reginia fell silent with grief. Tears fell from her eyes, this time in sorrow. She kissed William softly, so thankful he was alive. William felt exhausted and climbed into bed. Reginia had his supper brought to him. They talked for hours that night.

"The war is horrible, Reginia. The fields of Pennsylvania, Maryland, and Virginia are riddled with death and destruction. The foul smell of death and burnt buildings fill the air. The Confederate soldiers are holding the Union back, but I don't know how long this can continue. I have never seen such devastation. I had no idea this war would be so costly. The hatred in the North for the South is unbelievable. I only hope our John and Quincy are safe. Young Will is fighting with the Yanks. I can't believe we have a grandson supporting the North! Poor Alex, he is so torn by this war." William talked with deep sorrow and regret in his voice.

"Are Alex and Jacqueline safe?" Reginia feared what would happen if the Southern soldiers pushed their way east.

"Yes, for now, they are. How have things been here?"

"Fine. Stanley is doing a wonderful job. He has been a big help."

"How are Katie and Josie?"

"Our two young ladies are at odds with one another. I'm afraid we've spoiled our Katie too much. Josie's worked very hard to hold Holly Hill together. She's becoming quite a businesswoman. John will be proud of her. Josie refuses to take part in social activities and dresses modestly. It's her way of showing respect for the men at war. Katie just can't understand this. She may understand better when she hears of the lives lost for this cause!" Reginia told William all the details of the feud between the girls and how Katie had been rude to Josie from the day that John and Quincy had left.

"I'll have them both here tomorrow and talk to them together. We can't have this in our family." William was determined to have peace in his home.

The next day, William sent Samuel to bring Josie and Katie to the house. Josie wanted to see William, but she refused to ride with Katie. She bundled the children and took her own carriage to the Wildes'. Reginia had a big lunch waiting for everyone. William was delighted to see Katie, Josie, and the grandchildren. The conversation over lunch seemed pleasant enough, but there was obvious tension between Katie and Josie. After lunch, William asked Josie and Katie to join him and Reginia in the library.

"I understand there is a problem between the two of you." William began to speak his concerns, when Katie rudely interrupted.

"Father—" She did not get another word past her lips.

"Mary Catherine, do not interrupt me, again."

Katie knew her father was perturbed when he referred to her by her given name. She sat upright in her chair with her lips pinched tight, with feelings of resentment for being corrected. William looked directly at Katie as he spoke. His disappointment in her behavior was apparent.

"Your mother has informed me of your behavior toward Josie. I will not have this, Katie. You are a grown lady with a husband at war. You must behave as such. You have no idea of the bloodshed this war has caused. The fields as far south as Virginia are filled with the blood of soldiers and the land lies in ruin. The South is doing well to hold the North back. Let me tell you something, many soldiers from both sides have been killed or severely injured. Medical tents are full of soldiers mangled by this war. You can only hope for the safe return of John and Quincy. Now, I will hear no more of this feud between the two of you! Katie, I want you to apologize, right now, to Josie."

"But, Father, Josie grabbed me like some heathen and embarrassed me, right in front of my friends! She should apologize to me!" Katie retorted with angry humiliation at her father's lecture to her.

"And what did you do to Josie? I know you, Katie. What did you do? I want the truth."

Katie hung her head, with her lips puffed and pouting. She would not respond to his question. She did not want to tell William what really happened. Katie's disrespect, by not answering William, angered him. He rose from his chair and walked directly to face Katie. Reginia had never seen William so angry with the children. She just sat staring at Katie, fearing her daughter's stubbornness would result in a terrible scene!

"Mary Catherine, did you hear me?" William's voice became stern. "You're almost thirty years old, but you'll never be old enough to disrespect me! Now, what did you do to Josie?"

Katie was furious and felt betrayed by her family. She began to get up from the chair.

William put his hands on her shoulders and pushed her back down in the chair.

"Sit down, young lady. You'll sit here all day if you have to. Why, if you were younger, I'd turn you over my knee and give you a spanking you'd never forget!"

Katie was furious. Her face looked as red as her hair! She shouted at the top of her lungs, "I slapped her. She deserved it. Carrying on like a man and dressing like some poor backwoods woman. Why, you should have seen her! She is a dishonor to this family!"

William looked at Katie with disappointment in his eyes. "I'm very ashamed of you. You're the one that's dishonored this family, with your lack of respect and concern for our nation. Josie has done nothing but take very good care of her family and show the respect that my son deserves. I'm proud of her. You should do as well. You're spoiled rotten and that is my fault. But it stops here. You'll receive nothing more from your mother and me. Yes, indeed, I'm having Samuel bring your two house slaves home. You'll fend for yourself, until you beg pardon for your actions and I see some change in you. Until then, I will not have you in my home. Samuel will take you to your house, immediately!" William stormed from the library to give Samuel his instructions.

Josie sat with her head hung in sorrow. Katie looked to Reginia for support. Reginia looked at Katie with disappointment in her eyes. "Katie, you brought this on yourself. There is nothing I can do. Your father is right and only you can help yourself. You would be wise to consider your father's wishes."

"This isn't like Father. Why, he wouldn't even listen to me!"

"He has seen hatred, death, and mutilation. This war should not be taken lightly. It isn't so much your feud with Josie that angers him as it is the lack of respect for his wishes and your ho-hum attitude about this war. There is fighting across this country and the last place he wants this is in our family. We should be supporting one another. Can't you see how self-centered you are acting?"

Katie, jumped from her chair in anger, flipping her red curls indignantly. "No, I cannot. I'm not a child and I can do as I please." She stopped and stared coldly at Josie. "Well, you got your way! Didn't you?

This is exactly what you wanted. I will show you, if it is the last thing I do! You make me sick to my stomach!" Katie stormed for the door, screaming for her children. She did not want to spend another minute in her parents' home.

Josie expressed regret to Reginia. She was bitterly sorry for Katie. Reginia would not have Josie feel that way. Reginia and William meant what they said and were sticking to their judgment. Reginia encouraged Josie to disregard Katie. "Josie, don't worry. I know my daughter. It may take her a while, but she'll come around. Don't let this upset you. You've done nothing wrong. I'm only sorry we didn't do something earlier, before the problem got so hard to deal with." Reginia hugged Josie. Josie gathered her children for the ride home, still saddened by the occurrence.

Samuel took Katie and her children home. He spoke to the field slaves and gave them William's directions. They were to tend to the stock and field only. They were not to cut wood or do anything about the house for Katie. If Katie gave them any problems, they were to return to Auburn. Samuel departed, bringing the house slaves back to the plantation. Samuel hated to see the Wildes so torn. He knew what it felt like to part with a daughter. William gave Stanley instructions to stay away from Katie's house. He was determined to make Katie grow up and accept responsibility for her actions.

CHAPTER

FORTY

Katie sulked the first few weeks. She would not ask the field slaves for anything and give her father the pleasure of removing them too! She cooked and cleaned. Katie gave Jane and Quincy Jr., her two oldest children, small chores. Her cooking was terrible! The children frowned as they tried to eat her food. She built her own fires. "Thank goodness the wood had been cut," she thought. She was determined not to go to her parents with an apology. Katie missed Christmas with her family. She cut a small tree and placed it in her house. She had nothing to give her children. She made stockings and filled them with pecans and candy she had tried to make. The children did not understand why they could not see their grandparents. Katie was lonely. She could not possibly invite her friends for tea, and serve them herself.

The Wildes celebrated the holidays with Josie and her children, Joseph, and Golda. Jim and Betty surprised them with a visit. The Wades' sons had joined the Confederate Army and their daughters had married and moved away. They were all alone. Visiting their dear friends was such a pleasure for Jim and Betty. By now, William and Reginia were amused by Katie's stubbornness. They thought it did her good to do without. Perhaps she would appreciate the things she did have and come to see that life was not always easy for everyone.

William was proud of her for not crying for help. But he did wish she was not so headstrong.

Reginia enjoyed having Betty with her again. They reminisced of old times and talked about the war. Jim and William enjoyed talking about their businesses. Jim had made a big success with his lumber company and William's shipping business was doing well. Texas flourished during the early years of the Civil War. With the blockade by the Federal warships, Texas was the main source of shipping to the South. They shipped supplies to the Confederates all through the war. The Wades stayed with William and Reginia through the second week of January.

Meanwhile, Katie continued to burn with rage. Spring came and she had to make her garden. Her hands were chapped and raw from the hard work. She did learn to cook, after much trial and error. She scrubbed the floors and did her wash. She gathered eggs and killed the chickens for special dinners. Her first experience with killing the chicken was something to behold. She ran about the chicken coop trying to catch one. When she finally caught it, feathers flew everywhere. They were in her hair and sticking to her clothes. She didn't know how to kill it, once she caught it. The field slaves stood by watching, about to burst with laughter. She held the chicken by the legs, while the bird flinched and fought, pecking her repeatedly. She screamed with impatience to the slaves. "Stop that laughing and tell me what to do!"

"Sure, Missus, you's got to wring that chicken's neck!"

"Do what?" Katie could not conceive wringing its neck. She thought they were teasing her. The bird twisted and pecked her right on her cheek. "Ouch!" The slaves laughed even harder.

"Missus, take that bird by the neck with your free hand and twist it till it breaks. That's what you gotta do!"

Katie did as they said. She squinted her eyes, held her breath and twisted that poor chicken's neck until it finally snapped. The bird went limp. Katie held the dead chicken high in the air for the slaves to see what she had accomplished.

Katie held fast with her decision to show Josie and her parents. She was elated with her ability to survive without their help. She lost weight and was exhausted from her hard work. At night, she read to the children and collapsed into bed, totally fatigued. Spring and summer brought more work her way. More than she ever had dreamed possible. There was no time to rest during the day. She had to cook, clean, wash, and tend to the garden, the yard, the chickens, and the hogs. She traded a fine European vase for the hogs. She had no money. She began to feel like a pauper.

One warm, sunny day in July, two of her friends came for a visit. Katie was in the yard pulling weeds from her flower garden, when she spotted the carriage coming down the lane. Her hands were filthy and her old dress, stained with grease and dirt, hung limp on her bony frame. She stood and wiped her hands on her dress. Charlene and Maydelle sat in the back of the carriage, driven by a slave. They stared at Katie in dismay. Katie, seeing the ladies dressed in beautiful dresses with full petticoats, suddenly felt humbled.

"Katie, what are you doing and why are you dressed like that?" Charlene laughed at the sight of Katie, who looked a fright. Her auburn curls were pulled up and pinned in a bun. Some frizzy curls had fallen loose about her face. Dirt smudges were on her face and neck, where she had wiped her sweat with her filthy hands. "My goodness, you look worse than Josie ever thought about looking! We came to visit and have tea. We haven't seen you in so long." The ladies got out of the carriage. Katie had no choice but to invite them in. She sent them to the parlor, while she went to her room to clean up. Katie looked in the mirror. It was the first time she had really taken a good look at herself. She slipped out of the old dress and saw her bones peeking through her skin. The sight repulsed her. Josie looked like a princess compared to her. She washed herself and quickly fixed her hair. Most of her dresses were worn from working in them. She picked out the best one and threw it on without petticoats.

Katie fixed the tea and served Charlene and Maydelle. The ladies just stared in wonder. "Katie, where are your slaves? Have you and your family fallen upon hard times?" Maydelle was truly overwhelmed for her friend. Katie resolved to tell them the truth. She could not contain the humiliation she felt.

"My family is fine. They are all richer than ever." She had disgust and envy in her utterance. "My father has cast me out from his home. I refused to apologize to Josie for treating her as I did." Katie heard her own words "treating her as I did." Finally, Katie saw herself in error toward Josie. Realization fell upon her. She had acted miserably and paid the price for being obstinate.

Charlene and Maydelle hugged Katie. They felt sorry for her, but they both felt it was a lesson well learned. Charlene and Maydelle had not admired her smug attitude. The ladies sipped their tea and visited with Katie for a couple of hours before leaving. "Katie, if you need anything, you can always come to me." Charlene generously offered her help, with Maydelle nodding in agreement.

Katie lay in bed that night thinking about her actions and how exceptional Josie really was. Katie had ruined a marvelous relationship with her best friend. A friendship that could not be replaced. Katie's pride would not allow her to go to her family or Josie. Especially now, with the way she looked! She had no money to buy a new dress. She did not even know how to sew such a garment! She pushed her face into the pillow and cried herself to sleep.

William and Reginia missed Katie and the children. Reginia, weary from waiting on the tenacious Katie, insisted on seeing her. William agreed, but declared firmly that they would offer Katie no assistance.

They went to visit just two days after Katie's visit from Charlene and Maydelle. William and Reginia knocked on the door but there was no answer. They walked in the house, making their way to the dining room. There Katie was, busy scrubbing her floors, with Quincy Jr. trying to help her. Jane watched Splaine and Lathe while her mother worked. William and Reginia were aghast at Katie's appearance. Katie saw her parents and leaped to her feet. Water dripped from her wrinkled and callused hands, as she acknowledged them. She was exhilarated at the sight of them, but she was not about to let them know it! She fought to maintain a simple smile. "It is good to see you Mother, Father," she said cautiously.

"Your father and I have missed you and the children." Reginia tried to act unconcerned by Katie's appearance. She gazed quickly about the room. "I am glad to see you are doing so well. The house looks immaculate, as does your yard."

"Thank you. I am sure the house and yard look much better than I do!" Katie had to laugh at herself A faint hint of her wit appeared. William bent down and hugged Quincy Jr. Jane came around the comer and spotted her grandmother. She ran as hard as she could to her, gripping her around her waist.

"The children look fine, Katie. You must be feeding them well." William felt he had to say something to breakdown the barrier between himself and Katie.

Jane spoke up. "At first the food was terrible, but she cooks fine, now. We can at least eat it!"

Reginia recalled the prissy wit and charm that Katie had had as a young girl. She smiled at Jane. "I just bet your mother is a good cook."

"Why don't you take grandma and grandpa to the parlor, Jane. I will bring in some lemonade and cookies." Katie went to the kitchen and Jane eagerly took her grandparents to the parlor where Splaine and Lathe were playing. William and Reginia visited most of the afternoon. Jane and Quincy wanted to go home with their grandparents for an overnight visit. Katie explained to Jane that she needed her help with Splaine and Lathe while she did her work. William saw the disappointment in Jane's eyes.

"I tell you what. If it's all right with your mother, we'll take all of you home with us. Would you like that?"

"Oh, yes, Grandpa. Can we all go, Mother?" Jane was ecstatic.

Katie could see that Jane and the children really wanted to go. It had been a long time since they had seen their grandparents and she would certainly enjoy some time to herself. "I think that's a good idea. When will you send them home, Mother?"

"Why don't you let them stay through the weekend? I will drop them off after church. Besides, why don't you go to church with us, Katie?" Reginia thought it would be a good way to get Katie back in church.

"I might. Let me get their bags." Katie rushed to get the children's clothes packed. Church was the last place she wanted to go. She looked terrible and had nothing suitable to wear.

Reginia and William left with the grandchildren. Katie sat on the porch waving goodbye. It was quiet. She took a deep breath and released it slowly. They would be gone six days. Thoughts of free time sped through her mind. She would not have to cook unless she wanted to, there would be little to wash, and the house would stay clean! She could even read a novel if she wanted to! A broad smile formed on her gaunt face.

Katie enjoyed her free time the first couple of days. Then solitude set in. Late in the evening, Katie sat on the porch. There was not even a bird singing. She felt lonely. For the first time, she truly missed her husband. She had been too busy to give Quincy much thought. She missed his hugs and kisses. Katie simply missed everyone! She was so alone. She continued rocking, feeling sorry for herself when, across the field, she saw a rider coming. She stood up to see who it was. The sun was setting and she could not recognize the man. Fear came over her. She thought about getting the rifle, but then she caught a glimpse of his face. It was Stanley. She filled with excitement. She was glad she had soaked in the tub and was fresh! She had even combed her hair, letting her pretty long curls fall over her shoulders.

She welcomed Stanley eagerly, asking him to join her on the porch. Katie fixed them a glass of lemonade and the two visited for a long while. It was approaching nine o'clock before Stanley left. Katie asked him to come again. She particularly enjoyed his visit. He promised he would return and indeed he did, almost every evening!

Saturday evening, Katie prepared dinner for Stanley and herself. She prepared fried chicken, potatoes, and green beans. She poured fine wine to drink. The table was set with her best china. Stanley ate voluminously, impressed with Katie's cooking. Katie enjoyed having Stanley at the opposite end of the table. It had been more than a year since Katie had had a man sit at the dining table with her. After dinner, she poured them a brandy from the decanter. She had not drunk the brandy since Quincy had left for war. They sat on the porch with their spirits. The night was warm and the moon was full. The stars filled the sky. The evening was perfect. Katie chatted about everything from wringing a chicken's neck to the Civil War. Stanley felt sorry for Katie. She had to work so hard and had lost too much weight, but even though she was too thin, she was still beautiful. Her eyes had changed, he noticed. The mischievous sparkle was gone.

"Katie, why don't you reconcile your differences with Mister Wilde? There is no need for you to struggle through life as you are doing."

"I can't, Stanley. This has gone on far too long. I recognize it is my fault, but my pride just will not allow it."

Stanley took Katie's callused hands and gently lifted them. "Look at your hands, Katie. You are right about one thing. This feud has gone on far too long." Katie quickly pulled her hands away and hung her head with shame. Stanley picked her hands back up and kissed each one tenderly. "Never be ashamed of honest hard work, Katie. You have proven to be a lady of backbone. You admit you were wrong. There is nothing left to prove."

Tears filled Katie's eyes. "Josie would never forgive me and I can't blame her for that."

Stanley stood up and took her in his arms, comforting her until she stopped crying. He wiped her tears from her sun-weathered face. "Josie has already forgiven you. She hates to think of your suffering." Katie gazed into Stanley's brown eyes. She felt vulnerable and alone. She wanted Stanley to hold her again. She missed being held and loved. "Katie, let me take you to Josie or I'll bring Josie to you. You've got to overcome this anger of yours."

"Stanley, I'm not angry. It's been so long. I don't even know when I stopped being angry." Katie's voice was soft and defeated.

Stanley's heart filled with pity for Katie and he wanted her for his own. He lowered his head and kissed her. To his surprise, Katie returned the kiss. She wrapped her arms around Stanley's neck and kissed him again. Stanley realized he had gone too far with Katie. He took her by the shoulders and stepped back. "This isn't right. I can't do this."

"Stanley, I don't care! I don't care about what is right or wrong and I don't care about that silly old war! I need someone who cares for me, don't you understand?"

"Katie, you do care. That's what's wrong with you. It's not my love you want. It's your family's and Quincy's love that you miss so desperately. I am going to bring Josie here tomorrow after church. Everything will be fine, you just wait and see." He gave her a consoling and friendly embrace and left for home.

Katie went to her bedroom and prepared for sleep. She tossed and turned all night, dreaming of Quincy and the times she and Josie had spent gossiping and laughing. Katie slept late the next morning. She jumped from her bed at eleven o'clock. She could not believe she had slept so long. She only had an hour before Josie would be at her house. She bathed and dressed in the only half-decent dress she had. She stood in front of the mirror. She hardly recognized the person she saw. There was no trace of the high-spirited Katie, only a weather-beaten, heartbroken woman. She hated the person in the mirror. She put her hands on her hips and shouted at the creature staring back at her from the long mirror, "I have backbone! I'm strong and able to do anything I want. Why, I can cook and clean with the best slave! I have proven that! But I'm not going to do it any longer. I deserve better and so do my children!" She straightened her shoulders and stormed from her bedroom. She would welcome Josie, she would do whatever it took to have her family's love once again!

After church, Josie walked to William and Reginia. "I am going to see Katie today."

William smiled at her. "That is good of you, Josie. But you don't apologize. That's Katie's obligation, not yours."

Stanley, standing by William, interjected. "Oh, don't worry, Mister Wilde. Katie's ready to offer an apology. She misses all of you very much and she knows she was wrong." Reginia and William were both bewildered at how Stanley knew so much about Katie. They looked at each other with puzzled expressions.

"Let me take Katie's children with me." Josie wanted to be alone with Katie, without her in-laws. She felt it would be easier for Katie. Reginia and William agreed.

Josie loaded the children in the carriage and left for Katie's home. Katie lived near the church, only a few minutes away. Katie heard the carriage and rushed out the door. Jane ran to her and hugged her, telling her all about their stay with their grandparents. Katie hugged Jane, never taking her eyes off Josie. Josie still wore dark simple dresses, but to Katie, she now looked elegant. Josie got the children down and sent them off to play with the younger ones. She wanted to be alone with Katie. Josie walked slowly up the walk to her, stopping right in front of Katie. Katie looked into Josie's forgiving eyes for a moment. Katie's heart was beating rapidly with excitement. Her anxiety over this meeting left her. She was only thrilled to have her best friend back. She grabbed Josie and hugged her. Katie would not let go. She burst into tears of joy. "I'm so sorry, Josie. You're my best friend. I don't know why I acted like I did. Please forgive me. I love you so much. I can't stand being apart from you any longer!"

Josie held her, patting her on her back. "All is forgotten, my dear Katie. Let us go inside for a while."

Stanley had not exaggerated one bit. Josie observed Katie. She was thin as a rail and looked like a little orphan. "Katie, pack some things for you and the children."

"Why?" Katie could not understand why Josie wanted her to pack her things. Where would she go?

"I'm taking you to my house for a stay. You look terrible! I'm going to fatten you up and soak your body in oils. I'll have Carrie sew you some new dresses, while you relax and recuperate from all your hard work. You can't look like this when Quincy returns! He'll be expecting his redheaded beauty, not some redheaded farmhand!" They both laughed and hugged each other, again. Katie ran to pack their things, eager to have long chats with Josie once more.

Katie stayed with Josie for three weeks. She gained some weight and with all the oils Josie soaked her with, her skin was beginning to soften. Katie took long naps each day. The lines in her face, created from exhaustion, began to fade away. Carrie made her four new dresses. The dresses were simple, like Josie's. Katie didn't care. She thought they were beautiful. Every day they talked for hours. They had much to catch up on. The sparkle returned to Katie's eyes. After a couple of weeks, Josie invited William and Reginia for dinner. They delighted in having their family back together, laughing and loving one another. William sent the house slaves back to Katie. Katie had suffered, William knew this. However, he was proud of the fine lady she had become. Life was ultimately good again for the Wilde family. If only the war would end, and John and Quincy could return home. Life would be perfect.

CHAPTER
FORTY-ONE

Eighteen sixty-two was a busy year for Alex. His concerns for his native South overwhelmed him. He loved the East and his home in Boston. His best friends were "Yanks" and his family fought for the Confederate. He became torn emotionally over the war, in fact, he didn't believe in the war. He felt the States had their rights and the North should not force their beliefs on the South in the fashion of war. All he could see was a divided nation and the death of many good men.

The Copperheads were a group of men in the North that opposed the war. They organized secret societies, such as the Knights of the Golden Circle. These men discouraged Union enlistments and helped the Confederate prisoners escape. Alex had heard much about the Copperheads. He didn't approve of all their tactics, such as embarrassing the government by openly discouraging enlistments, and many were very radical on their stand against the war. Like the abolitionists, they demonstrated in the streets, often becoming rowdy and offending innocent people. They were, however, becoming very influential in the Democratic party and in the elections of 1862. Alex agreed with their mission to end the war and after great thought, he joined the Copperheads. If there was any way the Copperheads could succeed in ending the war, Alex would financially support them. Alex, however, kept his involvement private. He donated money as needed for the cause and aided the escapees' safe return to the South.

Alex passed a group of abolitionists one day in the late fall. The abolitionists had gathered in Boston, screaming to free the slaves. He stopped to listen. A lady was standing on the platform, boldly speaking her opinions. She was a beautiful white woman, very well dressed and obviously well educated. He heard someone refer to her as Ms. Barbeaux. Alex thought of Josie and wondered if there was any relation. The lady seemed to favor Josie in her features. The man standing beside her referred to her as Belle. Alex began to stare at her. Something about her seemed vaguely familiar. Was it her appearance, or her voice? Suddenly, he remembered Rogette's daughter, Belle. Surely, the lady speaking and his father's slave were not one and the same. Alex's curiosity overwhelmed him. He stayed until the rally was over and walked to the platform. Belle saw Alex. She tried to get away before he recognized her, but it was too late. Alex rushed to her, gripping her arm and stopping her.

"You are Rogette's daughter, aren't you?" Alex spoke firmly. He was sure she had run away by the underground railroad. "You are my father's slave!"

Belle looked about to ensure no one had heard him. "Please come with me. I will be glad to speak with you, only it must be in private."

"In private! You're a mulatto, posing as a white!" Alex was furious with her.

Belle kept her composure. "Please, you know nothing about me, although you think you do. I will tell you everything, if you will just come with me."

Alex did not trust her, but he agreed to follow. He walked by her side, worried that a gunman with the abolitionists might approach him. Belle noticed his uneasiness.

"Relax, you are safe with me. Believe it or not, as an assistant to a successful lawyer, I am respected by many of your fellow whites," Belle spoke with confidence. Alex just looked at her. He could not believe any of this. He wondered why she used the name Barbeaux. Nothing made sense to Alex! She took Alex to the grandest hotel in Boston. The manager greeted her warmly. Alex followed her up the stairs, to her room.

"Would you like something to drink," Belle asked, as she poured herself some wine.

"No, I don't want any wine. I just want to know why or how you got here and why you are using Josie's maiden name!" Alex became confused and irritated with Belle. He wanted the truth.

Belle sat in the chair and calmly told him about her life. "I am Rogette's daughter, this is true, but Samuel is not my natural father. Don Barbeaux raped my mother. That is how I was conceived. Josie is my half-sister. I am only one quarter black." Belle had no shame. She was too secure for that. She was proud of her success and wanted Alex to know it. Alex sat listening intently to every word Belle spoke. "My mother educated me and taught me manners. I watched your mother, with all her grace and sophistication. I wanted to be just like her. I wasn't accepted in the black or white world. I didn't belong anywhere. When Mother and Father told me the truth, I went directly to Josie. I must admit, she wasn't nearly as excited as I was!" Belle laughed, remembering that day. Belle became serious as she continued her explanation. "Josie is a good person. She accepted the truth, whether she accepted me as her sister or not. She talked to your parents and with their approval, she helped me leave Texas."

Alex found himself feeling sympathy for Belle. "How did Josie get you out of Texas?"

"It was easy. My birth was a secret. No one outside the plantation really knew about me. Josie insisted I take my rightful name—Belle Barbeaux. She took me to Houston and put me on one of your father's steamers. She introduced me as her sister. We do favor each other in some of our features. Josie forwarded a letter to her hotel manager, stating that I was her sister and asking him to treat me kindly. They were indeed kind. They rolled out the red carpet for me, because I was her sister! Josie gave me a large sum of money. I bought fine clothes in New Orleans and continued my travels to New York. I purchased a small home and put myself through school. I worked as a bookkeeper and taught French on the side. Today, I work as an assistant to a lawyer and have a decent-sized home in the city."

"I can't believe Father never told me."

"My mother begged their silence. She feared harm would come to me if anyone knew I came from a slave family. Your mother was always good to me, as was Josie. I truly believe they wanted the best for me. I have worked hard for freedom. Not only for the slaves, but for women. Women deserve to be treated as equals. We should all have the same rights. I believe everyone, regardless of race or sex, should have equal privileges and opportunities to succeed in life. I am accepted as a white, actually, as a French lady. I want to keep it that way. You see, Alex, when I was young, I always wanted to be white. Now I realize it was not the white race I longed for, it was the freedom it brought. I love my parents and am proud of the black blood I have. The truth is, I cannot achieve for my black race what I can if people know I have black blood. I would appreciate your silence, Alex."

Alex deliberated before answering. Belle was accomplished, successful, and certainly a lady. Rogette and Samuel would be proud of her. His parents would be proud of her too, even if they did not agree with her views. She fought for what she believed in, just as his son Will was doing. Alex had no opposition to slavery, but after listening to Belle, he had a better understanding of what freedom must mean to the blacks. She forfeited being able to see her family to fight for their freedom. It took fortitude to leave home and travel across the country to a place where she knew no one, at such a young age, and begin a new life. Alex felt admiration for Belle. "You have my word as a gentleman. I will not reveal your true identity." Alex walked to the door. He turned to Belle with his hand extended. Belle responded with a firm handshake. "Good luck, Belle. I wish you continued success."

Alex walked down the street, reflecting on his conversation with Belle. He wondered how many slaves could succeed on their own, if given the chance. He carefully thought about Abraham Lincoln issuing his preliminary Emancipation Proclamation. It would become effective on January 1, 1863. He dreaded Lincoln's decision, knowing his proclamation would greatly hurt any foreign intervention on the

Confederate side. Europe prohibited slavery and this would cause resentment toward any state resisting the proclamation. The South would never accept Lincoln's Proclamation and without the support of the European countries, especially England, Alex feared the South would fall. The New Orleans port had already fallen to the Federal blockade and Union troops had invaded the city. Both sides were winning battles, now. He wondered how long this war would go on? Belle had made Alex think about a lot of things as he walked the cobblestone streets to his carriage. Were all these deaths really worth it? He did not agree with the idea of a war settling a problem, anyway. Maybe slavery was a thing of the past and perhaps it should be. Jasper worked for wages and Alex never considered him a slave, but what would happen to the plantation owners if they had to free their slaves and pay all of them for their work. He feared it would be an end to the great plantations. The times were changing before Alex's eyes. He did not know if the changes were good or bad, but one thing he knew for sure—changes were going to occur.

Alex arrived home late that evening. Jacqueline waited upstairs for Alex. She was brushing her dark hair when Alex entered their bedroom. "Where have you been today? You are so late." Jacqueline continued brushing her hair looking at him through the mirror's reflection. She imagined he had to work late and was not concerned that anything out of the usual had happened.

Alex did not respond. He had never kept secrets from Jacqueline, and pondered whether to tell her as he walked to her and put his arms around her gently. He knew that if news got out about Belle's background, it would hurt his family, not to mention his own reputation!

"What is troubling you, Alex. I know that faraway look in your eyes. You have deep thoughts over something."

"Nothing. Nothing at all."

"My dear, I know better." She turned in her chair to face him. "Tell me what you are in such deep thought over."

Alex knew he could not keep this secret from Jacqueline and he knew she would never gossip. "I saw someone today, from Auburn."

"From Auburn? Who on earth was it?"

Alex hesitated before telling Jacqueline about Belle. The news astounded Jacqueline. She could not believe her ears. Being from the South, Jacqueline couldn't imagine what it must feel like to discover you have a mulatto for a sister. She had sympathy for Josie and Belle, both. She admired Josie's integrity. Jacqueline knew of no other Southern lady who would have acknowledged the girl, much less helped her leave the plantation! "I hate to admit this, Alex, but I could have never done what Josie did!"

"I understand, completely. I know, this must have been hard for my father to accept. He didn't even tell me about it. I'm sure he was embarrassed. I will say one thing for Belle. She sure has come a long way! I guess if I were her, I would have wanted the same thing. Jacqueline, have you ever considered what it must be like to be a slave? To be owned and worked without freedom. I never gave it much thought before speaking with Belle. Our family is good to their slaves and our slaves seem happy. Come to think of it, I would hate to be in that bondage. Do I sound like a traitor?"

"I wouldn't say a traitor. But don't forget where we came from. Our families depend on slavery, as all plantation owners do. I wouldn't want to be a slave, but then this is the way life is."

"But, should life be this way?'

"I don't know. Only the good Lord knows. It is late, Alex, we should get some sleep. I don't think this is something you and I will solve tonight."

Alex and Jacqueline were alone most of the time. Will joined the army just after finishing college. He was nineteen when the war broke out and Alex could not stop him. Alexander (they called him Zan) was entering college and living at home. Alex refused to let him participate in the battles. Zan, unlike Will, had no problem with slavery. He longed to visit his grandparents in Texas. His parents' stories of their lives on the Southern plantations intrigued him. To him, slaves just seemed to be a part of the lifestyle of the South.

All their children had dark hair and dark eyes, with beautiful olive skin. Jacqueline had taught her children proper etiquette, and had insisted they each receive a good education. Zan agreed to attend college, but was headed for Texas as soon as he graduated. Alex agreed. He knew his father would be thrilled to entertain his grandson at Auburn.

Will was a fighter for what he believed in. He wanted all the slaves freed and the Southern states to govern as the North did. Will deplored the secession of the South. This was a senseless action, as far as he was concerned. He had no understanding of the views of the Southerners. Will had dreams of returning from the war and involving himself in his father's shipping business. Will had graduated at the top of his class. He was as brilliant as his father!

Sarah studied the arts in England. She was an accomplished pianist and wanted to study with the masters. Art was her second love. What better place to study! Sarah was delighted when her parents told her they were sending her to England for her education. While living in England, Sarah often traveled to France, viewing the great paintings of the French artists. Her father's European business friends entertained her like royalty. She attended concerts and many social events, dedicating most of her time to the piano. She was granted an audition to study under Franz Liszt in Rome. Her talent impressed Mr. Liszt and he fervently accepted her as his student. Sarah rented a large apartment in Rome. It had large glass windows overlooking the city and at night, she loved to view the lanterns glistening against the moonlit sky.

Alex filled with pride when Sarah got accepted by Franz Liszt. He sent her money for the purchase of a concert grand piano. She put the piano in front of the big windows. Sarah loved Rome. It was such a romantic city and the arts were greatly appreciated. Her life became a dream come true. The French and Italian languages came easily to Sarah. Within two years, she could speak both languages fluently. Sarah was a genuine beauty, friendly and sophisticated just like Jacqueline. Sarah enjoyed people and had the ability to listen and understand others. She kept her personal thoughts and feelings to herself, speaking little about herself and then only when asked.

Sarah's charm and composed ways attracted the young men to her. The most eligible bachelors in Italy courted her. Count Pierre Dupree, a Frenchman who frequented Rome, was one in particular. His love for the arts attracted Sarah. He loved to paint and had a brilliant tenor voice. Occasionally, for his own pleasure, he sang with the opera. Sarah relished her time with Pierre. He loved to hear her play her piano. Often, they enjoyed an evening at Sarah's apartment. She would play for him, while he sat watching her adoringly. Sarah spent her days studying her music with Mr. Liszt, concentrating only on her piano skills. By the mid-1860s, Mr. Liszt had her playing with orchestras and giving small concerts. She would later become a renowned concert pianist, traveling throughout Europe. Sarah was often seen on the arm of Pierre Dupree. They attended important social gatherings and royal affairs. The handsome couple were the talk of Europe.

Meanwhile, the Civil War raged throughout the South. Texas held one of the only available ports for shipping. The ships traveled to Vera Cruz, Havana, and Europe. Cotton was sold and the ships were loaded with supplies for the return trip to Texas. The Texans could make up to sixty thousand dollars off the sales of the supplies. This money would be used to aid the Confederate Army. New Orleans had been seized in 1862. Josie was glad she had listened to Jacob and removed her money from the grip of the Union. She built up a large herd of cattle and produced immense crops of cotton. The Confederate money lost value and the Confederacy had accumulated a huge debt. She knew William had invested in the Confederate bonds and currency. Josie only hoped he would not lose his entire fortune. Josie had not heard a word from John. News of death and destruction filled the newspapers throughout the land. She feared for his safe return. She held her faith that John would, once again, walk through the front door of their home.

FORTY-TWO

John and Quincy joined the troops led by Stonewall Jackson. They enjoyed the victories their masterful leader obtained. John became a lieutenant and Quincy provided medical care for the wounded. Bim remained to help John, caring for his master with great respect. The first year and a half of the war had looked favorable for the South. John marched with Jackson's troops through the Shenandoah Valley, rejoicing as they defeated the Yanks and regained the Valley.

In 1863, Jackson received an accidental gunshot wound and died by a Confederate bullet. His death was a shocking blow to the Confederacy. Quincy joined the forces of General Jubal Early and John joined General Lee. January of 1864 felt bitterly cold. Late one evening, John and Bim sat bundled in blankets by the fire. A group of men sat talking a few feet from him. John heard a familiar voice. He lifted his head and turned to see who had gathered near him. He heard the voice again. "You know, Bim, that man sounds just like my brother Thad." He jumped from his seat and stared into the group of men. Lo and behold: the redheaded, rugged Thad stood among the men, controlling the conversation, as usual! He had grown a long auburn beard. His hair hung loosely down his back.

John walked up behind Thad and kicked him in the rear end! Thad's quick temper rose as he wheeled to punch his assailant's face. John threw his hands in the air, jokingly. "Woah, little brother! You think you can take me on?"

Thad stopped his arm in mid-swing. "John, what the hell! I can't believe you're here. I figured you would be safely tucked in with Josie, back in Texas!" He grabbed John and embraced him mightily. "How are you? Man, am I glad to see you!"

"I'm glad to see you too. Come on over to my tent, Thad. We've a lot of catching up to do."

"You have your own tent?"

"Yeah, I'm a lieutenant! Come on where it is warm."

"A lieutenant. Now, how about that." Thad smiled proudly as he followed John into his tent.

"Tell me, Thad, how were the mountains?" John longed to hear about Thad's wild adventures. Surely, Mark had not told them everything!

"They are magnificent. The peaks rise above the clouds, and the rivers are cold and clear. You should see all the trout! We found gold, you know. I gave some to the Confederacy, but I have a fortune in gold buried in Mississippi. I hid it on Uncle Ben's plantation. I plan to get it when this war ends." Thad continued his tales of Colorado. He told him of his reckless nights in Denver and the Indian girl he left behind. "Little Star was a pretty little thing! I hated to leave her, but when I read about the war, I had to go. You know, John, when we get near Atlanta, we will have to go in for a night of pleasure! We can get drunk, gamble, and find us some wild women!"

"That's a good idea. I could stand some good whiskey. But, I think I'll let you take care of the wild women!"

"Damn, John, you were always such a prude! You need to enjoy life. How can you stand being tied down to one woman all your life? Why, I bet you haven't had anyone but Josie! Don't get me wrong, I love Josie to death, it's just that you can't let your life be so boring. Life's too short."

"Oh, Thad. You and I are just different. You would never understand." John was right about that. Thad would never understand love and commitment to one person. Thad just shook his head and laughed at his straitlaced brother.

Thad marched through the South, by John's side. Thad loved to fight. The battles seemed to exhilarate him. He fought with vigor, shooting and slashing any Yankee that got in his way. He built a strong hatred for the Union, which justified his pleasure in killing the offending soldiers. The tide of the war turned. The Union Army succeeded under the leadership of General Grant. He was as brilliant as Jackson and Lee. His skillful tactics for maneuvering his men were winning all the battles. Grant and his Union soldiers marched through the South, burning homes and towns, leaving destruction in their wake. Food supplies for the Confederates were at a low and the soldiers were weary, but they would not give up!

The thirtieth of August found Georgia scorching in the heat of late summer. Lee's troops were camped outside Atlanta. Silence fell on the city that afternoon. Thad approached John with boredom in his voice. "John, what do you say about the two of us going into Atlanta for a drink?"

"That sounds good to me. There's nothing happening here! We can look for Quincy. I understand he's attending the wounded there."

Thad and John rode into Atlanta, going directly to the hospital to find Quincy. The sight they saw sickened them. Hundreds of men lay on the cobblestone streets surrounding the hospital. Women were all about tending to the wounded. The smell of blood filled the air. They walked among the wounded, finding their way into the hospital. John and Thad could not find Quincy. They asked a lady nearby if she knew him. "Why, yes, I do. He's over there." She pointed to the crowded corner that had been set aside for surgery. John walked ahead of Thad. He looked around the screen just as Quincy removed the leg of a wounded man. The man screamed with pain. John, shocked by the sight, moved quickly, turning his head away.

John grabbed Thad's arm. "Quincy is cutting the leg off a man! Listen to him scream! I have never seen so many injured in one place." John's stomach boiled with nausea. The possibility of the South losing the war suddenly became a reality to John. They waited on the opposite side of the screen for Quincy. John glanced about at all the injured. Thad walked among the injured, speaking encouraging words to them. John admired Thad, but all he wanted was to get out of there. It wasn't long before Quincy came out from behind the screen. John grabbed him by the arm.

"Quincy." John took Quincy's hand and shook it, pulling Quincy to him for a hug.

"John, I can't believe it's you! What are you doing here?"

"We're camped outside of town. Thad is with me." John pointed to Thad. "We're with General Lee. This is terrible, Quincy. There are so many wounded."

"The death rate's high. I've been working all night and through the day."

"Come with us. We're going for a drink and you look like you could use one. Come on. I have to get out of here. The stench is making me sick." John waved to Thad to join them. Quincy told the other doctor where he was going and that he would be back soon.

The three walked to the hotel nearby for drinks. They sat visiting for about an hour. Quincy hated to leave, but he had to go back to the hospital. "Stay a while longer, Quincy," John pleaded. "It may be a long time before we see you again."

"I can't, there are men who need me. This war has taken more lives than you can believe. I'm afraid we're losing this war. It needs to end," Quincy concluded.

This angered Thad. "We will not lose this war! I'll kill every last Yankee myself." Thad, slightly intoxicated from the whiskey, allowed his hatred for the Union to be heard!

"You probably could!" Quincy smiled at John. He shook their hands as he departed. "If I don't see you again, take care. God speed to you both."

Thad was determined to find a house of prostitution. "I need a woman! Come on, John."

"I'm not going with you to some house of ill repute."

"Oh, come on. You don't have to do anything. You can gamble with the men or just sit there like some goody two-shoes!"

"Damn it, Thad. You make it sound like I'm not even a man! I'll have you know, it takes a big man to say no!" John put emphasis on the word "big."

"Well, come on big man, let's go!" Thad laughed at his brother and grabbed him by the arm, dragging him from the hotel.

Thad practically pulled John down the street. "Let go of my arm, Thad." John became irritated with Thad's behavior.

"If I let go, you will run like a whipped pup the other direction! You've got to quit living like a prude and experience some life! Hell, you've never even seen a whorehouse in your whole life."

John couldn't argue with his drunken brother. Thad was too strong and quick-tempered to fight with. "All right, I'll go. But, I'll not take part in your shenanigans!" John shook his head with disgust and followed Thad to the house of sin.

A well-dressed black man opened the door for Thad and John. Thad walked in like he owned the place. John timidly walked in behind him. He had never seen such a place in his life. It smelled of smoke, whiskey, and cheap perfume. Everything looked red and gaudily furnished. A long ornate bar covered the side of one wall, with a nude painting hanging above it. Men sat at tables playing cards. Many of the prostitutes stood by the men draping their arms and legs on them.

Within a minute, Thad had a young, full-busted girl hanging all over him, offering him sexual pleasures. Thad grabbed her, stopping at the bar for a bottle of whiskey before going up the stairs. John thought the whole affair appeared disgusting. How he longed for Josie. John spotted two Confederate soldiers sitting alone at a table. He introduced himself and joined them for drinks and conversation. An hour or two passed, as Thad tarried upstairs. "God only knows what he is doing!" John thought to himself. His brother's actions were somewhat amusing to John. The smoke-filled room began to burn John's eyes. He needed some fresh air. He had no idea how long Thad would be upstairs.

John sat on a street bench outside the door of the hotel. Tired from the whiskey, he fell asleep. Dusk approached before Thad exited the house. He looked at John sleeping on the bench and laughed. Thad nudged him on the shoulder, waking him up. "Get up, big brother. Let's go back to the camp." John just looked at him in disgust. Thad had a huge smile of satisfaction on his face. "Man, do I feel good!" he exclaimed.

"One of these days, you're going to regret your sinful ways," John teased.

"You may be right. But right now, I feel real good! You should've tried it, John. You might not be so grumpy if you had!" Thad laughed with pleasure.

"You just don't know what it's like to be in love with a woman like Josie," John remarked as they walked to their horses. Thad would never change. It was little use in trying to show him the errors of his ways. They galloped the horses back to camp. Bim had beans cooked for them when they returned. They ate and went directly to sleep.

They awoke at daylight to the blasts of cannons. The camp stirred with the soldiers grabbing their rifles and running to battle. General Sherman had surrounded the Confederate soldiers. The sounds of battle rang through Atlanta! Georgians filled the streets to flee the wrath of the Yankees. Thad fought near John, who had Bim faithfully at his side shooting the Union soldiers to protect his master. It was difficult for Bim to fight against the ones that could bring his people freedom, something he had prayed for all his life. But he loved John, and John was still his master. Bim wanted freedom but he wanted no harm to come to John. The enemy pushed in, killing many of the Confederate soldiers. Many men on both sides were being killed as they fought for their beliefs. A young Union soldier galloped his horse toward Thad. Thad shot him, grazing him in the left arm. The soldier, ignoring his wound, leaped from his horse onto Thad. The two wrestled on the ground. Thad pounded him with his fists. The Union soldier struggled for his pistol. John ran to aid Thad. John kicked the gun from the Yanks hand. Thad knocked the young man out with a strong blow from his fist. He pulled his knife to slit the unconscious man's throat. John screamed in horror. "Stop. It's Will! It's Alex's son. Stop!" John pushed Thad off Will in a panic.

"He's a damn Yankee. I don't care who you say he is." Thad raged with fury.

"My God, Thad. He is our nephew! Get a hold of yourself." John knelt over the bleeding, benumbed Will. Sherman's men were past them, forging their way through Confederate lines toward Atlanta.

"Get his legs and help me carry him. We are getting out of here. Bim, get over here!"

"I am not going anywhere! I'll fight to the end," Thad exclaimed deliriously.

John grabbed him and looked into his eyes. "You listen to me, Thad. There is nothing you can do. Look, Sherman has passed us. This is a lost battle. All you can do at this point is die and I will not allow you to do that! Now, you help me get Will into that thicket over there, and I mean right now!" John spoke sternly to Thad, who had never heard his brother speak with such authority. He did as John said. They carried Will to the woods, where they hid until the next day. John did not sleep a wink that night. He bandaged Will with his shirt and watched over him. His thoughts were on home and Josie. He wondered if Quincy had survived Atlanta. The cannons lit the skies that night. Bullets and screams riddled the air. Blazes from the burning Atlanta brightened the dark night. Sherman captured Atlanta within two days.

The next morning, Will opened his eyes to the surprise of his uncle John by his side. Will was weak from the loss of blood and strained to speak. "What are you doing, Uncle John?"

"I am keeping you alive, that is what I am doing. You almost died at the hands of your Uncle Thad." John pointed to Thad, who stood by him.

Will looked at Thad. He never would have known him. "I tried to kill you, Uncle Thad."

"Don't worry about it, kid. You tried to kill a Confederate, just like I tried to kill a damn Yankee!"

"That is enough, Thad," John warned.

"Well it is the truth," Thad argued. He stared coldly at Will. "What in the hell are you doing fighting for the Union, kid. Don't you know your entire family is from the South!"

Will became angry. "First of all, I am no kid! And my family is from the East, not the South! The South wants it all! Big plantations and their 'niggers' to live in bondage and work for free! I hate slavery! It is barbaric." Will blurted his words through all his pain. His sudden exertion caused him to pass out again.

"Damn, Thad, why can't you keep a civil tongue. Help me get him up. We passed a plantation about three miles west of here. We will take turns carrying Will. Maybe we can get some horses there." John had a plan to get his brother and nephew home to Texas and no one would stop him!

It took them all day to walk the three miles. Sounds of gunfire and cannons echoed in the distance and they had to be cautious of lagging Union soldiers. They reached the old weathered and beaten plantation right at dark. A man in his fifties came to the door. He hurried the Confederate soldiers inside. Bim laid Will on the floor of the parlor. The man looked at John. "My name is Roth Styles."

"I'm John Wilde and this is my brother Thad. That is my nephew Will Wilde." He pointed to Will and explained what had happened.

"You're telling me that Yank is your nephew." Roth could not understand.

"Yes, sir. My brother moved to Boston years ago. He's in business with our Father in Texas. Will was raised up East. He just doesn't understand the South. He's my nephew, sir. I can't let him die. Why, he's my father's namesake. It would destroy my family if I didn't care for him. He's a good boy, he just has different opinions." John paused in thought for a brief moment. "I guess that's why we're in this war, all the different opinions."

"I understand. Loyalty to family is important. Even if one is a Yank. Stay as long as you need."

"Thank you," John sighed. "We'll spend the night, but we need to be on our way in the morning."

Bim carried Will upstairs to a bedroom. John cleaned the wound. The bullet had to come out. Mr. Styles said he could get the bullet out of Will's shoulder. He went for his knife and strips of cotton. Will would only wake up for seconds before passing out again. Mr. Styles poured whiskey over the knife to sterilize it. Thad and John held Will down, while Mr. Styles dug the bullet out. Will's eyes flew open. He screamed with pain.

"Hold on, Will. We have to get this bullet out," John told him, as he held him tightly. The bullet finally came out and Will laid his head back on the pillow. Thad poured Will a shot of Whiskey and told him to drink it. Will downed it with one gulp. John bandaged Will. Will asked for more whiskey. Thad poured him another shot.

An old black man walked in the room. "Master Styles, I've some beans and taters for supper. You want me to fix a plate for these soldiers?"

"Yes, Parks, that will be fine. I know these men are hungry." Parks took Bim with him.

Bim got a plate and brought it to Will.

Mr. Styles looked to John. "All the slaves ran off when the Union soldiers came. Parks wouldn't leave. The old slave has been loyal. My wife died before the war and I've lived here alone for the last six years. I don't know what I'd have done without old Parks!"

The men continued their conversation over supper. "Do you have horses we can buy?" John asked. "I have no money with me but I'm a wealthy man. I'll pay you back."

"The Yankees took my good stock. I've got an old buckboard and there's a ten-year-old gelding out there. Take him. He's old, but if you go slow, I think he can make it. Don't worry about paying, they aren't worth a plugged nickel. I don't know where you're from, but I don't know of anyone that has money. I don't mean to alarm you, but be prepared for the worst. The Yanks have taken everything and the Confederate dollar isn't worth much."

"We're from Texas, I don't think the Yankees have made it that far." John thought about the bank in New Orleans. He knew Josie's and his money would be gone. The Yankees had been there for over a year. But surely his father still had his wealth.

The next morning, they prepared to leave. Parks hooked the old horse to the buckboard. Mr. Styles gave them a cloth bag full of jerky and dried apricots and peaches. He had two loaves of bread for them and a bottle of whiskey to give to Will for pain. Mr. Styles drew them a map through the woods. It had been an old Indian trail from years ago. Only a few people knew about. It would take them safely for about fifty miles. He put *x*'s on the map showing other plantations. John took the bag and Thad took the map. They thanked Mr. Styles for his generosity. They laid Will in the buckboard on a bed that Parks had made out of hay and old blankets. They covered him and climbed on the seat of the wagon. Bim rode in the back with Will. They waved farewell and headed for the forest trail.

FORTY-THREE

They traveled for days, stopping at night along small creeks. They traveled slowly, so as to not tire or, worse, kill the old horse. They reached another plantation. This place had escaped the wrath of the Yankees. The Jones family welcomed and fed the men. They spent the night, before leaving the next morning. A young fresh horse was given to them to replace the old gelding. They cleaned and redressed Will's wound. The Joneses filled the bag with a smoked turkey and salt pork. They gave them potatoes and dried beans for their travels. John and Thad were grateful as they reentered the woods. It took another week to get through the thicket. According to the map Mr. Styles had drawn, Alabama should be only a few miles away. They no longer had the safety of the hidden forest trail. They traveled at night, hiding in underbrush during the day. People along the way were glad to help them.

Most of the South lay in destruction. John could not believe his eyes as they traveled through the ruin. Houses were destroyed or in need of great repair. The fields were barren and burnt. The cold breezes nipped the air of December. They finally reached the outskirts of Natchez. John drove the horse toward his uncle Ben's plantation. The place looked deserted! The fields were bare and the house looked as if it had not been lived in for years. The once beautiful plantation looked pitiful.

John stopped the horse at the front door. Elizabeth peeked through the window. She saw the ragged Confederate uniforms. She rushed to the door.

"Aunt Elizabeth," John called.

"Who is it?" Elizabeth did not recognize her bearded and half-starved nephews.

"It's John and Thad Wilde!"

"Oh, my goodness. Get in this house, boys!" she screamed with delight. They carried Will into the house and put him to bed. John instructed Bim to put the horse and carriage in the barn.

"Be sure to give him hay and water. Come to the house when you finish. Where is Uncle Ben?"

Elizabeth told them of Ben's death. John knew of his father's capture and release. It was the talk among the Southern folks, but he had no idea his uncle had been shot and killed. Elizabeth kept staring at the Yankee. Will burned with fever. "This is Alex's son Will." Thad told her the story of how they had come to be together. Thad had become fond of his Yankee nephew. He hated that he had come to know Will under those circumstances. He had regrets of being the one that shot Will, although he knew it was not his fault and faced with another Yank, he would do it again.

Elizabeth placed her hand on Will's forehead. "You are burning up!" She reached down and kissed his forehead. "My poor great-nephew." She took a wet rag and wiped his head and neck. "We need to get you out of these filthy clothes and get you cleaned up." Will was too weak to move. Thad and Will lifted him carefully from his clothes. Elizabeth removed the bandage. The wound oozed with green pus. "This looks like gangrene."

She called for Tom, her house slave. "Tom, I need you to fetch Doc Evans, and be quick about it." Tom had remained on the plantation with ten other slaves. All the others had run away to freedom. Elizabeth filled the tub with lukewarm water and instructed John to put Will in it. "We have to get the fever down and get his body cleaned."

Will's arm reeked! They stripped Will naked and put him in the tub. They looked in surprise as Elizabeth walked to Will with soap in her hand. "Don't look so shocked! You two think I have never seen a naked man before?" She scrubbed Will from head to toe. His limp head lay back on the tub. He could not have cared less what was happening, in his state of delirium. She cleaned the wound, as best as she could, before having John and Thad put him back in bed. She turned to her nephews. "Empty that tub and both of you take a bath. You don't smell much better than Will!" Elizabeth seemed a loving and caring aunt, but her sternness was something to reckon with. John and Thad didn't argue. They went directly to bathe. She took them clothes from Ben's armoire.

Tom returned with Doc Evans. "Pete, thank you for coming." Elizabeth welcomed her old friend.

"Tom tells me you have a wounded Yankee in your bedroom," Pete said with some disapproval.

"Yes, I do," she smiled." However, he is my great-nephew. It's William's grandson."

"William's grandson? You don't mean Alex and Jacqueline's son, do you?"

"Yes. Come see him, Pete. I am afraid he has gangrene in his arm." Pete changed his mind about the Yankee. He had known the Wildes and the Exaviers all his life. Why, he had delivered Jacqueline and Alex at birth.

Doc Evans examined Will. Pete turned to Tom. "Take my horse, he's fast. Run to my house and have Missus Evans send you my surgical bag, some ether, and morphine." Tom ran from the house and to the Evanses'. John and Thad entered the bedroom. They shaved and scrubbed their bodies. They both looked fresh and clean.

"Hello, boys, I haven't seen you two in years!" He shook hands with Thad and John, before breaking the bad news to them. "I'm afraid the gangrene has infected all of Will's arm. See how dark the arm is?" They nodded. "It's virtually dead. A miracle it hasn't spread into his shoulder. Actually, he's lucky to be alive. I have no choice but to amputate."

Thad and John just stared at each other. Thad hung his head and left the room.

"He'll be all right. I'll talk to him. Thad's the one that shot him," said John. John told Doc Evans about the battle at Atlanta and how Will had received the bullet. John left to speak to Thad. Thad waited on the front porch, with tears in his eyes. He turned away from John, so he could not see him cry. John put his arm around Thad. "This isn't your fault. You didn't even know who Will was. Those are the hazards of war."

"I know that. But he's my nephew. And now he won't have an arm when he wakes up! He's so young."

"But he will be alive. That's the main thing. Another Confederate would have killed him and you know that!"

"Alex will never understand how I could have shot his son," Thad worried.

"Yeah, Alex will understand. He's going to hate what happened to Will. But like I said, if he hadn't been kin to us, he'd be dead. And Alex will understand that." John continued talking to Thad. John looked down the lane and saw Tom galloping the horse. "Come on, Thad," John urged. "Tom's back. We need to help with Will."

Will lay in a deep sleep, as they moved his limp body to the dining table for surgery. Pete administered ether to Will. He pulled his saw from the bag. John and Thad could not stand to watch. Elizabeth told them to wait outside. She would assist Doc Evans. The two young men rushed from the room and walked outside.

Thad broke down. He could not contain his sorrow any longer and sobbed. John tried to comfort him, but Thad pushed him away. John stood by until Thad pulled himself together. "I've never cried in my life." Thad hung his head with embarrassment.

"There's nothing wrong with crying, Thad. It's good for the soul. I hate that Will is losing his arm. But, you can't take this blame. If I had not seen Will pulling his pistol, you would have been gut-shot. Now, would you lay that blame on Will?"

"No." Thad reflected on the past few years. "I'm ready for this war to end. The South is really taking a beating. Who would've thought it. Those damn Yanks. The South should've stormed the North. Hell, there's no way this war would've lasted so long if the South hadn't been cut off from supplies. How much longer do you think the war will go on?"

"I don't know. Grant's storming Virginia and Sherman has destroyed Georgia. Many other states have already been invaded. I fear the South's coming to an end." They were solemn as they sat on the porch waiting for Doc Evans to finish with Will.

Elizabeth and Doc Evans came to the porch. "Boys, Will's fine. He came through the surgery without any problem. He's sleeping. Come on in. I need you to carry him back to bed. I'll stay over tonight and be here when he awakes. I have a little more morphine. He'll feel no pain, I promise you that."

They carried Will to bed and returned downstairs. Bessy, the old house slave, had prepared dinner. They ate the modest meal of beans, potatoes, and cornbread. Thad and John didn't care. It tasted good to them. John slept well that night, but Thad got up frequently to look in on Will.

At five o'clock that morning, Thad was at Will's side. Doc Evans was asleep in the chair when Will awoke. He looked, groggily, at Thad. Will felt pain in his left shoulder. He reached for his arm. Before Thad could do anything, Will let out a scream. "My arm, where is my arm?" He looked at Thad. "What have you done?"

Doc Evans came to the bed. "Will, It's Doctor Evans. Your arm had gangrene. It was too decayed. I had to amputate. If it hadn't been for Thad's and John's care, you would be dead. You'll be fine, don't worry yourself now. You need to rest. I have some morphine for you." Pete gave him the medicine and Will fell off to sleep. "Let's get some coffee, Thad."

Thad walked out the door with Doc Evans. "Doc, I thought you were going to tell Will you had to amputate," Thad questioned.

"I did tell him. He was delirious. He probably didn't realize what I was telling him. Look, Thad, this is going to be hard for Will. But he'll recover. You'll see." Doc Evans only hoped this would not destroy Will's ambition to live. Pete would never let Will's family know this. They had to be strong for Will.

Bessy was up and had coffee ready. She fixed them eggs and biscuits for breakfast. Elizabeth had been awakened by Will's screams. She looked in on Will and joined Thad and Pete for breakfast. John slept late. He was utterly exhausted. Nothing could wake him!

Doc Evans stayed for a few days, until Will's pain began to ease. The next week, Will began sitting up and eating with appetite. The shock of losing his arm diminished. He was grateful to be alive. He held no blame for his uncle. Thad visited with Will constantly. The two were becoming very close. Thad was eager to get to Texas. Will, on the other hand, wanted to go home to Boston. If he could get to New Orleans, where the Yanks were, he could get back safely.

Elizabeth overheard the three making plans. "You're not going anywhere!" she reprimanded. "You wouldn't make it five miles without getting shot by a Southerner or a vagrant. Besides, the news is that the Yanks pushed the Mississippi troops clear across Louisiana and into Texas! Now, there has been enough death in this family. I haven't heard from Frank in three years and my other two sons are dead. Jolene had to return home with her husband. He returned without his legs! You'll stay here until the war is over and I'll not hear another word about leaving." They just looked at one another. Will felt lucky he had only lost an arm! He couldn't imagine losing both legs.

"Aunt Elizabeth, you're right. We'll wait the war out with you." John worried about Josie, but he would do her no good if he were dead.

CHAPTER
FORTY-FOUR

Things were not as bad in Texas. There wasn't the destruction that had occurred in the Southern States. The Union troops pushed the Confederates all the way to Brownwood. Katie's home sat on the path of the Union soldiers. Asa Rhome rode with his commanding officer late that evening. The light from Katie's home shone through the window. The officer told his men they would camp there overnight.

Katie heard the sound of horses' hooves coming down the lane. She stood at the window. She did not foresee Union soldiers coming to her house. There were too many horses. "What is going on?" she wondered. Katie couldn't see through the dark of the night. The commander rode to the front of the house. He handed his horse to Asa to tend to. Asa took the horses to the barn and got the men ready for camp. Asa had become filled with anger over the years. He had never recovered from the rejection by Katie, and that, along with the spoils of war, had contributed to his rage.

The commander knocked at the front door. Katie answered. Her face showed signs of fear as she gasped and jumped back. She had never seen a Yankee soldier! There was no one to help her. She trembled at the thought of her children upstairs. Apprehension raced through her mind.

"Ma'am, I'm Lieutenant Forrest Beane, with the Union Army."

Katie's strong will surfaced. She arched her back, raising her head with pride! She shouted at the lieutenant, "I want you Yankees off my land!"

Lieutenant Beane looked at her and smiled. "My goodness. You're a brave young lady!" Katie reached swiftly with her hand, slapping the lieutenant across the face. He grabbed her hand. "I mean you no harm. Now, calm down. My men and I are camping here tonight. We're moving on first thing in the morning. There's nothing you can do about it, so just relax."

"How dare you tell me what you're going to do," she screamed.

Lieutenant Beane laughed. "I admire your spunk." He still held her by the arms. He dropped his hands from her slowly and lowered his voice. He spoke softly, using his best manners. Beane removed his cap and bowed to her. He wanted no problems. He just wanted to rest for the night. "No harm will come to your family, I give you my word. My men are tired. They just need to sleep." Katie could see the lieutenant meant well. She hated the Union, but if she let him stay, maybe she could find out more about the war. Most of all, she wondered where Quincy might be. She hoped the lieutenant could answer her questions.

"Well, I'll let you stay. But, you and your men better not damage one thing on my homestead. Do you understand!"

"Yes, Ma'am. I understand. I'll instruct my men right now." Lieutenant Beane turned and walked out the door to check on his men, shaking his head, wondering what he was going to do with the fiery redhead!

The back door slammed. Katie turned quickly to see who had come in. There stood Asa. She stopped dead in her tracks. Asa glared at Katie. His eyes were contemptuous and cold. Katie didn't know that side of Asa. She took a step toward him. She actually felt relieved to have someone she knew at her home. "Asa, it's me, Katie."

"I know who you are, Katie," Asa spoke in a low, controlled voice. He began walking slowly toward her, staring into her eyes. Katie took small steps backward, keeping her eyes on him.

"Asa, what is wrong with you?" she pleaded.

"What is wrong with me? Why don't you tell me what's wrong?"

CHAPTER FORTY-FOUR

Katie kept moving slowly away from Asa. "Asa, I don't know what you're talking about."

"Shut up! Just shut up! You and your promises. Promises you had no intention of keeping. You made me look like a fool, you damn wench."

He began moving quickly toward Katie. Katie bolted for the door. He grabbed her and dragged her, by her long curls, into the parlor. She screamed.

He forced his hand over her mouth and shoved her to the floor. "Shut your mouth or I'll kill you and whoever else you have in this house!" He raised his fist and hit her in the mouth. Her mouth filled with blood; she saw stars. His hands tore at her clothes, ripping at her breasts. She fought to regain her senses. She felt his hand searching under her dress! He was on top of her!

She screamed at the top of her lungs. He pushed his hand over her mouth. She bit him until he bled. He jerked his hand back and she screamed again. He laughed at her and ran his hands over her struggling body. Katie screamed even louder. Lieutenant Beane was on his way back to the house. He heard her screams. He ran through the door and grabbed Asa by the back of the shirt and pulled him off Katie. He pulled out his gun and pistol-whipped Asa across the head. Katie desperately pulled her clothes back together. Lieutenant Beane ordered Asa to be tied to a tree for the night.

"I'm sorry for my soldier's action. He's been acting strange ever since we got to Texas. I don't know what's wrong with him." The lieutenant tried to console Katie. Katie was shaken and filled with anger. She was no longer interested in speaking with the lieutenant.

"You keep that lunatic out of my house. And you better be gone by morning." She went upstairs; gathering her children, she put them in her bed. She bolted her door and placed the loaded rifle by her bed. She sat in the chair, guarding her children and crying softly throughout the night. Katie felt violated and dirty. How would Quincy ever forgive her for allowing the Union soldiers to stay at their home? She did not fall asleep until the early morning hours.

Lieutenant Forrest Beane slept by the stairs all night, to ensure the young lady's safety. He never got a chance to know her name. He woke his men before daybreak. Asa had to ride with his hands tied behind his back. Another soldier led his horse. Lieutenant Beane rode up to Asa and threatened him. "You make one move and I'll blow your head off. Men like you are a disgrace to the Union." Asa stared coldly. Lieutenant Beane had good morals and had watched other officers allow bad behavior among their men and this was something he would not tolerate.

Katie awoke. She looked out her door. She couldn't see nor hear anything. She crept down the stairs and to the front door. The soldiers were gone. Lieutenant Beane left a note on the foyer table.

> *To the bravest lady I have ever met,*
>
> *I did not have a chance to learn your name. I want to apologize with deepest regrets, for the assault against you. Asa Rhome will receive a court martial, I give you my word. He is a disgrace to his uniform. God speed to you and Texas.*
>
> *Lieutenant Forrest Beane*

Katie read the note. Maybe she had misjudged the Union lieutenant. She remembered her times in Boston and how much she loved the people there. The war had made everyone crazy. She thought of Quincy and John, wondering whether they were dead or alive. She wished the war would end. She stopped and knelt on the floor. She lowered her head and prayed to God to bring Quincy and John safely home. Katie prayed for everyone, including the Yankees.

FORTY-FIVE

That spring, while Will recuperated, Thad and John worked on the plantation. The slaves helped them clean up the fields around the house and plant the garden. It was the middle of March. Thad and John were busy working in the garden. A man walked slowly up the lane. John stood up and stared, until he finally recognized his cousin Frank. Frank looked weary and tattered. "Frank, it's me. Cousin John!"

Frank looked up. His spirits leaped. He didn't know what to expect at home. He had received the news of his father's death while in Tennessee. He didn't know if any of his other family members were alive or not. He ran to John with all the energy he had left. John embraced him.

"What in the world are you two doing here? Damn, I'm glad to see you!" Frank spoke with excitement. What a wonderful surprise to see his cousins!

"According to Aunt Elizabeth, we're going to be here until the war ends," Thad laughed. "Actually, we had some problems while at Atlanta. Alex's son Will is a Yank. Can you believe it?"

"A Yank." Frank was surprised.

"Yeah," Thad continued. "You know he was raised up North with all their beliefs. I guess when you think about it, it isn't surprising.

Anyway, he was shot. To make a long story short, Will lost his arm and we are here while he recuperates," Thad stated. "I'll tell you all about it later."

"Yeah, I'd like to hear about that. Where is Mother?" Frank asked.

"Aunt Elizabeth is in the house. She's going to be thrilled to see you, Frank." John told Frank their story as the three of them walked to the house. John told him all about Will and their travels to Mississippi. "We really are staying here until the war ends," John added.

"You won't be here much longer. The Yanks have beaten us, John. It's only a matter of time," Frank told them.

Elizabeth heard Frank's voice. She ran to him, throwing her arms around him. She burst into tears of joy. Frank took her into the house. He set her down in the parlor.

"Mother, I have to tell you some bad news. It's about Benny and Tim."

"Oh, honey. I already know. Their names were posted a year ago. It's been you I've been so worried about. I didn't know if you were alive or not." Elizabeth hugged him again. "Stand up and let me look at you." Frank stood up and turned. "Well, you look just fine. All you need is a good bath and some hot food."

Frank bathed and returned for lunch. Will had begun to get around with ease. They all sat at the table exchanging war stories. Elizabeth hated the depressing talk. "Listen, boys. I'm sick of hearing about this war. You talk about something else!"

"Aunt Elizabeth, you want me to tell you some more stories about Colorado and the gold rush!" Thad loved to tell his stories.

"That sounds wonderful. Tell me all about the mountains. Tell me everything, Thad." Elizabeth enjoyed his tales. They laughed with Thad for hours. She enjoyed having the sounds of young people in her home again.

Jolene and her husband, Bob, came to stay. Jolene hugged Frank with tears of jubilation. "It's just you and me, Frankie." Jolene missed Benny and Tim. She thanked God He had spared them Frank. Bob had a great sense of humor. He made jokes about walking and his legs.

CHAPTER FORTY-FIVE

Everyone laughed. Bob's ability to enjoy life, despite his handicap, helped Will to see there was a lot to be thankful for. In the evenings, Elizabeth played the piano, while Jolene and the men sang.

"Aunt Elizabeth, you can really play that piano! You know, my little sister, Sarah, plays the piano. The last I heard, Father planned to send her to Europe to study." Will talked with pride at the mention of Sarah. Elizabeth wanted to hear all about Sarah and Zan. She thought back to Reginia's Sarah and the sweetness that had abounded in the child.

The men worked alongside the few slaves that remained, planting grain and corn. Bob scooted on the ground with a short hoe chopping weeds. Will used his right arm. He adopted Bob's sense of humor. "Look at us, Bob! Aren't we a dandy sight," Will exclaimed. "If we could put our bodies together we'd make a hell of a man!" They all laughed. Bob and Will cracked jokes every day, about themselves or anything they found amusing.

One day during lunch, Elizabeth wandered about searching for her apron. "What are you doing?" Bob asked.

"I'm looking for my apron. I can't find the darn thing anywhere!"

"I know how you feel, Mom. I've been looking for my darn legs for two years now and I still haven't found them!" Laughter filled the room.

Elizabeth slapped him teasingly on the back. "Stop that, Bob! I really need to find my apron."

"Not nearly as bad as I need to find my legs!" Bob chuckled.

"I give up with you boys. You're so bad," Elizabeth quipped.

"Aunt Elizabeth. Why do you keep calling us boys? Do you know I am thirty-five years old?" John teased.

"I know how old you are! But you're still boys to me!" Elizabeth loved having them with her. She dreaded the day they would leave.

On April 9, 1865, Lee surrendered to Grant at Appomattox Court House in Virginia. By the end of May, General Kirby Smith surrendered the trans-Mississippi forces in Texas. General Kirby was the last Confederate general to surrender. The Civil War was over!

Thad, John, and Will prepared to leave for Texas. John insisted Will go with them. He would get Will back to Boston on his father's ship. Thad had one more thing to do. "Come with me, John." He got a shovel and went to the big tree by the barn. He dug deep into the ground. There was the trunk. Thad and John lifted the trunk and opened the lid. Thad's big trunk was filled to the top with gold! John's eyes widened. He had never seen so much gold! They carried the trunk to the house. "I'm going to give Aunt Elizabeth a bag of gold. She can use it to restore the plantation," Thad told John. John agreed. They would also have to buy a wagon and mules for the trip home.

Thad took the bag of gold to Elizabeth. It was so heavy she could barely lift it. Her eyes welled up with tears. "Where did you get this?"

"I brought it with me from Colorado. I buried it here on my way to join the army. Uncle Ben helped me bury it, right before he left for England."

"Ben never told me. I didn't even know you were here."

"You were at Jolene's house when I stopped by. I was only here a couple of hours. Uncle Ben felt, for everyone's safety, that we should not tell anyone. If word of such gold got out, the place would be ransacked. Just thank the good Lord that I wasn't killed. That gold would have never been found! Seriously, Aunt Elizabeth, I want you to put this gold to good use. Rebuild your home. Frank and Jolene will help you. After all, this is the original Wilde plantation! My father would never want it in someone else's hands."

Elizabeth hugged Thad. "Thank you, Thad, ever so much. I will always be grateful to you."

Thad hugged his aunt. "I love you, Aunt Elizabeth."

"And, I love you, my darling Thad."

Thad and John purchased a covered wagon and a team of mules. They loaded the gold in three trunks, topping them with blankets and old clothes. Elizabeth, Frank, Jolene, and Bob waved as the young men left the plantation. Their stay had brought them all a family love for one another that would last a lifetime!

CHAPTER

FORTY-SIX

News of the war's ending reached Texas. Everyone waited patiently for their loved ones to return. Katie learned of the news first. She worked hard, trying to forget about Asa. Keeping the incident a secret became difficult for her. She had to tell someone and that someone would have to be Josie!

Katie took the children to Josie's to tell her the good news about the war ending and to tell Josie her secret. In spite of her own inner turmoil, she was exhilarated at the ending of the war. Quincy and John would be home soon! Katie rushed with the children into the house. "Josie. Josie, where are you?" she called with excitement.

"I'm here, Katie." Josie came from the back porch to meet Katie and the children. "The war is over!" Katie jumped with glee.

Josie stood in amazement. She leaped in the air and grabbed Katie. "It's over? I can't believe it!" They jumped and hugged each other like little children. Jane and Danielle, now ten and eleven years old, were running out the door with the younger ones at their heels. The children had little if any recollection of their fathers. All they knew were the stories and pictures of them.

"Tell me, Katie, have you any news of John and Quincy?"

"I saw a paper listing the dead. Their names weren't on it!"

"That means they should be home soon! I can't wait." Josie and Katie talked all morning, making plans for the return of their husbands.

After lunch, Katie decided to tell Josie about the Union soldiers and Asa. Katie told Josie the entire sordid story. Josie sat quietly listening to each detail. The thought of Katie carrying this burden for so long, disturbed Josie. "Why did you not tell me sooner?"

"I wanted to," Katie explained. "But I felt so ashamed."

"Ashamed of what? There was nothing you could do to stop the Yankees from camping at your place. And, Asa, my goodness, Katie. Just be thankful you did not marry the idiot!

"Josie, I don't know what I would have done if Asa had succeeded in raping me!"

"Put it out of your mind. He didn't and that is what you have to be grateful for. Be thankful for that Yankee lieutenant!"

Katie pulled the letter Lieutenant Beane wrote her from her purse. "Read this, Josie."

Josie took the brief note and read it. "He refers to you as the bravest lady he has ever known. What did you do, Katie, for him to say that?"

"Well," she smiled. "I bluntly told him no Yankee would stay at my home and then I slapped him!"

"You did what!" Josie burst into laughter. Katie had more spunk than anyone she knew!

Katie left early to go by her parents'. She wanted to make sure they had heard the war had ended. William had heard the news from Joseph. "What will this mean for us, Father, now that we have lost the war?"

"Joseph heard a lot of talk about this in Houston. The Confederacy actually fell after Lee surrendered. Each state is going to have to accept the reconstruction terms imposed by the federal government. What will become of the Confederate States? I don't know."

"What are the terms, Father?" Katie appeared bewildered and somewhat frightened for her future.

"I don't know them all. The first thing we have to do is free the slaves. We can no longer work them without pay."

CHAPTER FORTY-SIX

The slaves finally had their freedom. Many of them left the plantation without any idea of what they would do. They did not care where they went just so long as they were free. The idea of doing whatever they pleased overwhelmed them, even though they knew nothing beyond planting. They were slaves no longer!

Many of William's and Josie's slaves fled. However, over fifty Negroes remained on each plantation. They were free but they wanted to work for the masters they loved. The fields were all they knew. Those that stayed feared life without a home or place to work. Josie had money to pay the slaves, but William had lost an entire fortune with the Confederacy. He made an agreement to give the slaves a percentage of the cotton crops.

The Southern States had five years ahead of Reconstruction, a time of bitterness and resentment. Federal troops occupied the major cities. Large plantations were in ruins and the wealthy owners were penniless. Life was shattered for the Southern plantation master and his family!

CHAPTER
FORTY-SEVEN

The Civil War had its price. More than half a million men had died and another half million had been wounded and crippled for life. The government was in tremendous debt. The Confederate paperbacks were of no value and had to be replaced by gold or silver. The Union greenbacks were not redeemable at their face value in gold. Three hundred dollars in paper money was worth only one hundred in gold. The greatest problem, however, was to reconstruct the South.

Turbulent times lay waiting for the South. President Andrew Johnson attempted to follow Lincoln's moderate plan to allow each state to reestablish civil governments when ten percent of the 1860 electorate took the prescribed loyalty oath. However, this action by the Union was short-lived. Dissatisfied with the moderate provisions of presidential Reconstruction, Congress imposed military rule on the Southern States. The former Confederate States were divided into five military districts, giving the commanding general of each district total power over state laws and officials. Military rule was now in effect, along with the new amendment, giving national citizenship and guaranteed full civil rights to the freedman, for the first time. The next four years found Negroes and Negro-White coalitions controlling every state government in the South. The Southerners who cooperated with the Radicals, the dominate political party that enfranchised the Negroes, were called scalawags, and the Northerners who went south to take part in the Reconstruction were known as carpetbaggers. They were called carpetbaggers because it was said that they came south with all their worldly possessions in carpetbags. The carpetbaggers saw an opportunity to gain wealth by buying the plantations and businesses for taxes owed. The once wealthy plantation owner had been reduced to bankruptcy. Looters and vagrants roamed the area. Crime became rampant and the six-shooter replaced the law in Texas.

Josie had money to pay the fifty Negroes that remained on the plantation, but fifty men were not enough to work the fields. All summer, she and the children joined the freedmen in chopping the weeds and picking the cotton. She planted a garden to feed her family. Carrie stayed to take care of "her family." She had her hands full tending to the house. Josie never gave up. Her hands became callused, often cracking and bleeding.

"Missus, you shouldn't work yourself and those childrens so hard," Carrie scolded.

"I have to. I won't lose Holly Hill to ruin. I want things to be good when John returns."

Katie, in despair, came to visit Josie. Her slaves had run away. She had no help. Stanley did what he could for Katie, but he was busy with Auburn. Her land was overgrown with grass and weeds, and the cattle had wandered off. She planted a small garden and tended to her house chores. Her money was depleted and Katie could not go to her father, for he was broke. Josie had pity for Katie and offered her money.

"I don't want money from you, Josie. Hold on to what you have. We don't know what the future holds. You and John will need what you have. I can work like the other women. I just need a friend to complain to," Katie laughed. "After all, complaints are all we have now! The Union may have won the war, but they will not defeat me." That was one point both ladies agreed on.

"The newspapers are telling about the terrible conditions of the Southern States. We're fortunate Texas didn't suffer ruin. We still have our homes and our land wasn't harmed. We have plenty of food and the crops will be ready to ship soon. Things could be a lot worse, Katie. Your father will soon have his ships in route again and he will regain his fortune." Josie was optimistic. A view that would soon become a nightmare.

"I was told that John was released with many other soldiers." Katie paused briefly as she sighed with anguish. "He'll return soon. I only hope Quincy will be with him. I'm so worried about them. I hate that they're returning to such a sad land. The roads are overgrown, they're barely trails now, and the homes may still be standing, but they need repair and paint so badly. It just isn't the same as when they left."

"Nothing is the same as when they left, Katie, my dear!"

The planters, including Josie and Stanley, took their cotton to the ports for shipping; however, the Union military seized all the cotton. They claimed the cotton was there from the past to support the Confederacy. Their hopes for money diminished once more. Stanley returned to Auburn with empty hands. William was devastated. The loss of his fortune caused great despair for William. He was too old to start over. Shortly after, William received news that his ships were confiscated by the Union and Josh was killed trying to resist the Federal officers. His world crumbled around him. Auburn had been neglected, and was now overridden with weeds. Reginia had only Batha to help. William had sent all the remaining slaves on their way. Without the money he assumed he would get for the cotton, he could not pay the slaves the shares he promised. In return, William gave them land on the far southwest corner.

William gave Samuel twenty-five acres to build a home on.

"This is all I have to give you, Samuel."

"Master, you don't have to give me land. I'll stay here with you."

"No, you're free and you're educated. Do something for yourself, Samuel, while you have time." William felt beaten, as he sent Samuel away. Samuel was the same age as William, sixty-five. He didn't know what he could possibly do. The Radicals approached Samuel to work in an office. The respect that the slaves felt for Samuel, his education, and sophisticated manner fit the description the Radicals wanted. He took the job and tried to help other freedmen to find their way in the new world. He and Rogette moved to Houston.

Within the year, Samuel had become a success. He built a home on the land William gave him. He wanted to move there in a few years. It hurt him to see William suffering. William resented the Union government and their favoritism toward the blacks over the once-prominent white men of the area. The difficult conditions of life weighed against him. He could not bring his pride to conform to the Radicals' way of governing. Reginia hoped for John's quick return. Auburn was safe for a while with Josie's help, for she had paid the taxes on the land. Reginia wished she knew where Thad was. She feared she would never see him again. In desperation, she wrote to Alex, begging him to come home.

Stanley could no longer work for William without pay, so Josie hired Stanley as her foreman. She promised him work, until Jake returned. If, indeed, Jake would return. Josie changed her plans for planting cotton. She would expand the cattle business. There was demand for beef and she would take advantage of it. Stanley and a group of men rounded up cattle until the end of fall. There were a thousand longhorns branded. There were no fences in Texas. The open ranges were full of cattle that had strayed during the war. Other ranchers also rounded up cattle and branded them. Several times a year, they worked together separating the longhorns for shipping. Cattle drives sprung up between Texas and Kansas. Times were changing and Josie understood she would have to change with them to survive.

Joseph Riley died that fall. The loss of his slaves had placed a big burden on Joseph. He worked too hard and it had cost him his life. Golda was left with no money and had to sell some of the land for the taxes owed. She refused to sell to the carpetbaggers. Josie bought the land at minimum price. Golda's children were gone. After the war, they scattered to find a better way of life. She felt all alone. Reginia spent time with Golda, consoling her. Golda, being a strong German woman, would live off the remaining land.

Jake returned from the war in November. He stayed with Golda, working the land and building a small herd of cattle. Jake had no news of John and Quincy. He had joined the Texas brigades with them, but explained that late in the first year, they had become separated. He knew John had joined Jackson and he thought Quincy had gone with John.

Katie could no longer live without money. She had given all her money to pay the taxes on her home. She rode to Josie's to confide in her.

"Josie, I had to spend all my money to pay the taxes on my property. I can't lose our home. Quincy may not return soon. I only pray he's alive. I've made a decision. I'm sending the children to my parents', while I go to Houston for work." Katie knew she had to make some money and that would bring sacrifices.

"Katie, don't go. Let me help you. You can live here."

"No. But, thank you, Josie. This is something I have to do on my own. Quincy will come home and I must have a place for us to live and money to live on!"

"Let the children stay here. Your parents have enough problems. I would be glad to keep them, if you must do this."

"I spoke to Mother, yesterday. She's eager to have the children. She thinks it will be good for Father. He's so distraught. I must ask you one favor, Josie."

"Anything, Katie. I'll do anything to help you."

"Please make sure they have plenty of food. Batha and Mother work so hard. Thank goodness Batha is there. Have you seen Auburn? The pastures and yard look terrible. I cannot bare to see it this way."

"I know. It's almost Christmas. So much has changed in the last year. I hardly recognize our great state. I'll take care of your parents and children. They will have plenty to eat and warm clothes to wear. I wish John would get home. I can't imagine where they could be. They should've been home a year ago."

"I fear something dreadful has happened. I hate to think about it. I'll continue to wait for Quincy, until I get more information as to his whereabouts."

Katie sent her children to live with her parents and moved to Houston. Katie would not let the Scalawags and Radicals get the best of her. She could play their game too. Katie went to Samuel for help. He was surprised to see her.

"What in the world are you doing here, Missus?"

Katie smiled warmly. She was glad to see his friendly face. "I must be blunt, Samuel. I need help. I have no money and I need work. Can you help me?"

"I can help. And it's my pleasure. What did you have in mind?"

"I don't know. I'll do anything. I do know how to work hard, thanks to my father." Katie smiled.

"There's a mercantile store in town that needs help. Why don't I talk to Mister Tompkins for you? I'm sure he'll give you a job. You'll need a place to live. Rogette and I have a home in town. We have rooms we let for boarding. Would you stay with us?" Samuel knew Katie had concerns about staying where other blacks were. "It's a boarding house. The occupants are white Union agents. You're more than welcome. We wouldn't want you to pay anything, Katie. You're like family to us."

Katie was not eager to live with Yankees, but she enjoyed the thought of being near Rogette and Samuel and having free board. "Yes, Samuel, I would appreciate that. Thank you."

She moved into the large boarding house and went to work in Mr. Tompkins's mercantile store. Katie wore her beautiful smile and found it easy to sell goods. Mr. Tompkins soon relied heavily on Katie. He taught her how to keep the books and purchase wares. She worked all day in the store, rushing home in the evenings to help Rogette with supper. She saw her family only on holidays. She saved some money to buy gifts for Christmas.

CHAPTER
FORTY-EIGHT

Two days before Christmas, Josie was in the field with Stanley, selecting a tree to trim. In the distance, she saw a man on horseback. The horse turned slowly down the lane toward the house. The man had long hair and a beard. His clothes were old and worn. Stanley stopped to see who was riding up the lane. He did not know the stranger. Josie kept staring. Her heart began to pound. "Could that be John?" The horse continued at a walk toward the house. Josie ran across the field toward the rider. It was John!

"John. John," Josie screamed.

John stopped the horse and he looked at Josie for the first time in almost six years. He jumped from his horse and ran quickly to her, grabbing her and swinging her in the air. Her arms held tight around his neck. Tears of joy streamed down her face. John stood her on the ground and looked into her eyes. She ran her hands over his face, feeling his scruffy beard.

"I've missed you so much. I feared you would never be home! I love you, John!" She hugged him, afraid if she let go, he would disappear. "Come to the house. You have to see your children. They've grown a lot!" She called to Stanley. "Stanley, it's John! Please bring the tree to the house! It will be a grand Christmas this year!"

The children ran out to see the tree when they heard their mother shout to Stanley. They had no thought of their father being present. John stopped a short distance from the children, who stood staring at him as though he were a stranger. "They've grown. I didn't think they would be so big. Look at Danielle. Why, look at Elijah! He walks!"

"John, Elijah is seven years old, what did you expect?" Josie laughed at John's bewildered expression. They walked to the children, who were quietly looking on. Josie embraced them all in a huddle, facing John.

"This is your father," she said softly. "I told you he'd be home someday." Josie had told them stories of John every night before they went to bed. He did not look like the person in the picture. The children were hesitant in their reactions. John knelt by them and spoke of his love for them. He tried to hug them but they were reluctant to respond. John looked so disappointed, but he realized they didn't know him. He hated what the war had done. Josie anguished over the children's response and hugged John in sympathy.

"Don't worry," Josie comforted. "They'll come around, once they get to know you. Now come into the house and get cleaned up. Carrie will fix you something to eat."

Josie cut John's hair for him before he took a hot bath. She scrubbed his back as he soaked his weary body. "John, where have you been all this time? Other men got home just a few months after the war."

He told her his story, beginning with meeting up with Thad. He told her about Will and their escape to Aunt Elizabeth's. John talked for half an hour about their journeys during the war and on to San Augustine. Josie hung her head in sorrow. She could not believe their hardships. John got out of the tub and continued his story while he put on a fresh set of clothes.

"We stayed a few days, to rest, at the Wades'. We were preparing to leave when Union officers arrested me. I was a lieutenant in the war and the local Yankees found out somehow. Thad and Will stayed. They would not leave without me. It was a year before Mister Wade was able to get me released. He came to know a Union general. It was his friendship to the general that got me out of the prison. I'll be eternally grateful to him."

CHAPTER FORTY-EIGHT

"Where are Thad and Will, now?"

"They're at Auburn with Mother and Father. I didn't even stop. I came directly home."

"I know your parents are glad to see them."

"Now, you tell me what's been going on here."

"First, let me ask you about Quincy. Do you know where he is?" Josie knew Katie would want her to ask.

"Quincy? I thought he would be home by now." John had no idea what had happened after Atlanta.

"No, we haven't heard anything from him. All we know is his name is not posted on the death list."

"I last saw Quincy in Atlanta. We couldn't get him to leave with us. There were hundreds of injured men. He felt it was his duty to stay and help. The war was terrible there. I can't imagine what it must have been like in Atlanta during that battle. The Union burned the city." John could only think the worst had happened to Quincy. Josie begged him not to say anything to Katie, but John saw the destruction from a distance and knew Quincy was probably dead. There would be no reason to imprison him. He felt Katie should be told.

While John ate his meal, Josie told him all that had taken place in Texas, including the attack on Katie. "John, your father is destitute and is going through a severe depression."

"I'm not shocked by my father's loss." John had seen many plantations destroyed, their owners left penniless. "Texas had very little destruction, but the financial loss is across the nation. I must get Katie home. If we're financially stable, as you tell me, then we shouldn't let Katie be away from her children. Especially with the news I must tell her."

"I tried to get her to stay here. She refused. Katie wants to make it on her own. We're going to your parents' for Christmas dinner. Katie will be there. Maybe you can convince her to come home."

Danielle, Elijah, and Victoria came into the dining room. Danielle paused, looking at John, clean, shaved, and his hair cut like it used to be. She remembered her father and ran to him. He was thrilled as he pulled her to him and hugged her. Victoria and Elijah watched with apprehension. John looked at them. "I know you don't remember me.

It's been a long time. I never forgot you. I thought about you children and your mother every day. I just didn't realize how grown-up you'd be before I got home. I love you all very much." John knelt down with one arm still around Danielle and held his hand out to the other two. Victoria and Elijah moved slowly to him. He put his arm around them and gently pulled all three children close to him. John felt at peace, with his family by his side. Josie walked to her family and wrapped her arms gently around John's neck. They spent time with the children before dinner. John wanted to get to know his children. After supper, they trimmed the tree and sang Christmas carols. The children were becoming at ease with their father and enjoying their father's love.

That night, John tucked his children into bed. He told them stories about himself, Uncle Thad, and cousin Will. He said a special prayer of thanks for being home and at the end of the prayer, Elijah added a few words: "Thank you, God, for bringing me my father home. Amen." John hugged him and promised to never leave again.

Josie took her bath with mint leaves floating in the water, while John tucked the children in. She lay in bed waiting patiently for him. He opened the door and saw her bare shoulders protruding from under the sheets. Her long dark hair hung about her soft face. She looked radiant. The moonlight that glowed through the glass door shimmered across her white skin. He climbed into bed and snuggled his face on her neck. She smelled fresh. The familiar scent of mint filled John's nostrils. He took a deep breath.

"I love the way you smell." John began kissing her. He had waited five years to be with his wife. His heart pounded with excitement. The night was filled with passion as they rekindled their love for one another.

Thad and Will rode up the grassy trail toward home. Twelve years had passed since Thad had last traveled the lane. The dead winter grass covered the empty fields of Auburn. It seemed strange to see the vacant plantation that once yielded many slaves, cattle, and horses. Thad was distressed by the sight. The days of glory had long since passed. He knew he could not leave the plantation in such a state. Thad wondered if his parents were still alive, and if they were, what had happened to his father's great wealth? If the money was depleted, Thad would use his gold to restore the poverty-stricken Auburn.

The house appeared to be intact, but the yard was overgrown with winter grass and weeds. Everything was quiet. Thad and Will were apprehensive as they approached the front porch. Thad opened the door slowly. "Mother, Father," he called several times. "Is anyone here?" There was no answer. They walked throughout the house and found no one. Thad became angry and hurt. "This damn war. My parents have died and I wasn't here to bury them! Josie or Katie must be keeping up the house. Those poor girls." His voice filled with pity as he sat on the sofa. Will noticed embers still hot in the fireplace.

"Look, Thad. Someone has been here recently. There's been a fire. Maybe they've gone visiting."

"I don't think so. I'm telling you, I don't feel good about this. I'm going to the cemetery." They walked out the back toward the burial grounds. Thad dreaded finding new graves.

Reginia had gone with Batha and William to cut a tree for Christmas. Reginia wanted the day to be special for Katie, Josie, and the grandchildren. It was sad enough not having her sons and Quincy home for the holidays. The fact that they had no money would not stop her from having a tree and a good meal for her remaining family. William chopped at the small cedar growing just beyond Ransom's grave. Reginia stood facing the house. Thoughts of happier days filled her mind. Suddenly, the two men caught her eye. "William, there are two men walking from the house." William turned to see who it could possibly be.

"Hello, over there. Who is that coming from inside my house?"

Thad stopped and looked toward his parents. His heart leaped with joy. His parents were alive! "It's your son Thad! And I brought you a surprise." Thad ran toward his mother and father. William dropped the ax and walked quickly in the footsteps of Reginia, who rushed to greet their son. Reginia's eyes filled with tears of relief. She grabbed Thad and hugged him with all her might. She looked at the young man with Thad.

"Will! Oh, my goodness gracious!" She let go of Thad and hugged Will. "What are you doing here? Look William! It's little Will!"

William, who had been hugging Thad, took Will's extended hand to shake it. "He doesn't look so little to me!" They were so glad to see Thad and Will. They were thrilled to have Will at Auburn!

"Where are John and Quincy," Reginia asked quickly.

"John went on to Josie's and we haven't heard from Quincy since Atlanta. We thought he would be home. You haven't heard from him?"

"No," Reginia said, concerned.

"Atlanta was captured and much of the city was burned." Thad saw the worry in his mother's eyes. "I'm sure he's safe," he reassured her. "He was probably taken prisoner by the Union." He did not want to alarm his parents with the possibility of Quincy being dead.

William gave his grandson a big bear-hug. Something felt strange. He moved Will's coat off his left shoulder.

Reginia, watching William, gasped in horror at the sight and grabbed hold of Thad. William questioned his grandson. "What's happened, Will?"

"I lost my arm from a wound I received in a battle. I'm alive thanks to John and Thad." Thad could not lie to his parents. "I shot him, Father." His parents looked in shock.

Will began to laugh. "Actually, he shot a Yankee. You didn't even know it was me!" he laughed at Thad. "I'm fine. There are many men worse off than me. Poor Bob lost both his legs."

"Bob? Bob who," William questioned.

"Bob, Aunt Elizabeth's son-in-law," Will responded. "Thank goodness Thad shot me in my left arm!" He threw his right arm upward. "See, the most important arm works just fine!"

Thad laughed. Reginia and William just looked puzzled by it all. "Wait a minute. I'm confused," William declared. "How do you know Bob? And what in blue blazes were you doing fighting for the Union?"

"Grandfather, I was raised in Boston, remember? I never lived under the slave-holding regime. I don't even believe in it. All the Negroes I know are free and work for pay. I fought for what I believed in. As for Bob, we met him during our stay at Aunt Elizabeth's. That's where my arm had to be amputated. It's a long story. Could I tell you the rest after we clean up and maybe eat a bite?"

Reginia, still holding on to Thad, placed her other arm around Will's waist. "You certainly can. Come on to the house. You can tell us all about the war after dinner. Come on, William, let's take the boys in and let them get cleaned up. Batha, heat some water for our young men." Batha rushed to the house and built a fire. Within the hour, Thad and Will were scrubbed and clean-shaven. They joined Reginia and William in the dining room for a meal and told them their story in full.

Reginia looked at her son and grandson. They were no longer boys. They were men scarred by the war. She felt helpless. There was nothing she could do to change the pain Thad and Will had endured.

Thad was curious about Auburn. "Father, where are the cattle and your horses? Things look bad here."

"Well, son, I'll tell you. I backed the Confederacy with all I had. What horses I didn't send with the Confederacy, the Union soldiers took. The cattle have just strayed away to greener pastures. I had to send the slaves away that remained. I had no money to pay them. I gave them land instead. We are flat broke. If it hadn't been for Josie paying the taxes, I wouldn't have Auburn. Katie had to move to Houston for work, that's why we have her children. You have never seen them. They are good kids. Golda took them to her house for a visit. Jake and Trudy have two children they play with. They will be home shortly."

Thad hated seeing his father's anguish. The thought of Katie working and living away from her children saddened Thad. "Father. I have a lot of gold with me. Why, I'm a rich man! We'll hire help and rebuild Auburn."

"You have gold?" William questioned.

"Yes. I struck it big up in the mountains. We'll bring this old plantation back to glory! Where are your ships?"

"The Union confiscated them. They're holding them in Galveston."

Reginia interjected hopefully. "I've written to your father, Will, telling him of our situation. I pray he can help in some way. He has Union connections and maybe he can get the ships released. Alex and Jacqueline are worried out of their minds about you. We'll have to get word to them that you are here."

Alex and Jacqueline were indeed troubled over their missing son. Times were hard for them in Boston. Their friends gloated with pride over the Union conquering the South. Alex saw it as nothing more than brutality. He saw no need in burning and destroying the Southern cities and plantations. He hated the poverty it brought to the once-great cotton planters. The Yankees rushed to take advantage of the depressed South. They were buying the land for little money. Alex and Jacqueline considered the letter they received from Reginia, begging them to come home. Zan was eager to go to Auburn and Sarah was doing well in Europe.

"Why don't we sell our home and move back to Texas?" Alex wanted to go home. He had no use for Boston, the city he had once loved so much. "I could make use of my Union background. As far as they have to know, I'm going south to make my fortune, just like the rest of the carpetbaggers!"

"I'm ready, Alex. I feel betrayed by the North. They've killed my entire family. I have no love for this place." Her brothers had been killed in the war and her sisters were shot in their own home by Union soldiers. "We don't even know if Will is alive. They have given us no hope for his return."

Alex sold his home and made plans to relocate his shipping business to Galveston. Jacqueline wrote to Sarah, who was enjoying her life in Europe, and Reginia, informing them of their decision to move. Alex had all their belongings put on one of his ships bound for Texas.

CHAPTER
FORTY-NINE

Christmas at Auburn was a joyous occasion for the Wildes. Everyone gathered around the table for dinner. Thad shot a wild turkey and Batha prepared all the trimmings, including a sweet potato pie. Katie was glad to see her brothers. She questioned them about Quincy. John let Thad tell his explanation for Quincy's absence. He would talk to Katie in private after the Christmas celebration. He wanted her to have a few hours of happiness with her children and family.

The afternoon air was clear and crisp as John took Katie aside. Josie told the others what John was telling her. Katie was not prepared for John's news.

"Katie, my sister, I want to tell you something. It's hard for me to tell you this, but I feel you must know the truth."

Katie looked bewildered. "What is it, John. You know you can tell me anything. Why, I'm just thrilled you all are safe at home!"

"It isn't about us. It is about Quincy."

Her voice quivered. "What about Quincy?" She did not like the worried tone in John's voice.

"Honey, the battle was fierce in Atlanta, as we told you. We saw the city burning from the distance. His name was not listed among the dead or the prisoners of war, but I fear he lost his life in the blaze. It would be possible that he was not found. If he were alive, I believe he would be home by now."

"I don't want to hear this! You just got home! Quincy will be home soon, I just know he will!" Katie shouted.

John took her in his arms. "Katie, I'm not trying to discourage you. I just want you to be realistic in your hopes. You can't hold on to something that may never come true. I want you to come home. Your children need you. Josie tells me that the school needs a teacher. Evidently, Georgia has moved away. There are many children here that need educating. Please consider the position. You would be perfect. You helped Georgia many times in the past. If Quincy should possibly return, you need to be waiting at home, not in Houston! I'll take care of you, Katie. You're my only sister."

"I love you, John. Thank you." Katie cried as she hugged John, glad to have his support. "If what you say is true, my children do need me. I miss them so much when I'm away. But I do think Quincy will return, no matter what you say. I can feel it in my heart. I'll teach the children and keep my home ready for my husband."

"All right." He patted her shoulder. "I'll go with you to Houston and help you move home." John was relieved he had talked Katie into coming home. He only wished she would not cling to her ideas about Quincy. Then again, maybe Quincy was alive, who was he to say for sure. Katie remained in the library. She had to sort out her thoughts.

John told his family that Katie would be teaching the children and living at her home. Everyone was elated! What a wonderful Christmas it was. Reginia knew the Lord had not forsaken them. He was bringing her family back to her.

Stanley, who had joined the Wildes for Christmas, rushed to be with Katie. "Are you all right?"

"Yes, Stanley, I'm fine. I just need some time to sort things out. Do you think John is right and Quincy could be dead?" Katie's eyes were dewy as she fought back her tears.

"I don't know. It has been a long time. Perhaps he's injured and has taken shelter to recover." The thought seemed unlikely to Stanley, but he hated to see Katie worry over Quincy.

"I must hold on to my faith that he'll come home to me. But I'm going to go on with my life. I'll teach school and care for my children. John will help and things will be easier for me."

"I'm here for you, Katie. If you need anything I'll be there." Stanley felt deeply for Katie. If it were not for her devotion to Quincy, he could easily allow himself to fall in love with her.

"Thank you. I'll take you up on that!" Katie felt secure with the support of her family and Stanley.

Late that evening, John and his family, along with Stanley, returned to Holly Hill. Thad and Will occupied one bedroom and Katie and her children took the other two bedrooms at William and Reginia's. Everyone was content.

The next morning, Thad and Will joined William to make plans for Auburn. William delighted in their determination to restore the plantation. Thad sent Will to hire as many men as he could to work. He would give them good wages and a place to live. The old quarters were empty and all they needed were to be cleaned. Thad talked with his father about possible uses for the land.

Will was gone a week seeking workers for Auburn. He returned New Year's Eve with good news. "I hired twenty-five strong Negroes. Several are married. A couple of the black women can work in the house. They will arrive on the second of January. There are carpetbaggers in Houston seeking land and businesses. The Texans I spoke with are angry and are busy trying to occupy the vacant land. They don't want the Northerners to settle here. We need to help."

"You're beginning to sound like a Texan yourself," Thad laughed.

"Well, let's not go that far! Let's say I don't agree with anyone taking advantage of someone else's bad luck. I don't care who they are." The Northerners' actions had shocked Will.

The year 1867 looked promising. The workers arrived. Thad and Will showed them where they would stay. Thad instructed them to begin cleaning the quarters, working in the yard, and cutting the weeds off the lanes, while he and Will set out to buy horses. The Union officers had many fine thoroughbreds. They eagerly accepted gold from Thad, giving him the pick of the herd. Thad took twenty good brood mares, a fine stallion, and fifteen geldings for riding. He also wanted to round-up as much cattle as possible. They gathered their supplies and took the horses back to Auburn. William smiled with satisfaction as the two men brought the horses up the lane.

The cattle would be rounded up immediately. Thad wanted to get the first pick of the cattle, before the other people did in the spring. They took ten men with them. They were gone all of February, fighting the cold weather, to round-up the cattle. Thad branded over a thousand of the finest longhorns. He moved them to the old cotton fields between Best Creek and the Brazos. The green winter grass was high and he knew the cattle would stay. William still owned all ten thousand acres of Auburn. Thad's dreams of exploring were gone. He would become a cattle baron and Auburn would be a great Texas ranch. By spring, Auburn was beginning to show her beauty. Katie was teaching and John was breeding and raising his cattle.

Neighbors to the north of Auburn were losing their land to taxes. Thad rushed to the Humphreyses' just in time. Carpetbaggers were trying to occupy the land. The tax assessor stood waving the papers and ranting at the top of his lungs. Mr. Humphreys, with a rifle in hand, was refusing to let them come on his property. There was nothing Mr. Humphreys could do. He was destitute. Thad ran his horse to the front of the house, pulling him hard to a stop and almost running over the Yankee tax assessor. "How much land do you have," Thad asked of Mr. Humphreys.

"Why, I have six thousand acres. Who might you be?"

"Mister Humphreys, you don't recognize me. I'm Thad Wilde."

Mr. Humphreys was pleased to see Thad. "They're going to take my land for the taxes I owe. According to my notice, I have one more week to get the money for my taxes. I'll be damned if these Yankees are going to get my land!"

Thad wanted the land. The south end along the Brazos adjoined Auburn, with Jake and his family owning land in between. He turned to the Yankee. "Mister Humphreys will have the money for his taxes. Consider this now part of Auburn and from now on you'll be dealing with me. Now get the hell off my land!"

The tax assessor and the carpetbagger stormed away on their horses. Mr. Humphreys, who was elderly, stood in amazement. "Mister Humphreys," Thad spoke. "I want you to stay here. There is no need for you to leave your home. I'll pay the taxes and you can deed the property to me."

"Thad, I appreciate the offer. The missus and I want to move to the coast. She loves the water and I have a little money left. I think I'll buy us a small house in Galveston and live a quiet life."

"Well, if you won't stay, then I want to buy the land at its full value." Thad made Mr. Humphreys a good offer for the land and purchased anything Mr. Humphreys would sell. Mr. Humphreys left immediately for Houston, to pay the taxes and transfer the land to Thad. Thad rode home and told his father about the deal he made. William could not believe he had acquired Riverbend from the Humpreyses.

"Riverbend was a fine plantation. The ground is good there. We can plant a lot of cotton. I'm impressed with your wisdom, Thad. You've become a fine businessman."

"Thank you, Father. You know, Mother received a letter from Jacqueline stating that they were on their way. The Humphreyses' home is nice. It would make a good home for Alex. I know he wants to build the shipping business. It's closer to the road to Houston. What do you think?"

"I think you are planning too far ahead. It's an excellent idea. I just don't know what Alex wants to do."

"Yes, sir, you're right. If he doesn't want it, I might just move into it, myself. I need to have my own place, anyway."

"Whatever you want, Thad, is fine by me. We don't know for sure when Alex will arrive. They wrote that they would be stopping and searching for Will. I guess they didn't receive Reginia's letter telling them about him. If we can't get a letter to Alex, it could be a year before he stops searching for Will. I only wish I knew where they were."

"You're right about that," Thad answered. "Alex will look until he is satisfied that he can't find Will. It's a shame we can't get word to him."

Thad was good in business and left the next morning to meet Mr. Humphreys in Houston. He needed to be there to sign all the papers putting the title to land in his name. Thad was anxious to get to Houston. He still possessed a wild streak. He proudly wore his six-shooters on his hips and enjoyed an occasional weekend in Houston, at the old hotel, gambling, drinking, and cavorting with the women in the saloon. Thad became known for his quick temper and fast hand with the gun. Everyone respected Thad's ability with his gun. Thad walked cockily, exhibiting tremendous pride for his Texas heritage. He had no use for the scallawags and carpetbaggers, cursing them any chance he got. The Yankee officers called Thad "Mr. Wilde." They had come to respect him, if for no other reason than the fact that he had so much money. The Wildes were, once more, Texans of great wealth.

FIFTY

By spring, Alex and Jacqueline were on their way to Auburn. Alex advised the captain of the ship they traveled on to stop in all the southern ports. He hoped to find Will. In Savannah, General Pearson welcomed his Union friend, Alex. Alex told him about Will. Will's name was not on the list of the dead or missing Union soldiers, and he had not been taken prisoner. Pearson took them to the hospital. One of the Confederate doctors overheard Pearson introducing Alex.

"Your name is Wilde?" a doctor asked Alex.

"Yes. Do you know my son Will?"

"No. But, there's a Confederate soldier here. He's a doctor from Texas and attended the wounded in Atlanta. He received a blow to his head escaping the fire. I was told by a Texas soldier that he's married to William Wilde's daughter. Are you any relation to them?"

"Yes, he's my father. What is this man's name?"

"Doctor Quincy Tyler."

"That's my sister's husband! Where is he?"

"He's over here." The doctor took Alex and Jacqueline to his room. "I must tell you something. Doctor Tyler has amnesia. He remembers some things about the war, but nothing else."

"We are on our way to Texas. I'll take him with us."

Quincy lay in the bed. Alex and Jacqueline walked slowly to him. "Quincy, how are you?" Alex held his hand out to him. Quincy shook Alex's hand, wondering who the stranger was. "I know you don't remember me, but I am your brother-in-law Alex Wilde." Quincy just stared at Alex. He could not believe someone might know of his past. He sat upright.

"Explain yourself," Quincy demanded.

"Well, you see, you are married to my sister, Katie. You met her when you moved to my family's plantation in Texas. Your uncle is Tom Bradley, a doctor my father brought to Auburn. Auburn is our plantation. Does any of this sound familiar to you?"

"No." Quincy was intrigued and wanted to know all about himself. "Tell me more."

Alex smiled. "You're a doctor, as you know, and you came to Texas to take over Tom's practice. Your uncle wanted to retire and travel. You and my sister fell in love and married. You also have children."

"I have children? How many?" The thought of a family who cared about him gave Quincy hope for a future.

"You have four children. Jane, Quincy Jr., Splaine, and Lathe." Quincy could not recall anything, but he believed them. Alex told Quincy all he knew from his mother's letter and reassured Quincy that he was needed at home. Quincy agreed, even though he could not remember anything Alex had told him. Quincy realized he may never remember his past life, but at least he knew he had one. One in which people loved and needed him. Quincy prepared for his journey home and departed with Alex and his family.

Life for Katie was better. Stanley called on her frequently, ensuring she had all she needed. Katie enjoyed his company. She and the children spent weekends with Josie and John. Stanley frequently joined them for supper. They played poker with small sticks John whittled. John told them the story about Thad and their visit to the brothel. Josie raised an eyebrow but had to laugh at the thought of John's innocence. Katie and Stanley's time together was filled with fun. Katie began to rely heavily on Stanley, for support and friendship. John thought it was wonderful that Katie had found friendship with

Stanley. Josie was glad to see Katie happy but was apprehensive about such a deep friendship. The possibility of Quincy being alive crossed her mind.

By June, Katie and Stanley were courting. Stanley could be found every evening at Katie's. The children loved him. Jane had only a slight memory of her father. The weather was warm and they took long picnics on Sundays after church. Everyone could see the two were falling in love. Katie wanted a complete family. She longed to have a husband again, someone to share her life with. Katie loved Quincy, but she had given up hoping that Quincy would return.

One hot Sunday in July, Josie, John, Katie, and Stanley took all the children for a swim at the creek. They all swam and reminisced of days long ago at that swimming hole. Katie flashed to thoughts of Quincy. She knew in her heart that by now he must be dead. She loved Stanley. It was not the same as her deep love for Quincy, but it was a love she could live with for the rest of her life. She jumped from the water and ran to lie on the blanket under the old oak tree. She wanted to forget about Quincy. Stanley followed quickly behind her.

"What's wrong, darling?"

"Nothing, nothing at all. I just wanted to rest." Katie never wanted Stanley to know she still had thoughts of Quincy. She would never hurt Stanley that way.

Stanley put his arm around her and kissed her. Katie loved the affection. It made her feel alive. "Katie, I love you very much and I love your children like they were my own. I want to spend the rest of my life with you." He knelt facing her. "Will you marry me?"

Katie was quiet, which was very rare for her. She thought what life would be like married to Stanley. He was a good man, a hard worker, and would make a terrific father. She looked into his eyes. "Yes, Stanley, I will marry you."

He kissed her and jumped up, suddenly facing everyone in the creek. He screamed loudly so they could all hear. "I'm going to marry Katie!" Jane, Quincy, Splaine, and Lathe ran from the water screaming with delight. They all grabbed Stanley, knocking him on the pallet. They hugged him and rolled about with laughter. Katie watched. She knew she was doing the right thing. John was thrilled. Josie smiled discreetly. She hoped this was truly what Katie wanted and that she was not acting hastily.

The wedding was set for the tenth of August. News of the wedding spread throughout the area, but they would have only close friends attend. The local law and church would allow the marriage on the grounds of death in absentia. Katie had done all she could to try to find Quincy. He was presumed dead and the wedding could go ahead. Katie wanted to have the wedding at her house. She and Josie spent their days making plans. Approximately fifty people were invited. Carrie made Katie a beautiful wedding dress of off-white fabric. The Wildes were happy with Katie's choice. Merriment filled the air!

Alex took his time getting to Texas. With his search for Will, it was August before they reached Houston. Alex had told Quincy all about Katie, their children, and home in Texas. He let Quincy read letters Katie and Reginia had written about their lives and the letters all contained information about Quincy. He read of the deep love Katie expressed for him. He could not remember her, but he felt a bond to her. Quincy felt relieved to know about himself and to know someone loved him as much as Katie did. Alex went to see Jacob Crowe. He wanted to let him know he was moving the shipping business to Galveston and planned to buy a house there so he could be near his office. Alex asked Jacob to begin procedures to get his father's ships. Jacob asked what had brought him back to Texas. Alex told him about the loss of Will and about finding Quincy. Jacob was shocked to hear that Quincy was alive!

"Alex, your son Will is at Auburn with Thad and his grandparents."

"What! How'd he get there?" Alex couldn't believe all that time spent searching for Will and he was in Texas safe and sound. Jacob informed him of all Thad had told him, but did not tell him about Will's arm. He would leave that for Will.

"There's something else I must tell you. We all thought Quincy was dead. Katie spent a year and a half planning his return. She gave up, Alex. She's going to marry Stanley Groves. In fact, she's going to marry him in two days."

"She can't do that, she's married to Quincy! I have to get to her before she marries that man. Do you have a carriage I can use? I'll send for my belongings later. I have to stop this wedding!"

"Sure. Get your family together while I go get it. I'll meet you out front."

Alex hurried to get Jacqueline, Zan, and Quincy. He rushed them into the carriage, telling them about Will and the marriage. Jacqueline and Zan couldn't believe Will was alive, much less living at Auburn. Jacqueline was thrilled as Alex whipped the horses into a gallop. Quincy did not know what to think, nor did he know how he felt. He couldn't blame Katie for wanting to go on with her life. With his amnesia, he didn't really know her and was apprehensive about showing up at the wedding. He wanted to turn and go the other way, but Alex refused.

"You don't remember right now, but you will someday. My sister loved you with all her heart. She would never marry another man if she thought you were alive. I know she's marrying for convenience. You have to see for yourself."

Alex pulled the carriage to the front of his old friend Caleb McAlister's home. Caleb lived between Auburn and Houston. Caleb welcomed Alex and his family. He had not seen his friend in many years. They enjoyed dinner and a long talk. Caleb knew Quincy well, and could not believe his eyes! Quincy, however, didn't know him. Alex explained everything to Caleb. Caleb was to attend the wedding. "It's at noon tomorrow. This is one event I think I shall pass on. You'll need to leave before daybreak."

The next morning, they left at five o'clock. It would be the longest ride Alex ever took. They were running out of time. Alex whipped the horses into a run. He only knew that Katie's house was along the way to Auburn. He passed the church, looking frantically for a large home filled with people. In the distance, he saw the gala event. The large home stood alone with big trees surrounding it, just as his mother had described. He could barely see the people gathered in the yard. Alex whipped the horses again, urging them to gallop faster. They reached the house and Alex pulled the horses to an abrupt halt. Stanley stood with John at his side, in front of the minister. The door opened and there was Katie, holding the arm of his father. Alex shouted, "Wait! Wait!" Everyone turned to see who had made such a commotion.

Quincy stood by the carriage. He stared at the beautiful lady dressed in white, with her long auburn curls. He became captivated by her sight. The familiarity of the scene before him triggered recollections of his own marriage. Memories flashed through his mind. "How could this be?" he thought. Was he just imaging the memories because of all the letters he had read and conversations he had had with Alex and Jacqueline? He closed his eyes and slightly shook his head, but the thoughts continued. He recalled the flower-filled arbor at Auburn, the Wildes, and most of all, his bride. He remembered his spirited Katie and the love they shared. He opened his eyes and saw his wife. He could remember. Quincy felt strange. How could he have forgotten her; forgotten the love he felt for her. Perhaps it was his love for her that had sparked his memory. He did not care. He was only glad to remember. Katie was bubbling inside to have Alex and Jacqueline present for her wedding. Suddenly her eyes passed Alex to see Quincy. His blond hair and blue eyes caught her attention. He was as handsome as the day she had last seen him. Their eyes met. She forgot about Stanley and all the people gathered for her wedding. She picked up her long dress and ran to Quincy. He grabbed her, pressing her body hard against him. His amnesia was gone. He loved Katie and would never let her go. Tears of joy streamed down her face. Whispers passed among the crowd. Stanley stood still staring at Katie and Quincy. He flinched in disbelief. He had lost his dream of settling down with Katie and her children.

Will ran to his mother and father, grabbing Jacqueline for a hug. Alex stood in dismay at the sight of Will's missing arm. Alex hugged his son, with tears mounting in his eyes. "I had no idea that you lost your arm." He continued holding Will.

"I'm fine, Father. It was just the left arm. I didn't use it much anyway!" Will grinned, trying to soothe his parents.

"Will! How can you be so nonchalant? It's your arm for goodness sakes!" Jacqueline cried.

"I'm fine. Stop crying, now. I could be dead. Be glad I only lost my arm!"

William, Reginia, and the others rushed to Quincy and Katie. Quincy told them where he had been and about his amnesia. Everyone was thrilled to have Quincy home.

"Come with me, Quincy," William said as he put his arm around Quincy's shoulder and guided him to the house. William turned his head and looked at Katie, nodding toward Stanley. Everyone was at William's heels, eager to hear more of Quincy's whereabouts.

Katie, looking in the direction her father had nodded toward, suddenly remembered Stanley. Stanley still stood where he waited for Katie to say their vows. He was heavy-hearted and feeling somewhat awkward. Katie walked to him and held her arms open to him. Stanley looked away from her. She slowly dropped her arms to her side.

"Stanley, I'm sorry. Please don't turn away from me. I care for you deeply, but I can't forsake the love I feel for Quincy. He's my husband and he's returned. There's nothing I can do about this. You must understand."

Stanley didn't answer her. He just turned and walked to his horse tied by the barn. Katie ran after him. "Stop. I won't let you go like this."

Stanley turned to her. "What do you want from me, Katie? Quincy has returned. I know this is what you prayed for. But there is no reason for me to be here now."

"Stanley, you mean the world to me. You've seen me through a terrible time. I know you would have been a devoted husband and a wonderful father to the children. But, Quincy is home and he is my husband and the father of my children. Please listen to me, Stanley. Our love was based on friendship. I don't want that to change. The children love you. They will want you to be our friend." Stanley looked away without saying a word. "I know you're hurt," Katie continued. "I hate that. I would never have done this to you intentionally. Please, Stanley, please try and understand. I beg you to think this through. There is someone out there that will love you and give you your own children."

"I love you, Katie. Don't you understand that? I have eyes. I saw Quincy and the way you ran to him. You could never have loved me that way. I think that is what hurts me the most. I never wished death for Quincy and I do want you to be happy, but forgive me if I'm disappointed. As for the children, I will always love them and be their friend. I'll get over the hurt. I just need time."

Katie stroked the side of Stanley's face. "There's a place in my heart for you. A part of me will always cherish our time together." She put her arms around Stanley. He pulled her close and kissed her. Quincy walked out the front door looking for Katie. He glanced to the barn just in time to view them kiss. His spirits sank. Quincy knew he had lost his beloved Katie. He watched, wishing he had never returned.

Katie pulled back from Stanley. He looked into her eyes. "We would have had a good life. Well." He smiled. "At least one of us will have a good life and I'm glad it's you, my dear Katie. Quincy is a lucky man."

"Thank you." Katie smiled. Stanley got on his horse and rode away. She turned to the house and saw Quincy. She waved and began running to him. His heart beat rapidly as he ran to meet her. "I love you, Quincy. Never leave me again!"

"I love you with all my heart, my dear Katie. I'm home for good."

They returned to the house. Quincy had a lot of catching up to do. They visited with their family and friends all afternoon. The children played, not paying much attention to the father they did not remember. The children had come to love Stanley and resented the stranger putting an end to their mother's wedding. Jane was the only one who was old enough to even try to understand what was happening. Months passed before the children began to accept Quincy as their father.

The Wildes would once again have feelings of joy and sorrow. The return of one had caused another such grief. The most important thing to William was that his family was home and in good health. Nothing else mattered but the welfare of his loved ones. William hated the hurt that Stanley had to endure. But after all, Katie was his daughter and Quincy was the father of his grandchildren. Hard times were finally nearing an end for some, but just beginning for others.

FIFTY-ONE

The year 1868 proved to be better for the Wilde family. Alex, Jacqueline, and Zan moved in with William and Reginia. Alex was able to obtain and repair all their ships. He worked hard rebuilding the business, spending most of his time in Galveston. He purchased a large home on the island, overlooking the Gulf for himself and Jacqueline. Zan loved Auburn and remained with his grandparents and Will. Thad moved into the old Humphreys home, but ate most of his meals with his parents. Josie and John were busy with Holly Hill and Quincy resumed his medical practice. Life once again seemed positive for William and his children.

Thad worked hard building his cattle empire. He taught Zan how to ride Western and rope. Zan had accomplished equestrian skills in the English form of riding. Thad laughed as Zan bent his legs, using the pressure from his calves, to move his body gracefully in an upward and downward motion with the movement of the horse. However, this form of riding looked strange in the Western saddle. Thad would shout, "Sit down in that saddle. You look ridiculous!" Zan practiced sitting deep in the saddle, which was a difficult transition from the way he had learned to ride. His skills with a rope took even longer. Zan loved the land in Texas and idolized his uncle Thad, giving all his efforts to becoming a rancher. He purchased a pistol and wore it on his hip. Thad took him in the evenings to practice shooting. Before long, Zan became a master sharpshooter, quickly outdrawing Thad. Will refused to wear the guns. He had seen enough bloodshed during the war. He worked with Thad and kept records for Auburn. The three men were dedicated to rebuilding the homeplace. Will's thoughts of returning to the East had long since faded from his mind.

Thad had become restless on the plantation and planned a weekend in Houston to whoop it up. Zan insisted on going with him. "I want to go with you, Uncle Thad. I play a mean hand of poker."

"Have you had a woman, Zan?"

"What do you mean?" Zan put his uncle on the spot. He knew exactly what Thad meant. He just wanted to hear Thad explain himself.

"Well, uhh, you know. I was wondering. Have you ever been with a woman?"

"Sure. I escorted many a fine girl in Boston," Zan teased.

"I don't mean escort. I mean been with a girl. You know. Hell, didn't your father ever tell you about sex?"

"Oh, you mean that! Why, no, he hasn't. You tell me, Uncle Thad."

"Boy, I can't tell you about such things. You have to learn it from experience. How old are you?"

"I'm twenty-one years old."

Thad shook his head in amazement. "Well, it's high time you found out what pleasures a woman can bring you. Come on. Get your bag and let's go. I'll show you a weekend you'll never forget!"

Zan rushed to get his bag packed for the weekend. Reginia stopped him on the staircase. "Where are you going in such a hurry?"

"Oh, I'm going with Uncle Thad to Houston on business."

"Business? Don't you mean funny business? I don't think you need to go with Thad."

"Grandmother, I'll be fine. I want to go."

Thad walked into the foyer and put his arm around Reginia. "I'm taking this young man with me for the weekend."

"Thad, you have no reason for taking Zan. I think this is a bad idea! I know what you do and you should not be leading Zan astray. He's too young to realize what he's doing!"

"Grandmother, I'm twenty-one years old. I'm not some kid!"

Thad hugged Reginia and kissed her on the cheek. "Mother, Zan's a grown man. He can make up his own mind. I'll take care of him. Now, don't you worry your pretty little head over the matter."

"Thad Wilde, you are going to burn in hell for your sinful ways. Don't you dare get Zan into mischief." Disgusted, Reginia placed her hands on her hips and left the room.

"She'll be all right. Let's get out of here. We're burning daylight!" Thad was eager to get to Houston by Friday evening. The two rode off with smiles on their faces.

That night, they camped under a big tree by a clear creek. Zan quizzed Thad for hours about Houston and the women. He could not wait to get to Houston! Zan was playing the innocent for all he was worth!

Friday afternoon, Thad and Zan arrived in Houston. The proprietor of the saloon, known only as Miss Jones, welcomed Thad into her place of business. The hotel had a bar and was a place of gambling. Miss Jones was from the East and had come to Texas with her girls to find her fortune. She was not what Zan expected. She was older, probably in her mid-forties, with grace and charm. Miss Jones was a stern madam, demanding every man to be at his best behavior. Her ornate saloon and hotel seemed somewhat out of place for the Texas frontier.

The young girls quickly gathered about Thad, with their eyes fixed on the handsome Zan. Zan smiled, flirting with them and teasing them for their attention. Thad looked at Miss Jones and whispered in her ear, "Something tells me this is not the first time for Zan!" A cute blonde with blue eyes caught Zan's attention. She had a sweet smile and a look of innocence. She couldn't be more than seventeen or eighteen! He took her by the hand and offered her a drink. "I don't drink the whiskey, but I would like a sassafras, please." Her polite manners intrigued Zan.

"I'm Zan Wilde. What is your name?"

"My name is Ramona English. You can call me Ramie."

Zan and Ramie sat at the table having their drinks. Her soft voice and natural beauty captured Zan's attention. Ramie had perfect manners and a sophistication that seemed out of place in the saloon. "Would you like to go to my room?" Ramie asked.

"Yes," was all Zan could say. He was eager to find more out about the young girl. Ramie took Zan up the stairs to her room. The room had been painted white and the fabrics were pink. The cloth appeared to be dainty as if chosen for a young, innocent girl. Ramie did not fit in this atmosphere. Zan could not imagine why she had chosen this profession.

"Why don't we talk for a while," he suggested. He had become fascinated with the young beauty and wanted to know all about her.

A smile appeared on Ramie's lips. She felt relieved. "That would be nice. Most men don't care to talk!" she giggled.

"Where are you from," Zan asked.

"I'm from Maryland."

"You're from Maryland? How did you come to be with Miss Jones in Texas?"

Ramie told him her life story. She had been born and reared in Maryland. She was the fourth generation to be born at Mayfield, the family-owned plantation on the Potomac River. She had lost her mother to a fever and her father and only brother had lost their lives during the war. She was too young, at the time, to keep Mayfield. It had been sold for the taxes owed. Her education had been cut short by the war. Her aunt and uncle had lost everything and could not care for her. She was afraid and had nowhere to turn, when she met Miss Jones and the girls. They were traveling to Texas. Ramie wanted as far away from her past as she could possibly get. Miss Jones took her in and was kind to her, not pressuring her to work. Miss Jones had dreamed of having a family. She had always wanted a daughter. The man she had loved many years ago had been killed and this left her heartbroken. She had never fallen in love again and had given up her dream of having a family. As time passed, Miss Jones became very fond of Ramie, spending as much time with the young girl as possible. Ramie seemed like the daughter she had never had. Miss Jones wanted a better life for Ramie and found herself guarding Ramie from the men. A year passed, and Ramie began to feel guilty for not working and contributing to the business. Against Miss Jones's wishes, Ramie relented to working.

Zan visited with Ramie all evening and late into the night. He spent the entire weekend with her. Early Saturday morning, while Zan slept, Ramie went to have her morning coffee with Miss Jones. Miss Jones noticed the sparkle in Ramie's eyes. "My goodness, you seem very cheerful this morning."

"I am. I spent the evening with Zan Wilde. He is a real gentleman."

"I can tell you are fascinated with him. Listen to me, Ramie. I caution you to be careful. I don't know him, but I do know his uncle Thad. I'm telling you there are many women who have been smitten by his charm, but none that will ever be able to capture his heart."

Ramie looked disappointed. She had dreamed of finding someone to love her and care for her. "Zan seems so sincere. Why, he didn't even make an attempt to touch me. He only wanted to talk. He actually wanted to know all about me."

Miss Jones loved Ramie and didn't want to see her get hurt or disappointed. "Ramie, the Wilde family is a prominent family and well-known in Texas. I don't think they could understand their grandson being involved with you. I fear they would pass judgment on you." Miss Jones looked into her eyes with sorrow. "I wish I had sent you back East. I wanted so much more for you. That is why I didn't want you to work."

Ramie fell at her knees, placing her head in Miss Jones's lap. "No. I could never have gone back East. I like Zan and I think he likes me. If nothing else, I would treasure his friendship. I really want to get to know him. He asked if we could go for ride today. Can I?"

"You do what you must. I will always be here for you. Just remember what I have told you." She stroked Ramie's head. She knew this wasn't the life the young girl needed, but she hated to let her go. Ramie had brought joy into her life for the first time in over two decades.

Zan and Ramie slipped away Saturday for a ride in the country and a picnic. Zan became captivated by Ramie's charm. He found her to be honest and humble. All day they shared stories about their lives. They discovered they had friends in common, who were from Boston. Ramie's father had been active in politics and traveled to Boston on business. Thad hated that Ramie should end up in a saloon. Ramie spoke enthusiastically when recalling her days spent with her family at Mayfield. Zan stroked the side of her face, smiling at her. His trip for pleasure had turned into a time of falling in love. He wanted to take her to Auburn away from the life that had been dealt her. That night, Zan could not withstand the passion he felt for Ramie. He made love to her. Zan had never felt so good with anyone before.

Every Sunday, Ramie had gone to church and sat on the back pew. She had prayed for forgiveness and a new way of life. That Sunday, as she prepared for church, Zan asked if he could go with her. Ramie was thrilled at the idea of Zan going to church with her. The two went to church together. Zan could hardly hear the preacher, for he was thinking about his feelings for Ramie. On the way home, Zan asked her to marry him. Ramie could not believe this handsome man wanted her for his wife. She hung her head.

"You don't need me. You can have anyone you want. I'm not worthy to be your wife."

Zan gently turned her face toward him. "I love you. You're worthy to have anyone you want. I didn't expect to fall in love on this trip, but I did. I won't take no for an answer. I want to marry you right now!"

"You don't really know me! And what will your family think?"

"I know all I need to know about you. My family will love you just as I do. You feel the same about me, I can see it in your eyes. Besides, I have to make an honest woman of you!"

Ramie smiled and nodded yes. She, too, had fallen in love with him. Zan turned the carriage around and went back to the church. He would not hear another argument over the marriage. God had answered Ramie's prayers. Zan took Ramie by the arm and guided her to the preacher.

"Sir, I'm Zan Wilde and this is Ramona English. I would like you to marry us." The preacher recognized the Wilde name. "Are you related to William Wilde?"

"Yes, sir. He is my grandfather."

"I know your grandfather and your grandmother. Are they aware of this?"

"Well"—Zan paused—"no they aren't."

"Sit down and let us talk about this." The three sat down. The preacher was concerned and had questions. "Tell me why you are in such a rush to be married."

Ramie sat quietly as Zan spoke. He told the preacher how they met and told him about Ramie's past. "I love her, sir, and I want to marry her," Zan concluded.

The preacher smiled. "Wouldn't you like to introduce her to your family and have their blessing?"

Zan knew in his heart that he could not take that chance. He hated to admit to himself that they may oppose the marriage. Zan was also like the other Wilde men in the respect that when he made up his mind to do something, he did it. "I don't want to wait. Neither does Ramie. We know what we want and I want to take her home as my wife."

The preacher talked to them for more than an hour, exhausting every argument as to why they should wait. Zan was determined. His mind could not be changed. "I don't know why we fell in love as we have. All I know is that I do love her. I want to spend the rest of my life with her."

The minister finally agreed and married them.

Meanwhile, Thad had enjoyed the other girls and the gambling. Thad lay in the big bed asleep, where he had passed out from the whiskey. Zan and Ramie returned. Zan sent her to pack and tell Miss Jones, while he went to tell Thad. Zan knocked at the door of the room where Thad was sleeping. The woman let him in and Zan requested to see his uncle alone. He walked to Thad and pushed his shoulder until he awoke. Thad was suffering a hangover. He rolled over and just stared at Zan with a big smile.

"Zan, what are you doing? You look like you had a good time with that possum-eatin' grin on your face. You have been laid up with that young girl all weekend. Why, you didn't even come down for cards and whiskey!"

"It isn't what you think, Uncle Thad."

"Are you going to tell me you just sat in her room visiting for the last two nights!"

"No, sir." Zan paused. "You see . . . well, sir . . . we got married."

"You did what!" Zan's statement quickly sobered Thad. He sat straight up in the bed and looked directly at Zan. "What do you mean you married her?"

Zan explained the last two days and how he had fallen in love with her. Thad could not say a word. He was stunned and knew his mother would have his head for allowing something like this to happen, not to mention what Alex and Jacqueline would say!

"Well, say something, Uncle Thad. Aren't you happy for me?"

"Happy! How in the hell can I be happy for you! I bring you to Houston to experience life and have a woman. I could see this was something you had already encountered, the first minute you entered the building! Why, you flirted and left with that girl immediately! Now, tell me how you're going to explain marrying a prostitute to your parents and grandparents, young man! What's wrong with you? You don't even know her. I can't believe you've done this. Damn, I'll never hear the end of this from our family." Thad was getting out of bed at this point and putting his pants on. "I'll get this fixed."

"What do you mean, you'll 'get this fixed'?" Zan shouted. "Ramie's a wonderful person. She's had a difficult time and this is not her chosen profession, but a desperate situation. And you will not fix anything!" Thad's response disappointed Zan. He defended Ramie, telling Thad about her life and how she ended up in Houston. He planned to take a steamer to Galveston for a visit with his parents, before returning to Auburn. Zan was determined that everyone would accept Ramie and love her. "You'll like her if you just give her a chance. She doesn't belong here and I love her. That is what matters!"

"Love her," Thad mumbled to himself. "You do what you have to do. But I doubt that the folks will approve. So, don't expect it. Furthermore, you're a grown man and I refuse to take the blame for this from our family! I don't know about Alex and Jacqueline, but I can tell you one thing. Your grandparents aren't going to be happy. In fact, your grandfather will probably have a fit! If this Ramie is as good as you say, you may have a chance with Mother when she gets to know her, but I don't know about Father." He just shook his head. "You have your hands full." Thad suddenly burst into laughter at the thought of his father ranting and raving.

"What is so damn funny?" Zan scowled.

"I was just thinking about Father's reaction. I have to be there to see you explain this marriage!" Thad could hardly speak for laughing so hard.

"It isn't funny! This is serious and you're going to eat your words. I'm going after Ramie and we're leaving for Galveston. I'll see you at Auburn." Zan walked hastily to the door.

Thad laughed at Zan. "You bet you will! And I'll not give them any clue as to what you've done! This is all in your hands! I just want to be there when you tell them."

Zan ignored Thad and slammed the door behind him. He went to Ramie. Miss Jones was thrilled for them. She knew this was not the life for Ramie and wanted only her well-being. Ramie hugged her. "Thank you," she whispered in Miss Jones's ear.

"I should thank you," Miss Jones whispered as she hugged Ramie. "You have brought me more joy than you will ever know. I couldn't love you more if you had been my own daughter. Now, you go with your husband and don't you ever look back." Miss Jones fought back tears at never seeing Ramie again. She knew the young girl would be much better off if she was not in her life. Miss Jones had allowed Ramie to see her gentle side, something she had not allowed anyone else to see. She gave Ramie some cash as a wedding gift and wished them well.

Zan and Ramie arrived in Galveston late that evening. A carriage took them to the large home overlooking the Gulf. Zan became nervous. He thought about what Thad had said. He realized he had acted on impulse, but he did love Ramie and the last thing he wanted was for his parents to be rude to her. Zan would not tell them how he met Ramie until they got to know her and liked her. He thought that would be easier for everyone. He told Ramie his plan and convinced her to go along with his decision.

Alex and Jacqueline were excited to see Zan and welcomed them in their home. Zan introduced Ramie as his wife. The sudden marriage surprised Alex and Jacqueline. Zan told them all about Ramie, except that she was a prostitute. They stayed a week with his parents. Jacqueline took her shopping and had friends for dinner to meet her. Zan was grateful that his father's friends were not the type to visit the Houston saloon! A week passed and Ramie insisted Zan tell his parents about her life in Houston. She had been with only a couple of men, for most of the men wanted the girls with experience. She feared she would meet up with someone that knew her. She wanted his family to hear it from them. She cared for her in-laws and appreciated their warm hospitality. She wanted to tell them herself.

Ramie and Zan summoned his parents to the parlor. "We have something we must tell you," Ramie insisted. She told them her story of meeting Miss Jones and her desperate flight from Maryland. Ramie explained her entire ordeal. Tears welled in Ramie's eyes as she told how she prayed for forgiveness and a different life, one filled with love as she had at Mayfield. "Please forgive me. I never meant to deceive you." Alex and Jacqueline sat quietly. Neither said a word until Ramie finished speaking.

Jacqueline felt pity for Ramie. She walked to her and put her arms around her, wondering how many young girls were in this profession due to similar circumstances. Jacqueline assured her that everything was fine and she was a welcome joy in their family.

Alex felt the same way, but he knew his own parents would not respond so well. The war had left his parents callused to the new ways in the South. They both felt the war had corrupted many people. His father had always been opposed to prostitution and the fact that saloons were becoming so popular with men made William upset. He felt this behavior would only lead to trouble. Alex knew his father would be disappointed and would also express his opinion on the matter. He explained this to Zan and Ramie, assuring them that if they had problems, to return to Galveston.

Zan and Ramie slept peacefully that night. The next morning, they left for their trip to Auburn. Zan told Ramie all about Auburn and his family there. They arrived home three days later. He wanted to handle his grandparents as he had his parents. He would let them get to know Ramie before telling them the complete story. Thad had not said a word, just as he had said. He only told them Zan had gone to visit his parents. Zan feared his grandfather's response, and for the first two weeks, he kept quiet about his wife's past. Thad shook his head and teased Zan continually. Finally, Zan had to tell them. Everyone had gone. John and Josie were in New Orleans on business and Katie had had Ramie come for tea and meet the local ladies. Thad, the last person he wanted around, was tending to the cattle!

Zan took this opportunity to tell his grandparents. Reginia appeared shocked and William, as expected, voiced his opinion loudly after Zan told them how he had met Ramie.

"How dare you marry some prostitute and bring her into my home! I will not stand for this."

"She's not a prostitute, now. She's my wife. Besides, you liked her up until now!" Zan yelled.

"Don't raise your voice with me, youngster."

"I'm not a youngster!"

Thad entered the room unannounced as the argument heated. Reginia looked at Thad with harsh eyes. "This is your fault. Taking this poor child to Houston and introducing him to your wild life! He didn't understand his own feelings. He has confused lust with love. Just look what you've done! Are you happy now?" The news had clearly upset Reginia.

Thad remained calm. "Listen, Mother, Zan knew exactly what he was doing and furthermore the two of you have made over her like she is some precious cargo for the last two weeks. You're obviously very fond of her. Can't you overlook this little offense?"

"Little offense? She is a whore, for heaven's sake!" William jeered.

"You'll regret this, Thad. I begged you not to take our little Zan, but you wouldn't listen to me. We can't have this sin brought into our home!" Reginia was furious with her son. Thad had never seen his mother so angry.

Zan felt hurt and betrayed. "You all stop talking like I'm not here. I can speak for myself. I'm a grown man with a mind of my own! I'm ashamed of you. You profess to be Christians and yet you judge my wife. The Lord forgives all and says you must too. You not only won't forgive, but you won't even allow her a second chance at life! She loves the Lord and has a good heart. She sure hasn't judged you!"

His comments hurt Reginia. She stood quietly thinking about having passed judgment so hastily. The girl had had a hard time. She did go to church and loved the Lord. She was good to Zan and obviously loved him too. Perhaps she had acted too hastily.

William, however, fumed at his grandson's apparent lack of respect. "How could this whore possibly judge anyone, with such a life of sin that she has led!" he snarled as he stormed past Thad and out of the room.

"Father warned me about grandfather, but I didn't expect this from you, Grandmother. My parents told me to come to Galveston if I had any problems over this and that is exactly what I'll do. I don't care if I ever see you again!" Zan left the room and walked out the front door.

Thad did not find the confrontation between his parents and Zan as amusing as he had thought. He was disappointed in his parents. He had expected a big disagreement to end in hugs and acceptance.

"Mother. You and Father are wrong. Ramie's a good person and you had no reason to be so cruel to Zan. He loves her and so did you. He's right, you know. Everyone deserves a second chance. Maybe the good Lord sent Zan to her, answering her prayers. Did you ever think of that! What good does it do if you lead a moral life, but don't possess a loving and forgiving heart? This is so unlike you and Father." Reginia and William had disappointed Thad by their quick judgment. He needed Zan to help with the cattle and farming. He rushed after him. Reginia sat in the parlor stunned by the whole affair.

Thad caught up with Zan at the barn. He insisted Zan stay and offered his home to them as a wedding gift.

"I can't take your house."

"I don't need that house, but I do need you. Ramie can care for the house and make a home for the two of you. You can fill the extra bedrooms with children! Mother and Father will come around. I knew they would be upset, but I didn't expect them to react as they did. It isn't like them. I think all the hardships they went through have caused them to be unfeeling. I know they don't really mean it. They like Ramie. When they have time to sit back and think about it, they'll change their minds. I don't want you to give up your dreams. We have a big cattle business and will begin farming again next year. You can't leave. This is what you wanted. Will is expecting you to help us. Besides, I have no plans to marry. Auburn will someday belong to you and Will. Don't give it up."

"Where would you live, Uncle Thad, if we accept your offer?"

"Oh, I'll move back into the big house with Will and your grandparents. They won't stay mad long. You'll see." He smiled with a chuckle. "I eat all my meals there anyway!'

"This is so kind of you. Ramie would like our own home. Thank you."

"Don't mention it. Let's get your things moved and you can go after Ramie. It's best you take her to your new home. She doesn't need to be exposed to Father's anger!"

Will returned from the pastures. Thad explained what had happened. The three moved Zan's and Ramie's trunks to the new home and Thad returned with his belongings to Auburn. William would not say a word to any of them as they passed him sitting on the porch. A week passed with quiet suppers at the dining table. Conversations were focused on anything but Zan and Ramie.

Reginia missed Zan and wanted to see him. She lay in bed by William thinking about how she had reacted and knew she had been unfair. "Darling. I miss Zan. And I fear I was too hard on Thad and misjudged Ramie."

"You did not," he grumbled. "I do not want to discuss this."

"William, Zan is our grandson. We should not forsake him. After all, we did like Ramie and accepted her when we didn't know who she really was. My goodness, Alex and Jacqueline overlooked her way of life. Is it possible we are afraid more of embarrassment, than of forgiving Ramie for her past?"

"Embarrassment! The war has brought nothing but sin and corruption! I'll never approve of such behavior!" He rolled over and turned his back to Reginia for the first time.

Reginia wrapped her arm around him and took his hand, squeezing tenderly, as she spoke ever so gently. "My dear, the war didn't bring this sin. Why, prostitution has been around for a long time. We can't blame the war for everything. Ramie turned to it out of desperation. I hate to think that over the years we have become so judgmental and unable to understand circumstances. I don't want dissension in this family. It will bring nothing but heartache. This is Zan's choice and we must stand behind him, not against him. Ramie was young and scared. I can tell she had a proper upbringing. Maybe we should help her feel loved and welcomed. Tomorrow, I'll take the carriage to Zan's home and apologize. I shall invite them for supper. I would like for you to join us."

William turned to Reginia with his hand holding hers. "Is this what you really want?"

"Yes, it is. I don't know what got into us, reacting as we did. I feel like an old fool."

"We're not old fools. Maybe fools, but not old ones!" William hugged her and smiled. "It seems I have acquired a temper lately. I better try to do something about that. You have Zan and Ramie over, I'll join you."

She squeezed his hand and hugged him lovingly. "Thank you. I only hope for their happiness."

The next morning, William and Reginia went to Zan and Ramie with their apologies. William gritted his teeth and under his breath muttered, "You are welcome in the family." His pride would not allow him to say he was sorry, even though he was. Zan knew this was hard for his grandfather, as he shook his hand with acceptance. Ramie felt relief and joy. Reginia took her in her arms. She invited Zan and Ramie for dinner. They all rejoiced at being together again. It would take William time to completely accept Ramie's past, but he did his best to conceal his disappointment in his grandson's choice for a bride.

John and Josie joined their family for supper. They had returned from New Orleans with tales of excitement. Josie had refurbished the hotel and was making large profits with the influx of Northerners and travelers from abroad. Everyone enjoyed the evening, especially Thad. He was glad his father had decided to accept Ramie into the family. The cattle business had grown tremendously, and he relied on Zan and Will for their help. John joined them with his men on the large roundups. The Wilde men had become known as one of the largest cattle raisers in Texas. The tall, lanky longhorns proved to be hearty, but John and Thad wanted a breed that produced more beef. They discussed bringing in Brahmans and Herefords to cross with the longhorns. William agreed with them. The Brahmans were able to withstand the Southern climates and the cold, while the Herefords would add more beef. This cross should make a beefier breed and one that could endure the weather and long cattle drive. The evening grew late and Reginia insisted they all stay overnight.

FIFTY-TWO

The rest of the year was busy for the Wilde men. They purchased Brahman and Hereford bulls to cross with the longhorns. They branded them with the circle *W* brand that Thad used and the rocking *J* that belonged to John and Josie. The men planted winter grasses in the old cotton fields. The cattle roamed freely in the absence of fences. They hoped the grasses would keep them nearby, which indeed it did. The branding was successful for all the cattle raisers. After the large roundup in the spring, the men sorted the cattle according to the cow's brand. They branded the calves according to the calf's mother's brand. Thad and John shipped many longhorns. Thad took several men and drove the cattle with the others on the drive to Kansas. Zan longed to travel with Thad. It was a long trip but Ramie wanted Zan to follow his dream. She was pregnant, unbeknownst to Zan, when he and Thad departed with the cattle and chuck wagon.

Thad joined the Chisolm Trail south of Fort Worth. Adventure and misery beset the drives. The spring rains filled the creeks and rivers. Crossing them was often treacherous. Several men lost their lives. Storms often scattered the cattle, causing many delays. Dust storms filled the air from the sandy plains of the Oklahoma Territory. Nothing discouraged Thad and Zan. Their skill and fame with the six-shooters halted the cattle rustlers from stealing their cows.

It was a hot, dusty July when the drovers entered the Kansas stockyards. The stockyard pens filled with the longhorns. The cowboys shouted with joy. That night, they celebrated at the local saloon. Thad offered a round of drinks for all the men. A card game seemed like a good idea to Thad and Zan. The two played most of the night winning hand after hand. Sam Reagan had become known throughout the country as a gambler and marksman and had been known to have started many fights when he was losing a card game. He glared at Thad from across the table, shouting accusations of cheating. Thad was a lot of things, but a cheater and liar he was not. His quick temper flared. Zan noticed Sam easing his hand under the table. Zan discreetly reached for his pistol from the holster, preparing to defend Thad. Sam continued to taunt Thad. Thad lunged upward, pushing the chair down and slamming his fists on the table. He invited Sam outside. The people scattered to the corners of the saloon. Sam just sat with a wicked grin on his face. His arm moved slightly. Zan pulled his pistol quickly, aiming it right between Reagan's eyes. "Put your hands up where I can see them or you'll never see anything again." Zan cocked his pistol, daring Sam to make a move for his gun. Sam showed his hands and left the table with disgust and humiliation. He was no fool. He realized he should not take on the Wildes.

It was September when Zan and Thad returned. Ramie was six months pregnant and big as a barrel! Zan was overjoyed to find he would soon be a father. He hugged her gently and waited on her hand and foot. Ramie had grown close to Reginia and William while Zan had traveled to Kansas. She and Zan spent many Sundays with the entire family. Quincy checked on Ramie frequently. She continued to gain weight and her size concerned him.

The first of December was bitterly cold in Texas. The temperatures were in the low teens. Fireplaces blazed for warmth. Ramie lay in the bed suffering from cramps. She hated to send Zan out in the cold but she needed Quincy. Zan rode quickly to get him. He stopped at his parents to ask Thad to stay with Ramie until he returned. Reginia and William insisted they go with Thad. They would not miss the birth of their great-grandchild. Thad drove the carriage carefully to Zan's home.

The frigid wind blew harshly. The bridge had iced over and had become slippery, as the horses walked carefully across.

It seemed forever before they reached Ramie. Ramie suffered tremendously. The Wildes could hear her wails as they approached the house. Thad thrust the door open and rushed to her side with his parents behind him. Reginia could see it would not be long. She had Thad retrieve clean cloths. Blood stained the bed where Ramie lay. The cramps and bleeding were not normal. Reginia did not know what to do. She comforted Ramie and tried to have her relax so the baby would not come before Quincy arrived.

Several hours passed before Zan and Quincy arrived. Reginia met them at the front door and explained Ramie's pain and her bleeding. Just at that moment, Ramie wailed. Quincy rushed to the room. Thad held her as she passed out from the pain and exhaustion. Quincy could not wake her. She bled profusely. The baby was a month early and had not turned. Quincy waited and worked with her as long as he could. He looked at Reginia with sorrowful eyes. He had no choice but to take the baby by surgery. Reginia hung her head in prayer. She was grateful Ramie was unconscious and could not feel the pain. Her limp body seemed helpless. Quincy told them what he had to do and asked Zan to leave the room. Zan became horrified as he left Ramie's side. He became weak from the thought of possibly losing Ramie. William and Thad, who had waited outside the bedroom door, had to help Zan to the parlor.

Within thirty minutes, two small cries were heard. Zan jumped to his feet. The door opened and Quincy appeared with a smile on his face. "Well, Zan, you're a father."

"Do I have a boy or a girl? And is Ramie all right?"

"Ramie is sleeping. I think she'll be fine. And you, my nephew, are the father of a girl and a boy."

"Twins!" Zan looked at William and Thad. He was so excited that he could hardly speak. "Can I go in?" he asked Quincy.

"Yes. Just remember these babies are a month early and are very small."

Reginia held the bundled babies by the fire. Zan looked at his children, gently touching their foreheads. Seeing his babies overwhelmed

Zan. They looked so tiny and delicate. He felt blessed. He then took his place by his wife, as Reginia placed the babies in the bed beside Ramie. He stayed with Ramie, watching her and the babies sleep. Ramie awoke early the following morning. She had had no idea that they had twins. She was in pain but managed a smile at the sight of her two infants. They named the babies Thaddeus Saxon and Amelia Ann. Zan wanted to name his son after his uncle Thad, but would call the boy Saxon.

All the Wildes visited the twins frequently. Josie stayed with Zan and Ramie for two weeks, caring for every need. The cold spell passed and the ice melted. Alex and Jacqueline came for a visit. The thought of being grandparents was overwhelming. Time had passed all too quickly. The Wildes celebrated Christmas at Zan's home, because Ramie was still too weak to travel. All the family gathered. The house was full of children. The only one missing was Sarah, who was still in Europe.

March brought warm weather to Texas. Ramie finally recovered and wanted to attend church and have the children christened. The babies were beautiful and growing quickly. William and Reginia joined their family at the church. Alex and Jacqueline came for the occasion. Friends filled the building. Afterward, everyone gathered outside around the twins. Zan proudly exhibited Saxon and Amelia. Johnny Jackson, a cocky young man, walked to the Wildes with a sly grin on his face. Ramie looked stunned by his presence. He had once visited the bawdy house while Ramie was there. She hung her head in shame as he approached.

"Well, I'll be. If it isn't Miss Ramie." Johnny had always been jealous of the Wildes and saw an opportunity to offend them. "Just look at you, pretending to be an upstanding citizen. Why, Zan, you married nothing but a common whore?" he laughed cockily.

Before Johnny could say another word, William sent a hard right blow to the young man's jaw, knocking him to the ground. Everyone stood in shock! William was seventy years old, but obviously was still strong! "This is my granddaughter-in-law and the mother of my great-grandchildren. Whatever you think she did in her past, remains in her past! I will not hear another word against Ramie." William looked slowly at all their friends. "If any of you have something to say, I want to hear it right now!" No one said a word. William put his arm around Ramie and walked her to the carriage. "You are a Wilde now and I will never allow anyone to speak against you." William realized he had come to love Ramie. Her kindness and charitable ways had won his respect and loyalty.

Zan bent down over Johnny, still stunned on the ground, and whispered, "If I ever hear you talk about my wife like that again I'll kill you." Zan walked away without saying another word. Johnny knew Zan meant what he had said. Johnny got up, wiping the dust off his pants. Everyone stared at him. He couldn't say anything. He was embarrassed by his own cockiness.

FIFTY-THREE

The next two years sped by. The Reconstruction period for the States was nearing an end. The United States reinstated Texas and removed the military. Cotton became king again, yielding more than ever. John and Josie bought more farmland and built another large cotton gin. Thad, Will, and Zan shipped large herds of cattle and farmed many fields of cotton and corn. Texas was on the rise and the Wildes were growing in wealth. Katie helped Quincy with his medical practice and they also invested in the shipping company. Sarah married Count Pierre Dupree and continued her career as a concert pianist. She and Pierre planned a trip to the United States. She was to hold a concert in New York and Boston before visiting her family in Texas. John and Katie's children had grown and the girls had left home. Danielle moved to New Orleans to pursue her own life. She moved into the hotel suite and worked with the manager to learn the hotel business. Josie wanted her to learn all she could and if she liked living there and enjoyed her chosen career, she would give her the grand hotel. Victoria attended college in the East and Elijah lived at home working with his father. He loved Holly Hill and wanted to ranch and farm. Jane, Quincy, and Splaine attended college in Ohio. Jane wanted to teach, Quincy Jr. followed in his father's footsteps of medicine, and Splaine studied law. Lathe left for Galveston to live with

Alex and Jacqueline. The ships fascinated him and he wanted to begin working with his uncle while finishing school.

Alex and Jacqueline sat on the front porch looking across the Gulf. The afternoon was muggy and hot as they drank tea from the crystal glasses. Life had been good for them and the move back to Texas had been rewarding. They were close to their children and the business was booming. They spoke of times past and of the future. The only thing missing was their beloved Sarah. Alex was proud of his daughter's success and prominent marriage. The sound of horses' hooves came from the distance. Jacqueline stirred in her chair with anticipation. The carriage stopped in front of the house. A handsome young man opened the door for the beautiful and regal Sarah. Alex and Jacqueline rose from their chairs.

Jacqueline stared at Sarah with pride, before rushing to her and exchanging tender greetings. Jacqueline held her daughter lovingly. She had not seen Sarah in over a decade.

The evening was filled with laughter and joy. Sarah entertained her parents with an intimate concert on the piano. Memories of Sarah as a little girl filled Alex's mind. What a tremendous talent she had. He never regretted a moment sending her to Europe. Sarah was eager to visit her brothers and grandparents. She wanted to see Texas and show Pierre the land that her family had pioneered.

Alex arranged for a small steamer to take them up the Brazos to Wilde Landing. The winding river was full from the spring rains, so traveling was easy. The trip was beautiful as they passed the large plantations and fields of cotton. They arrived at Auburn late in the day. Will and Zan waited a bit impatiently. The excitement of seeing Sarah and Pierre had them pacing the dock. The fact that their sister, whom they had played with as youngsters, had become a countess and famous concert pianist was amazing to them. They could not envision the beauty she had become. Will and Zan affectionately hugged and kissed their sister. They were pleased to meet their brother-in-law and gladly received him into the family.

Reginia and William waited for their family at home. Pierre enjoyed the delicious country dinner and the friendly ways of his Texas in-laws. Reginia had planned a reunion for her family on the following day. She wanted to use her fine china and crystal for the luncheon. Reginia could not wait to see their entire family all gathered at Auburn. A grand celebration was scheduled for the following afternoon with the gathering of all their friends and neighbors to hear their granddaughter play. Even Jim and Betty Wade would arrive unexpectedly, just in time for the party.

The next morning, Pierre awoke to the wondrous aroma of the pig and calf roasting over the open pit. He woke Sarah. "Sarah, take a deep breath. Doesn't that smell wonderful?"

"You woke me to smell the pig cooking?" she laughed and told him they had been cooking all night in preparation for the party. She thought she should prepare him for what he might expect from the Texans. Pierre was impressed with the kindness shown to him. John, Katie, and Zan came with their families for an early brunch. All the grandchildren were present. They wanted several hours of family privacy before all the guests arrived. Pierre was welcomed into the family by all.

William had purchased a grand concert piano for the occasion. That morning, they carefully moved the piano to the front porch. Sarah ran her delicate fingers across the ivory keys. It sounded magnificent! She was proud to have the opportunity to perform for the Texans. By four o'clock, over a hundred of the Wildes' friends had been welcomed to Auburn. Count Pierre Dupree and the Countess Sarah Wilde Dupree were introduced to everyone proudly by William and Reginia. Jim and Betty were a blessed sight. Their long friendship had endured over forty years. The day was festive, filled with dancing, good food, drinks, and fellowship. A band played waltzes and jigs all afternoon. The Wilde family gathered in front of the old plantation home, still beautiful in its appearance, for a family photograph. All the friends looked on with admiration and respect for William and his offspring. Pierre had never seen anything like this in his life. The Texans whooped and hollered and passed cheers among themselves in a proud flamboyant manner. Their generous hospitality, and their ability to relax and have fun, made Pierre feel at home. He thoroughly enjoyed the dancing and cheers. He found the Texans friendly and knew this was a place he would want to visit often.

Evening fell and lanterns lit the sky. Sarah proudly took her place at the piano. Everyone gathered to listen. She played the concertos with grace and ease. Everyone listened as if they had never heard a piano played before. Reginia, William, Betty, and Jim sat in the rockers on the front porch listening intently to the beautiful music. Suddenly, Sarah shook her head and paused briefly. She looked teasingly into the crowd and began to play Dixie. The Texans cheered and sang along proudly. Sarah continued the medley with "Amazing Grace." The song touched the hearts of everyone. "Amazing Grace" had been written in 1779 in England by John Newton. By the mid-1800s, the song was sung in churches across the United States. They sang the hymn softly, as they stood under the glow of the lanterns. They were proud people. They were proud to be Texans and proud to have been part of the Confederacy. There was a moment of quiet as Sarah finished her concert. Sarah sat still. One could hear only the sounds of the crickets in the background. She had stirred their souls with her music. The crowd began clapping softly, many with tears in their eyes, then with gradual exuberance, they began clapping louder and louder. William stood proudly clapping his hands as hard as he could for her. With her own hands trembling, she stood up and bowed. Never before had she felt such appreciation for her music and talent. Sarah had put every emotion she had into this concert. Pierre stood with adoration for his wife. He had seen her true American spirit. He felt as if he had seen the innermost part of his wife for the first time. What a glorious night it was for the Wildes and their friends.

The evening continued with dancing and festive toasts. William and Reginia sat holding hands on the front porch and visiting with their dear friends Jim and Betty.

"I believe this is the grandest party I've ever attended," Jim told them.

"What is grand, is having four generations gathered at Auburn and living to see it!" William laughed.

That night, after everything was quiet, Reginia and William retired to their bedroom. Reginia walked to the large family Bible and opened it up. She took her pen and entered the marriage of Sarah and Pierre. She looked at all the names entered, their births and marriages. Only one death had been entered, and that was little Sarah, her first daughter. Reginia thought of Sarah and how much she still missed her, but she also felt fortunate for all her other children, grandchildren, and great-grandchildren. She would give the Bible to Katie to continue the family genealogy. She wrote one last line in the old Bible she had cherished for so many years.

When these few lines you see Oh think of me,
Though far apart we may be.

Reginia Stuart Wilde

Reginia climbed into the bed beside William and took his hand. "What were you doing?"

"Writing my last entry into the Bible. I plan to give it to Katie tomorrow. We're so fortunate, my darling, to have such a wonderful family."

"Yes. We've been blessed with a good life."

"Texas proved to be a rewarding adventure for us. A place to be proud of." She thought of her days with him, it had been good and she knew she would not have wanted it any other way.

"Yes, indeed. I only hope that many more generations of Wildes will take pleasure in Auburn and their Texas heritage."

Reginia kissed him tenderly, adding softly, "And it all began with you, my dear William Wilde."

www.ingramcontent.com/pod-product-compliance
Lightning Source LLC
Chambersburg PA
CBHW030629020726
47493CB00006B/1633